BEAUTIFULLY

LEESA BOW

ISBN: 978-0-6456871-0-1

Editing by Swish Design & Editing
Proofing by Swish Design & Editing
Editing by Lauren at Creating Ink
Cover design by Letitia at RBA Designs
Photography by Rafa G Catala
Cover Model is Alejandro Caracuel
Cover Image Copyright 2022

Please join my mailing list to be notified of Leesa's latest releases.

You can learn more about me on my website.

If you're on Facebook, I haver a reader group where I chat about books, offer giveaways, and sneak peeks of upcoming books.

You can join here.

For Shauni,
Your strength and fight to live made me view the world
through different eyes.
I love you and am thankful for small blessings every day.
To the friends you met at the Adelaide Children's Hospital who
lost their battle to childhood cancer, this book is also for you.
To Jenna, Will, Michael, and your parents, your emotional
toughness in the face of fear will stay with me always.
Writing this story gave me the strength to cope.
A mother—afraid, finding hope.
My beautiful family and friends showed me the way.
Lynden, Jamie-Lee, Ashleigh, Demi, Mum and Dad, and
Vickie were always by our sides.
Fear remains. How we cope is our strength.

A NOTE FOR THE READER

This book's heroine is Australian, and, as such, some euphemisms and slang words that form part of the UK/Australian spoken word are included for authenticity.

Please remember that the words are not misspelled or incorrect.

If you would like further explanation or to discuss the translation or meaning of a particular word, please do not hesitate to contact the author. For your convenience, contact details have been provided at the end of this book. Also provided below is a limited dictionary of explanation for your convenience.

DICTIONARY

Bloody – British slang meaning 'very' but can also be used as an expletive.

Dickhead – Idiot or jerk.

Footy – Football. Australian Rules football.

Stuff up – British and Australian slang for a big mistake.

Mum – Australian for Mom.

Tepui – Flat top mountain found in Venezuela.

INTRODUCTION

Fear (noun)
Feeling of anxiety
A frightening thought
Terror

Fear (verb)
Be afraid
Be apprehensive
Be frightened
Feel reverence for somebody or something

Fear often stems from one's past, the unknown or
something bad happening in the future.
My journey is about conquering fear.
The challenge lies in taking risks to remove the power
fear holds.

PROLOGUE
SAMUEL

Undisclosed location in the rainforest of
Venezuela

Large dark lips pucker around a bamboo pipe. Tattooed cheeks puff round.

A tiny smoke cloud momentarily blocks his view of the shaman's face. When their eyes meet, Samuel lowers his gaze. He knows his place. The upper-class society he was born into holds no ground here.

Words are spoken in a foreign language, one he had to learn and isn't taught in any educational curriculum. Many indigenous tribes inhabit the Amazon and other rainforests, only this one is unique. Their laws are a stark contrast and incredibly extreme compared to his California lifestyle. Yet he's chosen to remain here to live a primitive lifestyle for five years and build trust with every passing month or every full moon, as time is perceived differently.

Trust.

Another measure he had to overcome to substantiate

his manhood. Every time he leaves the village and returns, he places the entire village at risk of disease. It strains the trust between him, the shaman, and the elders.

Samuel's ventures beyond the village boundary have lessened over the years. By remaining in the village, the shaman's trust in him grew. This year, old friends demanded he make an appearance. They were worried about his mental health.

He reciprocated the same opinion of them.

Kneeling before the shaman asking permission to return to the village reminds him of his younger years at an expensive private school. Only here the repercussions could be life or death.

"O'win nuno." *One moon*. One month. Wrinkled fingers rise toward the sky. A prayer follows the spirits living among them, a divine power in the tree vines and beneath the soil.

"Waküpe-küruman." *Thank you*. Samuel understands that if three full moons pass, his re-entry will be rejected. A new sacrificial ceremony will be required, and Samuel isn't sure he has the strength or stamina to endure the interrogation of another initiation. When he first came to the village, he was a driven, younger man with a pharmaceutical scholarship. Finding a cure to terminal illnesses fueled his passion for science. Now the only person who holds answers sits before him, a library of knowledge captured inside the mind of the shaman.

The shaman scoops red paste with his finger and wipes it behind Samuel's ear to where the chief had tattooed him. Another line is drawn across his forehead, representing how the shaman will follow Samuel by his thoughts. He lowers his gaze and nods once, rising to his feet only after the shaman walks away.

He strides to his hut, grabs his backpack, changes into cut-off cargos and a t-shirt, and slips on his sneakers. Outside his hut, the sun is directly above him. He waits until he passes the village perimeter before breaking into a jog, ignoring the pining gaze of a young female native American. He makes his way along a narrow dirt path between thick shrubbery, careful not to touch any spikes on unruly vines. Some needles can cause paralysis in minutes, and thanks to the shaman, Samuel's now wise enough not to take on the overgrowth in these parts.

He stands on a sandy embankment where tree limbs overhang the water's edge on either side. Asoo will pass the river fork soon. A weekly occurrence. He's alerted to the faint roar of a motor, a sound similar to a Yamaha motorbike. He waves to the driver of the dug-out motorized canoe.

"Ciudad Guayana?" Asoo asks. Asoo is of *Pemón* descent—a similar tribe to the Ularans.

Samuel shakes his head. The cities north of Canaima are collection points for parcels and letters about his research. Places where he posts exotic plant species to a professor in Caracas. "Rio for a couple of weeks."

Asoo's black eyebrows lift. "Rio? For Carnival?"

Samuel curses under his breath. It's the last thing he wants to do. The hundreds of thousands of people lining the city streets are a threat. Being in Rio can jeopardize the health of the indigenous people he has grown to love. Even a common cold threatens their survival.

"My friends are traveling from California and New York. We're meeting up in a matter of days."

Asoo breaks into a song, chanting "*New York.*" Samuel

shakes his head. A fairy-tale city to many. A place where dreams come to life.

Living in a large city no longer interests Samuel. He has found his destiny by trying to escape the one his father had set up for him in Los Angeles.

He considers his sacrifice. Like a priest married to God, he too has dedicated his life to a divine power. Here he learned about ayahuasca, the vine of the soul, while living primitively and in the name of medical research. From a Western medicine perspective, Ulara is a world that made little sense to him, a perspective he has learned to overlook, for Ulara preserves secrets, which potentially can save lives.

1

EDEN

Adelaide, Australia

Everyone imagines the moment you tell your boss to shove the damn job. Some create composed and reasonable exits, and others are much more dramatic with extensive cursing.

To me, it's merely a dream because I work for the family business, and my father is the boss. I'm not whining, especially since I'm not unhappy. To be honest, it's a great job with an opportunity for an upcoming promotion. Did I mention the location is by the beach?

I'm often distracted and gaze out of the window of our small office. Days like today, the ocean is simply mesmerizing. The water is flat, barely a wave, and like glass—the perfect day for paddleboarding. Waves drift in and out as quiet as the office, except for the subtle tapping on the keyboard. It's quite serene, and I can't visualize anything to make me angry enough to want to quit despite the feeling in my gut telling me it's time.

Time to make my own choices.

My father walks out of his office, and I turn from the window to meet his glowering look. "I trust you're smart enough to stay out of the jungle." His tone holds a warning, and I'm guessing he finally read the email with the attached itinerary of my upcoming holiday.

Angling the monitor from his view, I minimize the email on vaccination schedules—specifically, yellow fever, rabies, and our options on malaria prevention.

"Of course," I say in a level voice.

As if someone upped the cooling, the temperature around us turns icy, reminding me of the winter wind blowing up from Antarctica. Where we live, vineyards lie to the east, north, and south of the city. Adelaide is no jungle.

His executive assistant coughs. I assume she senses the tension between us. "I have the December report you're waiting on, Mr. Monteford. I'll forward it to you now."

"Thank you. I'll run over the figures in my office." Blue eyes reminding me of my own, hold my gaze in a warning that this discussion will be continued.

When the door to his private office closes, I swivel on my seat. "Thanks for the distraction. I have no idea why he's so hung up about this holiday?"

"At least he didn't make another underhanded comment about letting him down. Remain calm because you'll be there in no time and leave all this behind," Dana says, extending her arms wide. She lets out a gentle laugh. Her brown eyes crinkle at the corners as we share an understanding.

I smile at the sound of her laughter because it quickly warms the mood in the small room. "Guilt-tripping isn't going to change the fact he'll need to hire someone. I mentioned my sister could help out, only he wouldn't have any of it."

Dana pushes short strands of hair behind her ears. Her classy-styled bob-cut never has a hair out of place. Her mascaraed eyes are always perfect. "No need to hide your true feelings to me. For years I've witnessed a different set of rules for your sister than you."

And my younger brother, I want to add. Only I keep the thought to myself.

Our office is located on the bottom floor of the apartment building where I live. It's ideal in the sense I don't have to worry about time or expense in getting to work. Not so ideal when it comes to the time before or after work to clear my head. When I clock off at the end of the day, I've made a habit of walking along the esplanade to level my thoughts, and breathe in the clean ocean air. I love this time before twilight when everyone is capturing 'me' time. Skaters whiz past. Cyclists ting their bells and call out, "On your right." The Bay is one of Adelaide's popular beachside suburbs, and we need an extra lane on the path for this amount of foot traffic. I pass groups of fitness enthusiasts doing star jumps on the grass. Further along, families picnic on rugs spread out over the grass and wicker baskets within reach. Others prefer fish and chips enticing the seagulls to behave erratically.

Before entering our apartment complex, I stand out front and admire the white stone building. Built in the early 1900s, my grandparents purchased it in the late 1950s and passed it onto my father. Part of me is proud he trusts me to handle business matters, but the other part is regretful I didn't seek my own adventure.

The white façade has several cracks in the faded paintwork weathered by the ocean climate. The popular hotel a few buildings down—all modern glass and steel—gleams in the sunlight. Our smaller building has weathered some tough times and regained popularity, mainly for the renovated interior that has incorporated the vintage appeal crossed with a crisp bohemian design. We manage the eight apartments. The hotel on the corner has one hundred and eighty rooms. We are no threat, and yet we're fully booked until Christmas next year.

The external flights of stairs are stringed with tinsel and fairy lights. I love this time of year when everything sparkles. Choosing to take the internal staircase, I make my way up the three flights of stairs to the penthouse.

The front door creaks as it opens. The cry of a child comes from another room.

"We were just talking about you," Faith says as she stands.

My sister is visiting. *Fantastic*.

"Why?" I focus on my father sitting opposite my mother at the kitchen table. A few seconds is all I need to acknowledge Mum has been to the hairdresser—freshly colored mocha hair sits motionless under a can of lacquer.

"We were discussing suitable applicants to replace you while you're gallivanting in another country." Faith's tone is condemning. She doesn't wait for a response before heading toward my parents' bedroom, where her sleeping toddler has awakened.

"Let me get him. I haven't seen him in weeks."

Faith crosses her arms. "He's not the happiest when he wakes."

I ignore her and open the door. My nephew raises his arms for me to pick him up. So adorable. I lift him out of the portable cot and love how he curls into my chest. "How long have you been sleeping, little man?"

"Two hours," Faith says. She leans on the doorframe. Brown hair borders her face before falling to her shoulders. She's the clone of our mother with her alluring eyes—pools of melted chocolate.

They're both extraordinary businesswomen—go-getters in life, confident, and resilient. Our parents named us, as though in hindsight of the future. They always had faith in my sister to succeed and do the right thing in life. My name, Eden, has a meaning of pleasure and delight. My father keeps a close eye on me as if I'm going to become a bohemian hippie if he turns his back. Ironic when I have an average personality and life.

"Are you sure it's not possible to shorten this holiday? Instead of taking all your leave at once and leaving Dad in a predicament, you could split your leave and travel to Europe next year?"

"I'm not interested in Europe at the moment. And you fail at being subtle." I stride past her. "Why don't *you* work a couple of days a week, and Mum could look after Seb? You always say my work isn't that difficult."

"You can't expect Faith to work in the office when her morning sickness is at its worst."

I blink several times at my mother before turning to Faith.

She raises her hands at Mum. "Not how I was going to tell her."

With my free hand, I hug her. "Congratulations. You'll be busy. Have you extended your leave from work?"

"I didn't expect to fall so quickly. I'm thinking of resigning and returning to work when the kids are at school. Jake has always wanted three kids, so..."

I gape at her. Our parents funded her university education to study law. It's where she met Jake, whose parents own a law firm, and subsequently employed her to work alongside their son. She took her career seriously until they married. Has she forgotten what my parents gave up for her? What I gave up?

I wasn't 'allowed' to study full-time—only online because our father needed *me* to work for him. I also worked weekends while at school and did anything to save my parents money by not hiring extra staff. For the last few years, the business has turned over substantial profits, so I'm taking extended leave to work out what I want to do with my life. My father has created a new position in the company in marketing and building development. The position is mine if I want it.

"My leave isn't debatable. I suggest you hire a temp for the eight weeks I'm away." I take a breath. "I'm going out to meet my friends for a couple of drinks and to discuss our upcoming trip." I kiss my nephew on his cheek before handing him to my sister and make my way to my room. Before I reach the door, I pivot to meet my father eye to eye. "Why are you hung up on the jungle? If I take precautions, is a small tour so bad? It's part of the Iguassu Falls tour we have booked."

Scarlet heat rises along his neck, masking his pale skin.

"Eden, this also isn't debatable." Mum's hand rests on her chest. "You have no idea of the possible danger."

"I told you she's *just* like her grandmother," Dad grunts under his breath. Only we all hear, and by Faith's expression, she's as confused as I am.

It's not the first time he has related me to Gran. But I'm twenty-four, not sixteen, and thankful to be moving out on my return. Even if it means moving in with Yasmine and listening to her daily meditating chants and spells and taking all the herbal concoctions she swears by.

"For once, I wish you'd trust me like you do Faith and Will." The door closes with a thump behind me before giving him a chance to respond.

2

EDEN

"Evening, Eden," Dave says when I reach the doors of The Shores bar. We're on a first-name basis since the bar is only a half a block from our apartments, and I'm here most weeks. The Shores is a trendy hotel, including a nightclub, cocktail bar, and restaurant. "Your friends are already inside."

"Thanks," I say and offer him a smile. I weave around the booths and tables to find my girlfriends sitting in the usual seats by the window with an ocean view.

"Sorry I'm late." I plop down on a comfortable lounge chair and stretch my hands over the padded armrests.

Amy stops mid-conversation and stares at me. "What's pissed you off?"

I sigh loudly and shake my head. "Nothing. Just my father trying to guilt-trip me again."

"Here." Yasmine pours a glass of sparkling wine and hands it to me. "Medicinal bubbles always help."

"Medicinal?" I smile at Yasmine.

"Good for your heart, your skin, your cognitive brain, and it will improve your mood." She beams her white teeth at me. "Bottoms up." She raises her glass to me and takes a sip.

"Cognitive thinking?" Amy muses. She runs her fingers through her long blonde ponytail and adjusts it to sit over her shoulder.

I down the glass in one go and let out an appreciative sigh. "I'm feeling better already." I wipe any residue from the corners of my mouth.

"Only three glasses a week to improve your memory," Yasmine adds as though we all need educating.

"You don't need to sell it to me," I say. "You had me at boosting my mood. As for improving my memory, I'd rather forget some things. Tell me, if I drink more than a few glasses a week, does it reverse the effects and wipe out my memory?"

Yasmine shakes her head, and dark spiral curls bounce as she does. "If you lived with me already, then you could use my essential oils and have access to my motivational books."

"Be careful." Amy smirks. "She only wants to practice her spells on you."

Yasmine rolls her eyes. "You need to have an open mind."

"I do. Just with other things," she says. Her eyes fix on the dark-haired, handsome man walking past our table. "I'd be willing to be open with him."

Ugh. "You don't even know him. He could be someone waiting to spike your drink and then have his way with you." God, I sound like a prude. I'm not. Because of a certain someone, I now have my own trust issues after he stomped all over my heart.

She gives a devilish grin. "And I wouldn't object."

"This is why we need to talk about our holiday," I say

to Yasmine. "We need to be sensible and have group rules. We can't be going to an exotic part of the world where crime is high and think it won't happen to us."

"Bree will have it covered," Yasmine says as though she's undeterred. "We need to talk about what we want out of this holiday because we all have different needs."

"Men," Amy blurts out and sits forward in her seat as though we're now discussing a topic that interests her. "Those gorgeous Brazilian men. I want to know if there's any truth in the stories."

God, did she just wink? "Seriously?" I roll my eyes, yet I'm not surprised. "You can get laid anywhere, Ames. Don't you want to visit the old churches and see the architecture of another culture?"

She shrugs her shoulders. "I'm not objecting to those things. I'll go with you if that's what you want, but I also want the party. You can't go to Rio and be like, 'the architecture is wonderful, darling.'" She says the last few words in a high voice and as if she has the olive from her empty martini glass in her mouth.

"I wouldn't say it like that."

"This is good. We're talking," Yasmine adds. "I want it to be a spiritual journey. Come back wiser and stronger for it."

My phone rings, and I glance down at the screen.
Bree.

I swipe the screen and press speaker. "Hey. You called at a good time. We're all here at The Shores."

"Drinking medicinal bubbles," Amy adds with a smile.

"Hey, girlfriend," Yasmine pipes in. "We're talking about the holiday. I think we need to consider what's important to each of us so we can cater to everyone's needs."

"Good point," she says in a serious tone. "I've been thinking about our first-aid kit and collecting items from the hospital."

"Bree, are you stealing from your workplace?" Amy teases.

"No. I'm paying for everything."

Amy grins, well aware Bree would never do anything dishonest. "How's Sydney?"

"I wouldn't know. All I do is work and study."

"That sucks," Amy groans.

"It's why I can't wait to get away. Are your vaccinations up to date?"

"I have one more," I say. "When you get a break, text the group what's important to you in case we need to make any last-minute amendments to some tours."

"Honestly, I'm so exhausted I'm happy to lay on a beach and drink cocktails, so long as we're safe."

"Safety is your priority," I conclude.

"Absolutely. Sorry, I have to get back to the ward. I'm so jealous of you all there, together. Have a drink for me."

"Bye, Bree," we all say in unison.

"Talking about safety, my father is giving me a hard time about staying safe."

Amy's eyes round. "Seriously, when is he going to treat you like an adult?"

"He does treat her like an adult. It's obvious he has trust issues," Yasmine adds.

"Yet he's not like this with Faith and Will." I shake my head. I have never done anything for him not to trust me.

"For fuck's sake, it goes further than that. He's pissed you split up with that dickhead. In his eyes, you and

Ethan were meant to be together, and I wouldn't be surprised if he believes you'll get back with him."

"Not going to happen," I say firmly. "Although his behavior of late has nothing to do with Ethan. He's worried about the jungle, of all the places."

Yasmine smirks. "Not Rio and getting shot or at the very least mugged for your purse?"

"Oh, he's already warned me of those dangers."

Yasmine blows air into her cheeks. "I'm glad my mother stays out of my business."

"You have the privilege of not living at home." After living with Ethan for eighteen months, I found it difficult to adjust to living with my parents again. I was distraught and desperate and needed somewhere to live after throwing the key at him and storming out. "If I weren't saving every last cent for this holiday, I'd be out already." I refill my glass, emptying the bottle, and then signal the waiter to get us another.

"Same. I mean it's great to save money, but my little sister's drive me crazy. The other day Alex used my expensive nail polish on her bloody dolls," Amy exclaims. "As soon as I receive a permanent teaching contract, I'm moving out, hopefully with my new Brazilian boyfriend."

We giggle at Amy's optimism and clink our crystal flutes.

"On that positive note..." Yasmine says, "... I want to talk about our first days in Salvador. There's something that interests me, and I don't want you to feel uncomfortable."

"I'm interested in what would make us uncomfortable because I'd be surprised if anything does."

"Butting in there, I've booked my last laser and then a

tan appointment. I. Am. Ready." Amy angles both hands toward her pelvis.

"It's a wonderful thing to be comfortable in your own skin." Yasmine smiles at Amy. "I want to point out our holiday will be an adventure, and we're filling it with wonderful experiences, and not all experiences are good." She shrugs. "Not bad either. Some could make you uncomfortable. What I'm saying is if an experience isn't enjoyable, it isn't reason enough not to do it. It's all about opportunities and trying different things. Some we love, some we don't. The important thing is to do it. Try everything and give your inner courage a chance to bloom."

3

EDEN

Salvador, Brazil

Three weeks later...

We arrived on the first day of February in time for the Candomble tradition. Attending the festival of Iemanjá is a tick off Yasmine's bucket list. It reminds me of the times we celebrated Yemaya back home.

"What time is it?" Amy moans. White foiled strands of hair fan over her pillow, giving an angelic impression.

"Eight thirty."

A steady drumbeat creeps closer, accompanied by unapologetic singing.

She pushes up onto her elbows and stares toward the window. "Sounds as though the festival is underway."

"Yeah. I can't wait to be part of it tomorrow." Plucking a brochure from the table, I flop back on the bed.

"Pelourinho," I say. "It looks interesting."

"I'm keen," Amy says, now upright.

"You sure? It's the historical center of the city, and I

don't expect you to obsess over the architecture with me. I can take a bus."

"We don't go out alone," she reminds me. "Bree's rules."

I smile at Amy because I know she's making an effort for me. This isn't her thing. I already knew Yasmine and Bree were staying at the hotel for Yasmine to prepare for the offering. Preparation for these ceremonies brings out Yasmine's creative side, and she enjoys doing it. So, I expected to go out alone. Shit. It's only day one, and I'm contemplating breaking a group rule. Who the hell am I?

A short time later, Amy and I are squished like sardines in a bus, our skin similarly smeared with sweat since there's no air conditioning on the bus. Staring out the open window, her blonde hair blows wildly around her face, uncaring about knots when it's the only source of air. As the bus chugs up sloping hills, pastel-hued buildings snare my focus, the mismatched colors beautiful in their uniqueness. I'm enchanted with the people and their bright clothing.

Baroque churches are our first stop on my list of tourist sights, and here, it isn't a case of 'you've seen one, you've seen them all.' Even the photos I take on my phone are jaw-dropping. The Cathedral Basilica, trimmed with gold, is considered one of the finest examples of the wealth of Portuguese Baroque architecture.

"There's something about the beauty of a church," I say from the street and turn to take one last shot with my phone. "It's inspiring and calming."

"Architecture... inspiring and calming." Amy holds out a hand as if weighing something on an imaginary set of scales. "Working for your father and slaving away at the family business... busy and demanding." She tips the scales and pretends to overbalance, and I laugh.

My chest warms, knowing I have eight weeks to discover the beauty and thrills of this country and learn a little more about me.

Time gets away as we wander through walls of art, mesmerized as though we have time-traveled to another world. Here in Salvador, I sense I'm going to lose track of time every day.

We make a final dash along a pebbled road and then come across Foundation House, a place where the famous Brazilian author, Jorge Amado's book covers are housed in his honor. Four floors inside the blue colonial building hold the entire archive of his work. Discovering small treasures like this adds to the adventure, although we are unable to stay long for already the sun is descending toward the horizon.

We pass a museum for African-Brazilian art and artifacts. We have enough time to wander inside before the bus arrives. The exhibits reflect the African cultures of the region and deities. I lead Amy to a carved wooden statue of Iemanjá.

Amy fixes her gaze on the statue, then reads the inscription. "I'm beginning to understand why it means so much to Yasmine, knowing it's part of her heritage."

"Yeah." I've always understood Yasmine, and yet right now, I'm a bit jealous of how she's in touch with her spirituality in this exotic place. I've followed her lead because she offers the best advice and is always feeding us girls with word porn that's healthy for our souls.

We arrive back at the hotel to find Yasmine has purchased frangipanis and other white knick-knacks to divide amongst us. She instructs us to tie them to our letter when offering it to Iemanjá. Tomorrow, if the ocean swallows our offering, it means the deity has accepted our gifts.

All our wishes differ. My friends have written long lists, but mine is simply asking Iemanjá to guide me in finding happiness and a sense of purpose.

Lord knows I need it.

4

SAMUEL

Salvador, Brazil

The weight of meeting his friends plays on Samuel's mind. Unable to sleep, he shaves and cuts his unruly hair to appear more civilized before wandering out to buy breakfast.

A sea of white packs the street, blocking his path.

Dressed in a red t-shirt and cargos, he stands out like blood on a chef's white apron. He'd forgotten about the ceremony when he decided to stay in Salvador overnight before flying on to Rio.

He's witnessed it all before and respects their belief. It still intrigues him, so he decides to mesh with the crowd. Pulling his t-shirt over his head, baring his tanned chest in an attempt to blend. He follows the mob toward the beach, watches them load small boats filled with gifts— gifts to please the Iemanjá so she'll grant a favorable fishing season among other personal blessings.

The chanting continues, repetitive singing and white flowers adorning hundreds of offerings. The people follow wading and jumping the waves to leave their tributes and asking for blessings.

A voice with a sweet accent catches his attention.

Laughter.

Blonde hair that's whiter than his.

The crowd parts momentarily, and he allows his gaze the luxury of lowering. Subtle curves in a white swimsuit knock the wind out of him. The swimsuit style is cut to her navel, revealing the swell of her breasts. He forces his gaze to lift and meets the most beautiful blue eyes as rich as the ocean's color.

Caught in her spell, he's unable to look away. His entire body hums, and for a second, his world tilts. He's quick to shut it down and blames lack of food and sleep. He resists the urge to take a step toward her and wills his feet to remain in the sand.

Her friend steps forward and severs the pull between their eyes.

He lets out a breath and wills his heart to slow. Samuel turns in the direction of the hotel, his place of refuge. For too long, he has denied the feeling that shook his core, the pull of need reminding him he's still a man —*desire* from a single glance, an understanding of lust.

Years of constraint incinerated in seconds.

He blames the Brazilian sun and seeks shelter behind the walls of his hotel.

For him, safety is *not* in numbers.

5

EDEN

"What is it?" Yasmine takes a step closer and blocks my view.

"Nothing," I say quickly and sidestep around her to wade through the ocean to the sand. Only it wasn't nothing. In those brief seconds, I was walking on clouds.

I search the crowd after losing sight of the shirtless blond with the intense stare. For a few seconds, my balance wavered with the pull of lust. Only it wasn't just lust. On another level, I felt more, which is odd for me since I don't know him. Heaven forbid I mention for the first time in countless months that my libido came alive. I imagine my friends celebrating the resurgence of my sex drive by dropping to their knees and giving thanks to whatever deity is a sex goddess. Hmm, maybe this is something I should know about. I could be praying to the wrong god.

"Eden!"

Ignoring Yasmine calling my name, I wade out of the shallow water only to stop on the sand, finding myself caught in a group of people repeating a mantra over and over. Did I imagine him? Am I that desperate to find happiness that I'm now hallucinating? Suddenly, I'm shuffled forward, and I am feeling out of sorts with the constant singing messing with my head. I am more of a silent worshipper, usually concentrating on a prayer for longer than a few minutes makes me fidget. In the moment, overcome with emotion and in a strange country, I'm struck with uneasiness being out of my comfort zone. Seriously, and what's with the humidity here? Coming from a city that feels closer to the rim of sea ice in the Southern Ocean than the tropics, extreme humidity is a quiet hell, heating from the inside out.

A man standing before me flops to the sand. His eyes roll to the back of his head, and the rest of his body shakes. A hand lands on my shoulder, and I jump. Yasmine gives a subtle head shake.

She knows me well, as my first instinct is to drop to my knees to assist him. I glance around. Other followers keep chanting and praying.

My gaze shoots back to the man who has collapsed near my feet. I'm scared he'll choke right beside me, and the crowd is overlooking him. Bree appears on the other side of Yasmine, and Yasmine presses her hand on Bree's stomach to stop her from going to him. Bree is a medical student. If something goes wrong, at least she'll be able to help.

The imposing sound of a hundred people chanting out of sequence clouds my thoughts. Drums echo from the street. What the hell is happening?

The guy stands, brushes sand from his clothes, and smiles as though nothing happened, or something has, and he now feels the better for it. To my surprise, he raises his arms toward the sea with gratitude in his expression.

Amy is now standing on the other side of Bree, and by their expressions, they have the same concerns as me.

Yasmine whispers, "He believes the queen of the ocean has freed him from whatever demon kept him captive."

I nod and take a step back. In a bid to stay out of the way, I take another step back when other followers hug him and pat his back affectionately. Questions sit on my tongue. I itch to ask Yasmine, only the look she gives me yearns for understanding. I respect her belief and so remain quiet and attempt to push out my own insecurities.

I'm not denying I am completely out of my depth. It makes me nervous, and I'm attempting to embrace it. My father taught me being uncomfortable is the first step in learning something new. Funny, on this occasion, his advice echoes Yasmine's words. Immersing ourselves in different cultural experiences is all part of why we came to Brazil. This ceremony is the beginning of us encompassing it.

Still, I need to down a few caipirinhas, regardless of the time.

6

EDEN

Rio de Janeiro, Brazil

Two days later...

Bare golden shoulders shine with a film of sweat, a combination of one's own perspiration and that of strangers from pushing through the crowd on Copacabana Beach. At twilight, the heat is somewhat more bearable. Yet, the air remains thick and makes it difficult to breathe among the hundreds of thousands of partygoers along the shoreline.

Despite the heat, happiness is contagious. Yesterday my heart settled into a quicker beat from the time the plane descended, and the Christ the Redeemer statue came into view. The memory is etched into my brain—a false sense of security, maybe with the protector overlooking the city, arms open wide embracing every living soul.

The drums.

The singing and dancing.

The vibrant colors.

Rio de Janeiro has met our expectations and more. Salvador prepared my mind and body for the deluge of excitement buzzing inside of me.

Swallowed up by the crowd, my reticence dissolves. My hips sway to the beat—the drums demanding it—and I hum to an unfamiliar song in a foreign language.

Yasmine returns with caipirinhas to pep up our mood. We down the cold liquid in minutes. Amy and Yasmine return to the bar for refills.

Bree wipes her face. "Argh, I don't know why I bothered with bronzer."

I snort a laugh. "You're tanned. Your skin's flawless. And in this heat, why bother?"

Seriously, every guy would want her to be his doctor. She's tall and slim, long dark hair, and the most caring brown eyes framed with long lashes—the ones where you don't need mascara.

She shrugs. "Part of the getting-ready-to-go-out process."

I rub the skin along her jaw to blend powder where she rubbed off the color. Over her shoulder, my gaze locks with a guy with dreamy dark eyes. Not the same eyes that captured my attention in Salvador, the blue-eyed hottie who stole my breath. Instead, this guy's eyes hold a familiar look and one I recognize from the men looking for a hook-up back home. Here, it feels soul-boosting.

Tanned. Sculpted shoulders. Dark hair shaved close to his crown. His lips curve, and I swear Rio is under a spell. Apart from the flattery of him checking me out, I still find it uncomfortable. I inhale a breath.

You don't know him, and it's absolutely fine. It's acceptable, so chill.

When I glance up at Bree, there's a flirtatious twinkle in her eyes. A tall, athletic-looking guy is smiling at her. He has the same olive skin, dark eyes and hair, and a heartbreaker smile like most of the guys in Rio.

"A linda garota gostaria de dançar comigo?" the hot guy says to Bree. He takes her by the waist, his pelvis connecting to hers.

She smiles at me, eyes wide. "He said, 'Does the beautiful girl want to dance with me?'."

Of course, Bree has already picked up the Brazilian Portuguese language. I wave her away. "Go."

I do my best to ignore the guy who's eyeballing me, and before an uncomfortable feeling of being alone settles in, Amy and Yasmine return with four Caipirinhas.

"I see Bree is making progress." Amy grins at me. I nod while sucking my cocktail down. Swift sucking through a straw is my new superpower.

"Slow down, girl." Yasmine takes my empty cup. "I volunteer to refill again."

It finally clicks. "What's the attraction at the bar?"

"Same attraction as here." Yasmine nods in the direction over my shoulder.

I look to the guy sending me his best let's-fuck look. He raises his chin and gives me a you-know-I'm-sexy wink. Ugh, could he be any more obvious? He's now getting on my nerves. In the open air on the beachfront, another band takes to the stage.

"Let's dance," Amy says. She takes my hand, and we create space allowing our hips to move to the beat like our bodies are charmed by a musical spell. Soon, it's simply us four girls dancing, and for the next hour, we barely give our feet time to rest.

By the time the next band comes on stage, my friends are grinding hips with random males. I dance alone. The quick samba step tests my coordination, especially after downing several Caipirinhas.

It's a click to midnight, and my thoughts are in another zone where my head is light, and my heart is brave.

Watching my friends, I pray the rest of our holiday isn't about hooking up with hot guys. Visiting an exotic country is about much more. Or is it because my heart is scarred from the last guy who destroyed my faith in men?

7

EDEN

"Unreal," I squeal at the top of my voice to the instructor as we glide off the mountain into the air and fly toward the city. With a bird's-eye view, I pinpoint Christ the Redeemer where we visited yesterday, Sugarloaf Mountain the day before, and the white stretch of beaches where we lazed other days. The night is all about the beach bars. We have already been in Rio for one week, and I have loved every minute.

"What's next for the Aussies?" the pilot asks. His voice is lost in the wind.

"Iguassu Falls and the Carnival," I yell back.

He veers the pole of the hang glider like a steering wheel. The surrounding mountains and vast rainforest are as beautiful as the city. My insides spark with excitement thinking about Iguassu Falls and being in the rainforest, enjoying the natural beauty of this country. "You're lucky to do this every day. The view is breathtaking."

"Yeah. I appreciate the tranquility," he says in a thick accent.

Below, there's a vibrant city. From up here, it's a whole other world. "I love all the green of the forest. It's appealing to the eye."

He chuckles. "Nature's trap to lure you in. Many don't find their way out."

"From down there?"

"No, we have walking trails down there. If you visit the Amazonia rainforest. She's beautiful, but if you're thinking about a trip to the jungle like many tourists, you need to understand what it takes to survive. Foreigners come looking for adventure, thinking they'll find it in the jungle and aren't prepared for mishaps or deviations to their plans. The weather can change rapidly. Everything looks the same, so you need an experienced guide to find your way out. Numerous animals and insects are a threat, so getting fast medical aid becomes a bigger problem."

"Are you speaking from experience?"

He nods. "Banana spider. I lost my daughter at three. I prefer to admire the beauty from up here."

My gut turns thinking about his loss.

Thank God we have Bree and her extensive medical supplies.

Nothing excites Amy more than a music festival. The blocos, or street parties, are popular during Carnival, and this is one reason why Amy wanted to visit Rio during Carnival. I'm sure party-'til-you-drop is her middle name. With more than four hundred to choose from over the carnival days, there are blocos on practically every corner.

Choosing which bloco to attend even has Amy overwhelmed. Bree suggested we head out to the shops to buy costumes as part of the fun in Rio is dressing up. The receptionist at our hotel recommended a street market for cheap costumes and accessories, so after a quick dip in the pool—because it's the only way to combat the heat —we head to the Saara market.

In a matter of hours, we're back in our cramped apartment dressing into our colorful animal-print outfits. And by colorful, I mean neon pink, yellow, and blue with a black background.

We decorate our faces in a dark bronzer before applying the glitter and colorful eye makeup to match our costumes.

"You know this makeup isn't going to stay on once we head out into the heat, right?" I say as I stroke mascara to my lashes.

"You should have fake lashes. Foolproof," Amy quips. She bats her synthetic ones to make a point.

"If I were to glue any now, it would melt in this humidity, and by the end of the night, I'd probably find it on my cheek."

"She has a point," Bree adds.

Amy ignores Bree. "Done." She twirls in front of the mirror. "Girl, we'll be picking up tonight."

I stare at her in the reflection, my hand frozen mid-air. "Here? In this tiny apartment? Do I need to remind you we're sharing a queen bed?"

Amy shrugs, causing Yasmine and Bree to grin at me.

"Hope there's room for three in your bed," I remark to their reflections.

"There is. I'm not that big," Amy replies.

I roll my eyes.

Yasmine smiles at me. "I'm popping the champagne now."

"I'm glad we have only two more nights here." I bump Amy with my shoulder. All four of us trying to use a single bathroom mirror isn't ideal.

After popping two bottles of champagne, we head to Ipanema Beach. With the alcohol pumping through my veins, combined with the excitement of partying with fifteen thousand other revelers, I swear I'm close to wetting my pants.

Forty-five minutes later, I clamber out of the taxi holding my stomach because I spent the entire ride squeezing my pelvic floor.

Amy appears by my side. "If it makes you feel any better, I was scared for my fucking life!"

Bree joins us. Her face is also pale. "That ride was an experience."

Ignoring us, Yasmine walks past with a spring in her step. "I can hear the band."

We don't question, only follow.

"I have to pee," I tell Yasmine. "I need to find some form of restrooms first."

"C'mon," Amy yells from outside the cubicle when I'm taking the longest pee in the history of urination. "I'm dying of dehydration out here."

"Okay, ready," I say when I join my friends outside. There's no doubt where the action is. The crowd is thick along the beach, and we have no clue where to even look for the bar.

It doesn't take long for us to infiltrate the membrane of the crowd.

"How the hell are we supposed to get drinks when we

have to snake around partygoers, and all I see is people dressed in drag with twenty-inch heels, or they are propped for the Samba parade with a ten-foot headpiece?" Amy whines.

I chuckle because we have always teased Amy about her height. "That's why Bree is leading us," I say and wink. Even though I'm almost as tall as Bree, I fall behind because this body on body and being surrounded by sweaty skin isn't as fun as it looks.

We get to a point, and no one moves to allow us through. We can't see beyond them or where in the crowd we're stuck. "Can you point us in the direction of the bar?" Amy asks a group of guys.

A guy stares at her with a confused look.

"Bar," she repeats and mimes drinking from a cup.

"Sim." *Yes.* "Bar," he points toward the beach further along.

"Thank you," she says.

"Obrigada," Bree adds. *Thank you.*

"Seriously?" Amy says to Bree with her hands on her hips. "You didn't think to help me then?"

"Babe, you had it under control."

We all laugh and head in the direction the guy pointed.

Periodically, I catch the scent of salty air drifting from the ocean. It's a welcome relief from the musky human odor hanging in the air.

Half-naked, exposed skin glistens, and toned bodies move to a rhythmic beat. The laughter, singing, and positive vibe are contagious. Never have I been so overwhelmed with emotion, and learning to ride it is a new skill I'm yet to master.

After buying two caipirinha's each, we make our way

toward the beach side of the stage. Too far away to see the band, we dance in our little group and enjoy the music despite not understanding the foreign lyrics. Two drag queens dance beside me. After downing both drinks, my hands are free, and I have the confidence to dance with them. Bree and Yasmine head to the bar again. Amy joins us, and the dance moves up a tempo, and our new friends take the challenge. I'm laughing at Amy's competitiveness. She grinds her hips and drops to the ground, and with a quick rebound, she springs up showing her hip-hop style. Taller, and with bigger breasts and longer lashes, they just do sexy better. I stand back and clap at the three of them when Yasmine taps on my shoulder and tilts her head for me to follow.

"We have found some American guys," she says. "They asked us to hang out with them."

"Sure." After waving goodbye to our dance competitors, we weave a short distance to four guys standing together, dressed in plain street clothes.

"We met them at the bar," Bree explains. "This is Michael." I nod and smile at the guy a little taller than me with dark hair. "And this is Sean." I wave at the blond guy with a beard. Bree is smiling at Sean, and I already sense a connection between the two.

Yasmine jabs her thumb toward the next guy. "Harrison," she says, and he smiles. His eyes, skin, and hair are a darker shade like Yasmine's. Harrison nudges the fourth guy who's looking toward the ocean and disinterested in the bloco and apparently also in meeting us. He's tall, with beach-blond hair, lean, and tanned. Beneath the sleeve of his t-shirt, defined muscles contract with his movement. I take an extra look. His physique is different—strong, not bulky like a gym buff but more natural or earned from hard labor.

"And this is Samuel," Michael announces. Michael steps to the side as though he's not going to force his friend to interact.

Samuel turns, his big beautiful blue eyes lock with mine, and my stomach flutters—not of butterflies but the bloody uncoordinated flapping of an emu trying to dance.

"Hey, I'm Yasmine," Yasmine says in a polite voice. "This is Bree, Amy, and..."

I sense Yasmine staring at me.

"Eden," I finish. I force the blue haze of a spell his eyes cast over me to clear.

It's him.

The guy I saw in Salvador.

The guy who made my body hum like I was having an out-of-body experience and floating on the clouds. From the way he's staring at me, I assume he remembers me also. Something passes between us. The air crackles with physical electricity, and even in this heat, my insides warm. Something zings low in my stomach, reminding me of the joy I've deprived myself. I force myself to look away and check on my friends. They're chatting with the other guys, unaware this man—without even touching me—has awakened my female organs.

I smile at Samuel. "Nice to meet you. Are all four of you from the US?"

He nods. His brow pulls tight as though I've given him a vibe. Going by his expression, he's not pleased. His scowl flusters me.

"As you can tell, we're Aussies..." I pause, yet he gives me nothing. "We're here for Carnival and then heading north. What about you? Are you here for Carnival?" Damn, I keep tripping over my words.

He closes his eyes in a slow blink, and by the way his shoulders slowly rise and fall, he's either taking a deep breath, or it's a sigh.

What. Am I boring him?

"Please excuse me," he says in a smooth, deep voice. His gaze leaves mine. "Michael, I have to go." He waves at Michael before turning and disappearing into the crowd.

My mouth gapes. I push up onto my toes to find him, but it's useless. What did I say?

I turn back to the group and stand next to Samuel's friend. "I don't know what I said to upset your friend, but he's gone," I say to Harrison.

Yasmine looks at me, and I shrug.

Michael glances from Yasmine to me. "Don't worry yourself," he says. "Samuel's not one to stay out."

I nod as though it's nothing.

Did I say something to upset him?

I shake my head, hoping to find some clarity. I mean, who walks away from someone you just met? It wasn't like we didn't have chemistry. I felt it and know he did too —what a rude jerk. Well, Mr. Rudey Pants, it's your loss. I huff to myself and decide to think nothing else of him.

Only I can't stop thinking about him.

Bree must notice my mood because she grabs my hand and dances with me in the middle of the group.

We continue dancing late into the night.

Samuel.

I say his name over and over in my head.

In Salvador, I thought I imagined him and didn't believe I'd see him again. Yet here we are in Rio, and now my friends are hooking up with his friends. My alcohol-fueled thoughts are telling me I can be anyone I want to be. Rio is the city of love, after all. I raise my cup and stare into the liquid as though it holds answers. If I could have that time over, what would I say to him? I need to be prepared for the next time I bump into him.

Now my friends are with his friends, there will be a next time.

8

EDEN

Two days later, I'm throwing summer tank tops in a case and sorting through dirty clothes, even sweaty clothes from the clean ones. I zip up my case, and simultaneously on the floor beside me the phone brightens with a notification.

Ethan.

The jerk who broke my heart and one of the reasons I needed this holiday. I'm even more pissed my father hired him to replace me.

Since there's a slight chance it could be work-related, I open the message.

Hey...

Hope you're enjoying your holiday. It's weird working here. Sitting in your chair. Using your computer. I keep staring at the frame on your desk—the one of you and your friends. You're everywhere. I'm waiting for you to walk through the door and kick my ass and tell me to get out of your seat.

Dana's grumpier than I remember.

Your dad looks sad like he misses you even though you have only been gone two weeks. I'm grateful he's given me this position while you're away. It gives me a chance to work out what's next for me. When my internship ended, I thought the law firm would keep me on. My second biggest mistake. You think I'd have learned not to take things for granted.

I still regret what I did and hope one day you can forgive me. I do appreciate you saying we're friends. So, as a friend, I'm grateful to be working with your dad and seeing constant reminders of you, even though it hurts.

Stay safe, possum.

A storm of emotion tightens my chest.

The hurt.

The anger.

The embarrassment.

I toss my phone on the bed as if it's the cause.

Possum!

"Bree and Yasmine will meet us downstairs," Amy says, emerging from the bathroom.

I retrieve my phone and drop it in my bag because nothing will dampen my mood. The Copacabana Palace Hotel awaits us. We're living it up for the last two days of our stay in Rio. It's a highlight of our holiday, and the idea of experiencing the grandeur is enough to dismiss Ethan's text. Even more exciting, our new American friends secured tickets for us to attend the Magic Ball— standing tickets only. So, we need to shop for masquerade masks. Yesterday we ventured out and hired long gowns and shoes for the evening. Something we didn't pack since we never expected to attend. We were simply happy to be staying in the thick of the celebrations.

Hours later, with glittering masks packed in our cases, we head to the Belmond Copacabana Palace Hotel. I'm clinging to the seat of the taxi with every corner taken too fast and too hard, the Samba music blaring.

"Holy fuckeroni," Amy whispers when we pull up out the front of the hotel.

"It's even better up close," Yasmine says, eyes bulging.

"Ladies." Bree's sharp tone pulls us back. She coughs and nods to the doorman standing near the taxi. It appears most guests arrive in Mercedes, BMWs, and other luxury cars.

"*Obrigada*," Bree says, handing cash to the driver. *Thank you.*

Standing outside, I stare up to the hotel's imposing cream façade—a representation of elegance and sophistication. The doorman guides us inside to an opulent lobby. The sparkling chandelier grabs my attention first before a white-gloved hand lifts prompting us toward the reception desk. There are walls of fine marble and floors in mosaic. I consider the rich and famous footsteps we're following in as we're led toward the elevator.

We take the elevator to the third level. I stand at the door with Yasmine and smile in anticipation. Bree and Amy walk a little further along the hall to the room next to ours.

We open the door to polished antique furnishings, a marble bathroom, and chocolates on a period desk to welcome us. In unison, we drop our bags and stride to the double doors opening to a Juliette balcony facing the beachfront.

Yasmine exhales dramatically. "Just wow."

Salt air assaults my senses. The view is enough to make me forget the humidity.

Yasmine opens her arms wide like she's impersonating Christ the Redeemer statue. "I'm never leaving."

"Neither am I." We giggle, then slip back to being mesmerized at the sight of the cerulean ocean, watching surfers and swimmers.

"Want to check out the pool?" Yasmine asks.

"Hell, yeah." Exploring the hotel is an adventure on its own.

We hang our ball gowns in the closet, change into swimsuits, then don the white bathrobes and slip-ons provided. After notifying the other girls, it's only a matter of minutes before we're all sunning ourselves on the loungers surrounding the pool.

Stretched out on the sunbed, the sun warms my ochre skin. The waiter delivers champagne in crystal flutes, and I feel like a friggin' superstar.

I take a quick dip in the water to cool off and then lie back on my navy and white striped towel.

"Look at us living the life of the rich and famous," Amy sings.

"I could get used to it, I guess," Bree says and chuckles.

Slowly, people vacate the pool area, and I assume it's to prepare for the ball tonight.

"Hey, I'm going to head up and shower first," I tell Yasmine.

I slip on the white robe without bothering with the

ties and hesitate at the winding marble staircase when I hear the elevator door ding. I stride past staff speaking anxiously in their foreign tongue. I assume the fuss is about tonight's ball.

The doors open, and I rush in then hit the button for the third floor without looking at the guy leaning on the back wall. He steps beside me, so we're both in line and ready to race through the doors. Awareness shoots along my spine. A forest scent combined with earthy male hits me. I tilt my head toward him, and fire flares inside of me when Samuel's pure blue eyes lower to meet mine.

A dent forms between his brows. "It's Eden, right?"

"Yes." I look away, doing my utmost to ignore the pull between us.

"Water refreshing?"

"Uh-huh." I keep my focus straight ahead.

"I understand my friends have purchased tickets for you and your friends to attend the ball tonight."

Is he serious? This is his first thought after what happened between us the other night. "We're paying Michael back for the tickets," I say quickly. "Will you be going?" I turn to gauge his reaction.

His eyes rise to meet mine, and we both know I've caught him checking me out.

"Under sufferance." He turns and stares directly ahead at the elevator door as though wishing it would open.

"I'm sure no one is forcing you."

The sarcasm in his chuckle matches my tone.

The elevator dings. The door opens, and I walk out without even a goodbye. Somehow, I managed to act cool around him, but the way my heart is pounding in my chest, I'm anything but calm.

My eyelids are artfully painted with powdered glitter. I've paid extreme attention to detail even though a lace mask will conceal half my face. I down another glass of bubbles, and joy pumps through my veins making me lightheaded with an understanding of what freedom is.

Not wild as my father believes.

Brave and free.

I pour another glass. This time, I sip it slowly while waiting for my friends who are still in the bathroom adding finishing touches to their makeup. My white gown fits like a glove, and I almost didn't choose it in fear of looking washed out with my fair hair. Here, with sun-kissed skin and a holiday glow radiating from within, I feel anything but washed out.

"It's time," I say, urging my friends along. I pick up my phone and take a selfie.

With alcohol fueling my thoughts, I tap out the reply to Ethan I had been avoiding.

Rio is epic. I don't want to come home. So, go ahead and get comfortable in my chair.

Btw, we all make mistakes. You need to learn from each one and not repeat the same shit. So, please stop calling me possum. The sweet taste of hearing you call me that soured a long time ago. Don't feel guilty about us because I don't. We are friends. That is all. Oh, and thanks for working for me.

I hit send and drop my phone in my bag, smiling from one jeweled ear to the other. I drain the last of my champagne and promise myself that tonight I'll prove that I'm over Ethan, once and for all.

9

SAMUEL

On entering the ballroom, Samuel makes his way to the balcony. He finds a space in the far-right corner and remains there. The position allows him to inhale the clean ocean air, keep his distance from the crowd growing inside the French doors, and be prepared for when *she* arrives.

He tugs at the bow around his collar and loosens the button beneath. It's been years since he wore this attire. It's a vast difference from the grass skirt he dons in Ulara.

He pulls at his shirt. The need to dress appropriately is impractical when the humidity is much the same as in the rainforest. He shakes his head. Society conforms many to unrealistic rules.

Samuel turns away from the ladies standing within arm's reach of him and clicking selfies on their phone.

He stares out to the ocean.

It's the one thing he misses, the one thing the rainforest doesn't offer despite the clean running water streaming from the tepui—crystal clear water unpolluted by man. He smiles, thinking about his *home*, and yet looks longingly to the sea. He makes a silent promise to swim before he leaves. He bows his head, his duty to his friends fulfilled for another year. He has proved his well-being. As for his sanity, they believe his anti-social behavior stems from living in solidarity. They know little of his life in Ulara.

Except Michael.

He's privy to more.

"What can I get you?" As though summoned, Michael appears and lands a hand on Samuel's shoulder, a crystal glass of beer in his other hand.

Samuel raises his glass of water. "I'm good, thanks."

"Sam, it's your last night. At least have one for old time's sake."

Old time's sake.

In college, he and Michael survived on booze, parties, and sex, usually all three in unison in the house they shared. And even now, he's cautious with Michael trying to pry more from Samuel about his lifestyle. There were times when Samuel wanted nothing more to do with him. Only he's a family friend and stood by Samuel when his parents were infuriated with his decision to throw away his career.

Samuel looks away to gather his thoughts and conceal his expression while pushing out judgment of his former self. "I'm honestly fine drinking sparkling water. In this heat, and wearing a tux—"

Words stick in his throat at the sight of her. Black lace covers her eyes, yet he recognizes her. She's laughing with her friends. It's as though his body has tuned in to the tone of her voice, the sound waves float across the crowd and, like a homing pigeon, find him. Every nerve ending is on high alert.

He's avoided the Western world's alcohol for years. Tonight, he needs it more than ever to calm his erratic thoughts. Tonight, he should avoid it more than ever to keep all wit about himself.

"Maybe one, then," he says without taking his eyes off Eden.

"That's my man. The old you is in there somewhere." Another slap to his back is hard enough for him to step forward.

Michael calls out to Harrison, who has already waved the girls over on the balcony, twenty feet away from where Samuel stands. A group of a dozen men and women close the gap between Samuel and his friends. His attempt at keeping a safe distance from people is pointless. The corner position allows him to watch her from a safe space and decide whether to retreat quietly back to his room after one drink. His brain tells him to do the latter. He has managed to shut out lust for years. Tonight, he struggles to control his attraction. A chemical overdose streams through him after being deprived for too long. He glances down at his hands. His veins bulge, and he understands why. The chemicals fueling his bloodstream are now controlling his bodily responses.

She speaks to her friends, and he hisses out a curse at the sweet sound. He closes his eyes and wills his heart to slow. No female has had this effect over him, ever. What the hell is wrong with him? She's another human only of the opposite sex, and he sees half-naked women in the village every day. He shakes his head, chuckles quietly to berate himself, and turns back to the ocean. He leans his elbows on the rail while he takes in the vista. To think he not long ago believed he had lost the urge, and now he's acting like an experienced fool.

"Michael said to bring this over to you."

At the sound of her voice, he spins awkwardly, almost knocking the glass of beer from her grasp.

"Shit, I didn't mean to spook you." Eden flicks beer droplets from her fingers and wipes the material of her dress.

"I apologize." He leans in and brushes droplets from the white fabric clinging to her hips. Her skin warms his fingers through the thin material. He yanks his hand away, takes the beer from her grasp, and nods. All rational thought is lost as he inhales her fruity scent.

"Okay, then." She fidgets seemingly lost without anything in her hands.

"May I get you a drink?"

Eden smiles, elevating Samuel's desire to touch her, a need his body longs for, and instinctively, he takes a step closer.

"Amy is getting me a glass of champagne. So..." She takes a step back. "You should come over and join us." She nods toward his friends.

"I need a moment." He pulls out his cell as an excuse. "I'm expecting a call."

"Right. Well, I'll catch you later." She turns and glides in her heels back to the group. His gaze roams over her bare shoulders, down a back crisscrossed with spaghetti straps. He watches her hips sway and makes out the swell of her rear beneath the white satin. He assesses the lines and realizes she's wearing a thong and imagines her naked in nothing but that thin piece of material.

Samuel has succumbed to the power she has over him. He leans over the balcony and closes his eyes. The way the band of his trousers has tightened around his hips, he'll need more than a moment.

For one night, he'll divulge in the pleasure of being close to her. Tomorrow he'll head back to Ulara and far away, not to be charmed by her presence.

He waits until he can straighten without embarrassment before finding his friends. Harrison is talking to Eden. His hand rests on her shoulder, and Samuel's pulse surges. He fights the urge to storm over and smack his hand away. He downs the cold liquid in three gulps and places the empty glass on the tray of a waiter passing by. Jealousy was never part of his makeup. He feels possessed and uncomfortable with how he's reacting. Panic builds in his gut in not having control of his emotions.

He starts for the door, weaving around guests.

"Hey." Sean pats his back and hands him another beer. "Wondering when you were going to join us."

He bumps Samuel in the direction of the group. "Got this for Michael, although you could use it more." With a hand on Samuel's shoulder, he walks beside him. Being close to Eden is like being on a high and craving the pleasure of dopamine to be rewarded with euphoria. It's a warning for him to remove Sean's hand from his shoulder and call it a night. Instead, he accepts the beer and walks toward *her* as though he has lost all control.

When they join the group, Eden turns and makes space beside her. "Did you take your call?"

"I did." He looks to Michael.

Michael gives him a smug smile. "Not so bad after all, is it?"

10

EDEN

My stomach cartwheeled the moment we entered the ballroom, and I'm still amazed we secured one of the hottest tickets in town.

Decorations sparkle on the walls and ceiling. Under the lights, a band plays a catchy jazz tune, and the smile hasn't left my lips. Along with every guest, I talk at a higher octave, my voice joining the hum of excitement in the room and on the balcony.

"Thank you," I say when Yasmine hands me another glass of champagne before she stands beside Michael. I don't miss the way she looks at him, hanging off every word he utters. He has dark hair and brown eyes with *that* look and a muscled physique—a tell-tale sign he works out. And I know Yasmine's thoughts are tick, tick, tick. I understand as I'm doing the same standing beside Samuel. My heart is racing, yet I'm doing my best to act cool around him. When Michael convinced me to take him a beer, the change in him could give a girl whiplash. For some reason, I now feel like I have the upper hand.

Michael makes another joke about his travels in Peru.

Yasmine pulls a face. "I call bullshit."

"I kid you not. Have you been there?"

Yasmine shakes her head. "We will be in a couple of weeks."

"Michael." Samuel has barely uttered a word, and yet this sounds like a reprimand. My breath catches momentarily.

Michael frowns at Samuel. I'm not sure what's happening between the pair but note the silent message conveyed.

"Well, I'm up for an adventure in Peru because I fell in love with Iguassu Falls and the rainforest," I say to lighten the conversation.

Michael rolls his eyes. "You haven't experienced anything until you venture into the heart of the jungle." His gaze flicks to Samuel, and he shrugs. "Just saying."

Samuel stiffens beside me.

"You don't like the rainforest?"

His brow arches at my question. "I'd like to hear more about your trip to Iguassu."

I smile as I recall the details of our trip only days before. "Invigorating. Breathtaking." I shake my head in wonder. "Seriously, you have to go there. It was two hours by plane and well worth the journey." His lips curl a little at the edges. "I'm not joking. It's been a highlight so far."

"The humidity and oversized bugs didn't bother you?" He grins at me as though he's waiting for me to concur.

I wave my hand acting blasé. "You don't even notice because you're in another world. The power of the water surging over the cliff. The rainforest surrounding you and all the noise of the creatures fade because the roar of the water is deafening."

His eyes lock with mine. After a moment, he smiles

all perfect white teeth, and the joy reaches his blue eyes. Damn, he needs to smile more. "You like waterfalls?"

"Yeah." I smile back. "It was different than anything I've experienced. When we walked through the rainforest, we even saw a toucan."

"Impressive. Where are you headed next?"

"After the Samba parade, north along the coast to Ilhéus. Then a short stop in Caracas before Margarita Island. From there, on to Peru and hopefully, Galapagos, although we haven't booked the last week in case we decide to extend our days in Peru or head to Colombia." I didn't sound like someone who lived a sheltered life and was afraid of change. It feels good not to be that person and be adventurous. I raise my chin and look into those beautiful eyes with newfound confidence. "Have you traveled to any of those places?"

"A while ago." He loosens his collar beneath his bowtie, takes several mouthfuls of his beer before looking sideways at me. "How long will you be in Ilhéus?"

"About a week to explore the coast and have some downtime."

He nods while looking into his beer. "There's this place. It's quite a bus ride to get to, but it's worth it for the caves, smaller waterfalls, and a mystical lake."

"A mystical lake?" I grin at him. "I must remember to mention it to Yasmine."

"A non-believer?"

I snort quietly. "I'm a visual person. I like to see things with my own eyes. Though some things..." I pause, thinking of when I found out my ex had cheated on me. "Some things I believe if the information comes from a good source." I glance at Yasmine, thankful to her for having my back.

His eyes never leave my face. Under the heat of his gaze, I'm reminded of the first time I saw him on the beach in Salvador. I'm sure it was him, except the way he acted at the bloco—

"Can I get you another drink?"

I glance down at my empty glass. "Were you in Salvador a few weeks ago?"

"What?"

I glance up. "In Salvador. At the Iemanjá ceremony?" I watch his Adam's apple bob. "We saw each other, didn't we?" I'm thankful for the alcohol fueling my courage.

He takes the empty crystal from my fingertips and turns toward the bar. In perfect timing, a waiter walks by with a tray of beverages. Samuel takes a glass of champagne and a beer, swivels back, and hands me the crystal.

"Yes," he says and takes a swig without looking at me.

I knew it.

"Why were you rude to me at the bloco?"

"Not to you. I didn't want to be there."

"You were a grump."

He smiles into his glass. "I've been called worse."

His gaze lifts and meets mine. There's something about the different shades of blue in his hues that mesmerizes me, and I struggle to look away. In a moment of contentment, I know Samuel has come into my life for a reason. Judging by his expression, he senses a connection as well. He leans in. I lick my lips and lean closer. His lips are so close to mine—a whisper, a kiss away. What would they feel like on my skin? My neck? My décolletage? I raise one hand to touch his face—

He jerks back.

Freezes.

His eyes dart up to his friends as though he requires backup.

What just happened?

"I'm sorry if I gave you the wrong impression." He holds one hand up at his friends in farewell.

Shit. He's not into me?

"Night, man. Sleep well," Michael shouts.

His friends don't seem surprised Samuel is leaving.

"It was nice meeting you," he whispers.

Before he turns away, there's a flicker of regret in his eyes.

What the actual heck?

"Yeah." I want to say much more, only the shock of him bailing has words stuck in my dry throat.

I withhold from turning to watch him walk away.

Michael is watching me curiously. "I know his room number if you're interested."

Yasmine catches on and gapes, then a smirk creeps over her face. "Go on, Eden."

"He's not interested," I manage to rasp out.

Michael laughs. "I'll ask you again at the end of the night."

11

SAMUEL

The last time Samuel checked his cell, it was close to midnight.

Laughter echoed behind his door with tipsy guests bumping the hallway walls heading back to their suites.

He rolls over, stares at the window, and groans. At this rate, he'll get no sleep. It's not the noisy guests he blames. His thoughts are relentless of Eden and what could've been. Ecstasy for one night could open the gates of desire. More of what he can't have. He'd forgotten the buzz of lust and attraction and the thrill of pleasure hormones circulating and fulfilling certain areas. Now he's suffering and unable to sleep, wanting a release.

He reminds himself of the promise he made years ago —not to get involved with a woman while he was committed to the Ularan people. It's not their way to divulge in casual relationships, and he's now one of *them*.

A bang on his door has him listening for revelers. Another, and he realizes it's no mistake. He jumps up, pulls on shorts, and steps closer to the door.

"Samuel. Open the door."

His heartbeat soars at the sound of her voice.

The knocking grows louder.

"It's Eden."

He flicks on the light before opening the door. "Is everything okay?"

"No." She strides past Samuel before he has a chance to object. He catches the sweet aroma of wine on her breath. "Michael and Yasmine are getting it on in my room. I'm not into watching. And Amy has hooked up with Harrison, and Sean with Bree. So, it leaves you. I know you're not into me, but I need a place to sleep."

A better idea would be to pay for another room for her to sleep because he won't get any rest with her so close. He locks the door. Her hips sway beneath the white gown as she moves toward his bed. She looks even more beautiful than she did a few hours before.

Eden unzips her dress. He struggles to breathe, yet he can't look away. He should tell her to leave. Tell her she's right, and he's not interested. Only it would be a lie.

"Stop," he hisses.

"You can't expect me to sleep in this." The dress loosens and slides over her curves to pool around her feet. She pauses and looks longingly at him. He holds her gaze, and yet he sees all of her. His peripheral vision is outstanding—rounded breasts bounce freely, and the skin-colored flimsy piece of material on her hips barely covers anything.

His chest expands in a greater need of air. He's aware of other parts of him expanding too.

He retrieves a t-shirt from his case and hands it to her. "You'll be more comfortable in this."

There's a glimmer of sadness in her eyes.

He slides under the sheet to hide his attraction. "There's toothpaste in the bathroom if you need it."

Under the safety of Egyptian cotton, he watches her bare rear as she pads to the bathroom. Hell, she's truly perfect.

"Hinting about the toothpaste..." she calls out from the bathroom, "... could mean you want to do something," she mumbles with the toothbrush in her mouth.

He sits up, but she's out of his sight. "Are you using my toothbrush?"

"Is it the little white one in a pack?" she says with a mouthful.

"No." He flops back onto the bed, remembering his is in a bag, and the complimentary brush remained next to the basin. The back of his wrist rests against his forehead, and it does nothing to ease the sexual thoughts tormenting him.

"Stop avoiding my question." She gargles water. "Are you intending to kiss me?"

"Being a gentleman and providing you a place to crash, and then offering for you to freshen up isn't an invitation to hook up," he mumbles, even if it's what he craves. He inhales a breath, and all he smells is the sweetness of Eden, and the scent is enough to send his thoughts into overdrive.

Moments later, she clambers in beside him. "What is it about me guys don't like?" she whispers.

"I have no idea what you're talking about?" Keeping a safe space between them, he slides onto his side, so he's facing her.

"It's Rio, for God's sake and not one kiss."

"You want someone to kiss you?" His voice cracks on the words.

Eden nods. "It doesn't have to mean anything."

Only it will, and knowing so, Samuel ignores the warning in his head of the commitment he has made. He wants to reach out and touch her cheek and tell her what he truly feels. She's a beautiful woman, and yet the pull between them is beyond physical attraction. The short time he has spent with her has given him time to see the colors of her aura. The kindness and passion of her heart emanate from her soul. How he sees and senses it is beyond explanation, and it's getting harder for him to resist the burning attraction between them. He leans in until his lips are inches away and hesitates. Her eyes hold him captive, pools of blue capable of drowning him. He stops fighting what he wanted to do the moment he saw her on the beach.

He starts slowly—a gentle kiss. Soft, moist lips reciprocate. She sighs into his mouth. It triggers a reaction, and he presses his lips harder to hers. Her tongue finds his, and he loses all coherent thought. *How long has it been since he has kissed a woman like her?* If he is being truthful, he's never met anyone like her.

His body presses against hers as he gives into lust. His hands move over the swell of her hips and higher to find her soft breasts. He pulls back and stares into her eyes.

"Don't stop."

He doesn't want to. Only he remembers how much she has had to drink, and if anything happens between them, it will be under the influence of alcohol. Reeling in emotion, he rasps, "Not tonight when you've been drinking."

She flips up, throws a leg over, and lands on his hips

in one smooth action. She settles where he feels it most. Eden smiles down at him. "You do like me."

"More than you'll remember tomorrow." He grabs her hips to keep her from moving deciding to speak honestly —there is a high chance she won't recall anything he says when she wakes. "You're right. I did see you on the beach, and I wanted you then. I've been fighting it the entire time. Right now, I want nothing more than to be between your legs." Her eyes widen. "But it won't happen. I'm not taking advantage of you. You're killing me right now, so please..." he grabs her hips tighter, "... don't move, or we both might do something we regret."

Eden hasn't taken her eyes off of him. She frowns as if her thoughts have caught up. "I wouldn't regret it. I should be angry with you. You were an ass."

He wishes she were. He could handle her anger better than her advances. "You have every right to be."

"You've liked me all along?"

He nods while assisting her in lying beside him. He strokes her face, runs his hand along her neck and shoulder. "You're truly a beautiful woman."

She smiles, and he likes how it reaches her eyes. "So not tonight," she whispers. She closes her eyes. "I'll see you in the morning."

"I'll be looking forward to it. Are you heading to the Samba parade tomorrow night?"

She makes a purring sound. "Uh-huh, then onto Ilhéus. I'm looking forward to staying at the resort on the beach." Samuel continues to stroke her face until her breathing slows, and she sounds like she's asleep. He kisses the tip of her nose, knowing he won't be resting anytime soon.

12

EDEN

"Desculpe." *Excuse me.*

"What?" I moan and roll over in bed.

My eyes open, and I gasp. A maid is standing by the door. I jerk up and realize I'm not in my room, and snippets of last night flash in my mind. I'm staring at the maid.

"I'm sorry. Did Samuel order breakfast?" I straighten the t-shirt over my chest and stroke my hair, wishing it would behave.

We exchange confused glances. "Mr. McMahon checked out," she manages in broken English.

"Pardon." My stomach tightens, trying to comprehend what she's telling me.

She bows her head and takes a step backward to retreat.

"No, no." I scan the room for my clothes. "If you give me a minute, I'll be out of here." I hold up one finger. "One moment."

She nods. We stare at each other for a brief moment

before she leaves—long enough for pity to settle in her eyes.

I clench both fists and want to scream. "Fuck you, Samuel McMahon." I take a deep breath. Who does that? Who bloody checks out while I—whatever I am to him—am still in the room? I pull off his t-shirt and slip into my white satin gown.

I gather my shoes and purse. I glance back at his t-shirt on the bed. I'll claim it too. With the Brazilian soccer team logo on the front, it's like my personal souvenir.

Waiting at the elevator, I have no idea what floor I'm on until the number above the door lights up.

"Asshole" plays over in my head like a mantra.

I tap on the door before I use my room key to open it.

"Yasmine," I whisper and peer around the corner. Two heads are on pillows with sheets covering their bodies. I sneak in, grab some clothes from the closet before heading to the bathroom.

Yasmine lifts her head. "Edes." Her voice is thick with sleep. "What are you doing? The plan was to sleep in, remember? We're going to be up all night at the Samba parade."

I glance at the clock. It's just gone seven in the morning. Oh, for heaven's sake. "Well, we didn't explain that to Samuel before he decided to check out at some ungodly hour, and the maid woke me believing the room was vacant," I spit.

Michael groans. "He what?" He sits up, and the sheet falls away to reveal a tattooed muscled chest.

I swallow down the ball of hurt once more. Tears sting and threaten to spill out the corners of my eyes. "Samuel checked out."

"Are you sure?" He rubs his hands over his face and sighs.

"Yep."

"The jerk." Michael reaches for his phone, but the screen doesn't light up when he touches it. "It's dead." He tosses it back onto the bedside table. "I'll find out what the hell is going on later. I'm not surprised, though. He's... different."

"You don't say." I fold my arms.

"He does this. It's not you." Michael rubs the back of his neck and shakes his head.

"Is he married?"

"Not to a woman." He chuckles when he sees Yasmine's and my expressions. "Or a man," he adds. "To a way of life." He pauses. "It's hard to explain."

"You better start trying harder," Yasmine threatens in her best tone.

"I'm going to shower." I raise my hands in the air. "Please find a way to explain it because I'm feeling pretty shitty."

Behind the door, I ignore the murmurs of Yasmine and Michael in a discussion.

Under the water, my thoughts clear. Memories of last night flash back. He wanted me. He did from the moment we saw each other. I sob into the water spray remembering his words, his touch.

What's wrong with me?

13

EDEN

Ileus, Brazil

Two days later...

Under the Brazilian sun, I roll my shoulders and stretch my neck from side to side. I'm grateful that Yasmine discovered the coastal town and booked the beachside resort so we could rest after Rio. Only now, with what happened in Rio, busy is better to keep certain thoughts at bay. The brochures are spread out on the sand so I can plan my days. My thoughts wander to the mystical lake *he* mentioned. Now, I'm determined to find it—to take something positive out of our negative interaction.

"There's a chocolate factory. And we can go on a tour of an old cacao plantation," Bree says beside me.

"Oh, and look. You know *Jorge Amado,* the author we saw in Salvador? He came from around here." Amy hands me another brochure. "There's a bar, the *Vesuvio,* named in one of his books. It looks popular."

"I can rely on you to find a reason to go to a bar."

Amy winks at me. "I've had enough of the beach. I'm heading up to the resort pool. Anyone keen?"

"I will." The wind has picked up, and I'll find it easier to read through the pile of brochures in a sheltered area.

Amy hands me the brochure on the *Vesuvio* bar and gives me a pointed look. "We need to go out and let loose."

"You know, you're right."

🌴

The following morning, Bree rolls her eyes at Amy. "Someone go a little hard on the Caipirinhas last night?"

Amy plucks the straw from the glass and sucks the acai smoothie in a slurp. "I had fun. Oh shit." She glances down at the purple spots on her white tank top. "I need to change."

"You have ten minutes before the bus arrives," I warn her. "And we're not missing it."

When Amy races off, Yasmine piles the laminated menus on the table. "I'm going to brave the Dourada tonight."

"You're going to try catfish?" Bree asks, her voice a higher pitch.

"Yep."

"I'm not sure why we're discussing dinner at breakfast." I laugh. "If we're eating lunch at *Vesuvio,* I might not need dinner."

Bree starts in on the nutritional value of the exotic fruits available here. "They are a rich source of Vitamins A and C and minerals calcium, iron, phosphorus, magnesium, and zinc," she says and continues on until Amy returns.

"Okay. Let's get this tourist stuff out of the way for Edes, so I can get back here to the pool," Amy says, out of breath.

"I found more churches as well." I ignore the eye-rolling. "Don't you find the architecture interesting?"

"I guess." Amy shrugs. "I find *other* things more interesting. We have five weeks left, and it's about meeting guys, adventure, and fun."

We make our way to the front of the resort in time for the bus.

"Michael and I are staying in touch," Yasmine says, taking a seat beside me. "We message several times a day." She bows her head as though she has a secret. Or maybe she's embarrassed. "He gets me... like really gets me. I think even more than all of you." She peers up. Her eyes convey an apology.

"What do you mean more than us?" I whisper, my voice cracking on the last word. I'm not sure whether it's hurt or anger that she believes a guy she has just met has a stronger force of understanding than a decade of friendship. What did he say to her? I can't help thinking he has an agenda. I'm overcome with wanting to protect her, except it's Yasmine. She has always looked out for my friends and me. She's the one who's strong in her beliefs and convictions, even more so than Bree because Bree still doubts herself and her ability even though she's borderline genius.

"It's like we're searching for the same thing." She shrugs. "There's more to our personal being. More to this life," she says in an even quieter voice. I tilt my head, so my ear is closer to her face. "We talked a lot in Rio about life and our individual journeys. He wants to meet up again before we get to the island."

I had noticed she was spending more time on her phone, which is also unlike her. "What makes you think he knows you better than me?"

Her eyes scan my face, and I know I'm failing at hiding my concern.

Her head tilts to the side. "I'm different."

"In a good way," I say.

"If I tell you what I want to do, you'll get mad at me."

"Why would I? You're my friend, and I trust you."

Her shoulders rise and fall. "I'm considering meeting Michael in Peru."

I nod quickly to portray I understand. "Peru is part of the itinerary."

"I want to go further than the outskirts of the Amazon. I want to travel deeper into her heart. Experience what she has to offer."

"If you've considered it, then I know you have weighed up the facts and know the pros and cons. I'm not sure why you thought I'd be mad."

"Because I'm going to experience it all. You know I believe there are more dimensions to our world. The Amazon is a place of life. The people, their simple way of life, their beliefs... it's a multitude of everything... race, color, plants, diversity. The jungle holds the secrets I've been searching for, and I want to try the medicinal plants. I know you're freaking out, but Michael will guide me."

Admittedly, I'm a little scared for her. Hell, Bree *will* freak out because she understands what could possibly go wrong and will do all she can to deter Yasmine.

"It's what my soul craves, and I want to do it with Michael. I don't want negative thoughts to block my spiritual journey or you all telling me what can go wrong, not how wonderful I'll feel after."

"Okay, then," I whisper. "If you feel this strongly about it, then I'll have your back." I reach and touch her arm. "We go together," I emphasize. "I'm not going to let you do this alone, but we need to learn more because we definitely have to be cautious, and I'm not being negative."

Yasmine smiles, then turns to gaze out of the bus window. Her smile doesn't fool me. She's lost in her thoughts, and I sense she isn't telling me everything. We're traveling together yet embarking on our personal journey, which might mean doing some of it alone. It's not what we promised each other before this holiday. Nor my father. I push out the thought because right now, I need to do what it takes to look out for my friend.

🌴

The following day, I'm sitting on a hot bus while my friends hang at the beach. I promised them I'd be fine and needed some time alone. A tour inland to a mystical lake—the one Samuel suggested—and to waterfalls didn't interest them, especially after they hit the bars again last night. Amy insisted on coming until Yasmine told her to give me space. When I didn't go out with them last night, my friends realized I was still upset about Samuel. I used the time to call my parents, reassuring them I was fine.

"Fishing is a means of survival here." The sound of the tour guide's voice brings me back. Pressing my nose closer to the glass, I make out small fishing villages dotting the edges of a large lake. Canoes line the shore. The tour guide speaks about folklore and the floating islands on the lake. Tales of an underwater kingdom and mystical beings—hence, why it's known as the Enchanted Lake. He tells a story of how fishermen never returned if their boats sailed near the floating islands at night. It intrigues me as to how some small communities have a strong belief in folklore and how these myths influence their lives and cultural tradition compared to our dependency on science, fact, and statistics. I struggle with the legends since I'm a visual person. I snort, thinking how I'd be the fisherman venturing out because I didn't believe and possibly never return. If only Yasmine had come with me. She'd enjoy hearing about the folklore.

I close my eyes momentarily and wish for some things in my life to change.

The bus bounces along the dirt road. "The first waterfall is Salto de Apepique," the tour guide says. "This waterfall is popular for rappelling."

The cliff edge isn't high, so a dozen of us are taken through the steps of a quick safety instruction before rappelling the rock while the others relax with morning tea.

The rope supports me when I push off the rocky edge. Water sprays my face, refreshing and awakening the fact my life is in the hands of one rope. No sooner do I reach the bottom, I'm clambering up the rocky cliff to do it again and again.

"We now have a short walk, so I apologize to those who have wet shoes," our guide calls out.

My feet are squishing in my sneakers. Ugh. Blisters will not be fun, but after an experience like that, it's worth it.

"Where are you from?"

I smile at the middle-aged lady beside me, both of us stumbling as we trample over pebbled rocks.

"Adelaide, South Australia."

"We're from Sheffield in the UK. By the way, I'm Kim."

I'd picked the English accent. "Hi, I'm Eden."

The guide stops and points to a cave. He talks in Portuguese first, then Spanish, before addressing us in English.

"Please gather in, people. We're to enter the cave. I'll explain the next activity. In the cave, I'll give a command. Then everyone is to remove their top and swap it with the person closest to them."

What?

I look at Kim, wide-eyed.

"You won't be able to see inside the cave. When we exit the cave, you're to find the person wearing your top. This person will be your partner for the remainder of the tour."

Surely, there are occupational health and safety issues with sharing clothes? This is worse than any team-building and trust exercise I've ever done.

I withhold my grumbling and offer a fake smile when laughter sounds through the group. I look around at the couples and consider how awkward it is for some. Hell, I don't have a partner. I follow one couple in, afraid to turn and check who's behind me. I don't want to establish what top they're wearing or if there are any sweat marks.

I remember Yasmine's words about not all experiences are enjoyable.

C'mon, Eden. It's an adventure, so try and roll with it.

Chatter and laughter echo as we approach the opening of the cave.

"Watch your step," our guide warns, shining his flashlight into the cavern. "Find a rock to sit on." I stumble on loose stones before regaining my balance. I walk about thirty steps in darkness, a dim light reflecting the outline of the stones. Taking a seat on the cold, moist pebbled ground, I rest my forehead on bent knees then lift my head when the guide speaks. I strain my eyes when he turns off the flashlight.

In the dark, fear creeps in. I've always been afraid of the unknown, of what I can't see. I remember being a little girl afraid of spiders, unlike my fearless gran. Her words echo in the back of my mind. What if I'm sitting next to a scorpion right now? I re-curl and place my head on my knees and wrap my arms around my thighs to block out the world and concentrate on my breathing.

"Sorry... sorry." Whispers come from behind me as someone stumbles to find a seat.

In the dark, our guide continues with his folklore stories relating to the Enchanted Lake. The musky air tastes wet, and with only blackness around us, it creates an eerie presence. Goosebumps prick up along my arms, and an unnerving tingle runs down my spine. Yet, I visualize his words. I see the calm waters of the blue-gray lake and the boats sailing across the water without a motor and feel the serenity in the stillness of night and of a single breath while watching these slow-moving islands drift into another dimension.

A weird sensation rolls over me. In the darkness, I'm reminded of nights I've cried myself to sleep. How in those times, Gran's spirit talked to me in my dreams. It's weird I'm thinking of her now.

The guide claps his hands, and I jump. "Now is the time to swap your top."

Would anyone know if I didn't play along? After all, it is dark, and no-one knows me...

I jump again when a hand rests on my shoulder. *Shit.*

I close my eyes, which is pointless really, except it helps me suck up what has to be done—remove my tank top. Soft material lands on my shoulder. I hold my tank out until it's yanked out of my hand. I fiddle with the top, trying to find a tag, not wanting to be the person everyone laughs at because her top is inside out or the back is the front.

When I reach the cave opening, my eyes burn in the light. A green t-shirt falls to my hips. I don't recall anyone wearing it. I search for the person wearing my yellow top. Laughter erupts from the group as people discover their surprise partner. The giggling continues as tops are turned from back to front and inside out. Some men have squeezed into their female partner's clothing.

In the distance, I spot a guy sitting alone with his back to me. A topless figure, a rock with yellow material thrown over his shoulder. The stranger is wearing a hat. He's facing away from the group looking out toward the rainforest beyond the cliffs. I look back to the group as I walk toward him, checking no one else is wearing my top. Everyone else appears to have paired up.

With every step, awareness zips up my spine. I recognize those shoulders. I want to believe it possible and curse myself for showing vulnerability.

I'm pulled closer by an invisible whirlpool.

When I reach him, I gasp.

What the actual hell?

Samuel's gaze is lowered as though giving me a minute.

My eyes laser in on him. I'm holding my breath waiting for him to say something.

His eyes lift slowly to meet mine. Gone is the

confident asshole. His eyes hold apology as he searches my face.

"Is this a sick joke?"

His brow pulls tight, then he shakes his head.

I fold my arms and glare at him. "Then why are you here?"

"It's not something I can explain in a couple of sentences. First, I wanted to apologize."

"For what? You just checked out early. It was your room, after all."

His mouth opens as if my nonchalant response surprises him.

"Oh right, for your shitty behavior. I remember now. In fact, I remember *everything*."

He stares at me, and his silence pisses me off even more. He nods to the group. "We should join them." He holds out my tank top. "I believe this is yours."

In a swift action, I pull his tee up and over my head. His gaze lifts to my bikini. "And I assume this is yours," I say bluntly.

He takes it from my grasp and doesn't put it on. He pushes up and uncurls to stand. Like dominoes, his muscles contract with movement from his arms, down his chest, to the ripple of his abs.

I'm dead.

I close my eyes momentarily before forcing my feet to move. I need a moment because my every cell crackles like live wires craving him. I hate myself for wanting him when right now I need to remain angry and hurt him like he hurt me. It's immature maybe, but my thoughts are all over the place. Mostly, I'm surprised as to why he's here.

Our guide points to the door of the bus. I take a seat at the back, and Samuel follows in silence, sliding in beside me. The window is now my focus, my shaky hands pushed under my thighs.

"Our next stop is *Saltos de Almada*. Here you can relax and take a swim," the guide announces.

The other tourists cheer.

My gaze doesn't falter from the glass. I don't want to be on this bus and this close to him when all I want to do is scream. "Why would you promise me morning and then leave before I wake?" I turn to meet his gaze. "You're nothing but an ass."

14

SAMUEL

Samuel didn't think she'd remember the words he spoke in Rio.

"You'd been drinking," he says gently.

"Not so much that I forgot."

He looks out the window to what has her interest and sees their reflection in the glass. She's watching his every move.

He sees the indent between her brows, and yet there is sadness in her eyes. "You're angry. I understand." He witnesses an eye roll. "The other night..." He closes his eyes momentarily with the memory. It was only five nights ago, yet it feels longer. "You surprised me. It put me in a position, and I needed time to consider my action."

She turns and glares. "Most guys would jump into bed with a naked woman given a chance," she hisses under her breath. "Especially the one I gave you. Unless I'm—"

"I'm not most men," he says. "I don't indulge like our friends."

She stalls as though comprehending what he's saying. Her expression softens, and he hopes she's considering his words.

She turns again to the window like it's a safety barrier even though both of their expressions are visible.

"Did you know I was on this tour?"

He nods. "Wait for the next stop, and I'll explain..."

As best he can.

How does he tell her the truth?

He can only explain how she has haunted him from the moment he first saw her.

Even from the time she took a seat on the bus, her scent filled the small space, and he knew it was her before he caught sight of her long, blonde ponytail flowing from the base of her cap, the same fruity, floral scent on her skin she wore to the ball. It taunts him with the memory of her lying close to him, and the soft curves of her body beneath his hands.

She obliterated his armor in Rio, armor he had built up over the years to resist women so he could focus on his work. His duty. He has never expected anyone to understand his way of life or his choices. Years of restraint and the willpower to get to this point in his life all vaporize when he's around her. He doesn't know why he gravitates to her like a bee to a flower. Not any flower. She has evolved from all others. Her scent and beauty attract him in a combined complexity, controlling his thoughts and manipulating his behavior. She's his weakness, and now he has her scent ingrained in his memory—his brain has selected her. The overwhelming need to understand *why* was enough for him to change his flight and head to Ilhéus to find her.

"I wanted to say hello before you hurried off to climb

the waterfall, only I didn't know how you'd react seeing me—"

She turns her head in a snap-like action. "You've been on this bus the entire time?"

"At the back," he confesses.

Eden removes her hands from beneath her bare thighs and wipes her palms on her tank top. "I don't know what to think."

The bus pulls to a stop, and the guide announces they have thirty minutes for a quick swim at the rock pool and to stay close by. Samuel stands when the rows before him file out. He glances at Eden and holds out his hand to help her slide across the vinyl. Her gaze remains fixed on the glass, and she stays seated. He leaves her to walk ahead. When he reaches the stream, he finds a smooth boulder to sit on away from the group.

He observes the other tourists splashing in the water to cool down. He catches her in his peripheral vision. She strips down to her bikini and wades into the water only several feet from him.

Tossing his t-shirt on the rock, he sits on the edge so his feet can dangle in the water.

For days, he contemplated what to say when he saw her again. His heart and mind have endured a battle since the morning he left her lying in his bed.

He grits his teeth when a voice tells him *you're weak*. He is threatening everything he's worked for, endangering the lives of those he now calls family. Simultaneously, his gut tightens the moment Eden rises from the water and takes a step toward him. Water drips from her sleek body, moisture glistening on golden skin in a goddess form. Right now, he believes she's one. It's the only explanation for the hold she has over him. The dark shadow of weakness consumes him.

Lust.

Desire.

And more.

It has sparked and ignited his soul. He had tried to ignore it and disregard the voice calling to him to do what he shouldn't. A voice reminding him of the one he hears in the dark of night when he sleeps on the jungle floor, a voice more powerful than any living being.

He sucks in more air as she approaches. She's six steps away. He braces himself for the impact. Their eyes lock. He sees her and is aware the moment her nipples peak beneath thin nylon. She squeezes moisture from her hair.

Three steps...

Two...

She sits beside him.

Her floral scent crashes through his barrier. He moves slightly to give her more room, ensuring her skin doesn't brush his. The slightest touch threatens his thin web of restraint. His manhood shifts a gear to drive his thoughts. He closes his eyes to give himself a moment.

For hours, he has prepared several short excuses as to his sudden appearance. Now she has infiltrated his senses, his composure flails. Yet hers has strengthened. Her strength impresses and nevertheless weakens him further.

"How did you know I'd be on this tour?" she asks without looking at him.

"I noticed your name on the booking sheet for the bus at the resort."

Her head snaps to face him. "You're staying at the resort?"

Samuel nods, hoping she doesn't make an assumption. "I'm not trying to scare you. After all, I did tell you about this tour. Yasmine revealed the resort where you're staying to Michael. I wanted to see you, so—"

"Then why did you leave Rio?"

"I can't explain it here. We need to be away from everyone."

"Do you hear how crazy you sound? You have stalked me, you treated me appallingly, and now you're asking me to be alone with you so you can *try* to justify your actions?"

A smile pulls at his lips. She thinks he's crazy *before* he explains.

15

EDEN

I need to keep a level head.

It's not easy to do when he slides into the seat alongside me, and inside the confines of the muggy interior of the bus, I'm overcome by his manly forest scent. His heat radiates too damn close, inciting desire, and it's building quicker than I can control. I wage an internal battle—the thoughts of *what if*? My face warms thinking of the night in Rio. Physically, my body craves him, but hell, he pursued me, and I'm in an unfamiliar country where laws differ from home.

A half-hour passes before I level my thoughts and ask one of many questions. "So, what do you do for work?" A question a stranger could ask on a greeting, and it's less intrusive than my other thoughts. I turn to catch his expression as though I have an internal lie detector.

"I'm a doctor."

I nod. "Where did you study?"

"Stanford."

He didn't hesitate.

His chin lifts slightly. "What do you do, as you put it?"

His eyes flick over my face like he's assessing me. If I lie, he'll know it.

"I... work as a marketing coordinator for a hotel company."

"Where?"

"Adelaide," I reply. "And you? Where do you work?"

His brow lifts. "Now?"

"Yes."

He nods ahead, and I peer through the large glass windshield of the bus to the road. "This is my stop."

We're in the middle of nowhere. I shoot him a blank look. I thought he was staying at the resort.

"The path here leads to the beach. Would you like to take a stroll with me so we can chat?"

The resort must be at least a half-hour drive away. "Walk?"

He nods, then stands. He holds up a finger at the guide.

"I don't know you?" I rasp.

"I'll answer your questions as best I can if you come with me."

I stand, ignoring my father's voice in the back of my head, and allow my gut instinct to guide me. Generally, it's on point, and I hope this is a time when my intuition doesn't let me down.

The bus slows, and we both walk the aisle. When we reach the guide, he places a mark beside our names on his notepad.

While we wait for the bus to pull to a stop, I reach for my phone and send Yasmine a message.

> I'm with Samuel. Samuel McMahon. Can you google him? He studied at Stanford. We're taking a walk along the beach. See you later!

Before stepping off the bus, I shoot a look toward our guide, hoping he'll remember my face.

Here goes nothing.

When the bus pulls away, I'm met with unruly green overgrowth on both sides of the narrow road.

"Where are we?"

"Not far out of town," he says before we turn onto a dirt path wide enough for a car to navigate despite the green wall of the forest threatening to swallow it up. Apart from the blue strip of sky directly above us, the forest walls impede vision, so I see nothing else.

"Is this someone's land?" Hell, you'd never find a body here. The way the plant life grows, you'd swear it rained steroids.

"It is. I met the owner several years back. He doesn't mind people using this track to the beach so long as you don't trash it."

"Trash it? I think it would win. Digest anything you threw at it."

He chuckles lightly, and damn, it ignites a beautiful emotion deep in my chest.

He picks up a piece of dead wood and smacks the overgrowth, allowing us to pass with ease. The vines are literally freaking me out as I'm torn between second-guessing my decision and simultaneously looking out for snakes and spiders.

"How long is the walk back?"

"Three hours."

What? I glance at my Fitbit. "It will be dark before we get to the resort."

He nods, then directs me to the right when the path forks. The path is narrower, and at times, branches and vines block it. Samuel pins down wayward stems for me to squeeze past. I can hear the ocean, and it's enough to calm my thoughts because the notion of being trapped in this overgrowth is beyond unsettling.

Every time I brush past him, warmth envelops me, melting my fear. This time his eyes connect with mine as I slide past.

"Wait up," he says, smiling. Naturally, I smile back because one thing I've learned is Samuel rarely smiles. "I want to watch your reaction."

"My what?"

Samuel steps ahead of me and pushes another clump of vine aside. I step past onto white sand to meet the ocean. I inhale a deep breath to fill my lungs with clean, salted air. "Wow." I take a few steps and look from left to right—what a sight. The ocean is a bright azure blue meeting white sand, bordered by a green rainforest. Never have I seen anything so beautiful. Untouched.

Samuel points, indicating the direction we'll be walking. "We need to keep moving."

"Because it'll be dark before we arrive back?"

He stares down at me. "And the tide leaves little space to walk."

"Right." I pick up my pace. *Holy shit.* "You didn't think to mention this before?"

He smiles at me. "We'll be fine and maybe have time for a swim."

"I'll wait and see because this tide thing is freaking me out a little."

We keep walking at a steady pace. There is barely a wave, and even from here, the water is transparent in the shallows. The whole setting is serene, yet when I glance up, there is seriousness behind his eyes. "You look like you're carrying the weight of the world on your shoulders." This man has me curious, and I want to know what's going through his mind.

His gaze is fixed ahead. "Some days, it feels that way," he says in a softer tone.

"Is it your work?"

"Relatively. It's more when I'm not at work I feel the pressure to return."

"Ah, a work-a-holic."

With his eyes trained to the path ahead and a serious expression, he doesn't confirm or deny it.

"Do you work in a hospital?"

"Not anymore."

"A private practice?"

"In a way, yes."

"What state do you practice in?"

"As in the United States?"

I nod. "Where did you say you're from?"

"California."

"I've always wanted to visit LA and San Fran."

"Why?"

I shrug. "It's exciting. I've watched heaps of shows and—"

"Tourists believe it's like what you see on television and in the movies? It partly is, but there's a whole other side."

"It's not exciting to you because you've always lived there."

Samuel drops his backpack and retrieves a water bottle. "Would you like some water?"

"No thanks. I have plenty." I find my bottle while he guzzles several mouthfuls before placing it inside the backpack.

He wipes his brow with the back of his hand before continuing. "Have you always lived in Adelaide?"

I nod. "Apart from a quick trip to Bali, this is my first serious overseas holiday."

He peers at me sideways. "Serious?"

"Well, it's a risk coming to a strange country. We received a shitload of vaccinations. And there's crime and guns and—"

"So not for work. Serious enjoyment." He smiles down at me, and although I'm sensing a touch of sarcasm, I like seeing him smile.

I bump his side with my hip. "Enjoyment is a serious matter, don't you think?"

Our eyes meet. For a few seconds, we allow ourselves to assess each other before he drags his gaze from mine.

"You're yet to explain *why* you're here. So... did you follow me?"

"Since I was here first, I don't believe it's following you."

"You knew I was coming. Don't make me categorize this as stalking."

He chuckles. "Fine."

"After Rio, what changed your mind?" I quicken the next few steps, so I'm ahead of him, then turn and walk backward so I can observe his expression as he answers.

He slows the pace. "What is it you want to hear?"

"I don't want you to tell me what I want to hear. I want to know what changed for you?"

He glances to the ocean as though it holds answers.

I slow up, and it forces him to stop in front of me. "No lies," I whisper, and our gazes meet once more.

He takes a step forward, and I lengthen my neck to maintain our connection. We're so close, his breath tickles my face. "You've been under my skin since Salvador."

It's a moment of weakness, a moment when he should kiss me, only he steps back.

"You make me sound like I'm an irritation."

He chuckles. "You have a way with words. Unfortunately, if we don't keep moving, we'll be forced to leave the beach." His hand lifts to caress my cheek. I close my eyes and take pleasure in his touch for a brief moment and tilt my head toward his hand before opening my eyes. "A little further, and we'll reach a bay. There we can swim. And chat." He turns, links his fingers with mine, and like that, we're walking hand in hand.

It surprises me since only hours ago he was guarded. Yet we continue on in silence, and I use the time to mentally prepare more questions.

The coastline changes, and a bay comes into view.

"Over there." He nods ahead. "We'll stop for a rest."

In the distance, the colonial buildings of Ilhéus and residential houses rise from the shoreline. Although I feel somewhat safer, my stomach sinks in disappointment.

The physical attraction I have for him doesn't change the fact that Samuel is a stranger. So why am I breaking my own safety rules and hoping he seduces me?

16

SAMUEL

Gray storm clouds roll in over the ocean, blocking out the blue sky. Samuel considers the possibility of rain since it's not uncommon in the afternoon.

He slows his pace and unlinks his fingers from hers. "We should swim now before twilight."

"Finally. I'm so bloody hot."

Samuel smiles at the sound of her Australian accent, his grin fading when she pulls her tank top over her head and adjusts her bikini top. He notices more than he should since he can't keep his eyes off her body.

After wiggling out of her denim shorts, she runs toward the water. He watches her rear as she rushes off. Her bikini barely leaves anything to his imagination, and the way his body is zinging, it's best he visualizes her in a onesie.

He makes his way to the water. Are onesies still a thing? He has no idea, no idea of where the world sits in the fashion industry. He's in tune with the planet yet out of touch with society. It concerns him if their conversation is guided by modern-day trivial news since he has no idea what's happening and what is current.

Eden dives into a wave, surfaces, and swipes her face. She straightens, and the seawater streams over her curves. "The ocean is different here. Warmer," she says as she wades closer to shore.

He dives beneath a wave. A safe fluid membrane lies between them. When he surfaces, he feels the pull, caught in her current. It's like she's created her own riptide. She glides closer, barely making a ripple in the water.

Soft hands land on his chest.

"Kiss me. I want you to kiss me," she murmurs. Her hands slide to the back of his neck, and she guides his lips to hers.

For years he's fought the release of what men need, trained his mind not to be tricked by desire and lust.

With her, he feels every sensation tenfold.

He doesn't fight it. He knows the kiss will be different from when she was drunk, even though he remembers how she tasted and how much he wanted to take more.

She moans into his mouth the moment their lips touch. Her kiss is delicate and slow. He follows her lead, and it turns frantic and needy.

Eden cups his face. Her tongue finds his. Her hands slide into his hair and grip the ends. In response, he lifts her until she straddles him.

She gasps as she slides down against the length of him.

He dips beneath the water and adjusts her position so she's not riding his groin. Hell, that will send him over the edge quicker than he could control.

She breaks the kiss, gasps for air, and offers him her neck. He dots kisses along her moist skin. Dizzy with the taste combined with salt, he craves more. Supporting her back, he sucks his way to her breast. His nose moves the flimsy material aside so he can take her breast in his mouth. She moans in pleasure, the sound causing him to thrust against her.

"Yes," she whispers.

He moves to the other breast, her whimpers goading him on. He flicks her nipple with his tongue before taking her breast into his mouth and sucking until she moans, "More."

More.

Samuel chose a secluded beach. The younger version of himself would be on a home run, taking her on the sand. "Not here," he whispers. "I want you to know who I am. And I'm not a guy who has sex with women on a beach."

She leans back. There's sadness in her eyes. "Okay. We'll talk first."

He nods. "We need to make our way to the streets. It'll be dark soon, and I don't want you on the beach."

"I'll be with you."

"You will. I'd be more than happy to spend the night alone with you on the beach, a fire burning, only I wouldn't be getting any sleep."

"You say it like it's a bad thing. What are you afraid of?"

"It's more what you'd be afraid of. Snakes? Thieves? Or if the police found us? This isn't the place."

"The police finding us? Doing what? It sounds like you've thought it through."

He leans in and plants another kiss on her lips. "I

have. Unfortunately, we need to leave. Not far ahead, there is a path leading to a quiet street. From there, we can arrange for transport back to the resort."

"And then?" she whispers.

"We'll have dinner and talk."

Yet, in his mind, he has already surrendered to her.

17

EDEN

My stomach tightens when the taxi pulls into the resort. "Give me a half hour to shower," I say quickly. "Wait. What room are you in?"

"Twenty-four. You go ahead. I need to talk to reception about something."

I hesitate.

"Eden, I'll come to your room in twenty."

"I'm in room eight." I let go of his hand and move briskly along the path. Hell, thirty minutes to wash my hair and apply makeup, and what am I going to wear?

I reach for my phone. "Amy, I'm back. Come to my room. I need a dress for dinner," I say, puffing out the words. My heart hasn't slowed since the cave, and now I'm beyond remaining calm.

"Eden, what the hell's going on?"

"I'll explain soon," I say and end the call.

I pull out my key, and before I get a chance to unlock the door, it swings open.

"Girl, what's happening?" Yasmine's brow pulls tight. She steps aside for me to pass.

Bree is standing near my bed, arms folded.

Amy is going through my cupboard. "Nope. Nope. Nope," she says as she pushes dresses aside.

"Yeah, there's not a lot to choose from. I was hoping you had something."

"Hers are undersized and too short for you," Bree adds.

I shrug. "It's *that* kind of dinner. I want to... you know..."

"Impress him?" Bree's eyes round.

"Entice is more the word." I step closer to Amy. "Do you have anything? I don't want to look like... *me*."

Yasmine sits on the bed before me. "Edes, I've spoken to Michael about Samuel. Going by what he said, your clothes are fine. He likes you because you're different. And he's different. Don't overthink this."

"No," I shoot back. My stomach is in knots, and I barely have time to explain. "Tonight, I need to do this. I can't afford to let him 'get away' without knowing... argh, trust me, okay?" I spin back to my closet and throw clothes aside. "I have nothing."

Yasmine strolls to her side of the room and reappears holding one of her dresses on a hanger. "How about this?"

I take it from her and smile. A white, lacy boho dress, ankle-length with a low cleavage cut to the waist. "Perfect."

"I'm hitting the shower. I want to tell you everything except I don't have time. I'm meeting him in a half hour," I say as I head to the bathroom. "I can explain tomorrow."

I shower and wash my hair with mango-scented shampoo and finish in record time. With a towel around my head, I open the bathroom door to find my bed dotted with jewelry. Amy's makeup is spread out on the table.

"We can help." Amy sings. "Since you're the only one with a date tonight, we're all helping to make it perfect."

"And we can chat about what you're getting yourself into," Bree says in warning.

"Bree..." I say, searching for understanding, "... not tonight. Let me enjoy it."

"I googled him like you said," Yasmine says.

"Should I be worried?"

"If you were me, no. But you're you, and—"

"Then I'm not. We'll discuss it tomorrow."

18

SAMUEL

Samuel raises a hand to knock and hesitates when laughter echoes beyond the door. He smiles, liking the sound, taps twice, and hears hushing.

The door opens. His entire body stiffens taking in the sight of her. Her eyes remind him of the Brazilian ocean, framed with long lashes, and the sweeping lines of kohl accentuate her beauty. Straightened blonde locks fall over slim shoulders to caress her breasts.

Breasts.

He pauses a moment too long. He sees the pretty white dress, only his gaze is drawn to her chest.

"Hi." She gives him a knowing smile.

"You look beautiful," he says honestly.

"Thank you. Shall we go?" She pulls the door closed behind her and links her fingers with his.

He glances over her shoulder to the window and nods to her friends peeking through the blinds, then he glances down to his board shorts and polo and feels underdressed beside her. Eden deserves him in a tux. The one he rented and returned to reception in Copacabana. He didn't count on being away this long.

He never saw her coming.

The ultimate distraction.

The ultimate threat.

"Your friends—"

"Can talk to you later. I'm not willing to share you yet. Though it wouldn't surprise me if they rock up at the restaurant." Her fingers tighten around his. "Would it bother you?"

He smiles. "Spying isn't beneath them?"

"Amy would resort to worse." She laughs as though it evokes a memory. His insides tighten with the sound of her laughter.

Parrots zoom past to roost. She ducks as though she's on their radar.

Is she superstitious? Spiritual? What would be her opinion be of him if she knew the truth?

He can't ignore the idea he was meant to find Eden. He closes his eyes, knowing whatever they have will end in a few days, so why does it matter?

Yet he *is* here, with *her,* allowing a male instinct to guide him.

She squeezes his hand, bringing him back. They stroll along the path to the resort's open-air restaurant. It reminds him of his jungle home—his place of belonging with a peaked ceiling and no walls. The breeze flows in from the sea.

The waiter leads them to a small table where they overlook palm trees and the gentle swinging hammocks connecting them.

"I like it here. I mean, I loved Rio, but here I feel more at home."

The breeze catches her fruity scent, and he takes a deeper breath, closing his eyes momentarily. "How long are you staying in Ilhéus?"

She pulls a face and grins. "Your stalking skills disappoint me."

"I didn't plan anything beyond seeing you on the tour. I believed you'd send me away."

Her eyebrows rise. "After telling you how I felt in Rio?"

"You were drinking. We had mutual attraction except..." He shakes his head.

"Are you having second thoughts?"

He holds her gaze. "No."

Her nod is gentle.

There's a sense of caution, which he respects.

"Where are you headed after here?"

Her sentence holds a question as to 'what happens' next. It's subtle and wise to ignore it at the moment. "North."

"Same. We're heading to Margarita Island before Peru."

Samuel nods. "To meet up with Michael, Sean, and Harrison?"

"I was hoping you were also heading there."

He decides on some honesty. She deserves some truth as it may help with understanding when the time comes for him to leave. "My vacation has ended for now. I was heading north to return to work."

"Where?"

"It's not well known."

"Are you working in medicine or doing some work to help pay for your travels around the country?"

He raises a brow.

"You know, like bar work or living in backpacker quarters."

He stifles a chuckle. "No. This is medical work and with..." he pauses, "... another scientist."

Further explanation is saved when the waiter approaches to take their order.

Eden picks up the menu and points. "This pizza is amazing." She smiles at the waiter before her mesmerizing eyes meet Samuel's. "Have you eaten here? I can vouch for the wood-fired pizza. Best in the world, in my opinion."

"Sim." The waiter grins. *Yes.*

Samuel nods at the waiter and raises two fingers. "Make it two since the lady recommends it."

"It's a safe choice. Some things I'm just not ready to try. Although, all the fresh fruit and vegetables are fine."

Samuel takes a mouthful of water. "What foods have you tried and dislike?"

Eden pulls a face. "Cuttlefish in its ink." Her hand goes to her throat. "Amy found a restaurant, and we tried a few dishes like eel stew." She shivers as though the thought repulses her. "I didn't mind those snacks made with cassava flour."

"So, no dishes like buchada?"

She shakes her head.

"It's made of the animal's internal organs."

Her eyes widen. Samuel doesn't react. If she lived like him, would she be open to trying the food he survived on?

"No more talk about food. Tell me about you. Do you play sports? Follow any teams? Are you an artsy guy?" she asks.

"I played basketball in high school. Then my studies became a priority. Although I like to run... I competed in track in college." His physique was suited to long-distance running, and the activity facilitated his hunting skills. "What about you?"

"I played some basketball socially. I was never a sporty person. Although my ex..." she hesitates and meets his gaze. "He played football. I didn't fit into his world."

Hairs rise on the back of Samuel's neck with someone taking advantage of her good heart. "I imagine you'd fit in anywhere. Where is he now?"

She sighs. "In Adelaide working for my father." She rolls her eyes. "He loves Ethan. Hoped we'd end up together." She shakes her head.

Samuel picks up the knife and twirls it in his fingers like it's a spear.

"Even thinking about him makes me angry, and that my father has employed him. But it's a story for another time."

A story Samuel wants to eventually hear.

No. He can't invest in the emotion.

The pizzas arrive.

"What are your plans for the rest of your stay here in Ilhéus?" Samuel asks before taking a bite.

Eden swallows a mouthful of pizza. "What are yours?"

"I asked first."

"Okay... to be with you."

He nods. "Then I'll see you tomorrow."

Eden's gaze flicks over his face. He senses doubt.

"I'll see you tomorrow," he promises. "Tonight, I need sleep as I barely slept last night worrying about today and how you'd react. We have the rest of the week to be together."

It's all he can offer for now.

19

"I find it weird he has no social media presence," Amy had said last night.

"I find it refreshing," I'd replied, although it did spook me a little, almost to the point he doesn't exist. When Yasmine googled him, the searches popped up from ten years ago detailing his medical achievements at Stanford and around six years ago at a hospital in California. We found images of his father, a renowned hematologist. He possessed the same fair hair and blue eyes as Samuel and an identical browline.

The nerves in my stomach haven't settled at the idea of us sleeping together. Yet I sense him holding back, and it confuses me for most guys I know sprint to third base for a home run.

Even the way he dresses baffles me. From our internet searches, his family has money. Except for the tux he wore to the Copacabana ball, his fashion choice indicates he's barely getting by. I'm not being judgmental, only trying to understand his character.

I step out of the bathroom to Yasmine waking with a weary moan. "So, you're meeting him for breakfast. Then what?"

I shrug. "Last night he mentioned the beach."

Yasmine pushes up onto her elbow. "I can head into the town center, so you have the room to yourself." She offers a smile, although I know she senses my uneasiness.

"No need. He has his own room if it comes down to that." I turn to the mirror and pull my hair into a messy bun to keep it off my neck. I adjust several strands ignoring the way her eyes study my reflection.

Dressed in denim shorts and a white tank, I leave my friends for the day. And, the night, hopefully.

"Hey," I say and smile when I meet him on the path outside my room. "How did you sleep?"

He scratches at the whiskers along his jaw. "Not as well as I'd hoped." He takes my face in his hands and kisses me. Warm, soft lips caress mine, conveying why he didn't sleep. "You hungry?" he says against my mouth.

A double entendre.

"Always."

He takes both my hands and gazes down as if our linked hands hold answers. His expression retains anguish behind happiness.

"How cute." I point to a domestic cat on the path, crouching and staring into the tropical garden.

Samuel releases my hand and steps between bromeliads and leafy heliconias. He bends and scoops up a baby parrot. It squawks and flaps its wings. Samuel envelops it with both hands, the cat meowing. "I'll take this guy to reception before he's lunch."

He strides off, and it takes a moment for me to register and follow. "What's wrong with it?"

"It looks like it has an injured wing. It may have fallen out of the nest. They can notify an animal rescue shelter."

"Can I see it?"

He stops, smiles at me, and opens his cupped hands to reveal a calmer chick with blue and green feathers.

I smile and look up at him.

"You go ahead and grab us a table in the restaurant. I'll meet you there soon."

After finding a table, I keep looking at the entrance anticipating his arrival, and expecting he'll do a runner. The warning in my gut tells me not to fall for this guy. This is a holiday romance, and I know it will inevitably end, but my heart is all in ready to embrace the thrill of the ride.

Samuel returns, and we share a platter of exotic fruits.

"Are there any foods you don't like?" He holds a piece of seriguela between his fingers.

"I love all the exotic fruits here but reluctant to try some of the fish dishes, and battered foods never sit well with me." I scoop pitanga berries onto my plate and pop one in my mouth. "What about you?" I stare at his lips.

With every word coming from his beautiful mouth, I didn't hear a word he says. I'm mesmerized by watching him. He has to be one of the most handsome men I have ever met in my life. Points to him for acting like a gentleman by getting to know me better before wanting to get me between the sheets. Only I'm dizzy with the pent-up need inside of me and wish he'd take it down a notch because all I want to do is fast forward to tonight.

🌴

We head to the beach and lie side by side on a mandala towel. I'm supposed to be relaxing under the sun, only every cell is on fire being this close to Samuel. I sneak glances at his rippled abs. Our fingers brush, and the zing shoots to my toes. I trace the contour of his sternum, and I can't help ogling his bare, broad chest and defined shoulders. I visualize those arms framing me. I run my fingertips lower and rest my hand on his taut stomach.

His eyes meet mine with the familiarity of someone who knows what the other person is thinking. A hunger burns behind his blue hues. "I'm going to take a swim," he rasps. I follow him into the water, wading through calm seas until I reach him.

"Come here." Without hesitation, he pulls me into his arms. Large hands cup my face. "I want you so much it's nearly killing me."

My chest flutters hearing words I've longed to hear. "Then why are we waiting?" I whisper.

"To be sure."

"Sure of what?"

"We're doing the right thing."

The right thing?

I'm not going to say *it's just sex* because, for me, it won't be. I've never been that girl. Yet, he's bringing out a different side of me.

"Does this feel right?" My mouth hovers close to his. Our eyes connect one last time until our lips touch. It was going to be a gentle kiss. In seconds, he switches to wildfire, the kiss broken with breathy gasps, and we can't get enough of each other. He tastes of saltwater and the sweet melon he ate earlier. "We need to leave," I moan against his lips. "Take me to your room."

"I'm going to take you in my room," he says. "All of

you." His fingers link with mine as he leads me out of the water.

We collect our belongings from the sand and wander along the path lined with coconut palms back to his room. He unlocks the door and dumps everything on the floor where we stand, and kicks the door shut with a bang.

He holds my face in his large hands and kisses me hard. "You're right. This..." he murmurs against my lips, "... feels right."

"You taste like the beach." I lick my lips and savor the saltiness. A taste that will forever remind me of him.

"Taste," he murmurs. "It's another thing for us to explore." He leans over and sucks my neck, my ear lobe, and then my lips are his once more. Our kiss heats up, and I moan against his lips. Samuel pulls away, and a cold space surrounds me. I open my eyes to seek reason, only to find his eyes flicking over my face.

"Eden... I," he stammers. Then he takes my hand and leads me to the bathroom. Samuel steps out of his boardshorts, and I can't look away.

Samuel is gloriously perfect.

All of him.

I strip fast to match his readiness. There's a hint of a smile on those sensual lips. Samuel flicks on the shower and adjusts the water temperature. I step in first and wet my hair. It's cool. A little too cool, and I'm not sure if it's for his benefit.

Under the spray, his hands glide effortlessly over my curves while his mouth tracks along my neck to my breasts.

"You're a beautiful woman," he murmurs against my skin.

"Samuel…" I moan. His name sounds like pleasure the way it rolls off my lips.

He makes a rumbling noise in his throat, and then his fingers caress the spot that yearns for him. Using his shoulders for support, I circle my hips, enjoying every sensation whipping through my body and making me weak at the knees. Right before I come, his lips find mine, smothering a scream, and then my knees buckle at the right moment of pleasure.

The shower turns off.

And I'm awakened from my moment of lust.

A towel is wrapped around me.

Samuel dries quickly.

I should dry off, only I'm still coming out of the haze and questioning why we stopped. This can't be all that's happening? If he gives me the gentleman's speech, I'll lose my shit.

He pulls me close, so I feel his length, and there's no denying he's aroused. I go to drop to my knees, only he stops me.

"We're not done," I say gently.

"I know." His smile reaches his eyes. "I need you in my bed."

He whisks me off my feet and carries me to the wooden framed bed. A slight scream escapes my throat in surprise because I can't remember the last time a man has carried me like this.

I link my arms around his neck and admire his handsome face. The slight dent between his brow deepens. "What is it?" I whisper.

"You." One word, yet I hear the torment.

"I want this." I keep my voice low, but I let him know there's no mistaking my intent.

He lowers me gently to the white sheets, then crawls and hovers over me, his eyes fixed on mine.

"As do I. It's been a while since I've felt the longing of how I want you."

I wiggle my ass down the bed. "So let's not waste another second."

"You make me feel like a young boy again. In, that there are no repercussions."

"Repercussions?" I let out a snort. "I use contraception if that's what you're worried about. And I visited a doctor for a check-up after the last time, which was years ago."

He frowns, then his eyes glaze as though he's lost in his thoughts. What other repercussions is he talking about? Finally, he closes his eyes, and when he opens them, I feel the heat as his gaze tracks over my face.

His lips crush on mine. His hands are between my legs, moving and shaping my body to fit his. He eases into me with gentleness, and yet the air rushes out of my lungs. I moan the first sigh of pleasure of having him inside of me, and as each movement gains momentum, so does my breath. Our breaths and sighs mix with the rhythm of our bodies.

He builds, and the lust climbs higher and higher. "Faster," I moan, almost there. The sound of my heart races in my ears. His pulse races equally with mine—the spot on his neck pulsates with every beat. "Samuel," I cry out, and then my body melts into the sheets as my orgasm waves over me in a delicious sensation.

The dent between his brow deepens as he pumps faster, shudders, and collapses over me. He dots my shoulder with kisses, finding his way to my lips.

The table lamp provides a mellow light, creating a

shadow against the wall. I sigh with every touch and kiss as though he has awakened the part of me that has been dormant for over a year.

I never imagined being fulfilled to the point beyond speaking. We catch our breath as Samuel lies beside me. We both stare at the ceiling in quiet appreciation. His hand reaches for mine—a gentle squeeze. "I need to be inside you again," he whispers. "I want to make love to you over and over."

I turn my head, and even the simplest look has electricity sparking between us. "And I don't want you to stop."

🌴

Leaning against Samuel's chest, I take his hand and study it. The bathwater has softened his skin. I run my thumb over the whitish outline of calluses on his palm.

"Did I hurt you?" he whispers, dotting my neck with kisses.

I roll over, so my body aligns with his, and my chest is pressed to his. The scented bath water cocoons us. "No. In fact, I'd like these hands to keep exploring." I guide his palm to my rear and crane my neck so our lips meet. "First, tell me what you did to get hands like you've been wielding an ax all your life?"

"Maybe I have," he whispers.

I kiss, then bite his lip. "I'm serious. Can I ask you a question?"

He slides up. Bathwater spills over the edge with the sudden movement. "What do you want to know?" A tell-tale dent forms between his brows.

"Where do you work? I know you have to eventually

return, and I want to visit you." I push away to put space between us, hoping I can accurately read his expression.

"Visiting is... difficult. I work in a remote area in Venezuela."

"As a volunteer?"

"Not really, although I do volunteer some of my services."

"What's your favorite thing about it?"

"I'm questioning your employer's credentials. It's clear you can't count."

"This is conversation."

He smiles at me. "More like an interrogation. Hmm, one thing? The waterfalls. Have you heard of Angel Falls?"

I shake my head.

"Maybe you should visit there if you and your friends have time. It's the highest waterfall in the world. The locals know it as Kerepakupai-merú."

"Really?" He pronounces the unusual phonics easily. "And you get to go there often?"

"I try to."

A few seconds pass before I speak again. "Your turn to ask me something."

"One thing? Hardly fair," he says and chuckles. "Although there is one thing not sitting right with me. Why do you allow a past relationship with a douchebag to control the way you see yourself?"

"Sorry?"

He takes both my hands. "The moment you mentioned your ex, something changed in your expression. I saw a glimpse of unhappiness, not for loss of love but more the loss of self-appreciation. What did he do to you?"

"You mean what did I allow him to do to me? I'm a wiser woman now."

"A wise and beautiful woman who deserves much more." He pulls me close and kisses me until I forget what we were talking about.

20

SAMUEL

Samuel holds the lock until he barely hears the click of the door. His gaze shoots to his bed, to Eden lying beneath the white sheet. Her hair splayed over the pillow blends with the crisp cotton. He closes his eyes, remembering last night. Even a day and night with her isn't enough to cure the insatiable desire pumping through his veins.

More than anything, he wants to crawl back under the covers, allow her to ruin him over and over, and remind him what he has sacrificed. Show him paradise. Her paradise.

"You have coffee?"

He nods, coming out of a daze. He goes to her, sits on the bed, and hands her the other cup. "I thought you might need this."

"Thank you." She rises, the sheet slipping. She catches and secures it with a hand under her breasts. The white linen sits low over her tanned breasts revealing enough cleavage for Samuel to lose focus and remember how his mouth had claimed each one equally last night.

Or was it this morning? Either way, it's the reason he rose early and hired a Kombi at the receptionist's desk. He needs to get them both out of his room before he loses all coherence.

Every minute spent with her last night sparked something within him to question his future. His commitment. Yet he wants her by his side for every second until his inevitable return.

The Ularans know nothing of selfish ways. He *should* leave. Save them both from heartache. Only the incredible power she wields, or perhaps selfishness on his behalf, is allowing her to control him.

"It's a good brew."

He smiles at her accent. It's thicker on different occasions. "I have a surprise for you today."

Her eyes light up, and his chest expands knowing he gives her happiness. "Tell me."

"It requires you to wear clothes and sneakers. Pack your swimsuit in case."

"In case?" She takes another sip of coffee.

"There's a river you can bathe in after I show you the surprise."

Eden throws back the covers. "I can shower here, and you could join me."

He sucks in air. "I need to make some calls, and you need to be quick as I have a booking at a certain time. If we shower together, it won't be quick."

She smiles, knowing what he infers, then frowns, comprehending. "You have a phone?"

"Doesn't everyone?"

"You never use it. I assumed you borrowed one in Rio."

"I use it when I need to."

She nods as though she's thinking about his words while she slips into her shorts. "I'll head back to my room to freshen up and inform the girls where we're headed. Which is?"

"Nice try."

She giggles, and it fills his heart with warmth. Swiping her key from the table, she says, "I'll be back soon."

It surprises him when she taps on the door twenty minutes later. He assumed most women took longer. He reminds himself Eden isn't most women.

Taking her hand, he guides her to the front of the resort, where a pale blue Kombi awaits. He jingles the keys. "Our ride for the day."

She lets out a little squeal and bounces on the spot.

He chuckles at her reaction. He opens the passenger door and takes her hand as she steps up to the seat.

"Where are we going?" she asks before the keys are in the ignition.

"Did your parents ever explain what a surprise entails in order to keep it one?"

"Of course." She fiddles with the radio dials, and Brazilian music blares from the small speakers. The sound is distorted except for the signature quick drumbeat, and on cue, Eden wiggles in her seat.

He indicates to pull out onto the road. "For your own safety and mine, I'll ask you to refrain from dancing."

She raises her arms and jiggles her chest while tapping her feet. Samuel lets out a sigh and is thankful he hasn't yet veered onto the road.

Heading south, they pass beachside resorts and endless fields of coconut trees.

"You know I'd hoped to watch the Samba parade with you."

"I apologize again for my behavior in Rio," he says. He glances at her and notes her attention is to the window. It reminds him of her sad face a few days ago on the bus tour. "My decisions aren't rash, and yet sometimes I make bad choices."

"Sometimes?" She grins, and he hopes it's to lighten the mood.

With Ilhéus behind them, the scenery changes to the blue ocean on one side and green vegetation on the other.

"If practicing your Samba in the car makes you happy, then do it. I want you to be happy."

For now, small talk works well between them. He points ahead. "Did you know much of the coastline had thriving cacao farms, and this area was known for producing some of the biggest traders in the world?"

"Do they farm cacao beans now?"

"Not to the same extent."

"It's a beautiful country." She smiles at him and continues humming to the music, their conversation now about the landscape.

"What's this?" Eden points to the sign ahead, her focus away from their conversation.

He smiles. "Your surprise." When her eyes light up, so does something inside him.

He thought the Uno Ecopark might bore her. To Samuel, this part of the Atlantic rainforest is similar to his 'home.' A sanctuary for wildlife and rich in biodiversity, it's one of the most endangered ecosystems in the world. He believes the park stands to nurture as does his home village. He told himself it wouldn't be a test, only now he wants to observe how she reacts to the things he loves.

He takes her hand and leads her into the park to a walkway bridge suspended one hundred feet high among the treetops.

"We're going up there?" Her hand rises to her throat.

"We are. Are you afraid of heights?"

"Now I am..."

"I'll be right beside you."

She looks up to meet his gaze. A tingle forms at the base of his skull and travels down his spine, and like an electric force, shoots to his arms and down his thighs to his toes.

He closes his eyes.

He's falling for her.

🌴

"My palms are sweating."

With every step, Eden grips onto the bridge's rope. Netting below her waist is the only thing to stop them from falling through the barrier. The bridge is held by ropes overhead and nearly wide enough for one person. With every step, it sways a little.

Resting his palm on her shoulder, he remains one step behind at all times and reinforces their safety.

"I didn't believe I was afraid of heights until today," she whispers.

"Rest a moment." He points into the distance and places a finger on his lips.

She stares at the green treetops, her expression blank. Samuel wraps his arms around her shoulders, leans in and whispers, "A golden-headed lion tamarin. Do you see it?"

"I do."

"You'll only find them here."

"It's so cute."

He hears the fondness in her voice. Every moment they share, he's learning a little more about Eden. He leans down and kisses the side of her neck, wraps his arms tighter, so her back presses against his chest. Whatever way he holds Eden, she molds into him like a perfect fit. He closes his eyes with contentment filling his core.

Underneath the happiness, he worries she'll consume him, and he'll never want to go back.

21

EDEN

"You're all packed," I say to Yasmine when I arrive back at the resort. Her case is by the door, and the room is the tidiest I've seen it.

"Yep. I'm going to wear this tomorrow." She indicates to her skirt and an off-the-shoulder top.

"Where are you going for dinner?"

"We're heading into town. We didn't think you'd be joining us since it's your last night with Samuel."

Our last night.

"I'm hoping it's not. I intend to talk to him about getting more time off from his work and joining us on Margarita Island."

Yasmine nods. There's something amiss in her expression as though she knows something I don't.

"What?"

"Nothing. I want you to be careful, that's all."

"I am." I file through clothes deciding on what to wear tonight. "I'll chat to you tomorrow because I doubt I'll be coming back here tonight." I throw a wink her way.

"I didn't expect so. Be contactable, okay? We need to leave here by ten."

"I'll pack up my gear now. Tell the girls I'll see them tomorrow."

When the door closes, I throw clothes into my suitcase. Time is scarce, and I need it to prepare myself for the sweetest night with Samuel.

I told him I'd meet him at the restaurant.

When I make my way along the winding path, I can't ignore the thoughts in my head warning me not to get my hopes up. This is only a holiday romance.

I want it to be more.

By the way his eyes sear me when I walk into the restaurant, I know he feels the same way.

"Wow," he says, standing to greet me. "You're stunning."

I give him an easy smile. "What are you drinking?"

"The local beer. What can I order for you?"

"A white wine."

Our conversation remains safe, and we continue to banter about trivial things as though we're catching up like long-lost friends.

Coldplay's "Viva La Vida" sounds through the speaker, and I smile. "I've always loved Coldplay. Watched them perform live in Adelaide."

"A great band."

"What's your favorite song?"

"A "Sky Full of Stars.""

"Same," I say as though we're playing a card game of Snap.

Only his expression is serious. His eyes hold mine captive as though he's searching for more. "Where's your happy place?"

"Depends. There are many places that can relax me. Back home, I love nothing more than sitting out under the Southern Cross and looking up at the stars. No building to block my view, only the sound of the ocean as a reminder I'm not in heaven."

"You live by the ocean?"

I smile, sensing it pleases him. "I do. Have all my life and can't imagine not living there. It has a sense of calm and excitement, depending on the time of day and the seasons."

"I know what you mean."

We're interrupted when our food is delivered.

"What's your favorite food?" Samuel continues.

"Depends," I say with a mouthful of pizza. I wait a moment before answering. "If I go out, I love Greek or Thai. Japanese, too. At home, I snack on avocado and tomato on toast and other times fruit."

"What fruits?"

"Anything really. Depends on what's in season. We have some of the best stone fruits in the country. Apricots are one of my favorites."

"Do you like exotic fruit like acai, pawpaw, and dragon fruit?"

"Absolutely, but they can be expensive. What about you?"

He holds my gaze when he answers, "I live mainly on fruit."

"Ah, that's why you look so fit." His brow pulls tight. It seems he missed the compliment I intended.

The waiter places the dessert menu on the table, and Samuel declines and asks for the bill.

"You don't want dessert?" Damn, I could go for something chocolaty tonight.

"I'll be having dessert in my room." The seriousness behind his eyes has my insides tightening with anticipation.

Dropping the napkin on my plate, I push up from the chair. "Ready when you are."

🌴

Walking hand in hand to his apartment, it seems like we've been together our entire lives. I was meant to take this holiday and find him. Even from the moment I saw him in Salvador, I knew he had come into my life for a reason. My gut tingles with a strange sensation— anticipation and acknowledgment equally. I'll be getting to know him better once we reach his room, only I can't help thinking what happens after tomorrow. I don't want this to be the end of us.

I used to mock people who fell in love at first sight. Lovers who thought they found their soulmate after a couple of dates. I believed they were fools, yet here I am, feeling the same pull of need to be with someone beyond a few weeks. I need more time because after moping around the last eighteen months, I've come all this way to discover someone who's everything I have wanted in a man.

Samuel opens the door and stands aside like the gentleman he is. He follows me into the room, and the door lock clicks. He takes my hand and tugs, so I'm pressed up against him. He kisses my neck and sucks gently on the nape. "So sweet," he murmurs. "One taste, and you could put chocolatiers out of business."

"Ha." I smile at him. I overlook the excitement growing between my thighs for a moment, so I can talk to him before we spend all night making out. "Can I ask you something?"

He pulls away and stares down at me as though he's missed something. "Sure."

"You seem familiar with Venezuela and Peru."

"I have traveled there..." He steps back and gives me a quizzical look. "Why is that?" He pours two glasses of cold water from the fridge and hands me a glass.

"You seem to know the best places to visit, so I hoped you might like to be my personal tour guide?"

His arm freezes with the glass halfway to his lips. "I thought you were going straight to Margarita Island?"

"Well, yes. But with the latest protests, we're avoiding Caracas and instead flying to Guayana City for one night before heading to Margarita Island. I'm hoping you could show us some of the sights and then come with us to the island?"

"Guayana City." The crease relaxes between his brows. "It's the gateway to the tepuis and a great river system. Pity you're not staying longer. You'd love the Angel Falls tour."

My stomach flutters with a window of hope. "If I stayed longer, would you take me?"

"Eden, I—" His lips are on mine. His kiss has me losing my train of thought. Strong arms tighten around me as though he doesn't want to let go. "Let's talk in the morning. I'll glance over my plans then. I don't want to waste tonight with us going back and forth."

"So, you'll try to come to Margarita Island with your friends?" I rasp against his lips.

"I will."

Then his open mouth claims mine. The kiss is needy, and I can't shake the feeling it's a last kiss.

A goodbye.

He walks me back until my knees hit the bed, and I'm lifted onto the mattress, losing my clothes and my thoughts to his passion.

I shiver despite the tropical air basking us in a light film of sweat. His touch is gentle, his eyes unwavering except to study my body in appreciation. Running my hands through his fair hair, I grip the ends and whimper when he sucks on my breast.

He lifts his gaze and stares at me as if he sees me for the first time. "I want you so badly."

I bring my mouth close to his, so we share the same breathing space. "And I want you. Now. So please don't stop."

"I'm not going to stop," he says in a low, deep voice. "In fact, I intend to make love to you all night long."

Everything about him feels so right. We can't end after tonight. When we're together, it's like nothing else in the world matters. The feeling of freedom I have with him is like nothing I've ever experienced, and tonight is even more of a reason to absorb everything he has to offer.

"Fine by me," I murmur and bring his lips to mine.

22

EDEN

As I roll over, my arm reaches out, searching.

It takes a moment for me to acknowledge its morning and the empty space beside me.

I sit up. Like yesterday, I assume Samuel has slipped out to get us morning coffee.

I pad my way across white tiles to the bathroom and notice the absence of his toiletries. I let it absorb for a moment. A heavy feeling grows in my chest. We're both leaving today.

After washing my hands and splashing water on my face, I head back into the bedroom, deciding whether to wait for him in bed or get dressed so we can have breakfast together. The closet door is ajar. I have no idea why, and yet I open it, and every bit of air rushes in and then out of my lungs.

I spin and find no sign of a packed case. "Not again," I moan.

No, this can't be happening.

My heart is thumping in my chest as I open and close

every closet. Every drawer. I look to the kitchenette, and on the bench is a note.

My chest tightens, knowing what it says without even reading it. The hopeful side of me whispers it's a note explaining he's getting me a coffee. I read the first line and *hope* can go to hell.

I don't get past the first three lines before I screw up the letter and throw it at the wall. "You bastard," I scream.

A note, a text message—it's all the same.

Gutless.

I dress in the same clothes from last night, grab my clutch and key, and dash out without closing the door behind me.

Passing families on the path as they head to breakfast, I keep my head down and swipe at my tears, hoping I don't look like the fool I am. I swallow down the emotional lump scratching the back of my throat before it explodes inside my chest.

I need my girls.

Then it dawns on me.

Did Yasmine know?

My gaze shoots up to the door in sight, and I run, ignoring strange looks as I gasp for air. In one smooth action, I turn the knob and push the door open with more force than usual.

Yasmine stands from the end of the bed and throws her phone on the crumpled sheets. Her eyes pop, her mouth opens, but she says nothing.

My body trembles in a combination of hurt and anger. I grip the door to balance myself. "Did you know?" The words fall out in accusation.

"What did he say?" she asks. Her voice is calm, yet her eyes tell me otherwise.

I flick the door closed and take a step closer to her. "Did you know?"

"What happened, Edes?" Her voice holds the worry I'm holding in my gut.

I make an exasperated sound in my throat and throw my arms in the air. "He left," I shout. "I mean, what did I expect?"

Yasmine rushes to my side. I stumble, and she wraps both arms around me, guiding me to the bed. She pushes strands of hair away from my eyes, stuck with tears to my cheeks. "What happened?" she says with a familiar warmth that's consoled me many times over the years.

"I woke up, and he was gone. Not even a goodbye." I turn and bury my face into her shoulder and let the tears flow.

"He couldn't, babe. He's fallen for you, too."

"Then why didn't he give me something? Like a phone number, email, anything? Not an *I'm sorry* note."

The door swings open to Bree and Amy mid-conversation.

"Who's up for breakfast?" Bree sings.

Amy stalls. A panicked expression flitters across her face. "What happened? What did he say?"

"Nothing." I run my thumb under my nose and sniff hard. "It's the whole problem. Nothing."

Both girls' gazes flick to Yasmine as if they're waiting for her to say something.

I do the same. "You do know something."

"He left a note," Yasmine says to Amy.

"But you were talking to Michael last night. What did he say?" Amy's voice holds blame.

I gape at Yasmine. "What did he tell you?"

"I'll grab us some coffees from the restaurant," Bree says quickly before leaving the room.

"To be fair, I didn't know what Samuel would do." Her eyes seek understanding because we have always believed in honesty with our friendship. "Michael told me Samuel wasn't joining them on the Island. He never was. And he already pushed limits on his work contract to meet up with you here. In truth, he said he never expected him to come to Ilhéus. Work has always come first for him."

I nod. "And you didn't think to mention it to me?"

"Did you want me to barge into your room last night? C'mon, Edes, you both knew it was your last night together."

I let out a sigh. "You could've warned me."

"It was up to Samuel to tell you. I'm pissed off at him like you are. He should've explained it himself."

"Yasmine's right. He did a shitty thing." Amy tightens one arm around me.

I appreciate their hugs, only it's not enough to numb the pain in my chest.

"And now I'll never know anything more about him," I rasp.

"You could talk to Michael when we get to the island," Amy suggests.

My gut sinks knowing it will be for nothing because Samuel will have already returned to his work. If he wanted to see me again, he'd have mentioned it. I need to let it go and understand it was merely a whirlwind holiday romance.

It's not a simple act of letting it go because I'm furious I had no say in this. He had all the control over how we said goodbye. I hate how he ended us and didn't give me a chance to show him we could try a long-distance *friendship*. Because the idea of never seeing him again cuts through to my fucking soul.

In perfect timing, Bree returns with four coffees. "Girls, we should go check out," she says as she passes us all a disposable cup. I down it in one shot and wish it contained something harder.

"I have to shower first and get his scent off me," I snap.

Bree nods like she's a bloody dashboard doll, her head bobbing continuously.

Under the shower, I let my frustration go. I cry uncontrollably, the water washing away tears of heartbreak. I trusted him to let me go gently, not leave me alone with a fucking note to end us. It's not as bad as the breakup with Ethan, yet it hurts more. I expected more because he acted like a gentleman and not a twit like my ex.

We weren't together-together.

Still, I trusted him to do it right this time since he left me the same way in Rio. My chest heaves with hurt, a stab wound to my heart, and for the first time, I wished I had never met him.

On the drive to the airport, I barely speak.

We board the plane, and I'm seated beside Bree.

I lock away my hand luggage, and before sitting, I lean over the seat and look Yasmine in the eye. "Can you find out from Michael where he works?"

Yasmine nods. "I'll do my best, babe."

She's not to blame, and yet I can't help the anger and disappointment inside me believing she could've probed Michael more since she didn't seem surprised that Samuel up and left me this morning. Is she hiding something? I know Yasmine is good for her word, and if she promised Michael, then there's no way I'll get her to reveal anything without his consent.

I let out a sigh.

It's her relationship with Michael I envy and how she trusts him despite our friendship spanning a decade. I glance out the window and, at the moment, acknowledge I'm the same as her. I trusted Samuel just as quickly as she did Michael, only Michael has proven himself not to be a douchebag like Samuel.

Halfway through the flight, Bree digs into her pouch and holds a crumpled piece of paper folded in an attempt to smooth out creases. "I went to his room. The door was unlocked, and I found this on the floor."

My heart skips a beat, realizing what she's giving me. I look down at the piece of paper.

"I can't." I shake my head. "Not here. Can you hold onto it until I'm ready?"

"Sure." Bree tucks the letter under the top to the pouch holding her passport.

"Did you read it?" I whisper.

Bree's eyes hold mine. "Only the first few lines to make sure I had the right piece of paper." She squeezes my hand, then lets it go.

I look out the window at the clouds. We have begun our descent, and beneath the clouds are vast stretches of green. The tight ball of anger in my chest softens. Rivers are like snakes, winding and dividing the land. I'm filled with an inner calling.

I can't help thinking Samuel is down there.

Somewhere.

The question is, am I capable of letting him go?

23

EDEN

Ciudad Guayana, Bolivar, Venezuela

Guayana City isn't like any other place we've visited. It's a river city with modern architecture and pretty patterned lawns.

We checked in to a Euro Hotel. While the receptionist organized our rooms, I browsed through the rack of brochures on display. It turns out we're in the heart of the city and close to Llovizna Falls. The truth is, regardless of what this city has to offer, I want to stay in my room, be alone, and hide under the covers. I need time to process why I fell hard and fast after months of locking away my heart.

"I hear there's a nightclub downstairs." Yasmine smiles, and I'm aware it's her way of trying to pull me out of a dark place. I smile back at her, and yet it holds no joy. Out of habit, I grab a handful of brochures before following her and the others, who are chatting excitedly about how to spend our two days and one night here.

"I need food," Yasmine says.

"And a swim in the pool," Amy adds.

"What do you have there?" Bree nods at my hand holding the brochures.

"I might go exploring rather than stay in and wallow." I can hear the sarcasm in my voice.

"Cool. Let's get settled, and we can check them out," Bree says, sounding upbeat as we walk into our room next door to Yasmine and Amy's.

I'm checking out the minibar when Bree says, "This is fascinating. Let's head there now."

I spin around to ascertain what it is she's talking about. "Look. Two rivers combine here. The confluence has distinct colors of dark and light. There are heaps of information about the importance of the rivers and a tributary leading to the Amazon."

I smile at Bree's excitement. Science is her thing, and although she took the medical field, she has David Attenborough's passion in her voice when discovering something unusual.

"Now?" I ask.

"Why not? We're not here long, and we can check out Llovizna Falls while we're out."

A waterfall. I smile at her. "Okay. You message the others."

Waterfalls remind me of him, and I'm still hanging onto hope.

The minibar can wait.

🌴

We arrive back at the hotel and order a cheeseburger for dinner at the restaurant downstairs. After downing it with a glass of sangria, we head up to our room for the girls to shower. I close my eyes in a false sense of calm while they thicken their lashes and style their hair. They don't question my decision to stay in.

God, what must they think of me?

When the door closes, I rise and head to the minibar. I pour straight scotch into a glass and down it then shiver when it burns my throat. I don't want to think about the next couple of days. The island no longer has the same appeal knowing all three girls will pair up with Samuel's friends.

Yasmine had messaged Michael. He told her Samuel was back working and in an isolated location. He couldn't tell her more other than it involved medical help with an indigenous group.

I pour another shot of scotch and throw it down my throat. I groan, wishing it had the same effect as it seems to in the movies.

I'm drawn to Bree's bed, where she has fanned the brochures over the covers. They showcase beautiful beaches toward the coast, zoos, and a range of botanical gardens. The brochure on Canaima catches my attention —it's a national park south of Ciudad Guayana with tours to Angel Falls.

I stare at the brochure and recognize the name. I read it front to back then repeatedly flick the piece of paper in my hand. What am I thinking? I can't do this tour. It requires at least two days. I can't be traveling south when my group is heading north. And it's Bree's last days before flying home. I shake my head, only I can't stop thinking I need to take this trip.

The letter from Samuel sits on my bedside table. I stare at it, wishing it would burst into flames.

With a quick swipe, I grab it and walk to the corner of

the room, slide down the wall, and curl over as though it will help in some way to shield my heart by hating the words he wrote. Tentatively, I unfold the piece of paper.

Eden,

Last night when you drifted off to sleep, I thought about our goodbye kiss. It was difficult to imagine kissing you one last time because I don't want to leave you.
Over the past week, I've thought over and over about how we could make it work, how we could be together. We could if we could visit each other because that's what couples in a long-distance relationship do, right? They survive on phone calls, so they can hear the other's voice until they can see each other again. They plan when they can next visit, depending on their work and finance restrictions.
My work involves a greater depth of limitation when it comes to visits and phone calls. There is no internet service. And visitors are forbidden. I can leave to meet others in a nearby camp, but it's risky, and I'm committed to work for at least another year with no breaks.
I was hopeful until I considered how everything will change when we return to our normal lives. You'll be in Australia and so far away. In another year, so much can change, and I'll be just another memory of your holiday.
I have been awake for hours watching you sleep, and I know I have fallen for you. I want to wake you and hold you, listen to your voice one more time, kiss you one more time, only I can already feel the pain of goodbye. I'd be the source of your pain, and seeing you hurting because of me would crush me even more.
So, I'm choosing to leave quietly. It's the only way even if it

means you hating me because I can deal with your anger more
than heartache.
Believe me when I say, I'll think of you every day.
You're the best thing that's happened in my life for many,
many years.
I hope you'll still want to be friends when I visit Monte Hotels
on the esplanade of Glenelg in another year or so...

Yours truly,
Samuel

Tears fall, blotting the paper.

He knows where to find me.

Yet it means nothing because my heart hurts with more than the pain of an ended holiday romance and knowing they are just words. He has one thing right. So much can happen in a year, and I'm not going to live with the hope that maybe he'll come find me.

Liar.

Ugh, I'm frustrated he believed leaving quietly would be best for both of us. I shake my head. I know what we had was right, and we could have worked through anything.

Why doesn't he want to be found?

Work commitments—I won't accept it as a reason we can't be together.

My father always said, *if there's a will, there's a way.*

And I have the will.

I need to find the way.

Before boarding the plane to Canaima, I check my yellow fever vaccination certificate is in the back of my wallet. After sending apologetic messages to my friends, I turn off my phone.

Apart from not joining them on Margarita Island, I broke important group rules. I'm traveling alone to somewhere unknown and not on the itinerary in *Venezuela*. In the current economic and political climate, we made rules about staying safe. The risk is now intensified with limited internet and poor communication channels.

No roads lead to Canaima. You can only travel there by plane. And it's the smallest plane I've ever traveled in.

I take in a deep breath and blow air out slowly.

Who the hell am I?

If my father taught me anything, it's to follow through with a plan.

The texts I sent him and my sister are unread—a message informing them I've changed my travel plans and won't be with the girls for a few days. I know exactly what he'll say before hearing or reading his response.

This is the most erratic decision I have ever made. My heart is thumping hard in my chest, and it's not at the sight of the small aircraft as we walk out onto the tarmac with the sun rising on the horizon, ready to board.

At least my friends know where I'm headed if I don't return.

Hell, what am I saying?

I'm following a strong instinct to visit a remote area on the edge of the Amazon jungle. Shit, my father will freak. At least he doesn't know details—only that it's a national park.

I remind myself it's *my* journey.

"Este camino por favor." *This way, please.* A uniformed woman smiles at me. "We're boarding now."

I nod at her before taking a step forward into the unknown.

My sole resource—courage.

Flight time is over thirty minutes.

"I'm doing the right thing," I murmur when we're above the clouds.

The brochures portrayed the landscape below as stunning, and on attempting to peer out the tiny window, I'm hit with nausea and a wave of lightheadedness.

I close my eyes, hold onto the armrest, and pray for the next twenty minutes.

24

EDEN

Canaima National Park, Bolivar, Venezuela

Canaima base camp's dirt landing strip did nothing to reassure me that my decision was a safe one. But a jovial man with a strange English accent greets us, and my erratic heartbeat—matching my decision-making—slows. Maybe it's reassurance in knowing someone here speaks English.

"I'm Victor, and I'm taking some of you to your accommodations." He points to an oversized yellow jeep. For a moment, I'm stunned because the body is painted with large random spots like a jaguar, and we're heading into the wilderness, thus requiring camouflage.

"Eden Monteford."

My name is read out loud, along with a few others. Out of the five passengers on the plane, three of us are staying at the lodge.

We board the jeep. There are no windows or doors. There are four rows of bucket seats, face to face like the other passengers and I will be seated on a train.

I take a seat along with a middle-aged couple.

"What brings you to Canaima?" The woman's broad smile is unwavering.

"It was a last-minute decision. I decided to tick Angel Falls off my bucket list before traveling on to Margarita Island."

"A good decision. I've been waiting years. When we traveled, I promised myself to return and visit Angel Falls. My husband is wary with the political tension, so we avoided Caracas." Her American accent thickens the more she speaks. "Are you taking the aerial view or by foot?"

"Um, by foot." Only option with my budget. "Canoe, I believe."

"Curiara," she corrects. "It's the indigenous term."

"Right."

"Are you taking the Sapo Falls tour?"

"I believe it's part of the package." I shrug.

"Helen." Her partner interrupts, and I turn in the direction he's pointing.

Wow.

Flat-top mountains rise through the vastness of a green forest breaking through the heavy clouds. I've entered an emerald world. It's like the heavens have poured green paint as thick as lava from above, and it has coated everything it touches. As we head closer, a lake comes into view, and our accommodations sit on the edge of the water with the waterfalls in the distance. The jeep slows, and the squawking echoes around us. Birds and monkeys overpower everything else.

I'm fixated by the beauty of the lake blending in with the surrounding landscape and the low-lying fog hovering above the water.

While checking in, we're offered refreshments and informed about the morning tour to the waterfalls and lagoon ride.

Every step toward my room I'm besotted with the beauty of nature surrounding me. I step onto a terracotta-tiled patio that joins each hut, all facing out to the lagoon. A hammock is tied to posts outside the door, an invitation to relax and take in the magnificence. Before unlocking my door, I pause for a moment to take in the view of Canaima Lagoon and the waterfalls in the distance.

My room is nicely decorated and cool despite the humidity. There's no phone, and I have no reception reminding me of our isolation. I change into sneakers, apply Deet because the mosquitoes are already making their presence known, and head to the restaurant for breakfast.

Walking the tropical gardens, I spot a macaw on a low branch. Its head is tilted, watching me, and I it. It hits me how the bird symbolizes paradise, and looking around, I realize I've found it.

🌴

Breakfast is a smorgasbord of exotic fruits spanning a table in the dining room. Exotic fruit, one of the things I told Samuel I enjoy, and right now, there are some I fail to identify. Regardless, I try everything. I want to taste every piece of fruit on offer. With every bite, I think about our conversations during our days together, trying to remember if he hinted at where he could be.

A voice brings me back to the room, and our small group is guided to a seated lounge room where we're briefed about the ecology of the area and being mindful of leaving a footprint.

Our host, a local indigenous man, is dressed in cut-off cargo shorts and a loosely buttoned khaki shirt. I'm surprised he's wearing solid boots in this heat. He fiddles with a sturdy broad-brimmed hat in his hand.

"Hello. I Asoo. I ask you respect our culture and land. Twenty thousand Pemón live in Gran Sabana," he explains. Thick lashes frame his dark eyes, his straight black hair is long enough to cover his ears, and his skin is a deep bronze. "Treat environment with care, it's a fragile ecosystem." I nod, barely understanding his pronunciation even though it sounds rehearsed like he's trying to remember the correct words. "Bring your trash back to lodge and dispose appropriately."

The 'respect and be mindful' mantra demands reflection, and I'm already glad I decided to take a risk and explore this area.

Asoo leads those of us on the tour to the lake, and we begin by boarding the *curiara* anchored at the muddy edge of the lagoon. After seeing our mode of transportation, I'm a little nervous. The canoe serves a purpose, and it's not designed for comfort. It's a long, narrow shell of a tree trunk, carved and hollowed out with wooden planks as seats. A portable outboard motor sits at the back of the canoe.

Asoo revs the motor, which sounds more like it belongs on a motorbike, and we jerk backward with the absence of support. With a burst of nervous laughter, I grab hold of the plank of wood under my rear.

We make our way across the lagoon, and I exhale quietly in gratification. The breathtaking scenery alone makes it worth the effort to get here. I'm filled with awe and know *this* is what my soul seeks.

The waterfalls come in full view. In the background, three table-top mountains hover in low-lying clouds. Asoo explains these are tepuis, and the word is from the Pemón language meaning 'House of Gods' significant to Pemón mythology.

We reach the shores of the main island. "Anatoly Island, where the river system splits coming down from the mountains," Asoo says, using his hands to emphasize his words. He nods at me. "My English ... Victor say... rusty."

"You're doing fine," I tell him.

We disembark for a fifteen-minute hike across the savannah to reach the first waterfall. The air is heavier with moisture, and we pass rocks, moist with slime. It's the end of the wet season. Large red ants scurry near the trail, so I tread cautiously and don't know whether to look up or down.

We reach the first waterfall, Sapo Falls. From the top where I stand, it gives me an uninterrupted view down the length of the waterfall.

Asoo instructs us to tread carefully as we take the trail down the side of the waterfall. "Down is another path leading behind waterfall. Everyone wait. Ground slippery."

We follow the wet, rocky path behind the waterfall, and the spray makes visibility difficult. I'm completely soaked, and then I skid in the mud. "Shit." I reach for a rope strung on the side of the path. The man in front of me turns and wipes water from his face.

"Are you okay?"

"Yes," I say and shoot out a nervous giggle. I stop and absorb the energy and acknowledge the water's power as it surges over the cliff. I remind myself why I'm here, remembering only a few days prior how I decided to shed the skin of the old me, take a risk and go on an adventure, and just maybe find a trace of where Samuel is working.

My concentration reverts to the man ahead as I follow him along the path leading to the base of the waterfall and to a small pool of clean water to swim and escape the heat.

"The water safe to drink," Asoo tells us. Still, I opt for the bottled water in my bag.

We move on to the next smaller waterfall. The water is significantly pinker, and I wonder why.

After a quick lunch break of sandwiches, we begin the return journey, retracing our steps and head back to our accommodations.

It's late afternoon when the curiara hits the sandy shore of the resort. With weary legs, I tread the path and clamber into the hammock on the porch. I close my eyes and simply listen to the constant noise of the jungle. I have no idea how much time passes before the mosquitoes force me to retreat indoors.

After a quick shower, I collapse on the bed, not bothering about dinner. The information about tomorrow's trip to Angel Falls is on the bedside table. I read over it again, paying particular attention to the paragraph on Pemón communities. Dotted on the map are the known communities around the Gran Sabana. I keep reading the lines of *funding by international aid*.

Specifically, *the help of volunteers, medical supplies, and visiting practitioners.*

I sit up and stare out into the distance toward the tepuis.

He's out there.

How in the hell am I going to find him?

25

EDEN

Low in the eastern sky, brushstrokes of yellow, pink, and orange break the horizon. I barely make out the lake for the dark shadows. I follow the silhouettes of a few tourists walking the path toward the main building.

I'm early for my tour, so I take the opportunity to send Amy a message while I'm close to reception to use Wi-Fi. I send a quick text because I don't expect any of my friends to be awake at dawn, especially now that they are on Margarita Island with Samuel's friends.

> I'm safe and will call you later.

Seconds later, my phone buzzes in my hand.

"Are you completely insane?" Amy screams into the phone.

"Maybe..." I whisper. "I don't know how to explain it, but something has drawn me to this place."

"Shit, Eden. You have broken all our rules, and I thought you were the responsible one?"

"I'm sorry—"

"Bit late now to apologize. We're worried about you. You shouldn't have gone alone. Why didn't you mention it to me? I could've come with you, for fuck's sake."

"Would you really have come?" I murmur.

There is silence for a few seconds before she responds, "We probably would've talked you out of it."

"Exactly. I can't justify my gut instinct to stay, except there's something about this place I need to explore more."

"Stay? C'mon, Edes, what are you saying?"

"I'm doing another tour today, and then there are these indigenous communities along the river I'd like to visit—"

"You're looking for him, aren't you?"

I let out a sigh. "I might not make it to Machu Picchu, so I'll meet up with you in Arequipa or Lima. Definitely before you get to Iquitos."

"You were the one who was keen to tour Peru. So, you've just wasted your money?"

"It's not about the money, Ames. I'm following my heart."

"I don't know what to say to change your mind. I'm scared for you."

"Don't be. I'm having the best time. It's like I'm meant to be here," I say, now smiling. "I'll keep in touch, but for most of the area, I won't have coverage."

"Have you spoken to anyone else?"

"No. Please tell the girls I'm okay and say goodbye to Bree. I'll call and message when I can. I love you, and I owe you."

"I don't want to end this call not knowing when we'll

144

next meet up." I understand her apprehension, and yet I can't give her an answer until I know myself.

"I'll be in contact and will send the contact details of the lodge in Canaima where I'm staying. They have email and a landline."

"That's hardly reassuring."

"It's all I can offer for now. Bye, Ames. Don't worry, I'm truly fine."

I press the end button and stare at the screen while going over the conversation in my head.

Am I insane?

There's warmth flowing through me as if I have suddenly developed the freedom to be courageous. Holding onto the sensation, I scoop up my pack and follow the path around the lake until I meet at the sandy beach with the other tourists.

A few more travelers had arrived overnight requiring two *curiara's* to transport us. I climb aboard Asoo's boat, taking the same seat position as yesterday.

My backpack is wrapped in plastic and sits at my feet. It contains a bottle of insect repellent, sunscreen, snacks, bottles of water, and a towel along with a change of clothes and shoes. My phone is for the purpose of taking photos. Stuffed at the bottom is a mosquito net in case things don't go to plan. If not viewing Angel Falls by plane, there are two parts to the ground tour. A day trip— my choice—so it will be late when I arrive back at the resort. Others chose to stay the night and sleep in a camp at the base of the falls, not in a hotel but a wall-less hut with hammocks strung from poles. Local Pemón assist the tour guides and provide the traditional dinner and breakfast. In energy-sucking heat, no further bedding is required except a mosquito net. Although I'm taking anti-malarial medication and regularly applying personal repellent loaded with DEET, the mosquitoes and I have already developed a close relationship, and it's one I don't appreciate.

Banter fills the air as we chug across the lake taking a similar route as yesterday. The sun rises, and the sky turns blue, and again, I'm awestruck at the backdrop of three tepuis jutting up through the clouds. The plateau of the flat-top mountain is invisible. Asoo spoke about the myths of these mountains yesterday. Myths aren't what attracts me to this mystical place, and yet there's something eerie, a warning looming in the clouds.

"Are you taking the tour by plane tomorrow?" the woman seated in front of me asks.

"No, only today's tour."

"Are you staying overnight?"

I shake my head.

"I thought most of us were."

I shrug. "I'm on a tight schedule."

She turns to her partner, no doubt realizing I'm of no help. "Did you pack extra snacks and water? I'm not sure I'm going to agree with the food on offer."

I smile at her and consider asking to trade places. Only it's not part of my plan.

We sail into the Mayupa rapids and disembark to cross on foot. Asoo and another helper ride through the rapids to meet us on the other side. Two guides lead us through grassland, a safer journey than trying to navigate the rapids.

We board the curiara and sail upstream. It's more what I imagined in my dreams with thick tree growth bordering the river's edge, overhanging into the water.

Walls of green vegetation block the world like a never-ending jail cell locking us into her heart. My trust is now in two strange men to get us safely to our destination regardless of what the river, jungle, or Mother Nature throw at us. There's not a cloud in the sky. We're not fooled after Victor's warning about how weather conditions can turn in the blink of an eye and how downpours can turn calm water into raging currents.

Monkeys howl, and it sounds like an alert to our presence. I'm engrossed, looking beyond the vines choking the branches trying to see one. I imagine snakes, spiders, and scorpions inhabiting the thick growth of the jungle floor and other dangers residing in the trees. I shouldn't be focused on trying to see a monkey. How anyone could survive in the jungle is beyond me. In a moment of truth, I realize the life jackets strapped to our bodies are useless with anaconda, piranha, and dangerous parasites inhabiting the murky water below. All would threaten my safety before I could make it to land. Or have I watched too many horror movies?

We approach a sandy river beach and disembark for morning tea on Orchid Island. Colorful wild orchids line the forest doorway intertwined in the trees and vines. The purple, pink, and white flowers growing near the sandy river beach almost trick me into believing we're in a wonderland. We don't venture far. After a quick break, we board the canoes and continue our journey along the Carrao River. The river forks, and Asoo explains the new route along the Churun River, preparing us for the smaller rapids.

A woman seated at front squeals when the canoe thumps the water while another guide helps navigate the rapids.

"*Auyán-Tepui* is origin of Angel Falls," Asoo says. "Water produced on top of tepui has no land water source. All water comes from clouds and squeezed out of the cloud onto tepui. It pools and feeds all waterfalls."

"Incredible," I murmur.

He shoots a smile over his shoulder before focusing again on navigating through the rapids. "*Pemón* named Angel Falls *Kerepakupai Merú*, waterfall of deepest place."

I remember Samuel telling me this. Could I be on the right track to finding him?

"*Pemón* myths say tepuis are home of gods. The *Mawari* spirits of dead, and people forbidden," he continues.

The mountain is associated with spirits of the dead. Well, that just confirms its eeriness.

The rapids ease, and Asoo signals an end to our river journey. After leaving the canoe behind, we find several man-made base camp shelters, structures where hundreds of hammocks can be hung from its many poles. Asoo had mentioned over five hundred visitors used to come to the waterfall daily. Now it's a handful of people every week. My heart goes out to the people here, knowing from our own family business the importance of tourism for survival.

Unusual flowers reminding me of red luscious lips and orchids line the path as I wander back to the group.

Our small group makes the uphill trek. It's more difficult than I anticipated, and I find myself falling behind, tripping on ribbons of exposed roots and slipping on dead foliage coated in mud. I stop to look ahead, tilting my head to gather my bearings on the steep hill. The largest palms I've ever seen fill any void. Thorned bamboo towers so high it bends at the peak, further growth obstructed by leaves of the taller trees. Small shrubs and new growth sprout everywhere I look. Thorned leaves on vines weave around trunks and branches or dangle down like rope searching to attach and attack anything solid. Yellow moss covers most tree trunks. Dampness thickens the air. I have to take deeper breaths, which worsens the higher we climb. Keeping my gaze low to maintain my balance, I spy mushrooms sprouting beneath the decaying foliage. Even though I'm following the person in front of me, I remind myself to glance up occasionally in case I need to duck away from a web, with what I imagine might contain an abnormally large spider. Ugh. I shudder.

Swiping sweat from my brows, I blink through the salt burning my eyes.

"You stay?" Asoo asks me.

"I can't."

"Omar, my helper, will stay night. I go with you and meet group in morning."

"How do you find your way around here? I mean, everything looks the same."

White teeth glow against his dark skin. "I live here many years. Your home in city scary. I get lost."

I laugh. "We all do at times."

I stop in my tracks before bumping the guy in front. Omar has his hand in the air signaling for us to halt and remain silent. Asoo points to a colorful toucan in a nearby tree. We take more photos before moving on to an unfenced lookout to view the falls.

I let out a sigh of achievement.

With my phone in my hand, I click away admiring the waterfall streaming over the cliff edge more than a mile high, so it's impossible to capture its entirety.

The steep rocky decline leads to Angel's Stream and a pond fed by a second cascade. We moan in unison at the disappointment of the cloud hovering above and blocking our view to the peak. Asoo encourages us to hike down to the pond for a swim, and no one objects in the sweltering heat.

Following Asoo's lead, I scamper down the rocky drop and strip down to a swimsuit, which is now like second nature to wear under clothes. I shower under the second fall and climb slimy rocks to walk behind the cascade. After a swim and feeling significantly cooler, I clamber out of the pond and sit with Asoo.

"It's breathtakingly beautiful. I only came here because a friend recommended it, and I'm glad I took up the offer." We exchange smiles of appreciation. "My friend, he also talked about the Pemón communities around here. Their traditional way of life interests me."

Asoo frowns. "Most have European influence." He gazes up without elaborating, and when I do the same, I'm amazed how the clouds have dispersed, and Angel Falls is now in full view.

"Unbelievable," I whisper. The sheer height of the falls is mind-blowing from the ground.

Asoo and I sit back on the rocks, and in a trance, I realize I'm on the adventure my heart seeks so desperately. It's only now my journey has truly started. I stare at the falls for I have no idea what length of time, and my thoughts drift, wondering if my past has led me to this day. The clouds pass by overhead, slowly thickening, and in a short time, our view is blocked once more, as if white-out has removed everything above the green.

"Eden," Asoo says, bringing my head out of the

clouds. "You lucky. You see her beauty. Now, we head back."

The way down, I assume to be quicker, only I slip even more on the tangled roots than I did before. Asoo maintains a good pace, the gap between us widening. By the time we reach our curiara, I'm out of breath. Asoo waits for me to board and pushes the canoe out into the river. I scramble over seats to sit with him at the back and chat while straddling my seat to observe our approach and him because he's been frowning for the past half hour.

"Something is bothering you," I say, more of a statement.

Asoo points to the sun.

I nod. "We don't need to stop for breaks. I have fruit in my backpack."

"My helper say rapids safe. We travel alone."

"If it's faster, then yes. It'll be quicker than me walking."

I turn to admire the view of the river snaking through a never-ending garden. The awareness of danger dissolves with an inner peace of being here in the Amazon. Her gardens are the lungs sustaining all life. I take in a deep breath and smile.

We turn the bend, and Asoo takes a tributary river, the fork disguised by overhanging tree branches narrowing the entrance to twenty feet wide.

If I ever considered my mind and gut could work in unison, it would be now. My thoughts race knowing this isn't our route. He's focused on navigating the canoe, but nothing in his expression hints not to trust him.

Sensing me staring, he nods to a package at his feet. "I deliver parcel to friend."

I draw my gaze from studying his expression to the river ahead. The current is significantly slower with a narrower river and sharper bends. Retrieving my water bottle, I guzzle down a few mouthfuls. Pushing my drink inside, I stumble on my seat at the crack of thunder directly overhead. Asoo shouts in a language I don't understand. Clouds roll and thicken, and it's as though I'm watching a storm on film in fast forward. In a matter of minutes, the skies open and cry heavy tears on us.

The rain pelts my shoulders and back. I'm all for getting wet to cool down, only the sting is like a high-pressure hose.

Asoo points to a small bowl and indicates to bucket it out. I do it quickly with the water pooling around my ankles, not watching ahead.

"Stay low," he warns. I fall forward when the boat hits an embankment. "Stay low."

Before I respond, he's out of the curiara and heading toward a figure. Positioning myself on the seat, I look up to the rainforest surrounding the river's edge except for the narrow bank of sand stretching for approximately one hundred and fifty feet.

I squint through the rain. Asoo has met with a man. He's naked except for something covering his groin. His skin is a golden bronze. Not of indigenous heritage—skin changed by the sun.

I stand and raise a hand to shield my eyes. Like a switch, the rain stops. Blue sky peeks through the gray clouds dispersing as quickly as they formed. My breath hitches on hearing a familiar voice. The boat rocks with my ungraceful moves to clamber to the front. Ignoring Asoo's warning, I jump onto the sand. With every step, the conversation between both men becomes clearer.

Asoo looks sideways and holds up a hand. He's standing several steps away from the man as though it's a safe distance between them.

The stranger's head snaps in my direction.

His eyes pop.

I still.

As though in quicksand and further movement will thwart my safety. My heart pounds in recognition.

Samuel takes a few steps toward me, and I do the same.

I want to run to him. Only my thoughts don't line up.

I want to scream at him for leaving me. Something holds me back.

I'm caught in his gaze, struggling to believe it's him.

Asoo places a hand on my shoulder to turn around, only something in me fights the delirium and refuses to obey.

Samuel shakes his head, bewildered. "How?" he rasps.

"You left me clues," I blurt out.

"Eden, stop," Asoo demands.

I push past him and march through the sand until Samuel's strong hands grab my shoulders, keeping us an arm's distance apart. His gaze roams my face, searching, as though answers will magically appear.

Before he speaks, the branches rustle. An oversized headdress catches my attention first. Red and black grass strung high in a semi-circle. One glance, and fear hits me with an unfamiliar world beyond the trees. A long, decorated stick thumps the ground demanding attention. Bones and beads rattle with the force.

"Don't be frightened," Samuel says gently and falls to his knees. "Follow my lead," he whispers, head bowed.

I kneel beside him. "What's happening?" Samuel doesn't look up, only stares at the indigenous man's feet and waits.

"Eden," Asoo shouts from the boat, its motor revving.

Samuel speaks unrecognizable words and sounds.

Peering over my shoulder, I foolishly wave Asoo on. He throws my backpack onto the sand. "I come back tomorrow," he shouts.

"Keep your head down," Samuel instructs.

Long, rough fingers wrap under my chin and tilt my head until I'm forced to look into the eyes of the man before me.

"What do I do?" I whisper.

"Nothing." Samuel glances at us before lowering his gaze once more.

Dark eyes lock with mine. The aging lines around his eyes deepen as he studies me. White paint slashes each cheek. Beneath each slash are shadows of old tattoos. Thin strands of gray hair fall to his shoulders, camouflaged by the grass and feathers framing his face. He speaks words not intended for me.

Samuel responds, and my chin is set free.

"Follow me."

The man waits while Samuel leads me to a small A-frame structure made of branches and palm leaves. Samuel glances over his shoulder. I don't need to look to know we're being observed. I sense it, along with Samuel's concern. I take his hips, wanting to pull him close. His hands land on my shoulders, firm enough to keep us apart.

Worry lines crease at the corners of his eyes. "Remain here until I come for you."

He bends and scoops up his backpack and the

package, and walks toward the man. I'm a little stunned as to what's happened. Yet I can't pull my gaze from his near-naked body as he walks barefoot over the sand. When he reaches the native American, they disappear into the trees.

I cough after inhaling the smoke from a small fire. Near it is a canopy of dried palm fronds, and it's high enough not to catch alight. It protects the flame somewhat from the downpour of rain, although the fire smokes as if rain has seeped in. Wood is piled under the cover, so I place another chunk on to burn. Not because I'm cold, but more to warn off insects and other things I don't want to think about.

The sun is getting low. I have no idea where Samuel has gone and how long I'm to wait here. I remember my backpack and sprint down to the water's edge to retrieve it. I stare toward the direction Asoo traveled in. There is no sign of him or anyone else. Monkeys howl in the trees above. Insects screech with impending nightfall. I unwrap the wet plastic from my backpack and shake it to rid it of the water.

Under the shelter, there's a hammock and a log. Then I notice string tied to a stick and fish bones scattered in the dirt. Beside the bones are pieces of dried skin from some type of fruit or vegetable. Through the branches, a vine grows bearing fruit reminding me of passionfruit. Knocking the vines and branches aside, I take a few steps into the overgrowth checking for webs and other creatures living in the trees. After choosing several pieces, I retreat and take a seat on a log under the shelter. There's a sense of safety here in the clearing where I'm able to observe my surroundings. Splitting the fruit with my nail, I break it in half. The yellow flesh with black seeds is familiar and safe. It's sweet. With every mouthful, I gaze up into the distance awaiting Samuel's return.

More time passes.

I stand, pace, glance to the river, and allow reality to set in.

I found him. No matter what joy and accomplishment I feel, I acknowledge this is his place of work.

The place he tried to keep a secret.

Going by his lack of clothes and the strange man's tribal headgear, this isn't one of the Pemón communities Asoo had mentioned.

Asoo. My gut tightens remembering his hasty exit and how overwhelmed I was with finding Samuel to care.

Sticks snap, and I look beyond the trees.

"Who's there?" I shout.

Did I expect anyone to answer?

Visibility is poor through the maze of green and failing light. I kneel behind the small fire, peer through the smoke, and add a few more pieces of wood, not wanting the flame to burn out.

My chest tightens.

Don't be scared. You are fine. Samuel knows you're here. You're not alone. My thoughts steamroll like a checklist accounting for my actions. *Shit.* There was no kiss. In my head, I deliberated how I'd react when I saw him and contemplated the million questions I had. Mostly, I imagined the kiss.

What if he doesn't return?

And what was with him falling to his knees bowing to the strange man like he was some kind of god?

I turn to the hammock. Is this where he's been sleeping?

I reach for my water bottle. My hand trembles, and

water dribbles from the side of my mouth as I gulp down mouthfuls, trying to swallow the dry lump in the back of my throat.

Yes, I found him, and he's disappeared, again.

The reality is night is falling, and I'm *alone* in the middle of the damn jungle.

26

SAMUEL

Ulara

Beyond the hut, Samuel looks to the leaves glistening under the moonlight shining through the tree canopy. Trapped droplets from the rain shine like tiny diamonds, the rainforest's unique jewelry store. His surroundings have always calmed him, only tonight he feels something else.

Samuel places a gloved hand on the young girl's forehead. She groans and rolls over crinkling the twine mat beneath her as she does. Her fever is easing. The shaman had spent hours grinding plants for her medicine and placing wet palms on her body. Occasionally, their medicine fails, and that's when the shaman asks for Samuel's help. A seizure caused the shaman to panic. His niece's daughter has never suffered seizures in the past.

A simple over-the-counter Western medication eases her temperature. It doesn't help with knowing the cause, though. He expects a bad gastric virus, hopes it's not measles as it would mean community transmission. The latter is of concern because the village is hidden from the rest of the world.

Until he speaks further with her family to account for the past week's activities, he can only treat her symptoms.

Samuel stands when one of the Ularan warriors approaches his hut. He creeps out and nods to the young man. He has estimated his age to be around twenty, and he's yet to find a wife. Rare, as most men here find a partner after initiation—a celebration when a boy becomes a man. Samuel assumes Timenneng wants to learn from the shaman. He hopes he doesn't take a page from Samuel's book—thirty-two years and no partner. The shaman has no partner, a pattern of devotion. And yet, the shaman has a daughter. Samuel has never asked about her mother. Asking is taboo. One day he expects the shaman will tell him the story, like many other stories he's privileged to hear.

Samuel speaks to him in the language the Ularans understand, a dialect similar to Pemón.

"Safe?" he asks in their native tongue. The dialect is clear even with the mask covering his mouth and nose for their protection. He couldn't be more thankful for a bright moon, knowing Eden is alone.

Timenneng tells him Eden sleeps. The other warrior, Wayara, remains on watch, hiding in the rainforest, a request by Samuel to the chief after the shaman requested the girl to remain.

He didn't expect it. He'd been overwhelmed at the moment. His heart had been torn, wanting to speak to her and ask her to leave, for she didn't belong. No matter how he feels about Eden, the latter is the truth. The shaman had surprised him by permitting her to spend a few days but only on the outskirts of their community. Maybe the shaman sensed what she meant to him or if he rewarded Samuel for returning and required his immediate help. Could the shaman's dealing with Eden's arrival be a rash decision? He didn't believe it. The shaman never acted on impulse.

"Is she afraid?" he asks.

The warrior remains silent, a strange word to them. Their world knows only personal growth, along with survival and acceptance, mostly coming to peace with your inner emotion and thoughts. Her isolation is a health and safety measure and a test. One Eden was unprepared for.

Her safety is what matters.

Samuel nods to dismiss the young warrior before returning to the young girl's side.

On first arriving in the village, Samuel learned his social status. His family's wealth and expensive college education were insignificant to the people and useless as a means of survival.

Eden will also learn her place.

Time isn't regarded here in the same way it is in the outside world. There are no clocks—only the sun and moon to guide hours, days, and years. Yet the tick-tock of the clock fills Samuel's head with how much time he can spend with Eden.

Never has he expected any woman to live the way he has chosen. His gut tightens fighting desire- fueled thoughts, threatening all logic. Eden *can't* be here. Yet his imagination fills with hope of her staying longer than a few days.

Gathering his thoughts, he checks the niece once

more before taking a mat near the far wall to get a few hours' sleep.

🌴

A whimper wakes him, and shards of sunlight streak through the trees.

The young girl is sitting, holding her stomach. Her mother stands outside the hut, her dark brown eyes plead to his. He nods for her to enter and stand at her daughter's side. The niece indicates she's hungry. Samuel smiles. He was told for many days she has suffered and not eaten. Last night was the second seizure. After administering an antispasmodic medication, he suspects the worst is over, and their indigenous medicine can replenish her energy.

He tells the mother she's to remain here for another day. The mother can feed her tea and *oo*—cassava bread made from yuca—and remain by her side. He points out the wooden bowl of water for her hands.

Samuel leaves them alone and makes his way to a nearby stream to wash before visiting the shaman and chief. It will give him time to consider his words when asking the chief to grant Eden a longer stay.

He doesn't want to think about the alternative and if he's refused permission to see her again.

27

EDEN

I roll onto my side, curl into a ball, and continue dreaming. Only this morning a slight roll causes the bed to sway beneath me. I jerk up remembering where I am. In the process, I tangle my arms and legs in the mosquito net wrapped around me. Alerted to buzzing above, I kick harder to untangle myself, forcing my eyes open and to focus.

"Oomph. Oh, for God's sake," I say when I land on the ground. I bounce back up onto my feet, shove the net aside, and look around me for anything crawling at my feet.

Rubbing my eyes, I groan and stretch out the kinks in my back. I had more energy and got more sleep after a hard night of partying than I did last night. Stumbling across the sand, I head to the river, scoop handfuls of water and wash my face. I stand and search the river bend for any signs of life. I'm grateful for the absence of movement in the river in the form of *caiman*, a smaller alligator found in these parts because that would send me over the edge.

Birds squawk high in the trees, and the monkeys squeal. I quickly glance over my shoulder to the vines and strangler figs choking the trees. The river divides the jungle's domination apart from the stretch of sand below my socked feet. I can't help my overwhelming sensation of vulnerability and consider how many souls are lost in here. The water before me isn't so much an escape—rather a potential death trap misleading you as a path out. No one knows what lies in those muddy depths.

"Why did I allow Asoo to leave me here?" I mutter. Oh, that's right, for the man who left me alone *all* night in the wilderness with nothing more than a smoldering fire.

"Why am I so surprised?" I say with sarcasm.

My stomach growls needing food, preferably the type prepared and ready to eat. Already I'm missing the luxury of Uber Eats—even a fast-food drive-through seems like a treat. Unzipping my backpack, I pull out nut snacks, a banana, and my anti-malarial meds. I take a tablet and guzzle water from my spare bottle, then peel down the banana skin and savor every piece then I head back into the forest edge to pick more.

Standing beside the vine, I'm on alert for bugs near my feet or movement above. I snap off a piece, then gaze ahead past the foliage while splitting the skin. I feel like I'm in a tunnel, the vegetation surrounding me is so thick. Yet through the web of green, I spy a man. Dark hair catches my eye first. It's cut like a basin framing his face. His skin blends with the rotting leaves on the forest floor. Strangely, I'm not alarmed, only aware. He's grasping a stick to balance, or it could be a spear. Squatting on his heels, he's as still as the tree trunks surrounding him. I have no idea how long he's been watching me. I recall Samuel telling me not to be afraid, so I take a tentative step toward him and then another.

He doesn't move until I take a few more steps, winding a path around trees until we make eye contact. His long legs uncurl in a slow, controlled movement. He holds his ground, maintaining his stance the closer I come. Then he shoves his stick forward, the base remaining on the ground. I'm not sure if it's for his protection or in warning.

"Where's Samuel?" I ask in a low voice. "Samuel," I repeat when he says nothing.

The piece of wood rises. He pulls out a small spear from his grass skirt. It's the size of a dart, and he places it in the hollow opening and blows hard. I shriek and jump on hearing a thump behind me. The man runs past me. A huge snake slithers on the ground, and I scream as loud as my lungs will allow. The native American drops to his knees, hands over his ears before turning wide-eyed to stare at me. I'm still panting when he snaps the head of the snake, and its long body falls limp. Gathering the length of it, he slings the creature over his shoulder. Words stick in my throat as a vile taste coats my tongue. Without thinking, I run, pushing vines out of my path to my camp and sit by the smoking fire.

"Eden." Samuel runs toward me from further along the river, and I sprint to him. He takes me in his arms and holds me close. Stroking my hair, he whispers, "What happened?"

"A snake," I croak. I point toward the trees and hold back the tears threatening to undo me. I thump his chest in blame. "Why did you leave me here alone?"

His expression wears the same sleepless mask as mine. "There was no other way."

"I was afraid," I rasp.

"I know," he says, stroking my hair.

"Iwoi." *Snake*. The indigenous man appears wearing the reptile wrapped around his shoulders like a necklace and a wide smile.

"I see you've met Wayara. He watched over you all night."

I cringe knowing there were times I had to pee, and unaccustomed to bush squatting, I removed my shorts to do so. "Where did you go?"

He takes my hand and leads me to the place I slept, and Wayara follows. He points to the fire, and Wayara throws the snake in the cinders.

"First, we eat."

"The snake?"

"You'll be surprised by the taste."

My hand rises to my mouth. If I ever considered being a vegetarian, now is the time to speak up. In perfect time, my stomach grumbles.

"Pretend it's chicken. You'll need the energy."

Hunger can provide the mental strength of visualization of what I wouldn't even attempt under normal circumstances. Choosing an alternative on a menu isn't an option here, so tricking my mind into believing I'm eating chicken is easier than I thought.

Sharing a meal of smoked snake with Wayara and Samuel, dirt on my face, my rear on a log, is far from any version of glamping I had previously imagined.

Wayara stands, and Samuel nods. "He needs to return to the village," Samuel tells me.

For a brief moment, I anticipate we'll have some time together to talk.

"I have to go with him, explain to the chief that Wayara has been in contact with you, although not closer than five feet. And I need to check on someone."

I glance down at my crinkled clothing. His words startle me as though I'm dirty and contagious. The men stand, and I do the same with only the fire dividing us.

"Please don't leave me again?" I plead.

He stops, and his brow furrows. "I'll be back soon. Does it help to know someone is always watching?"

I look toward the trees. "In a way..." I'm confused and have no idea what I'm doing.

"Did you bring repellent?"

"Yes, and I've enough Doxycycline to last me a while."

"Good."

It's his final word before both men run into the forest and disappear beyond the skyscraper trees.

"Wait. Why do you want to know?" I call out. High in the trees, the monkeys shriek and drone out my voice. "What am I supposed to do now?" I shout to the forest and then plonk my rear back on the piece of log with a huff.

28

SAMUEL

"Oko Weju." *Two suns.*

On bent knees, Samuel closes his eyes and quietly thanks the universe.

The chief has granted her another two days but no contact with the Ularans.

Samuel lifts his chin and meets the chief's gaze. Deep wrinkles exacerbate the scowl in his expression. His reasons for not wanting Eden to stay are understandable. For anyone else, he'd send them away.

Wings take flight in his stomach, and he pushes through the excitement to find reason. What does a few more days achieve? She cannot stay—wouldn't *want* to stay. And he can't *be* with her. Unmarried and sleeping together, he'd risk banishment.

Scarlet, hyacinth blue, and yellow feathers of the macaw point up to the heavens, secured by an embroidered band around the chief's crown. Red paint slashes his cheeks and dots his nose and chin. The dotting art continues along his bare arms, chest, and midriff.

Trophies in the form of teeth hang around his neck. There are several strands, including some from caiman and jaguar. The size of the incisors indicates a larger breed. Samuel has no doubt the chief himself won a battle with each.

What surprises him is the shaman's support. He senses fear, as with any outsider, there's the risk of disease, including yellow fever. Any virus is a threat when there is no built-up immunity in a community. The Ularans avoided the Spanish invasion and associated diseases. The original village resided deeper in the jungle. The decision to migrate was made because of tribal war before the shaman was born. The newer community remaining untouched thanks to the mountains and the hidden waterways behind the village to hide. In southeast Venezuela, myths of their folklore hold warning, and fear has kept intruders out.

Samuel rises to his feet and brushes dirt from his knees and then from his hands. The shaman watches him with intrigue. Since his arrival, and after proving his worth in a useful element to the shaman, Samuel has emphasized the importance of clean hands and wound care. His ways still fascinate the shaman. One scratch from a vine has infection potential. The Ularans have a plant for almost every ailment, except the common cold, a virus that could kill many.

The thought takes Samuel back to Eden in quarantine. He can't see her tonight with the first of many celebrations in preparation for their upcoming expedition. A special dinner and sacrifice to ask the gods for a safe passage and return and to find the plant Samuel seeks. The journey will begin in several days on the next full moon phase to light the jungle at night.

The shaman gives Samuel a knowing look. Samuel bows his head to both the shaman and the chief before following the shaman to the outskirts of the village and into the rainforest, keeping a safe distance between them.

They walk a short distance before vines, trees, and low vegetation engulf every space. To an outsider, it's a jungle requiring a machete to make a path. To the shaman, it's a medicine cabinet where every plant is beneficial to his people.

Today the shaman's entire face is painted white. The horizontal lines over his chest remind Samuel of an x-ray exposing ribs. The shaman's long thin fingers reach out and touch a vine growing abundantly among the trees, the vine, the mother of all healing plants.

To the Ularans, ayahuasca is a plant that heals the body and cleanses the blood. In order to heal, the mind must be open and cleansed of past traumas and emotions to allow the body and mind to work in unison in healing. For this to happen, the third-eye chakra needs to be open, to experience a celestial realm. Ayahuasca is controversial in the Western world, and yet it's part of the Ularan existence.

Samuel refused the ceremony ayahuasca for many months. A scientist and non-believer, he tried other healing plants on himself and on the younger children with good effect. When a child in his care nearly died, and the shaman introduced the same medicinal plants with the help of ayahuasca, he witnessed a miracle—an understanding as to how it opens the body's energy for other medicinal plants to have a purer effect.

Tonight, the warriors will drink the brew made from the vine. Samuel's body remains *poisoned* by the Western society foods after his trip to see his friends, and he needs to detoxify before drinking it in a shamanic ceremony.

The shaman cuts the ayahuasca vine and the chacruna plant and sings a harmonic tune in words Samuel is yet to understand. He comprehends words of gratitude and hope, and Samuel quietly thanks the vine. The spiritual power astounds Samuel, and over the years accepts that some things can't be explained.

The rumbling of a motor carries through the trees. The shaman gives Samuel a nod, and he dashes toward the river, surmising Asoo has returned to check on Eden. When he reaches the forest edge, he remains behind a rubber tree and listens to their conversation before making his presence known.

"Did you spend night here?"

Eden stands near the boat. Her backpack remains under the shelter. He lets go of the air in his chest.

"I did. Not as scary as it sounds."

Asoo chuckles. "You're acquainted with the jungle."

"Not really. I'm to wait here for Samuel."

"For how long?"

She shrugs. "We haven't had much of a chance to speak. I guess I can go with him soon."

"Where?"

"To the village where he works."

Asoo shakes his head vehemently. "Ulara no place for you. Come to Canaima." He holds out his hand for her to climb aboard.

Panic tightens Samuel's chest, so he steps out from the trees.

"Eden. Wait."

29

"She'll be safe here with me." Samuel gives Asoo a stern look. Something passes between them—a silent warning.

"Why wouldn't I be safe?" I ask Asoo.

"Will she stay with you?" Asoo asks Samuel.

Samuel frowns at him. "I'll look after her."

Asoo nods. "Then I return tomorrow."

"Thank you, Asoo. I appreciate it," I say quickly.

It will give me time with Samuel before returning to Canaima and contacting my friends to check in before making alternative arrangements to travel to Peru.

I remain on the bank and watch Asoo's curiara sail away. I'm not sure I made the right decision, but I didn't come all this way not to discuss *us* with him. Turning to Samuel, I ask, "Am I safe here?"

"As long as you follow the rules."

Rules?

"You left me alone. How did you know I was safe? And don't say you had those men watching me. They don't understand English, so how could they know if I was in trouble?"

"They have eyes and ears, Eden."

I dig my fists into my hips. "Oh, please. They don't know what I'm feeling. Or how scared I am. What if I ate the wrong thing and was poisoned? Or a snake or spider snuck into my shelter? They are too far away to see it. I don't want to be here alone."

He leads me into the rainforest to the place I picked the passion fruit. He points to several trees bearing berries and fruit. "You can eat these. It's safe to wander here."

Stepping over mangled tree roots, I follow him to a vine choking a tree.

"This is poisonous." He points to a shoot dangling from the branches high in the canopy, searching for another host. "The spikes can make you ill within minutes. Even the tiniest scratch can cause severe vomiting and diarrhea. Please watch where you're walking."

I want to plead my case. This is a reason not to leave me alone, but it raises another concern—the lack of bathrooms. Pee squats are fine, only the day is ticking on. "And if I were to become sick?" I cough. "As in requiring extra assistance in hygiene…"

His lips curl up. "The jungle garden has everything you need."

We backtrack toward the river and then off to the side, and he points out two plants growing near the bank. "This one." He picks a leaf and hands it to me. It's soft and wide enough to use like paper. "You can squat in the river downstream or find a rock to dig a hole."

"What?"

"I usually pick a few leaves and have them ready, so I don't need to go searching."

I cringe, ignoring his smirk.

"This plant." He picks a leaf, and I follow him into the shallows. "Wet your hands and rub it between your palms."

The leaf foams, my hands filling with a forest fragrance. "Amazing," I say before washing the foam from my hands.

He heads toward my shelter, and I'm quick to follow. I watch as he adds another log to the fire. "Keep the fire burning at all times."

I nod.

"And keep up your repellent spray and malaria meds."

I nod again.

"Can you fish?"

I tilt my head at him.

"I'll teach you."

"What? No. Not now. I just want to be with you. Talk to you. Why aren't you taking me to your village where you work?"

A muscle ticks in his jaw. He looks to the river. "It's not that simple." He bends to pick up a long stick with an attached line lying in the dirt under the shelter. He unravels the line, muscles contracting in his forearms. "Come."

I follow him down to the river. "Why are you showing me this. You're going to be with me, right?"

"In the jungle, everyone needs to be capable and self-sufficient. You need to know what it takes to survive." He points to where I slept the night. "I weaved the hammock where you sleep. I constructed the shelter that protects you, started the fire, and chopped the wood to burn. There is an abundance of fruit to pick. The river provides a source of protein, and the forest a source of water. I'll teach you how to get both."

I gape at him. Is this how he lives?

I'm not sure what I expected, but it wasn't this. Not luxury but hell, he's talking about survival tactics. "You told Asoo I'd be safe," I rasp.

"And you will be. You need to learn how to stay safe."

"You're talking as though I'll be alone again tonight."

"I keep a few things here." Samuel unhooks some netting from one of the bamboo poles and focuses on attaching it to the line. He walks a short distance to some shrubs and grabs some sort of large beetle. Eww. He traps it in the net and throws it out into the water. I watch in curiosity before realizing what his silence means.

"Are you bloody serious?"

"There are rules I need to explain after I show you how to catch your food."

I want to scream at him and ask him why he wanted me to stay. Instead, I stomp up the sand to the shelter, grab my bag, and secure the strap over my shoulder. Samuel watches me for a few seconds before turning his focus to the water.

A ball of frustration grows inside me with him ignoring my little spit by continuing to fish.

We both know I'm incapable of going anywhere.

Dropping my backpack, I sit on a log by the fire. There's barely a flame. Only hot embers smoke. After finding a smaller branch, I place it on top of the others, watch the flame build as blue fingers wrap around the wood, and smoke dances and twirls toward the sky. The longer I watch, the slower my breathing becomes.

What did I expect?

Admittedly, I had no expectation—only to find Samuel.

Naïve *and* stupid, really.

Dammit. I shouldn't have devoured all the fruit. I need a restroom without an audience.

I stride forward to stand beside him and look out to the river to where his gaze lands.

"What were you saying about the restroom services here?"

He gives me a sideways glance and points down river. "Follow the river for thirty yards. You'll find the same plants growing there I showed you, and you're screened more so than here."

I nod and scurry off, picking some of the wide, soft leaves on my way.

Removing my shorts, underwear, socks, and shoes, I wade into the shallows and squat, all while focusing on the trees before me and checking behind me for anything untoward in the river. Nerves could slow the process, so I praise the jungle garden.

The leaves are soft, I muse before tossing each one into the river.

Finding the foaming plant, I pick a few and wander back to wash my hands.

I hear giggling and freeze. Thankfully, it's not at me. Two children frolic in the water, splashing each other in the shallows. I take a few steps closer and hide behind a bush to dress.

Black hair is cut around their mocha faces, which are dotted with red paint. Naked, the kids play without concern. I smile, hearing their excitement, and yet I'm unable to comprehend a single word they say. Nevertheless, their smiles and laughter tell all.

I push through the low foliage along the embankment to Samuel standing by the fire. Tiny fish on the palm leaves are cooking in the embers.

He smiles without looking at me. "Found the way okay?"

"I did. And saw some children playing in the river."

His gaze shoots up.

"I didn't approach them."

He nods and points to a log opposite him. "Take a seat. It's time we talk."

"Finally," I huff. "Because you're sending mixed messages. I hoped you'd be happy to see me. Be surprised, and, well, a little impressed with my effort in finding you since you disappeared without a goodbye. And hell, don't get me started about that. Piss weak to just leave. *Again*. If I were a fling, then you should've manned up and told me so, but we both know I wasn't, and that's why I'm here. This misbelief I couldn't hack your life is bullshit. We do have a future."

I stand and point a finger as though I'm jabbing him in the chest. "You're wrong not to believe in me. We're so right for each other. And I... I'm full of surprises. Hell, I've surprised myself every day on this holiday. And I *can* hack it. Just give me a chance to prove it to you." I stand with my hands on my hips, out of breath after ranting on about every little thing that popped into my mind. There's much more I want to say, only I need him to respond to the first fifty questions.

"Please, sit." A command, yet his voice is gentle. "First, we eat."

30

SAMUEL

"They are vegetarian piranha," Samuel emphasizes after her concerned glance. Since piranhas have minimal flesh, the meal ends quickly.

Eden expects an explanation.

He focuses on clearing his thoughts. He couldn't start at the beginning—there's not enough time. More importantly, he doesn't want to scare her. Leveling his gaze with hers, he straightens his shoulders, hoping she'll understand why he left her in Ilhéus when she still owned his heart.

"When I saw you yesterday, I thought I was hallucinating. I have dreamed about you every night since the day in Salvador. So, it wouldn't have surprised me if I imagined you on the beach because I hated myself for leaving you without saying goodbye."

He raises a hand when she attempts to interrupt.

"I need to say some things. Let me explain without offending or breaking my vow. If you don't understand, I'll try and explain it later. For now, allow me to speak." Her eyes round. "I'm not going to explain why I left my family and the luxurious LA lifestyle. I'll only say that I received a pharmaceutical grant to work with the missionaries in indigenous communities by providing pharmaceuticals to promote companies and offer better medical care in the community. Along the way, the companies heard about plants native to the areas, some rumored to hold substantial therapeutic benefit. After some time in these communities and working with a professor in Caracas, where I send the plants I find, the pharmaceutical company considered me finding other rare plants unique to the areas near the tepuis, which could provide medical breakthroughs, especially to certain diseases like cancer and diabetes."

Eden gapes at Samuel in a combination of surprise and adoration. She nods for him to continue.

"I was privileged when a renowned rock climber and local Pemón native American familiar with the Auyán tepui took me up the mountain in search of a plant they talked about in their stories. I'm sure Asoo has mentioned some of Pemón mythology."

"A little," she says with a fixed expression.

"These other communities have a Spanish influence, including adopting the Catholic religion. They also dress in Western clothing. We had ropes and all the climbing gear, and we tackled the easiest path up the tepui. It still took a few days to reach the top, and we found the unusual carnivorous flowers. On our trek home, I saw one of the Ularans in the jungle. His red body paint caught my eye. My guide was oblivious, and yet I knew he was from another time. Untouched by any other human influence in the way he dressed and the concern on his face, we assessed each other momentarily before I caught up with my guide, not speaking a word.

"A month later, I decided to search for these native Americans, curious as to how they lived. The shaman found me after my canoe ended up on their river beach, where I slept. He treated me for dehydration, and my relationship with them grew. Naïvely, I believed I could help by treating them with Western medicine. Over time, I have helped only when their medicine failed. Mostly, they have taught me more of who I am than decades of studying at the world's best universities."

He stands and indicates for her to follow him. More than anything, Samuel wants her to understand his life here, yet he can't allow his demeanor to crumble. He's confused because she wasn't part of the plan *now*. God, he wanted her, more than anything, only he can't afford the luxury of a lover until his work here was complete. When she learns the truth and the reality of his world, he expects her to run far away from him. In his note, he wrote how he wanted to be with her, come find her at her family's hotel when his work here was done. He meant every word.

After learning of the man he is here, he doubts she'll want him to come for her.

Behind Samuel, Eden treads loudly over the forest floor scaring any nearby tiny animals. He's thankful he's not hunting. He points to a vine and smiles. "The forest garden supplies everything you need to survive. You only need to be educated on what and how to find it. Ulara is kept from the rest of the world, hidden behind thick foliage with tiny tributaries from Angel Falls supplying fresh water and fish. These people don't need anything else or anyone for their survival. In fact, people like you and I carry disease." He hopes Eden understands this was a major factor why he discouraged her from visiting him.

"A common cold can wipe out families as their immunity differs from ours. They have plants to help heal, except viruses from the outside world are a different threat. As a rule, I quarantine myself every time I return to Ulara. I remain on the outskirts until enough days pass to ensure I'm not a threat, or I remain a safe distance from them. I also wait for Asoo to ascertain from the surrounding communities that no travelers have fallen sick after leaving Canaima. It's not just here. The surrounding Pemón communities are also vulnerable to tourists and international volunteers. It brings me to why you're here and why I can't be with you as much as I want to..."

He stalls, his eyes hold hers captive. Even looking at her sends him wild with desire.

He swallows hard and reels in his thoughts—the memories of their time together. He glances at her fingertips and visualizes the way she touched and caressed him. Only now, her skin is smeared with dirt, and her pretty nails are chipped. Samuel bows his head, remembering his place here is far from the freedom they had in Ilhéus. "We aren't at liberty to do what we please." He tilts his head and seeks understanding. "There are rules I must obey. Hugging and kissing aren't allowed unless a couple is married. Your unexpected arrival changes things. If we're to gain the trust of the chief, we need to show constraint."

"What?" she rasps. "I'm only here for two days. I have to leave and catch up with the girls."

He nods, breaks a piece of wood from a tree, drinks the water trapped inside, and offers her some.

She shakes her head. "It's fine. I still have some bottled water."

He nods, understanding her apprehension. "I don't expect anything of you or for you to understand why I do what I do. Even when my contract ends in a year, I might not return to my home in LA." Her eyes glisten with moisture, and he bows his head. "It's why I didn't tell you anything to encourage you. This is no place for someone like you." Her shoulders stiffen, and he hopes she didn't misinterpret his words. "I should've known not to underestimate you." He offers her a smile and shakes his head, still astounded by her efforts. "If anyone were to find me, I'm glad it was you. Although, I trust you'll tell no one, only that I work with the missionaries. There is more at stake than I can tell you."

"Of course, I understand. And I'm glad I found you, too," Eden whispers and dips her chin. "I'm frustrated with you because I thought I'd see more of you," she says in a louder voice. She sighs and takes a moment before her gaze settles back on his. "Although I shouldn't complain since I'm lucky to have such a luxurious place to sleep." A grin slowly creeps across her lips. "I'm alive, so, hey, it's not all bad." She shrugs.

"Eden." He stares at her, hoping she understands the extent of his words. "I want to be with you more than *anything,*" Samuel's voice cracks on the last word.

She reaches out, brushes her fingers across his. It's a gentle brushing of the tips of their hands.

He takes hers and squeezes it. "I wish there was another way."

31

EDEN

Morning sunshine breaks through the canopy. I open my eyes and see the white and yellow circles of sunlight as the rays reflect off leaves and dewy fronds.

Damn this heat. I was hot and bothered all night despite the absence of the sun. With a foggy head, I stand and stumble to the river holding my back.

Stretching my arms over my head, I attempt to iron out the kinks. It's going to take more than a couple of nights to get used to the hammock. And to be honest, it could do with a wash. I groan, thinking about bubbles and water. What I'd do now for a bath or shower. Even the river looks appealing, although I'm not yet brave enough to strip down and wash, especially here on a river beach and out in the open. Besides, I'm not convinced the river is safe, even with the children I saw yesterday frolicking in the water. I glance upstream. Slashes of red and purple color the Eastern sky. The current is slow along this tributary compared to the Churun River and more so the Carrao River to which it flows. I smile, thinking how Bree would be impressed with my geography knowledge of the area.

A wave of sadness hits me thinking about my friends. What are they doing? I glance down to my feet in the river sand and imagine it to be the crisp white sand of Margarita Island. What do they think of me? I close my eyes at the realization of my erratic behavior.

If only I knew.

It's why Samuel didn't want me to come after him. I understand that now. If only I weren't as stubborn as my father. I let out a long sigh, the disappointment still with me.

Asoo will be coming downstream from the north. I'm not sure when and only know to listen for the motor.

I wander back and sit on a log to slip on my socks and shoes. The fire is almost out, so I carefully lay another log over the top. I jump back when it hisses at me. Now hungry, I meander through the vines—with more shoots sprouting in the two days I've been here—to pick as much passion fruit I can hold in the material of my tank top. After collecting what I can reach, I head back and sit by the fire.

I pierce each piece with my nail. Good god, my hands are filthy. Thankfully, I don't have to touch the flesh I eat. With each mouthful, I stare into the trees. Will he come and visit me this morning? Or will he allow me to leave without a goodbye? I'm so exhausted, I don't have the energy to be optimistic. Samuel explained everything as best he could last night. I don't have a choice and have to accept he has a commitment to uphold. It is what it is. There's no happy ending. I just wish I had the patience and waited for him to come find me in a year or so. I could've kept working with my father, go back to my boring, dull life, and wait for the day when Samuel walks back into my life.

I blow out the air between my cheeks. "Yeah, right," I mutter. I bite into the gooey flesh of the passion fruit and keep eating it until each piece is halved and the skin is lying beside the fire.

I gather my belongings and roll the mosquito net into a ball and stuff it inside my pack. The plastic to cover my bag is rolled up in a ball in the corner. I unravel it and wrap it around my pack. In the distance, there's a muffled sound. I gasp realizing it's a motor, and I haven't spoken to Samuel.

I head down to the beach and wait. My breaths come fast, and I look to the trees. I want to run in there and call out to him.

The curiara putts around the corner. My shoulders slump, and I drop my pack onto the sand. I never got the kiss I wanted when I found him, and I sure as hell won't be getting a kiss to say goodbye. It hits me how he's going to let me leave because we both know I never belonged here.

"Eden," Samuel's voice comes from behind.

What? He's here?

At the far end of the beach, he strides toward me. I smile, knowing he's come to say goodbye. I want to run to him but know I can't. Oddly, he's wearing cargo cut-offs and a t-shirt.

He gives me the same smile that reminds me of how he used to be in Ilhéus. "Good morning. Have you eaten?" He hands me a banana. Steely eyes hold mine captive.

"Morning," I say quickly. "And thank you." I take in his clothes and backpack. "What are you doing?"

He waves out to Asoo. "Taking you to Canaima."

"I don't need a chaperone." I want to kick myself because, more than anything, I want time with him, but if we're going to move on without each other, prolonging the pain isn't going to help me.

"I know. I want to monitor the questions Asoo asks." He doesn't look at me when he says it. A muscle ticks along his jaw.

"I won't say anything to anyone," I whisper.

"I know."

"Then why are you really coming?" I'm not sure he hears me with the motor now revving closer.

He points to direct Asoo to the shore and then gives me a sideways glance. "We both know why."

I don't have time to respond before Samuel is guiding the canoe to the sand and throwing his sack aboard.

"Eden. Samuel." Asoo raises his hands in the air. "I happy to see you."

Samuel nods, jumps aboard with more grace than I ever could, and takes a seat in the middle of the boat. He points to the seat in front for me to sit. I do so after taking some water from the bag Asoo has packed for us.

"Keep your eyes peeled on the river. Asoo needs assistance to steer, and you can point out small boulders further along he may miss."

"Sure." I nod, remembering how the guides helped navigate the canoe through the rapids. And let's pretend nothing about this is weird at all.

"I appreciate you making the extra journey," Samuel says to Asoo. "I can pay you when we reach Canaima."

So, he has money even though it's useless to him in the village.

I turn around so Asoo can hear me. "I haven't booked a room."

"It fine," Asoo says over the rattle of the motor. "Samuel has room. Rooms for everyone."

Keeping my eyes trained ahead, I smile to myself, knowing Asoo might have a case of loose lips.

Samuel has his own room. I mull over his words a while.

"Your English is a little better," I tell Asoo.

"I practice," he tells me. "Victor has book and CD." He gives me a proud smile.

🌴

"Left," I call out. Both my hands clasp the wood under my rear as I hang on to stop myself from being thrown forward or back. Samuel stands to push us away from the huge boulders, several feet tall, while Asoo navigates us through a narrow path to dodge the smooth rocks protruding out of the water.

I barely speak to the men. Samuel communicates to Asoo in Spanish or Pemón, whatever it is, and it gets on my nerves. I understand communication between them is easier this way, yet I can't help the paranoia creeping in and questioning my sanity. Like a pendulum swinging back and forth, my thoughts alter from *I'm brave and did the right thing coming here* to *what the hell was I thinking?*

Fearless bordering on stupidity.

What did I achieve by having a couple more days with Samuel? Do I hope to find out a little more about him? Am I waiting for him to promise he'll come find me when his contract is finished? All I know is something inside my heart led me here, and it's like the instinct to find him overpowered every other logical thought. Every day with him has to be viewed as part of my intended journey. Otherwise, I could possibly be going mad.

Not every experience is enjoyable.

Yasmine has told me this many times.

It's not a reason not to do it. It's all about opportunities and trying different things. Some we love, some we don't. The important thing is to do it. Try everything and give your inner courage a chance to bloom.

I smile, thinking about her words. Thank you, my friend.

I grab my bag to find my phone and wait for it to power on. Twenty percent battery life is sufficient to take photos. I click away, taking snaps of the tepuis in the distance and the jungle overhanging the river's edge. It truly is an experience I'll never forget. I turn, and Samuel frowns when I point the camera at him and Asoo. I turn back and sneak in another with myself at the front of the curiara in the group selfie. I check the image and smile seeing my friends in the background. Hell, I look like shit. I pop the phone back in the plastic before we pass through the rapids.

By the time we reach the other side of the plains not far from Canaima, my thoughts are in a better place.

I'll have Samuel to myself.

Except he never clarified whether he intends to return immediately or stay the night.

32

EDEN

Wakü Holiday Resort
Canaima, Bolivar, Venezuela

The water spray dances over my face like tiny fingers massaging my forehead, temples, and cheeks. After the last two days, a warm shower hands down equals that of a luxury spa treatment. I'm going to make an appointment as soon as I get home, and right now, I don't give two fucks of the cost.

Home.

My stomach drops.

I owe my family and friends a call.

Lathering soap over my body, I cringe when soap stings the small scratches on my shins.

Securing one towel on my head and another around my chest, I check if my phone is still charged. My room is closer to the reception area than the previous one, and it picks up the Wi-Fi, albeit slow. I flop on the bed and send a text to my friends to confirm my safety. While I'm waiting for the little blue line to cross the top of my screen, I open the last message I sent to my father. It will probably take a while for all the replies from my previous texts to come through.

"Eden." Knock. Knock.

I spring up to open the door.

Tormented blue eyes lock with mine. A slight breeze carries his freshly showered scent into my room, and it jolts my memory of us together in Ilhéus. His Adam's apple bobs. "May I have a word?"

"Sure." I widen the door for him to enter.

"I see you've showered." He turns in a slow circle as though assessing my room.

"I did. There was room for two."

When his gaze shoots to mine, I turn away and casually towel dry my hair. "Are you heading to dinner? I'll be ready after I call my friends and arrange my flight out for tomorrow." I hate talking about leaving him, especially not knowing where we stand makes the effort in finding him somewhat pointless. I understand his commitment, but it doesn't have to be forever.

I push the comb through my hair with extra force. "Ouch." My knots are glued together since I haven't used a brush in two days. The wind factor from the river ride was a formula for hairspray.

"Is it what you want?" he questions and takes a seat on the edge of the bed.

I stop combing. "I'm sorry, what?"

"To leave?"

I shake my head. "I don't have a choice."

He stands and walks to the door. "I'll wait in your hammock while you make the calls."

I'm gaping at the closed door. He walks by the window and slides into the hammock on my porch with the slightest rock. He folds his hands behind his head and stares out at the lake.

I yank open the door. "Don't put this on me. You said I wasn't allowed in your village. There are restrictions, and you can't touch me."

He flies out of the hammock and pushes me inside. "Yes, we have limitations." He spins me. His lips caress my bare shoulder. His hands wrap around my waist, so I feel the length of him pushing into my back. "We don't have any here."

"Here," I repeat.

"What did you expect when you came searching for me?" His lips are close to my ear, hot breath caresses my neck.

"To find out if you cared about me as much as I you," I rasp out.

"You knew I did. I showed you my feelings in Ilhéus. You've complicated everything in a way I've never felt before." Hands tighten around my stomach and travel down and touch me where heat builds. "I don't want you to go. Is that what you want to hear?"

"Yes," I grate out. "Of course, it is."

"Then, you've won. You drive me crazy. I hope you're satisfied that I'm a mess."

I attempt to turn because I want to take him in my arms and kiss him. Only he halts my action, his strong arms keeping me still, my back to his front. We're both peering toward the window to the view of the rainforest beyond the lake and waterfalls.

"You honestly believe you could survive out there?" He raises an arm and points. "Live like me?"

After my short experience—no. I couldn't do it. If it

meant giving us a chance, an instinct tells me it's a place where I could find myself and truly question my happiness, challenge my abilities, overcome fear, and grow. It's what this trip is meant to be—a journey of growth. Finding Samuel and love was a bonus. Then it dawns on me why I wanted to find him so much. By finding him, I also found my strength.

"I'd like a chance to try," I whisper.

He stiffens behind me. His chest expands and releases faster with every breath. His forehead touches the top of my head.

I listen to him breathe for a while before his arms loosen around my waist. "I want to kiss you. We need to be careful, and you haven't been in quarantine long enough to—"

"Stop talking. If I do this, I'm not living on the outskirts. I'm coming with you into the village."

"We can't sleep together."

"I know. Wait. I thought the chief said no?" I push his arms off me and turn to face him.

"Turns out the shaman sees something in you." He smiles at me. "He has granted you time, and I'm going to request for you to stay longer." A dent forms between his eyebrows. "That's if you want to—"

"Longer, as in the rest of my holidays?" What's he saying? Shit, I have four more weeks.

Samuel's expression softens. "If you think you can handle the four weeks, then yes."

Pfft. If I can handle it. Does he even know me?

I'm smiling like an idiot.

Four weeks.

It's enough time to form a solid bond and see if we have a future together. Our initial connection can't be ignored, and now that I've made all the effort to bloody get here, I'm not going to walk away wondering *what if*?

"Yes, of course, it's what I want. Give me time to make those calls, then we can head over to dinner."

He shakes his head. "We don't associate with anyone, only Asoo, as he knows to keep his distance. No handshaking or embracing tourists. We eat in our room. I'll pick some fruit from Victor's organic garden and bring it to you."

I nod. Damn, I was looking forward to a schnitzel or steak and a glass of wine at dinner.

A small sacrifice, really.

"Do you have everything in your larger case to cover you for that amount of time?"

"Not malaria meds. I'll need more."

He nods. "I have plenty. Anything else? Lady products? I have bags for trash."

I gasp. What do the Ularan ladies do? "It's fine. I have an implant. I haven't menstruated in years."

I take his hand and step closer and look up into those serious eyes. I'm ready to challenge him and make those eyes sparkle with lust. "You and I have some catching up to do. Less limitations," I remind him.

When he doesn't tell me to stop, I untie my towel, throwing it aside on the bed. His eyes bore into mine, then lower and glaze over. I watch him take his fill as I take a few steps toward him.

When I reach him, he spins me, takes my hands, and places them on the bed. "I'll take it from here," he whispers in my ear.

Moments ago, the world beyond my room was alive with nature. Monkeys howling, animals screeching, and the insects clicking. With Samuel's every touch, the sound fades into the distance, and all I hear is the excited throb of my heartbeat in my ears.

Samuel's lips trail along my back as his fingers glide over my slit. He teases and caresses me before sliding his fingers inside.

I sigh loudly and tilt my hips toward him. "I want you," I say urgently.

For once, he doesn't argue.

He slips inside of me, thrusts deep and hard, and moans my name. "Keep your hands on the bed."

Samuel adjusts my hips, and his thrusts turn fast, deep, and erotic. His willpower is lost to animal instinct. Sexual desire is strong enough that neither one of us can fight.

I'm going to enjoy the bliss while I can, and since I'm already breaking all the rules, I intend to break a few more tonight.

His hand reaches around, rubs, and presses my clit. The excitement thrums through my body, rising and rising, and little orgasms explode inside me as I build to climax. My knees weaken. His cock is pounding me, yet I want more of whatever Samuel can give. Lust has taken over our minds, especially knowing I can't touch him like this when we are in the village.

"Harder," I rasp out between breaths.

"I hope you know what you're asking," he warns under his breath, and then he slams into me until I'm incapable of uttering another word.

🌴

My body aches in a desirable, sexy way. My clit's swollen, and there's a steady throbbing between my legs. I'm sore, and I couldn't be happier. Rolling off the bed, I push up to find my phone and finish sending the messages before I was beautifully distracted.

I owe my family a call and not a text, and since Samuel might be a while *gathering* dinner, I have time on my hands.

Flicking my fingers nervously, I decide to call Yasmine first.

It goes straight to Yasmine's voicemail. I hope they're having the time of their life, then I won't feel as guilty for leaving them. I try Amy next and pace the length of the room waiting for Amy to answer.

"Eden," Amy screams. "Are you okay?"

"Hey." I let out a long breath. "More than okay. I'm with Samuel."

"You found him?" she asks in a higher pitch.

A smile spreads across my face like a victorious child finding all the hidden eggs at Easter, anticipating the joy to come. "Yeah. It's why I'm calling... to apologize again. I'm not coming to Cusco."

"What?" she gasps.

"I'm staying here. You can go on without me. I'm staying for as long as I can, so I'm changing my flights."

"Edes." Amy makes a sound like she's going to cry. "I'm worried about you, and I miss you. It's not the same without you here. Bree left early. She changed her flight for work reasons, and Yasmine spends all her time with Michael since he has taken your spot on the tours. They're acting weird, whispering and going off alone. I'd rather be a third wheel with you."

I snort. "I doubt it. I'm staying in a remote village."

"Canaima looks great on the map."

"I'm not in Canaima," I whisper. "I'm closer to Angel

194

Falls." I really had no other clue to Ulara's location. "If you need me, call the reception at the lodge and ask to speak to Asoo. I'll send you the number. He can get a message to me. I'll be all right, I promise."

"I feel lost here without you. Can't Samuel come here with you? Do the trek? Because Yasmine is talking about heading into the Peruvian jungle with Michael."

I remember my conversation with Yasmine on the bus. This is part of her journey—something I understand better now. "I know she wants to. She mentioned it to me in Brazil. Listen, if you don't want to go, then wait for her at the hotel. Call me to leave any messages."

"I can't believe your father has agreed to this."

"He didn't." I twist a lock of hair around my finger. "I'm about to make the call."

"He's gonna lose his shit."

I know.

"I gotta go, Ames. Talk soon."

"Stay safe, babe."

"I will. Love you."

I end the call with a heavy weight in my gut, knowing how alone Amy feels. I'm torn between going to her or doing what my heart tells me—staying here.

I pull up Dad's name and wait for what feels like forever for Dad to pick up. It goes to voicemail.

"Dad, it's Eden. A quick call to let you know I'm okay. I'm staying in Canaima, as I really love this part of the world. I'm not traveling any further with my friends. I know you'll be mad, but please trust me on this as I'm doing everything to stay safe. I love you and will check in regularly, so you know I'm okay. Bye."

I need to speak with someone from my family, so I call Faith.

"Are you fucking serious?" Faith yells, sans any greeting.

"Hope your kid isn't around to hear your potty mouth."

"Whatever. Focus," she chastises me like I'm her child. "Dad's been beside himself. He's spoken to Bree now that she's home, and she said you're in a remote area of Venezuela. Of all the countries... do you know the Canadian embassy closed, so there's nowhere for Australians to go? If you get into trouble, you're seriously fucked. You'll need to get to Colombia."

I hadn't paid attention to the news considering it's in Spanish. "Thanks for the update. I'm calling to let you know I have a new itinerary because I've met someone, and I'm staying with him." I go on to tell her some things about Samuel, mainly his medical experience.

"And this is supposed to make me feel better. You're seriously out of your goddamn mind."

There are times I agree with her, but I also don't expect her to understand. Love came easy for her and Jake. Their lives fell into place like a fairy tale, and years later, he still idolizes the ground she walks on. Even when I was with Ethan, I still felt alone because he never treated me like I was a priority.

"I need you to explain a modified version of what I told you to Dad. Tell him I'm fine, and I'm messaging you regularly. I'll call in a week or two, or at least get a message to you. If you need to get in contact with me, then either send a text or leave a message at the resort's reception with Asoo. I'll text you the number."

"You know he's going to freak out, right? You're going *into the jungle*."

I remain silent a moment.

"Yeah. I need you to weave your magic. I owe you."

Faith sighs into the phone. "Yep, you do. He had an early morning meeting, so you could call him in an hour?"

Right now, I don't have it in me to listen to his disappointment. "I can't. I'm heading to bed."

"You're lucky Ethan and Dad are getting along so well. Another reason why Dad wanted you home sooner rather than later. He has Ethan's desk set up next to yours."

"Ugh."

Another reason why I'm *not* rushing home.

My phone buzzes on the bedside table, and it's enough to wake me. My thoughts are whirling, and I've barely slept even though Samuel is in my bed spooning me.

Samuel.

Lying beside me.

Maybe it's because my heart is beating too fast to rest. I'm grappling with how everything has unfolded over the last few days. Trying desperately to understand, I keep questioning my decision and doubting his and my sanity.

Lying on my side away from him, I read the text.

I blink twice to focus. There are four messages from Ethan.

I know you're probably sleeping and hope it's not too late. Not time wise. I hope there's something I can say to change your mind about putting yourself in danger and adding stress to your family. Bree said your decision to stay is because of a guy. She said he's odd and he lives in the jungle...

I'm struggling to believe you would want to be somewhere like that and stay in a third-world society. Didn't you want to advance your career and step into your father's shoes? You like the beach. There'll be no football on weekends, hanging with your friends, and heading out to bars at night and cafés during the day.

Seriously, Eden. What are you achieving? And for a stranger? No wonder we're all worried. You heard about that last cult, where people ventured into the jungle and then the leader shot everyone. Please tell me you're not part of one. And yes, I'm worried. I understood this holiday would be about fun, and I thought you would come home refreshed with clarity to where the hotel business is headed and hopefully ready to assess our relationship again. I love you. I always have.

I know I messed up. Give me a chance to make it up to you. To work for you, beside you every day. To show you how much I have changed. Your father knows how crazy I am for you. Every day I see how stressed out you've made him. Please come home. I'm scared for you. Scared of not having you in my life x

I release air from my lungs with a sigh then check if

the shine from my phone has disturbed Samuel. The dim light reflects onto his beautiful face. His gaze lifts from my phone and meets mine. He doesn't say anything, and yet there's apprehension in his eyes. I wasn't going to answer Ethan until my fingers start typing.

> Hey, Ethan. Thanks for your message. I'm lucky to have so many people who love and care about me. I assure you your concern is unwarranted because I'm fine. Very happy and on the adventure of a lifetime. Yes, I have met someone, and I'm learning so much about life from him. I miss everyone! I'll be in contact soon.

I place my phone on the table and roll onto my side. My face is close to his, and my lips tingle with the light breeze of his every breath. I kiss him, so our lips barely brush. He doesn't retreat, and I take it as a green light. My mouth slowly caresses his, and I shudder with need, a slight tremor to my touch. A hand takes my shoulder, and our bodies align. His kiss becomes frantic, the air zinging between us.

"I need you to make love to me," I whisper against his lips.

He rolls onto me and sinks between my thighs.

To hell with the rules tonight.

33

SAMUEL

What was he thinking?

In one week, Samuel is to embark on a journey to the top of the tepui in search of a purple flower, one to heal the cells of the body. He learned about the unique plant from the shaman, knowledge gained during an ayahuasca ceremony where the vines and trees communicate to reveal secrets of the forest.

The pharmaceutical company believes the purpose of his stay is to find plants to cure disease. Samuel's stay in Ulara has developed into something far more valuable. The people here have taught him the meaning of a soul, healing yourself from within, and connecting with all living things on earth in a way he never thought possible.

He has grown in character, in mental and physical strength, and learned to accept some things that can never be explained. His science-based thoughts questioned how and why with every miracle the shaman performed. Over the years, he understood some happenings have no justification by way of his education. He didn't believe in magic. Happenstance in the jungle is far more powerful and connected him with other worlds his former associates mocked.

He understands the jungle more so than his previous privileged society. And by leaving that society, he became a different man, one indebted to the Ularans.

So why did he entice Eden to return with him?

It seems his selfish ways remain with him.

Eden sits ahead of him on the curiara, pointing and smiling toward the endless green when a monkey or colorful parrot catches her attention. He and Asoo laugh at her excitement, his gut tightening, hoping she maintains her cheerfulness during her stay.

Her acceptance into the Ularan community is yet to be decided.

Samuel recalls his initiation was more like torture, his mindset then the strongest of his life. Yet during the last forty-eight hours, he has portrayed weakness and jeopardized the health and safety of the people he has grown to love.

Part of him is ashamed of his selfishness.

Yet there is no fighting the adrenaline soaring through his body, knowing someone will be by his side for the first time in years.

His heart beats in a quick Samba rhythm and not from excitement alone. There's an underlying fear in the chief rejecting his request. Asking permission is the biggest risk Samuel's taken in years, and his shaky hands know it.

Hours pass, and he hasn't prepared her. He leaves Asoo to navigate alone as he climbs over the wooden planks to sit beside Eden. She places her head on his shoulder, and a contented sigh escapes him.

"If you see a girl eating alone and keeping her

distance, it's not that she's unwell. She is being ostracized as a way of social control."

"What?" Her forehead creases with a frown.

"I'm telling you, so you don't go and sit with her because I know how you think."

There's a glimmer of defiance in her eyes. "You think you do..."

He smiles at her before continuing, "It's only for a couple of days. I need you to follow their rules. Otherwise, you'll be the one who's excluded."

Did she roll her eyes at him?

"I'll do what I have to if it means I'm with you." She pats his leg reassuringly.

He'll be there beside her when tested to her limit. He goes on to tell her other things. "The village is divided into a series of huts. Families sleep in separate huts. The shaman has his own hut. The young men, the warriors, sleep together in another hut. Girls sleep with their families."

"Where do you sleep?"

"I have my own hut. It's connected to my treatment room. I'll make sure you're with me. New huts have been built as the village is preparing for the upcoming wet season and another for ceremonies."

"Like weddings?"

He laughs at the twinkle in her eye. "It's a similar celebration of two souls uniting."

Her hand squeezes over his. "I'd love to witness one. I guess it's all the same, only without the hefty wedding costs. Wait, does the bride wear a dress of some sort?"

Samuel shakes his head. "It isn't a wedding celebration."

His fear rises with her curiosity.

He's said enough.

†

A jog turns into a sprint as Samuel takes the path, swiping at unruly vines and smacking low branches, his pack bouncing on his back.

He reaches the village perimeter and slows to a walk to catch his breath.

He emerges from his hut in a grass skirt and a beaded necklace strung over his shoulders. He inhales a long breath and then a slow exhale to calm his thoughts before finding the shaman, passing the women leaning over mud pots, smoke rising from the fire beneath. He nods to Kaikare. Years ago, he believed she was an outcast. Like him, she'd found no partner. In those early days, he'd find her sitting with the shaman listening intently to his words. The two were close, and initially he thought they were a couple, only she was many years younger. Then he discovered she was his daughter and an apprentice, like him, who understood sacrifice.

She nods in the way of the garden. Samuel snakes around more hut clusters until he reaches the village perimeter's farthest point from the river.

A song leads him to the shaman, peaceful sounds of vows repeated in a tune sung to the trees in gratitude.

Dropping to his knees, eyes closed, Samuel concentrates on the words and allows the tune to fill his thoughts. The melody calms his heart, and he bows his head and simply absorbs the sounds like medicine healing the soul. He opens his eyes when a hand rests on his crown, and the singing stops.

Samuel speaks first, his head bowed. He tells him Eden waits near the river.

Nothing more.

No explanation.

Consequences are understood.

The shaman asks Samuel to wait outside the chief's hut until a decision is made.

Samuel does so, and elevated voices carry through the village. It's not the usual calm way the Ularans communicate.

White fluffy clouds roll overhead and block out the sun. The sun breaks through momentarily before clouds shut it out again. It's Samuel's only way of knowing, at this moment, time is passing by.

Kaikare mimics his pose, sitting cross-legged beside him, mere feet from the chief's doorway.

She nods to the river and, in her language, tells him the children saw his Tamu'ne Akare.

He holds back a smile at the name the children have given Eden—White Tortoise. He assumed her white hair —like his—would garner attention. And after the warriors watched over her those few nights, they thought her to be a slow learner of their ways.

Kaikare's name is a combination of a jaguar and a tortoise, and he wonders if, in her younger days, she was also a slow learner of the Ularan way. Or someone they wanted to protect like the tortoise when it came time to lay its eggs in the sand on the riverbank. The jaguar part he didn't question for it's the most feared animal in the jungle.

The rattle of beads and bones on a walking stick indicates movement. Samuel rises to his knees. Kaikare is a little stiffer than he remembers. She ambles to her feet. He considers her to be in her late fifties. He'd thought arthritis restricted her movement at first, yet it's not a condition he often sees with the forest offering herbs as treatment. She hobbles away when larger mud-coated feet come into his vision. Cracked nails require taming. A bang on the ground and a rattle of animal teeth and beads demand his attention.

With his head bowed, he listens to the chief's disapproval of an outsider. His obligation is to protect his people, the location of the village, and how they have lived without the influence of outsiders to keep the spirits happy—no new sickness, no evil weapons, or their forests burned down. More importantly, no evil spirits known as Kanaima have entered the village in many moons. The stone mountains are satisfied.

Samuel's thoughts drift to the tepuis—the stone mountains—and to his upcoming journey where warriors will also accompany him to the base as they venture out on their hunt.

Samuel realizes his mistake.

Eden isn't welcome.

He'll be away from the village for possibly weeks. He nods, thoughts racing. His gut aches, torn between respecting their law and fulfilling his own selfish thoughts.

His demeanor is weak. His time here is waning. He nods, and before he signals obligation, the shaman speaks for him and places Eden on trial.

"Kapeá töuking enya." *Five full moons.*

Five months.

The shaman's lenience surprises him.

She can only stay weeks with the government's rule

on visas, but now isn't the time to explain the outside world restriction.

The chief thumps his stick. "Uarati." *Man.*

Samuel is fully aware of his place here and his duty as a *man*. His initiation into the community established his manhood and a responsibility to be a better person.

The chief dismisses him, and the shaman motions for Samuel to follow.

They approach the women preparing the yuca and stop for the shaman to wave his stick at Kaikare. All three walk into the forest. The shaman takes Kaikare's hand and juts her swollen finger joints toward Samuel.

Samuel asks her if she has suffered any fever over the past weeks like the young girl he had treated—dengue fever, yellow fever, malaria, Mayaro virus, ross river, swine, zika. So many viruses come to mind and none should have made their way into the village. It gives him cause for concern.

"Pupai?" *Head.* He indicates pain in his expression like a headache.

Again, she shakes her head.

He glances down to her abdomen. Beyond the paint and dirt, there's no hint of a rash.

The shaman is a healer beyond Samuel's explanation. Yet there are times he seeks out Samuel's guidance. When it comes to Kaikare, his daughter and apprentice, Samuel understands her importance to continue his work. He thinks the shaman to be around his mid-seventies and expects he'll make the century.

The shaman and Samuel walk further toward the unruly vines. Samuel points to plants, and the shaman snaps leaves and flowers from a variety of plants. Samuel is careful not to touch anything and maintains a safe distance from his friends. He tells the shaman to give the leaves to Kaikare to boil and drink in tea. It will purify the blood and has an anti-inflammatory effect.

With gratitude, the shaman informs Samuel that Kaikare will look out for his Tamu'ne Akare. So, this is now Eden's name.

In a slow nod, Samuel thanks him and dashes toward the river to find his *white tortoise*.

He slows to a walk when he reaches the jungle edge and takes the narrow path to the sandy beach. Eden stands and slings her backpack over her shoulder when he comes into view—there's no running into his arms.

He allows her time to peruse his bare body to assess the red and black beads around his neck, the string of caiman teeth, his trophy. Tonight, his body will be painted again and reapplied the night before the hunt.

Her gaze lowers to his grass skirt.

He speaks before his body reacts. "The chief has granted you permission to stay. Although you'll be on trial, so I'll make sure you're aware of all the rules before I—"

"There was a chance I wasn't allowed to stay?"

She doesn't allow him to add he's going on an exploration in a week. Seeing her reaction, he deems it best not to mention it now.

He nods, answering her question. "I wanted to take the risk. I'm sorry, it was selfish of me. Now you're here, you need to obey—"

"Obey?" she repeats.

His jaw clenches. "You're free to change your mind."

She reaches for his hand, her fingers skimming over his. A tingle pricks his fingertips, and new energy sparks.

Yin energy soars up his arms and through his body. She links their fingers, and he savors the warmth.

"I want to do this. Only... here I get somewhat rebellious. I can't help it. Maybe it's because you're dressed like this." She gives him a cheeky smile.

He holds her gaze. "Everything is black and white. There is no confusion. Please don't risk being sent away—"

"I won't," she promises, stepping closer to him.

Keeping hold of her hand, he leads her along the path he walked moments before, pushing branches away from her face, allowing her to pass. With every step, he leads her closer to the village, to a world where he belongs and the center of his universe. His axis tilted four weeks ago. Samuel hopes Eden's presence will realign his universe, seal the hole in his heart he never knew existed until the day he first saw her on the beach.

The chief expects her to conform and behave in an acceptable way—eat what they eat, work the fields, cook alongside the women, and dress like them. His gut tightens imagining her in a palm skirt with only beads covering her breasts. Remembering her in a swimsuit in Salvador, he understands the effect she'll have on the young men and what he must do to protect her.

34

EDEN

"Welcome to Ulara." Samuel grins at me, and we both turn and gaze at the village before me.

The excitement rushing through my body is like a *Welcome to Hollywood* movie set. We're standing in a clearing where several thatched huts form a circle, and more of the same huts can be seen in the distance. Smoke rises in the air above the grass structures, and I catch the scent of food. It smells good, whatever it is. Until now, I didn't realize my hunger. With only fruit for dinner and breakfast, I'm craving anything that can be cooked.

Following Samuel, I walk a dirt path at the back of a smaller circle of huts. Between each hut, I get a glimpse of a central fire pit. It's dry, and no one tends to it. Around us, the jungle squawks, the only applause for my arrival. The further we walk the snake-like path, the more the air steams. The hum of mosquitoes circling above my head never ends. I wipe my hands on my denim shorts before swiping my brow.

Samuel leads me to a long hut with open walls and

windows. Here, several fires burn. Some women lean over huge mud pots stirring the contents with a long stick while others squat, grinding or mashing.

The same carbon hair borders their round faces. The color matches their eyes. Slowly, the women uncurl their bodies naked, and take a step back. A soft chatter grows among them. I'm not sure what I expected, but fear wasn't one. From behind me, the children giggle. "Tamu'ne Akare."

Samuel says one word I don't understand, and they laugh back at him.

"At least the children like me," I say.

"They're fascinated by your clothes."

With legs like pogo sticks, they jump in front of me, pointing and laughing.

Samuel makes a noise, and they stop. "They have never seen long white hair."

"Right." I drop to my knees to give them a better view. Faded paint covers their dark skin, a combination of Vs and long lines on limbs and chest. Sneaking a glance at the ladies, they're all watching me with a little more curiosity.

A crack on the ground has them running, although the giggling continues. Samuel drops to his knees beside me. On our left, two older men with similar feathered crowns stand before us.

"Look down," Samuel demands.

I do, although not before my eyes meet with the man holding the decorated stick. My gut tightens seeing conflict in his dark eyes. It's a look that tells me he doesn't trust me combined with an expression of power.

A conversation takes place between Samuel and the

two men. One of them is the man from the river—the shaman—the one who's on *my side*. I slowly raise my chin and sneak a glance. The shaman is watching me, staring at me as though he's mesmerized. Maybe it's my hair? The other guy is more interested in speaking with Samuel.

"Is there a problem?" I whisper.

Samuel hushes me.

He nods repeatedly.

"Stand. Follow me," Samuel commands.

I do as he says and nod to both the older men. "Thank you for having me," I say.

"They don't understand English."

"I know, but I feel like I have to say something. Show gratitude."

"They'll be expecting gratitude in other ways."

"How?" I ask and keep up to his pace as we walk the snake-like path again.

"Showing your worth. Not being a liability."

I let out a sigh. "Oh, right. Because my survival skills suck. Wait, where are we going now?"

"To cleanse. There's a stream behind the village. It's the best place to bathe. The water flows from the tepui and leads to a pond before flowing into a cave."

"I'm not complaining because I'm bloody hot, only we both showered today, and we have less dirt on our skin than everyone else here."

"It's not about dirt, Eden. We need to be purified."

"Okay. I'm not going to comment."

"I find it hard to believe."

I'm not going to object to a swim in this heat. And swimming with Samuel.

211

"Tonight is a celebratory dinner. After I take you to your hut, you need to help the women prepare the food."

"What sort of food are we cooking?"

"Fish, potatoes, bread, and fruit. They call the bread from yuca, oo. I'm not sure if you've heard of it. It's only prepared by the women, not you."

"You think I can't cook?"

"Eden." He gives me a pointed look. "It's laced with cyanide and takes special preparation before you can eat it."

"Oh." Shit, even the food can kill me. The perils of the jungle tick over in my mind until we stop at a stream.

Samuel unties his skirt. "Take off your clothes." He wades in before I get a good look at his front, although Samuel's rear is just as pleasing.

After kicking off my sneakers, I peel off my sweaty top and bra before removing my shorts. I wade in, allowing the cool water to swirl around my legs, walking slowly toward Samuel. He doesn't look at me until I'm waist-deep and in the center of the stream. He turns slowly, keeping his gaze averted.

"The stream is relatively safe. There is no caiman, only the occasional snake, so keep a lookout."

I grin and wiggle my eyebrows. "A snake?"

"Focus. You're safe in the village, only there is danger around you. I'll teach you to understand the jungle and use it, so your surroundings become a way of survival."

Monkeys scream from the treetops, and birds squawk as though being attacked—noise pollution replacing the horns and loud V8 motors of my city jungle. In this moment I miss the city—home. Then I watch Samuel dive beneath the water, and a memory jolts my thoughts

—my grandma telling me, "*Home is never in one place, dear. Home is where your heart is.*"

If I cancel the rest of my tour, then for the remaining four weeks, my *home* is here with Samuel.

🌴

Ornaments hang from the walls inside Samuel's hut, reminding me of the beads around my neck.

"I'd feel more comfortable with a few more strands." I glance down to my exposed breasts, the strands of beads covering less than that of a bikini top. It's going to take time for me to appear in public wearing my birthday suit like many of the others here chose to do.

"I agree. I'll ask Kaikare for more strings of beads," Samuel says.

I nod, thankful for small things, including the two grass skirts around my hips for the extra layer of concealment. I roll my shoulders to ease the weight of the long, beaded threads, especially since some are doubled for a graded appearance from my chest to my waist.

My hair is tied back in a braid, still wet from our swim that was interrupted when the women delivered my *clothes.* I drip-dried while they dressed me, Samuel watching from the stream. Although by the look in his eye, I was well aware he liked my new adornments.

Every minute, we're tested to keep our hands off each other. I agreed to it, and even though I'm mildly uncomfortable with my new attire, I'm not afraid to be part of Samuel's life and to understand why he has chosen to live this way. For me, it's a matter of sucking it up and not being self-conscious about my body.

I slide into the hammock and stare up past the mosquito net at the peaked thatched roof. This is a special hut with the walls made of clay, not thatched grass like the other huts. The windows are an open space, and there's an open doorway. It's more private than others and sectioned into two parts. In the smaller section, I clamber in and sway in a hammock. The larger section is a treatment area. In the corner, a wooden table is piled high with books and notes. On another table some sort of equipment and a microscope. A locked case is on the floor beside a long wooden bed.

"Do many of your patients sleep here?"

He pushes off the wall. "Sometimes. Mainly the children." He takes a few steps closer to me. "Do you know how euphoric I feel right now, seeing you in my bed as though it's the most natural thing for you to do?"

The intensity in his eyes warns me we're stepping on shaky ground. I'm not going to risk anything on my first day, even in *his* hut. "I wish you could join me on your bed, although I understand it's not possible, for now."

"Trust holds power to change," he says before walking through the doorway.

I scramble out of the hammock and fall on my knees. "Where are you going?" I spring up to my feet and follow him.

"To find Kaikare and ask for more beads."

🌴

Twilight falls early with the jungle blocking eighty percent of the sunlight. Long, dark shadows creep over the village, indicating its dinnertime. Kaikare leads me to the cooking fire in the village center. She demonstrates how to gut a huge fish the men had caught earlier in the day. My stomach turns squeamish, and I want to cover my mouth and nose, so I don't inhale the stench. But I can't act like a liability when I'm supposed to be an adult in terms of skill.

Harden up, princess.

A dozen more fish lay on banana palms and are covered in fresh herbs waiting to be cooked. How many do we need to prepare? I finish one without heaving and place it among the others. Every time I glance up, I catch the other women staring oddly at me, or maybe it's at my technique.

Kaikare smiles at me, one of the few women who seem to believe I'm not here in the form of a bad spirit. She has a different look about her—her skin is a shade lighter, her eyes are a honey color and not the usual black, and her dark brown hair falls over her shoulders in waves and different from the jet-black dead-straight hair of everyone else.

Her body is marked with red paint on her extremities and abdomen, a pattern of Vs lines along the length of her stomach with more dots on her chest. Red, white, and black are the standard colors of embellishment, be it the beads or paintwork, except for the blue and yellow feathers in the crowns of the chief and shaman.

I'm given potatoes to chop. The object I'm handed is a fine, thin stone tied to a thick stick. It takes a few attempts for me to chop one potato, and I miss the ease of a sharp knife. The smiles and nods of other women after I achieve the simple task is strangely gratifying.

"I'm Eden," I say and jab myself in the chest.

Kaikare says, "Tamu'ne Akare." She smiles at me and

repeats it to the other ladies. I have no idea what it means. I smile and nod as it seems to please them.

More fires ignite from posts around the long hut lighting the cooking area. I wave my hand over the food, although the best repellent is in the form of smoke that wafts our way.

"Shoo." I wave my hand madly, realizing ants have made a trail toward the fish. I cough out a choke when I inhale the smoke.

The women laugh, enjoying my antics. In bare feet, I squish a few black ants with my heel in a quick action, trying not to get bitten.

Kaikare waves her hands at me to stop.

"No?"

"Besides being a source of protein, they add flavor." Samuel stands on the other side of the fire, grinning, arms folded, enjoying the entertainment.

"I'm to let the ants get to the fish?"

He chuckles at my response. "When the ants come, they slide the fish onto the fire, ants and all. You'll be surprised by the taste."

"I'll treat them like anchovies on a pizza and pick them off," I say and groan.

"I should warn you about the entrée, although I'm looking forward to seeing your reaction."

"Why?"

Excited screams come from children running out of the jungle.

"Ah, right on time," he says.

Each child carries a palm leaf curled into a handle. From this side of the fire, I can't make out what has incited their joy. Long thin sticks are handed to every child. Each child holds a twig, extended low and away from their body. Something black wiggles on the end. They run toward me to the fire dividing us and form a circle around the flame. Recognition hits me, and I stumble back, knocking a clay pot of chopped potatoes over.

"Christ," I yell, trembling at the sight of two dozen black tarantulas gored by sticks being cooked over the fire like bloody marshmallows.

The collective sound of laughter pulls me out of my frozen haze of fear, goosebumps pricking at the realization I'm the center of attention, not the giant spiders.

More men have gathered near the fire wearing toothless smiles, fingers pointing at me.

"They taste like chicken." Samuel chuckles.

"Everyone says that about shit you shouldn't eat," I snap. He's grinning when he should be consoling me.

Geez, I can hear the squeal as the spiders cook on the heat, the stench of burned hair filling my nose. Samuel walks around the fire to stand with me. The sound of popping is like corn in a pan.

"Hear the pop? They're ready. They'll offer you a leg."

"No bloody way," I say to him.

"I understand," he says, yet I sense him holding back a smile. "There'll be times you may need to eat something you're not comfortable with."

"Yeah? Well, it won't be a bloody tarantula."

In perfect timing, I turn to the kids gnawing on spider legs exactly like we would a chicken wing, and I wonder to myself if they are really so different from us? Maybe we're all products of our society. Taking my seat near Kaikare, I smile and shake my head graciously when she offers me a spider limb.

"Maybe another time."

The long hut is divided into sections. The furthest part from the river is open walls with only the cone-shaped thatched roof to protect us from the elements. The smoke from the fire warns off airborne insects, and here, the mosquitoes aren't as troublesome. Most of the people sit cross-legged on the ground or in a squat position. There are a few pieces of logs lying around, so I use one as a chair with Samuel squatting beside me.

When everyone gathers around to eat, I don't know where to avert my gaze. In the shadowy light, there is no mistaking testicles hanging in the dirt as men squat on the ground. In curiosity, I lean forward to check Samuel.

"What are you doing?" he says between clenched teeth.

I ignore him and glance up, my instinct right. I'd assumed the young girls opposite us were staring at me.

No.

In a squatting position, Samuel's bits are in full view to those across the room. Here, a man's testicles on view aren't an unusual sight, only I assume a white man a good foot taller than the average guy here and exceptionally well-endowed is unusual, and teenage girls are curious.

"You're turning the girls on," I remark.

"Don't be ridiculous," he hisses. "They've known me a long time."

"Really? And I bet some have come of age recently, and they notice certain things more so. Take a look for yourself."

He glances across the room, quickly changing his

position to cross-legged, so his skirt fans out over his thighs.

"There are some things I just know," I whisper.

He stands and collects food from near the fire and brings it back to me—unusual bread, potatoes, and fish on a palm fronds. It's placed in front of me on the ground, and with each piece, I chew slowly despite the hunger gnawing at my stomach. After some time, I notice Samuel not eating.

"You're not well?"

"I'm only drinking the tea."

"Why? I mean you told me it's okay to eat."

He chuckles low. "It is. In fact, the fish is my favorite meal. I'm... detoxing."

I frown at him. "For what?"

His smile fades. "I need to tell you something."

Hearing his tone, I stop filling my mouth with food. "What?" Like seriously. What the hell now?

"In a week, I'm leaving to go up the tepui on an exploration. It will be one of my final journeys and—"

"Am I coming with you?" I whisper, already knowing the answer.

He shakes his head. "Kaikare will look out for you. I should only be gone a week, maybe two."

I choke on the last piece of food sitting in my mouth. "I'm only here for four weeks."

"I know. It can't be avoided. If I find the plant, then my contract may end earlier, and that would benefit us both."

I turn away from him with tears stinging my eyes. He knew this before he asked me to stay. I press my fingertips against my forehead with the beginnings of a headache.

Being here alone will change everything.

"I feel nauseous." I close my eyes as betrayal settles into my chest. Again.

He takes my hand and squeezes it. "I'll walk you back to my hut, and we can talk some more."

"Väi Uarati Kún-imá," the shaman says to Samuel. *Sun man with long leg.*

"He wants to speak with me. I'll meet you back there."

"Take your time," I snap.

Right now, I want to be alone.

35

SAMUEL

Samuel assumes the raucous clicking of insects mere yards from his hut will hinder Eden's sleep. Stepping inside, he sees her silhouette in the hammock, the mosquito net twinkling under the moonlight like morning dew on the leaves.

She had walked on ahead when the shaman had asked to speak to him.

"Are you awake?" he whispers.

"Of course. It's not exactly peaceful."

Her banter is better than silence. "Do you need me to walk with you while you—"

"I was busting. So, I went alone."

He nods. Before dinner, he pointed out areas where she could relieve herself and didn't believe she'd venture out in the dark.

"I used the light on my phone. Not that I'm going to be able to do it much longer since it's barely got any battery left."

"Your eyes will adjust."

The hammock grinds with her movement. "In four weeks, I doubt it."

"Can you see me?"

"No. My eyes are shut," she snaps.

"Open them. Now, can you see me," he asks in a calm voice.

Her dark outline adjusts position. "Kind of."

"Close your eyes." He stands beside the hammock and waits. He hears a sigh pass her lips. "Can you sense me?"

"Your voice leads me."

"Concentrate." His fingers hover over her body.

Electrical energy pricks his fingertips with heat radiating from her body to his hand. He wiggles each finger lightly, imagining the energy flowing back and forth joining them as one force. He pads in a slow motion, each foot lifting as though weighed down with concrete in an effort not to stir the air. Hand flexed, it follows the contour of her body as he moves.

"There's a warmth rolling over me. I'm craving to be touched," she whispers.

"Only focus on the energy between us, not how it makes you feel. Allow it to seep into your skin," he says in a gentle tone.

He homes in on the sound of her breathing—slow and audible.

"It was selfish of me to ask you to stay, knowing I'll be gone for a while. I'm sorry, Eden. I know my apology doesn't mean much right now, but I promise to make it up to you when I return."

"It does mean something," she whispers.

He reaches for her hand. "I want you to try something... focus and remember this energy, how it flows between us. Feel me when I'm not around. Knowing you're here gives me a source of vibrancy I've never known. Your spiritual force will guide me home."

Soft fingers brush his hand before linking them in an unbreakable chain. "I feel you, Samuel. In my heart and all around me. Even when you left me, I could still feel you. Even though I'm not happy about being alone, I'll do it. Know I *can* do it. Your spirit, or whatever you want to call it, guided me here. I'm not going to run away now." Her grip on his hand tightens, "It's odd because I haven't felt this way about anyone, not even Ethan. I've been lying here sulking. Yet I know what we have is real even though it'll be challenging. Part of me wants the challenge because I need it. So, while you're gone, I'll be okay because I'll be finding out a little more about myself while I'm here."

In a moment of truth, he forgets rules, lowers his head, and brushes his lips over hers. "Here, you'll find a sense of power within and develop an ability to control your environment. Unlike the outside world, where material catastrophes happen every day and people feel they have no control over them, you can build what you need, and it changes your sense of value. Your sense of importance changes."

Soft lips silence him. "My journey has already started."

Fingertips skim the length of her body. Her breath catches in a sharp inhale.

"Good night, Eden," he says before finding the treatment bed to stretch out on until dawn.

Securing the mosquito net around him, he listens to her breathing, the sound taking over his mind. Every breath giving her life offers him meaning. Eyes open or

223

shut—it didn't matter. He focuses on emptying his brain of useless images and on connecting with the sounds around him. The jungle screech is his mantra, and he imagines his own wings flying through the forest, the trees whispering, guiding him to the tepui, high up on the rocky mountain. It's here the whispering stops, and he finds himself alone, no spirit to guide him on the tepui. At this point of his journey, it's important he focuses on Eden. Her energy will guide him to the flower and back to her.

🌴

Samuel spends the morning in the long hut with the older men who basketweave. He's drinking the tea, another day of fasting, and a day to weave a new hammock, the one he is making for Eden.

Samuel catches a fleeting glance of her while she cooks alongside Kaikare. He smiles at her and nods. After he checked on her several times this morning, the women shooed him away. It brings him joy knowing they are warming to her.

Tonight is another ceremony, one he hopes she understands. In a world where less is more, he's not to explain matters. Her journey is her own to understand matters when they happen in the moment and not by preparing her mind for prejudgment to learn their ways. It's the way he learned, and he wants her to experience it all like him.

Fascination has grown among the children. The girls want to learn to braid Eden's hair. After lunch, the women paint her limbs with long red lines. He grins when they lift her beads to paint her chest and abdomen, her head shaking and her hands moving in a stop action. She settles on her back to be the surface for a temporary tattoo, the women eager to paint lighter skin and showcase their skill.

By evening, everyone gathers near the fire, the children up front close to the shaman to listen to the stories about their ancestors and the land.

Wide-eyed, the children huddle closer as the next story explains the anaconda.

"Is this really a bedtime story for children," Eden says under her breath when Samuel translates the shaman's words.

"He's building up for the chief's story."

The shaman raises both hands to the night sky. "A-pantoní-pe nichii." *May you take advantage of this story.*

The shaman nods to Samuel. A cue to meet him on the other side of the long house. "I have a private meeting with the shaman. Kaikare will look out for you now. Don't wait up for me. These meetings can go into the early hours of the morning."

"I'm happy to wait for you," she says when he stands.

"I'd rather you sleep. You'll need your energy for tomorrow. I'm going to show you around." She chuckles with him, making it sound like it's another Hollywood tour.

Samuel walks the outside of the story circle to Kaikare, sitting with the women. He explains his absence for the next few hours and tells them to watch over Eden, making sure she doesn't wander to the ceremonial side of the long house.

In a thatched-walled room, Samuel and a dozen warriors kneel before the shaman. Trying to find inner peace, Samuel closes his eyes and listens to soft harmonic tunes, the shaman calling to the forest, asking her to accept her children kneeled before her and connect their souls to guide them in their upcoming journey.

The shaman's song drones out the screech of the jungle. The warriors hum a low 'mmm,' a mantra Samuel connects to and sounds out along with them. The shaman sucks the wooden pipe, blows smoke into his face, a different tune for each warrior, a new request for a spirit connecting to each soul.

These are men who, for weeks, have sacrificed meat, sugar cane, and any substance capable of hindering the absorption of the brew. There's been abstinence of sexual orgasm to preserve energy and align thoughts to focus on the spiritual dimensions ayahuasca demands. Samuel has failed to refrain for the required weeks, only days, and hopes his experience of training his thoughts on this occasion will be enough.

He allows thoughts of Eden's safety to melt away, knowing Kaikare will safeguard the ceremony. Men join the room, a support for each warrior. It's time to leave the quiet room and congregate in the *waipa*, an open-air round house where celebrations take place.

In two lines, the men walk in silence, the receiver and the protector side by side, ready to begin the journey of the mind.

Silence has fallen within the village perimeter, except for a steady drumbeat by an elder to remind one's thoughts to remain in the circle of the shaman. The fire beyond their walls flickers in the distance, no longer maintained by those who gathered hours before.

A quiet normality fills him. The usual shrill of mosquitoes circle around his sweaty crown. The thick, moist air forces extra effort on inhalation, almost a natural way for him to breathe.

The serene voice of the shaman prepares him for his volatile body reaction. His protector passes him a bowl of ayahuasca tea. Samuel downs it, shudders at the bitter taste, reminding him of tequila and lemon. He's handed another, and another, and another. Focusing on keeping the contents in his gut for as long as possible, he hums, eyes closed, his body trembling as the indigenous medicine is absorbed by his cells. The first sign of his stomach contracting forces Samuel onto his hands and knees, and he fills the large bowl before him. He swipes his mouth and settles back into a cross-legged position and is handed more brew. The slight tremor in his arms intensifies. The quaking in his gut radiates out until his entire body convulses, leaving him curled on his side, his protector lifting his cheek for vomit to flow freely.

"Water," he screams out, only in his head.

The brew can't be diluted.

Every synchronized vowel from the shaman's throat drones out the moans and puking of those around him. Irregular purple shapes form before his eyes, then turn into slow-moving lava blobs, switching to pink, red, and orange and morph in a kaleidoscope of color, mesmerizing his vision. He allows the colors to take control of his body, lulling him into a false calmness until the probing tickles his hands, tracking the veins along his arms. Long intrusive fingers find his innermost thoughts and sort through every memory like a filing system searching for the crippling memories haunting him most. Every ayahuasca experience rakes through memories and addresses different files of the brain. Emotions overboil until he sobs like a young boy denied his most favorite toy, only the energy is tenfold.

As a sixteen-year-old, he visualizes friends bullying a girl, and he *watches on*. He experiences pain through *her eyes*, not his privileged upbringing in wealthy Trousdale Estate in Los Angeles. The taunting, the teasing as though she was inferior, and then until she could take no more, his soul cries for her soul. He has carried the burden of letting her down along with the promise he made to her all those years ago to be a better man and not follow the same path as his friends.

His thoughts switch to sexual infidelities through his university life, then to rebelling against his parents and their attempt to influence his career. Every piece of his past has led him on this journey.

Why does he exist at this time, in this place, in the universe?

He sees the plants with extraordinary powers to heal. His work is to find meaning in his existence, the euphoria of finding the essence of *why*. He sees Eden's face, a sign she belongs—with him. In a flap of wings—turquoise, red, and yellow feathers—he finds the space above the trees and soars through the jungle, *his forest*, a place of belonging. Below him is a map lit up like New York at night. A satellite view of every tree, branch, and root interconnecting with the next like a nervous system, each trunk a spinal cord, blue neon lights pulsing with electric energy. The effects of the ayahuasca vine guide him, lighting a path through the forest floor, a network of roots coming together in a giant web of the Amazon. With the wind in his wings, he recognizes river systems, crossing into an unknown section, and his concentration intensifies.

A black jaguar sprints the same path below, joining him on the mission, intimidating predators daring to cross his path. A second black jaguar joins them, a surprise. His confidence soars as he approaches the tepui, a dark shadow rolling like thunder clouds inside the giant stone. He has heard of the bad spirits residing there —*Kanaima* and the *Mawari*, spirits of the dead. He has the shaman running below protecting him, and now he has another black jaguar, and something tells him the shaman's mate could possibly bring extra enforcement against the spirits of this mystical world.

Could it be Kaikare? Only she's not part of the ceremony.

Eden's cry sounds in the distance, bringing him catapulting to the ground. The black jaguar growls. The shaman's voice tells him to focus and continue. The second black jaguar is attacking, not in fight but more in reprimand. Feathers beat. He soars up the side of the tepui to the plateau, the network now highlighted in electric yellow dotted with red. His flight path is low. He searches for the purple flower among the red, the pull to find it overbearing. He stops when a third black panther dashes beneath him—a younger cat and not as fast as the other two. His focus is challenged by curiosity, *her* voice breaking through the vision in cries and screams, yelling abuse. He falls and tumbles. The cat padding toward him, a predator ready to pounce. It bounds past him, pulls up a few feet away beside a miniature lily-shaped purple flower.

The shaman's voice pulls him through a funnel of color, recalling him into his own body, the present, the round house. He moans in disappointment, the exhilaration of flying forged to his memory. A map of the tepui is ingrained into his brain. Getting there will not be easy, especially without flight.

36

EDEN

Samuel returns to our hut at first light.

It's a little after sunrise, although it's difficult to interpret the exact moment the sun rises with a canopy of tangled green blocking most of the light.

He tiptoes around, and yet he wakes me since my head is thick from barely sleeping. I'm still haunted after finding Samuel curled up like a fetus in the shaman's special ceremonial hut. The stench of acid lingered in the air, his stomach contents in a bowl by his side.

I had cried, tried to wake him, yelled profanities knowing the meaning would fall on deaf ears. It felt good to release my frustration until Kaikare took me by the shoulders after the shaman shooed me away.

His broad, muscular back tenses as he kneels to open his suitcase, busying himself with a map.

"What was wrong with you last night?" I ask, trying to hide concern.

He freezes, although he doesn't turn. Instead, he dips his chin. "I can't explain now. I need you to go to the fields with Kaikare and learn their ways."

I clamber out of the hammock. "But—"

"Eden, *please*, not now. You shouldn't have come. I'd asked you to stay here. Please go to the fields." He points to the doorway, and sure enough, Kaikare is waiting.

He hands me two bananas and a clay mug filled with water. "The women will cook something more substantial soon."

I down the water and hand the mug back to him. "Promise me we'll talk later."

He places a hand on my face and rubs his thumb on my cheekbone. "Okay. So long as you stop worrying about what happened last night." He leans in with a quick kiss to my forehead. "Kaikare will teach you today."

Kaikare and I walk side by side just as friends do, except the entire journey is in silence.

We keep walking beyond the village until we stop at a small clearing and join the other women dotted among the rows of prickled shrubs. I turn in a circle, assessing the fields. Some plants I recognize like sugarcane, capsicum, and potatoes. Toward the jungle edge is a cluster of pineapples and banana palms. Unfamiliar are the rows of woody branches dotted with small thorns and fanning leaves. Samuel had mentioned yuca as a main source of diet, so I assume—since no-bloody-one can enlighten me—these are the source, and it's our chore for the morning.

Kaikare tilts her head, holds out a long thick branch with a stone fastened by twine at the end. She points for me to dig the root. Remembering what Samuel had previously mentioned about the root containing cyanide, I crinkle my brow at Kaikare.

She points to her mouth and eyes, shakes her head.

I turn and observe how the other women harvest the

root, a technique without using garden gloves or protective clothing. My core switches on, and I suck in my bare stomach as much as possible because of the tiny thorns. Swaying the man-made pick over my shoulder, I whack the ground. Vibrations shoot up my arms to my neck and back. I let go with one arm and rub a point at the base of my neck beneath strands of beads that are becoming heavier by the minute. Ignoring sideways glances from the other women, I heave and take another swipe, barely denting the soil.

I can do this.

Several blows later, Kaikare nudges me aside and extracts the plant pulling out the entire root. She smiles at me before throwing it on a pile. She nods to the next plant growing beside the one I previously mined.

Two more plants are added to the pile. I wipe my brow, my attention captured by the giggling of young girls reaching for banana bunches. To my left, a pregnant woman plucks capsicums, and I can't help the pang of jealousy that she doesn't have to wield a blunt axe. I stop to inspect a blister on the thumb line of my palm. Kaikare points to the next field. Potatoes. I smile, although I need to relieve myself first.

Pointing to the jungle, I leave her and wander to the edge of the field. I weave around tree trunks, dodging the unruly vines, all while maintaining my balance on the black decay covering the tangled roots. Yellow butterflies erupt before me, the cluster forming a cloud. It's no surprise since the butterflies are everywhere, and even still, I smile every time it happens.

Inside the green walls, the sunlight tightens, and I'm thankful for the added privacy. A moan comes from the distance to my right. A younger voice. Female. I walk the opposite way even though defecating with an audience doesn't seem to bother these people as much as it does me. I stop walking and hear a deeper masculine moan. I turn and spy two figures leaning on a tree for support, one leaning on the other's back. Realizing what I'm witnessing, I still in shock. In seconds, the boy sprints away weaving through the wide trunks until he's out of sight. The girl straightens. My position makes vision difficult though she seems calm. She grabs a handful of leaves and attends to herself. She adjusts the beads around her neck before strolling toward the jungle edge of the fields.

Her hair is short in a bowl-cut like many of the other girls, so I wouldn't recognize her anyway. I have figured out the girl's hair is cut when she first menstruates, as the young girls in the village have longer hair. The older women have long, gray-streaked hair with thinning ends, longer because they are menopausal, maybe.

I keep walking, stumbling in my sneakers, my concentration hazed thinking about the young couple. There would be consequences if they were caught. When I find a palm adequate for my hygiene, I squat, checking the ground for poison ants, snakes, and anything moving.

In a vulnerable position, I hurry through the paces and rethink the path I took to get here.

I leave and walk back. The fields are near empty. On the far side, the last of the women with baskets on their heads disappear into the trees. Feet barely touching the ground, I sprint through the potato rows reminding myself not to be a dependent child and be mindful of the tasks of the day.

I reach the younger girls at the back of the rank, catch my breath, and follow the procession of baskets to the long hut. The men sit cross-legged on the ground weaving baskets and fishing line. The children play with a coconut, rolling it along the ground, jumping out of the way as though it's an object of tag.

Kaikare finds me and leads me to a space on the hard ground beside her. She coaches me to chop potatoes. She wraps the vegetables in palm leaves or chops others to boil. Curiously, I watch the women prepare the yuca root. Kaikare sees my interest, points to me, and shakes her head. "I know," I say, nodding. Aware I don't have the skill.

Damn, I nod a lot.

I continue to observe the process of grating the root and soaking it in a clay pot of water. Outside the hut, there's an area consisting of beams and ladders. I first presumed it to be a child's playground. The overhead poles are used to secure a long, tightly-woven tube where the root is stuffed inside and left to drain the deadly juice. Kaikare joins some of the ladies to empty the contents of the twine- woven tubes hanging for, I assume, several days. The vegetable is now flour-like and placed on a long clay tray spread out to cook on the fire.

"Heating it removes the last of the poison," Samuel says. I sigh, hearing his voice. "Next, it will be turned into bread."

"How are you?" I search his face.

He nods to Kaikare and answers me at the same time, "Fine. Have you finished your chores?"

"I don't have a list, but I've helped some."

There's a hint of a smile when he speaks to Kaikare.

"What did you say to her?"

"I asked her if you were productive. She said you're learning."

"I am," I say, indignant. "Without any orientation."

He chuckles low. "Let's take a walk."

We reach the far end of the village, and he continues along a well-trodden path of tree roots. "I thought you might want to bathe."

"I do because I worked up a sweat in the fields. And I have to ask why the men don't help?"

"They prepare the soil and grow the new crops from cuttings and seeds. Their job is to hunt, fish, weave the baskets, nets, and hammocks, make the darts, and harvest the poison for the arrows and darts. The women tend to the fields and cook the meals."

"And tend to the children. Which reminds me, I spotted some of the women with babies strung to their backs as they worked. Surely, the fathers who are basket weaving could watch over the young ones to save the mother's back?"

"The men don't help much at a young age. They tend to show their sons how to hunt and fish, and the girls follow their mother's ways until they marry. By early teens, they are promised to someone, and when it's time, the guy shifts his hammock into the girl's family hut. He then learns from and works alongside his new father-in-law."

I gawk at him. "Simply like that. No wedding."

"The only ceremony is for new warriors heading out on their first hunt, like an initiation or a celebration as told by their folklore or ceremonies as you witnessed last night."

"Are you going to tell me about last night?"

"I know you're concerned for me, but your being there could've ruined everything."

"Or I could have helped. You were in a bad way.

Vomiting. Crying out. Moaning. Seriously, I couldn't leave you like that."

"I knew what was happening. It was part of the ayahuasca process. Next time, please do what is asked of you. The shaman might not be so lenient if it happens again." He stops short. "Are you going to bathe?"

I hadn't even realized we'd reached the stream. I wade in while Samuel fetches the foaming leaves to wash myself.

"Am I going to be punished?" I ask, taking the leaves from his outstretched arm. He sits on the bank and watches, his masked expression showing no emotion.

"I only heard him say you didn't belong."

"At the ceremony?"

"No. In the tribe." He kneels in front of me. "My heart sank hearing his words. It broke me because more than anything, I want you here."

"Tell me what to expect tonight. I don't want to stuff-up again." I clamber over rocks wishing there was an Egyptian cotton towel to greet me. Useless really because, in minutes, the sweat will bask my skin and gleam like a wax coat.

Samuel offers his hand to hoist me up. He holds my gaze, and I see a glimpse of the longing inside of him.

"If you follow Kaikare's lead and do what I ask, you'll be fine."

"What happens tonight?"

"We eat. We drink. More stories. New warriors are initiated."

Something tells me it won't be that simple.

37

EDEN

The steady beat of a drum and the soft notes of a flute filter through the air. It's the most relaxed I've ever been while eating dinner. The people sit quietly, smiling at one another. No excitement, and yet there's a sense of gratitude even though the makeshift wooden spit is absent of an animal. The fish and vegetables are still satisfying, and I find my fill easily. What's surprising after nothing except fruit all day, my stomach is adjusting to this lifestyle. I'm not even craving chocolate.

The fire is stoked, and the flames climb toward the dark sky. The shaman utters a few words. Young and old gather closer to form a half-circle around the shaman. The blue, yellow, and orange flames glow behind him creating his own theatrical stage.

There are more sticks, reminding me of cat whiskers, protruding from his cheeks tonight. He's wearing a smaller headdress with more teeth and bones than feathers. Raising his hands, he looks to the heavens and tells a tale about *The Tree of Life*.

Samuel whispers the translation. The touch of his lips

near my ear is more gratifying than any story. When it concludes, I recognize the shaman's last words.

"A-pantoní-pe nichii."

"What does it mean?" I ask.

"May you take advantage of this story."

"Right. Like a lesson learned." I glance back and catch the shaman staring at me—again. "The shaman keeps looking at us."

"If he makes eye contact, don't look him in the eye. He'll take it as a threat."

"I looked him directly in the eye last night when I shouted at him. It's a good thing he doesn't understand English," I say under my breath.

"You hope he doesn't."

"Does he?"

"I'm not sure. He doesn't speak it to me, although he may understand certain words. He hinted at being offended by your actions."

Shit, I called him a bastard.

"I was scared for you and wanted to help. And before you say I shouldn't have been there, I was, and you were in a bad way, so what was I to do? Leave you lying in your own vomit?"

"Yes," he says firmly. "I know what happens, Eden. You have to purge to get to the next stage, which is the most important part of the ceremony. Knowing you caught me in an exposed position, well I…"

"What?"

"Did you ever consider I was embarrassed by you seeing me vulnerable?" He looks down at me, his gaze mellow. The reflection of the fire flickers in his pupils.

"I'm here for you," I whisper. "I was scared I was going to lose you. Then you didn't come home." *Home.* It's weird

I'm thinking of his hut as our home. "I only wanted to hold you and make sure you were okay."

He slides his hand under my elbow and along my arm until our fingers link. I want to lay back and melt into him until I glance around and note no one is showing any public affection. No arms on shoulders. No handholding. No teenage girls on boy's laps. No children nestled into their mother's chest for a cuddle. All private people.

The dom-dom of drums breaks my train of thought. Five young men march into the center of the large circle, their lean bodies freshly painted in long black lines and red Vs. Tonight's audience appears to be a full house. There are one hundred Ularans, Samuel, and me.

The shaman stands in the center of the young men, now on bent knees. Kaikare walks to the shaman and holds up a thick piece of bamboo. She pops the wooden plug. One ant crawls out, and she replaces the plug. The shaman takes it by the thorax and places the ant on a young guy's shoulder. He cringes a little, and I understand why.

"Jesus," I murmur, seeing the ant's body raised in the air, its pinchers latched onto his skin.

"Say nothing," Samuel whispers.

Kaikare pops the lid, and ant after ant is attached to his skin on both shoulders and down his back. The boy's expression remains stoic. The process is repeated on the next boy. When the last ant is attached, the shaman returns to the first guy. Kaikare gives him something small and holds a leaf.

"It's a piranha tooth," Samuel says.

The boy bows his head when the tooth is placed behind his ear. The shaman carves the skin, his mouth gapes a little, and his gaze is focused. He sings a melodic three notes. Dabbing a stick on the leaf Kaikare holds, he then blots it where he cuts.

"A tattoo?" I whisper.

Samuel nods. "He's ready for his first hunt. A step in becoming a warrior."

"He didn't make a sound," I say in awe.

"No. It doesn't help, and noise upsets others. They need to find the strength within. The ants helped."

"How?" I choke out.

"Apart from guiding them to find their inner strength, the burning sensation diverts the pain away from the tattoo."

"Well, I'd rather the tattoo," I blurt out.

His mouth leans close to my ear. "The tooth is sharp and stings like a bitch, yet nothing compares to the poison burning like a million hot irons."

I move Samuel's hair away from his right ear. It's there —an X with a line through the center. I'd seen the symbol on the baskets. "What is it?"

"Their symbol for a butterfly."

"Why a butterfly?"

"A representation of life. Endurance. Hope. Change for the better. Resurrection." He glances down and smiles at me as the thought gives him inner peace.

"I see them everywhere, and today I came across heaps of them like a cloud of yellow."

"It's called a flutter."

"Okay... a flutter of butterflies. Does it mean anything? I mean everything seems to hold significance here." My gran had told me butterflies were someone special we once knew, or something good was going to happen, except my father told me never to believe what she said about those things. Now I'm finding myself wanting to trust her words.

An arm slips over my shoulder. "It means you're on the right path." He kisses my forehead and then releases me as quickly.

The drumming stops.

The chief stands and holds his arms in the air. He gazes up to the night sky and speaks to the heavens. Or maybe it's to their god or ancestors. Wait. Are their ancestors the spirits in the tepuis?

Everyone stands, and the circle falls away.

There's no cheering. No congratulatory slaps on the young boys' backs. The ants are plucked from their skin and dropped safely inside the bamboo tubes. Families disperse in groups and return to their huts. Once again, I hone in on the monkeys' mindless chatter and the birds' piercing squawks as the background music. A near-full moon lights the way to our hut. Samuel slips his fingers in mine when we walk past a group of young men. My lips tingle with a smile at his ownership.

"This moving your hammock-wedding thing. I hope the men don't want to do this to me while you're away."

He squeezes my hand in warning. "That's not even funny."

Stifling a giggle, I snort and laugh at myself. "How do you stop it? I mean it sounds too easy, yet we're not allowed to *be* together."

He gives me a sideways glance, expression unchanged, not seeing the humor at all. Maybe he caught a more serious tone to the last few words I said.

"The shaman has to approve it first. Then the father-in-law."

"So, a couple has dated a while then."

"Not always."

Turning my body, I walk sideways so I can read his face when he answers my next question, "Are you telling me the girl has no choice?"

"Not always."

"Do any of them believe in falling in love, first?"

"Some. Only the decision lies with the shaman and the father-in-law. My intent is known to the shaman if it's what you're worried about."

I remember some international couples who I'd met in our hotel. They had told me they were married by an arranged marriage, which is common in their culture. Their love for each other is as strong as any other couple I knew. They told me their bond and love grew with time, and they couldn't imagine themselves with anyone else. What concerns me is the young couple I saw earlier today and if it's a secret love affair for a reason? Is one of them promised to another?

"I don't see couples holding hands and being in love."

Samuel glances at me as we reach our doorway. The light flickers across his tanned, muscular chest. "Like us."

"Yes. Like us"

Without an audience, he whisks me up in his arms and carries me through the doorway in a declaration of making our own rules.

"Our time will come," he promises.

Arms linked around his neck, I slide down his body and close my eyes with the sensation of warmth being close to him and stand a moment longer, making out his expression in the shadows. He leans down and kisses me hard. I didn't expect it. The need overtakes every thought, and I link my leg around his hips to bring our bodies closer.

Large hands grab my cheeks, bringing his forehead to mine, and he breaks the kiss. Sensing his torment, I slide my leg down his body putting space between us, my desire screaming in defeat.

At this angle, his face is hidden, but there's anguish in his labored breaths. "Every day you're here, I'm struggling to keep my hands off you."

"Do you want me to leave?"

He shakes his head, his forehead sliding on mine.

"Can you talk to the shaman?" I rasp.

"It requires *more* than a green light to sleep together. It's a commitment, an expectation we'll stay together. Be married here. I know that might not mean a lot to you at the moment, but for me..." he hesitates, "... I'm one of them now." He backs away from me until he's standing in his treatment room. "Could you live with me here?"

"Indefinitely?" I gasp. "I thought you had a contract?" My throat turns dry, so I walk to the bench and scoop out a few cups of water from the clay bowl on a narrow side table.

This is a conversation we need to have, so I ease my rear up on the hard wooden table, my legs dangling. "Have you changed your mind about eventually leaving? I mean, I assumed my being here meant there would be an *us* in the future when your contract ends?" An unspoken understanding when we were in Canaima.

He stands opposite me with both hands on his hips, only his gaze is lowered as though he's deciding on how to respond. "I thought you might understand that I don't fit in with society. I hate all the materialistic bullshit and drama. It's not a world where I want to live."

A ball of panic grows in my chest. "And you're mentioning it now?"

"You saw how I struggled in Brazil."

"There are many awkward people in the world. You were a different guy in Ilhéus."

"Ilhéus was different because I was with you." He smiles at me. "You have a way of settling me. Now you're here, it has made me think about the days leading up to the end of my contract and what I'll do. I want to think about a future with you, only I'm afraid to go back to a world where I was unhappy." He glances at me. "I was depressed for some time."

Samuel places one foot slowly in front of the other as he moves quietly around the room. "Years ago, when I was still living in LA, I watched a documentary on a young dentist who became an explorer and lived with the indigenous people in Venezuela. He helped them, as a dentist, and over time, they taught him how to live by means of using his surroundings. The idea appealed to me. So, I lodged an application and found a position in a Pemón village not far from here and worked as a volunteer physician. It felt like nothing else I've experienced. I learned more about myself during that time, so when I returned to LA, I searched for more volunteer work. My wealthy parents were appalled at the direction my medical career had veered toward, so they pulled strings, and I was offered several paid positions. I found a physician and botanist contract located around here. Of course, I jumped at the opportunity and stayed with different communities. The more remote, the more joy I found."

Questions sit on my tongue, but I don't want to interrupt him.

"When I found something unusual like a plant the shaman used, or one considered to be rare, I documented it and sent a sample to Caracas for analysis. Sometimes it was a new species." He stops and places both hands on the bed beside me. "Do you know how exhilarating it is to discover a plant never found anywhere else in the world and with medicinal value?"

"Wow," I whisper.

I sense his need to release all this information pent up inside of him for years. "For short breaks, I'd stay at Canaima. I bought my own room, so I could go there whenever I wanted. Back then, it was hard to get accommodation. Now with the political unrest, only a handful of tourists visit." He shakes his head. "It took me a while to adjust and live by these ways, so I don't have an expectation for you to cope in a matter of days."

"Is that a compliment?"

"It is. You're doing better than I imagined." He brushes hair from my face and offers a warm smile. "I'm proud of you. Even so, we still need to be careful. One thing I want you to promise is to keep an open mind. There's a mystery to their stories, but it's also powerful. Do you understand? Don't shrug off their tales as fairy tales."

"Okay," I say, nodding repetitively.

He walks to the doorway and peers out. "Living here has become a natural way to exist by using the environment and not money for food. There's no dependency on the internet, water, food, money, or where I'm ranked in society, and especially, not what university I attended. None of it matters. What does matter is my ability to survive. To make a fire. To make my own bed and shelter to protect me from the weather. To make lines and nets to fish and arrows and spears to hunt. To make a tool to cut your kill. Know where to find water in the plants and where not to drink because as much as the jungle provides, she can kill you in seconds if you're ignorant." He looks over his shoulder to me, I assume to see if I'm catching up, but my god, I'm having trouble comprehending it all. "I'm rambling now," he mutters. "I apologize. The tea is getting the better of me."

I didn't want him to stop, except there is a change in the air, and I'm not sure if it flows from him or me. I don't want to think about the jungle or what lurks out there, or the days he'd be gone, and I'd be alone.

Unlike him, I miss my family, my friends, the comfort of home, sunsets on the beach, and admittedly, I like the internet.

I wanted an adventure, and I'm living it. I wanted to find love, and I've found that too. Caught up in the excitement, I went beyond my comfort zone for *him*.

Do I want to commit simply so we can bang each other in the village while I'm here? Surely, it's not a promise to stay.

The Ularan stories are not fairy tales.

If Samuel doesn't want to leave this place, and I can't stay, then maybe I need to stop believing we'll have our happy ending.

38

SAMUEL

Two days later...

Samuel and the shaman stroll through the garden of healing. The shaman sings as they walk, words only for the forest to understand. His song instills an inner peace within Samuel like no other.

They stop to examine the plants infiltrating the soil of the medicinal ones, every shrub vying for space. Here, only the quality vines are allowed to survive. Weeds and toxic thorned vines slashed. Occasionally, a new plant surfaces, one Samuel has not seen, and the shaman takes a sample, and in a private ceremony, asks the tree spirits if this plant will heal or take life.

Samuel picks twigs, leaves, and flowers all necessary for his upcoming journey. Some are best dried. Even so, the list of what he'll need for medicinal use and first-aid purposes is extensive.

He's to drink the brew of ayahuasca and chacruna before he leaves in a ceremony the night before—one without interruption.

He picks a little extra for Eden so she can rub the insect repellent leaves on her mosquito bites, more spots visible since she ran out of repellent. He stashes it into his animal skin pouch that's secured with twine around his hips.

The shaman touches his hand.

"She distracts you," he says in his stilted language. "She distracts me."

Samuel frowns.

He tells Samuel she's like the sun and the moon together, her light ever-present. He waves his arm in an arc—Eden the golden light over the rainbow.

Samuel tells the shaman he is focused. Before the shaman has a chance to speak of her, he confesses he relies on her presence like one does air. To his surprise, the shaman's expression is unchanged, as though he already knew the depth of his feelings for her. He tells Samuel he was once distracted in his early days of training and almost chose a path with a woman instead of medicine.

Samuel acknowledges his words, disguising his surprise. He emphasizes Eden will know her place and not interfere with his work and asks for the shaman's blessing.

The shaman holds his gaze with fierce intensity, so much so, Samuel bows his head. He tells the shaman there is no risk, and if it comes to a choice, he'll choose the safety of the village.

The shaman's face lights up, an expression Samuel's rarely witnessed. He hears footsteps and follows the shaman's gaze to the one who treads heavy on her feet.

"Kaikare pointed this way, so I thought I'd find you

here," Eden says in a tone indicating she's pleased with herself.

Samuel spins to the shaman expecting him to be distressed with Eden in their sacred place. Instead, his eyes hold a twinkle, and it takes a moment longer before he holds up a hand.

"Stop," Samuel orders. She stills and looks around her. "You shouldn't be here."

She raises her arms and drops them to her side. "You need to give me a list because there are no warning signs to stay out."

He goes to her and leads her back over her tracks. "I assumed you were with the women in the field. I was coming to find you after I finished here as Asoo is due to visit today. Do you need some supplies because we could give him a list of things to collect in Canaima? Another thought, he could charge your phone and return it to you in a few days."

"Really? You trust him with my phone?" Her eyes round.

"I do." Samuel takes a path past the round hut toward the treatment hut. "You could give him your phone to read messages and let you know if anything is urgent."

"Good idea because I need to send messages to the girls and my parents. If they reply and my phone is in Wi-Fi, Asoo can bring it back to me."

"Grab your phone. I have paper and a pen in my case. I'll also ask him to get some insect repellent." They reach his treatment room, and he stills her to inspect the bites on her shoulders, arms, and back. Samuel pulls leaves from his pouch. "Rub these over your bites. It will help ease the itch and stop any infection. I'll get some sap for you to use on your skin to act like a natural repellent until Asoo returns."

Eden smiles, the relief hinting at her exhaustion. "You know I hated the rash I got from the repellent, only these bites are bloody killing me."

"You have plenty of malarial meds?"

"I do."

He flicks open the case and grabs the paper and two pens. "I'll arrange for Asoo to grab some supplies from my room at Canaima. Write your message for Asoo along with names, and I'll make a list of supplies."

Minutes later, he leads her toward the river to wait for the sound of the motor.

The tapping motor alerts them to its presence before the curiara putts around the bend, the gray-brown water streaming in a wide 'V' behind it. Asoo doesn't wave out like he has on other days. Sensing his concern, Samuel waits on the bank, putting distance between him and the canoe when he mounts the sand. With balance and grace, he glides over the edge and lands only feet from Samuel.

"My friend needs you in Camp Sundown. A measles outbreak. Some children have pneumonia."

"Are the people vaccinated?" Eden asks, her eyes filled with desperation.

"No." He ponders his risk, the Ularans risk of contracting it. "Are the volunteers issuing antibiotics? Quarantining those who are sick and their families from the community?"

Asoo shakes his head. "My friend, I messenger. I sent to ask for help."

"I can give you some of my supplies as I ordered more when I last visited Canaima. Is Doctor Robert still in the camp?"

Asoo closes his palms in a prayer gesture. "Yes."

"Give me some time to gather my supplies. If he needs anything else, let me know. Unfortunately, I can't help as I leave for an exploration tomorrow."

"Already?" Eden asks.

"It's a day early as we're leaving with the warriors at the beginning of the hunt. I'm sorry, I'll talk to you about it later. Give Asoo your message and explain what you need him to do." Samuel takes off to the treatment hut, his thoughts whirling between Eden, his journey, and the news from Asoo. He hopes the outbreak is contained and not spread further into the jungle.

🌴

Twilight. Night. Dawn. Daylight. The time in the jungle never alters in the constant heat and humidity. The wet season exacerbates the humidity and the balance of life, with the challenge of finding sufficient food if the river floods the village.

He ponders how the Ularans believe this is in the hands of the gods.

This season the Ularans dodged upsetting the gods, the river only creeping near the outskirts of the village. The elders fear the next wet season to be worse. Plans are underway to build huts further away from the river and high off the ground in the trees. Samuel overheard an elder mention the spirit of the Kanaima in their village lives in the white sun god. He hopes the others don't believe Eden's presence will bring them bad luck.

Tonight, at twilight, he's to prepare for the ceremony.

Eden has barely spoken to him since meeting Asoo. He can't afford to be distracted by her now. She doesn't understand the importance of his upcoming journey, especially tonight's spiritual one with the guidance of the shaman to lead him to the rare flower. In truth, as much as his own journey has led him to this day—the pinnacle of why he is in Ulara—Samuel also wishes for it to be over so he can only be with her.

🌴

Night has fallen over the village.

The jungle choir on the highest volume barely distracts Samuel from his purpose. Small fires flicker in the round house, creating enough light to see the bowl of fluid handed to Samuel. He drinks the brew made from the ayahuasca vine. He gulps down several bowls, waits for the moment his stomach turns inside out to rid itself of the vile tea. The purging begins, a severe headache takes hold, and he loses the ability to stay on all fours. Curled in a ball, he holds his temples, the pain taking over until he moans and cries, his voice overbearing the harmonic song of the shaman.

Two soft hands cup his rough fingers. The voice of his angel whispering in his ear. "You're safe. Go where you need."

In his mind, his thoughts connect with the voice, psychedelic colors purging his brain when he feels his soul, and his spirit travels beyond his childhood memories into another dimension—a tunnel of bright neon light, a kaleidoscope of dreams.

He visualizes his life in rewind, and it quickly switches to fast forward to the future where he spreads his yellow, turquoise, and red feathers and takes flight on a path he has already traveled. An inner peace fills him knowing his body is in safe hands with not only a protector, more so with love surrounding his aura.

With her, he's ready to take the journey into the unknown.

🌴

In the early hours of the morning, Samuel returns to his hut, passing Eden sleeping peacefully in her hammock. She disobeyed him again. He touches the side of her cheek and kisses her lips. "Thank you for your support," he whispers. "I was grateful to have you there to look after me." It was the first time he came to without any vomit on his cheek or shoulder. The shaman had revealed everything, including her washing him while he slept off the medicine. "I know you're worried about my exploration. Afraid to be here alone. You'll be safe. Kaikare will take care of you. Knowing you're here will guide me home because you own my heart."

She doesn't move beneath his touch. Her breath is heavy with sleepy sighs.

Sighs he wants to hear when he sleeps beside her. He now longs for the day to hold her in his arms every night.

🌴

Sometime after dawn, Samuel gathers his containers and kit to hold the plants and fills his bag with food and bottles of water. Sources of water can be found in the jungle, but with the length of their journey, he needs to carry extra and have a bottle ready to collect it from the trees and bamboo.

Around his waist, a twine belt holds a pigskin pouch.

Hanging from the twine are handmade darts, a knife, and in his hand, a long blow pipe doubling as a walking stick. A hammock is rolled into his backpack along with a mosquito net and Western medicinal supplies. For this exploration, he wears his sneakers because his feet haven't adapted to the long miles, the damp jungle floor, and the torturous rock they'll climb over for many days.

A small group gathers to send them on their way. Eden rises early to be with him. He kisses Eden on the lips for the second time in a matter of hours, knowing the shaman has witnessed their affection. "You'll be fine," he says, meaning every word. "I'll come home to you as quick as I can."

"I know you will," she croaks and swipes her eyes. They stand a moment assessing the other, both stiff-lipped. She watches him join the warrior circle, chanting and waving their spears, mentally preparing themselves for the hunt. Samuel and Timenneng will separate from the others after a day's journey to begin their exploration. Other men aren't so eager to enter the home of the spirits.

The green membranes pulsate with life. He turns before the green cavern swallows him up and nods to the only woman brave enough to experience this world with him.

He gives her a subtle nod, an unspoken promise of love.

39

EDEN

My chest is tight with a ball of panic growing inside it, threatening to unleash all my insecurities. The composed expressions of the women make it worse. They may live in a peaceful place without the stress of first-world issues, only this isn't my world, and being here *is* stressful. I'm not skilled in their ways, and I'm struggling to find water in the plants like they do. I snap plants the wrong way, and the couple of mouthfuls stored in the stem gushes out before I get my mouth to it.

Heaving my ax above my head, I slam it into the ground near the yuca. In a few sharp blows, I've excavated the earth and dug out the roots. I glance up to a young girl picking bananas and watch as she leaves her duties to wander into the forest with some other girls.

Getting Kaikare's attention, I point to my mouth, indicating I'm hungry and head to the palms hoping to find one yellowing banana. Since most are picked green, bunches strung to beams in the long hut to ripen, I don't hold out much hope. Reaching up, I move a clump to the side to inspect the skin and jump back when a large brown spider unfolds and emerges. I clutch my chest gasping. Willing my heart to slow, I remind myself not to panic. *It's only a spider.* Although this one doesn't look like the tarantulas the children brought back to eat. It's almost as large, hairy, and brown with a smaller thorax and abdomen. With spindly long legs, it moves fast over the bananas, and its red fangs flare. An outstretched arm lands on my stomach and pushes me back a few steps. Kaikare is by my side shaking her head.

We take another step back. With her axe, she flicks it to the ground, and it scurries away. She looks at me and shakes her head. Points to her throat and gags.

"It could've killed me?" I rasp. She tilts her head. I place my hand to my throat and gasp for air. She nods twice. "For fuck's sake." I want to cry. "Why didn't you kill it?"

Kaikare places a hand on my shoulder and strokes it gently.

"Thank you," I croak out. "Thank you for saving my life. I know you can't understand me, but—" I turn and look around. I want to curl up in a ball and feel sorry for myself, only where? A few tears spill out—from fear, disappointment, and second-guessing my decision in coming here. Most of all, the disappointment is in me.

I point to my throat and mime a drinking action. Kaikare nods and takes my hand, showing unusual affection as though she understands. Something I've never witnessed among the others. She leads me to the stream and where the water runs clear. There are clay bowls nearby filled with water, leaves floating on the surface. Hoping the leaves serve as purification, I scoop out some water with a clay cup and drink three full scoops. *Why didn't Samuel mention these large bowls?*

Maybe he did. Admittedly, I haven't taken on everything he'd told me as it was a lot of information to comprehend at once.

Further downstream, the children frolic in the area where we bathe. Finally, it makes sense. Upstream we drink. Downstream we bathe. The same rule applies with the river—closer to the mountain they fish while downstream is used for personal hygiene. She drinks a cup herself and rises to her feet. We backtrack through the jungle to the fields. Passing over the tangled decay of the jungle floor, I glance up at hearing a low moan. A flash of skin between the trees catches my attention. Kaikare touches my hand and shakes her head. I can't help but look back and realize it could be the same young couple. Kaikare leads me to rows of capsicum and spinach-like plants called aurosa. We pick and slice leaves, and when I place the vegetables in a woven basket on the ground, I catch sight of the young girl emerging from the jungle. I take in her features, the beads around her neck. I'm not the only one who notices. Kaikare lifts her gaze at the same time before returning her focus to her hands at work.

I can't help the curiosity and know better than to show it in front of Kaikare. I'll ask Samuel about the girl when he returns.

🌴

Come twilight for the past five days, I'm overwhelmed with nausea, knowing I'll be spending the night alone. Today is no different, and inevitably dusk descends.

The days pass quickly by working in the fields and cooking around the fire. I have company, but with limited communication, there's loneliness even when surrounded by people. At dinner, I eat the vegetables and bread on offer. Hours earlier, I had walked past the fire and saw a pile of headless monkeys—dark blood pooling on the ground—and covered my mouth to smother a heave. The pong of charred hair sent me rushing to Samuel's hut to hide out for a moment and reel in anxiety. It's all too much for my first week alone.

The moment I've dreaded is upon me. I wave my hand, refusing the meat, knowing it's a sign of rudeness. The deep lines around the chief's eyes almost join with those in his forehead. I glance down at the monkey paw on a palm leaf, rub my stomach, and shake my head again.

I accept the flat bread Kaikare hands to me, and I'm left to be insignificant once more when the shaman rises from the ground and stands in front of the fire. Bright-eyed, the children shuffle forward, and despite not understanding their language, I detect the excitement in their voices as they scramble toward the inner circle.

The shaman raises his hands and stares toward the heavens before beginning his story. His words capture everyone's attention. I gaze around, watching their reaction. What makes them believe these stories?

Fear?

Respect?

The sound of night creatures echoes from the tangled knot of green and black surrounding us. The squawking, clicking, and chattering never eases. Tonight, the sound magnifies, taunting me, a warning not to relax. My heart beats at a quicker rate, on alert after my close encounter with a deadly banana spider. I stare toward the pulsating gloom. Why did I ignore the advice of the people I love to risk my life in the jungle?

Answers I don't find before I hear the words, "A-pantoní-pe nichii."

The shaman's tale is incomprehensible for me to *take advantage of the story*. More importantly, I need to understand my journey.

And why I left my closest friends to come here.

Every night since Samuel has left, I've peed right here outside my hut, too afraid to venture into the green.

Wrapping the mosquito net around my hammock, it's difficult to ignore the deafening raucous beyond the walls, my so-called jungle lullaby. Only it doesn't lull me into sleep. Now that I am alone, I'm listening more so to specific sounds, an awareness to which are warnings. Without Samuel to guide me, I have to rely on my own instinct since there is no one else I can ask for help. It exaggerates the notion of being alone, and it scares the crap out of me.

40

SAMUEL

The days the journey took Timenneng and Samuel through the jungle were familiarly dangerous. He knows the signs, the sounds of possible threats, and can identify a poisonous plant with a single glance. He understands where to find water and which fruits to eat. The forest garden offers an abundance of food if you know where to find it, and it means he can keep the food in his sack for the days on the tepui. Still, he can't risk sleeping in certain parts of the jungle with only a hammock and small pocketknife for protection. He won't use it unless absolutely necessary so as not to reveal the knife to his warrior companion. Considering Timenneng has poisonous-tipped arrows in the animal-hide sack he carries on his back, he hopes no danger will come close enough for him to wield a steel blade. He packed it even though Timenneng knows nothing of knives or the metal objects from Samuel's world. Carrying the weapon isn't an insult to Timenneng, more a reason to live with the promise he'd return to *her*.

Yesterday the jungle led them up a steep slope toward

the tepui wall, a constant battle through thorny vines and over mangled muddy tree roots. It rained most of the previous day, and Samuel hopes it holds off while on the rock face of the tepui. Rain and storms aren't ideal when free-climbing a dangerous mountain, most of it unknown to man. Timenneng leads the way, and although Samuel has faith in his navigation, it was the shaman who conveyed Samuel's visions of the location of the purple flower to Timenneng.

They wake at dawn and clamber down the tree where they rested. They continue their trek and are soon face-to-face with the rocky wall of the tepui. Samuel and Timenneng gaze up to the clouds, a sandstone barrier overhanging toward them. To Samuel, the tepui appears unclimbable without the special ropes professional mountaineers used for safety.

Timenneng places one hand on the rock, his gaze lifted as though studying every crevice and crack in a game of chess. He places an ear on the rock, closes his eyes, and listens.

The House of Gods.

Samuel's common sense tells him it's a myth, only now he's wiser, a believer, and it's possible the spirits are guiding his warrior friend. If so, he hopes the gods steer them right.

Timenneng wanders for another thirty minutes keeping a hand on the rock as they wrangle past the trees growing close to the rocky wall, competing for space and seeking sunlight. Timenneng stills, assesses the rock, and with one hand, he then reaches up and hoists a foot, the other hand, and then the other foot into the tiny crevice. His limbs spread out like an insect, and as light as a six-legged creature, he scrambles up the wall.

He doesn't ask for Samuel to follow, and he doesn't direct Samuel to stay put. Samuel's not surprised since their culture expects you to understand matters when they happen in the moment—learn and adapt to being a warrior. Yet, the vertical path on the sharp, flat rock seems ludicrous.

Samuel searches the rock for a crevice strong enough to take his weight. He's slim but not built like a stick insect and uses his core to lift and then spread his weight, so it's distributed evenly between his limbs. His movement is slow and calculated. Periodically, he glances up to ensure his path is the same as Timenneng's, as one wrong move could be perilous. There's an overwhelming feeling of blending into the rock, like slow-moving creatures barely visible from the ground. Each time Samuel stops to catch his breath, he peeks over his shoulder to the sun on the horizon to check for clouds as a storm can roll in quickly with barely time to find cover. On the ledge would be a death wish.

"Konopo?" he shouts. *Rain.* Timenneng has a better view and is more agile to turn and assess their situation than the fleeting glance Samuel takes over his shoulder, so he doesn't overbalance and fall.

"Weju," Timenneng replies. *Sun.*

He sucks in a deep breath of relief that the sky is clear. Yet he can't relax when the sun will sink below the trees in a matter of hours, and they need to make the first rocky ledge to set up their camp before nightfall.

Above him, Timenneng calls out. "Ero po." *Here.*

He offers Samuel a sweaty hand, and he scrambles onto the narrow cliff. It's a ledge wide enough for them to stand and rest for the night. He lumbers to his feet, turns, and inflates his lungs with clean, crisp air as he admires the view with the last minutes the day has to offer before the golden orb sinks below the green horizon.

In a race against time, they pitch their hammocks to the sapling trees growing out of the rocks. They eat the food in their packs and drink from the bottles Samuel has supplied. His muscles ache, and the scratches on his fingertips sting. Samuel can barely keep his eyes open, so he clambers into his hammock, eager to fall asleep to the sound of the jungle hundreds of feet below them. Eyes closed, his thoughts wander across the treetops searching for her essence. The notion of her remaining alone in the village, waiting for him to return, gives him a sense of purpose and self-appreciation with a woman sacrificing as much to be with him. He drifts off to sleep, imagining the soft sighs of her sleeping beside him.

🌴

The following morning both men wake at first light.

Timenneng rolls up his hammock, and Samuel senses his eagerness to move on. Securing his own pack to his back, he prepares his mind for the mental strength to keep going despite every muscle in his body screaming in pain and his toes blue from the climb.

Timenneng points a finger to walk sideways across the rock. Green moss coats the rocky surface above them, making it slippery and unclimbable.

Samuel's nails are chipped, his fingertips battered and covered in cuts. His calves burn from side-stepping, all his weight bearing through his toes. His fingers splay, searching for a cleft in the rock to dig his fingers in before moving his leg. Rocks break and fall beneath him, the clash unnerving as neither men wear helmets.

Timenneng calls out to him, and out the corner of his eye, Samuel sees an object approach. It's a vine Timenneng has swung toward Samuel. He grabs it without levering his weight from his extremities and gives a tug to assess its safety. He winds it around his wrist before he takes another step to his left and then sees Timenneng standing on another rocky ledge waving to him. He clings to the vine, his feet gripping like a monkey, and uses momentum to swing toward the protuberance to join his friend. Timenneng grabs and secures the vine as Samuel lands and stumbles on the edge. He crouches on all fours and takes a moment to gather his thoughts and regain his mental strength to push on.

He pants out of breath. Wait, is that—

"Tuna." *Water.*

The sound comes from a small opening. Is this what Timenneng was listening for?

Both crouch onto all fours to enter the cave, eventually sliding on their stomachs over smooth boulders into the unknown. It takes a moment for Samuel's eyes to adjust and for his hearing to guide them toward the underground stream. The cave widens enough for them to stand, and then he finds himself in a damp cavern, a stream to their right and a cathedral-shaped dome ceiling above. Tiny potholes of light shine in from all angles casting enough light to make out the ground beneath their feet. Timenneng holds up a hand, points, and says a single word in a hushed breath. They follow the stream, walking opposite the current in an upward spiral path. Samuel can't help feeling an overwhelming notion of being an intruder to a sacred place where many myths originate about the spirit world.

Soon they come across a boulder wall, and Timenneng directs Samuel on what boulders to slide his body over so as not to disturb the supporting boulders as the structural balance relies on a fine thread of cohesive sand.

It seems as though they are going in circles, for every hour or so they stumble across another opening blocked by boulders, and they slide through a tiny space to get to the other side. Only the punctures of light in the rock above grow brighter. Previously, Samuel had only ventured to a smaller wall on the other side of the giant tepui, to an area more assessable to climbers. He's barely capable of this climb. Over the past couple of years, the area close to Angel Falls has become popular with professional rock climbers, and helicopters and planes zoom over the top with curious tourists every day. The journey to find the medicinal flower has brought them to a treacherous section of the tepui, away from adventure seekers.

Climbing the rock from the inside through unstable sandstone columns in the caves is a better choice than the unclimbable rocky walls of the tepui. Only he has no clue of time inside the cave, and it's messing with his sanity. Timenneng remains composed. Time holds less significance to the Ularans, as night and day are all that really determines their behavior, and his duty is to guide Samuel in finding the flower. He will do so until his body tells him to rest. As light streams in, Samuel can see more of his surroundings, including the giant-sized cockroaches scrambling near his feet, and he doesn't even have the energy to flick them away.

Finally, they scramble through an opening. "Whoa," Samuel yells and stops at the edge. They are surrounded by walls of a large sinkhole, the opening above them around one-hundred feet high. Circling below from where they stand is a miniature forest, home to unique and varied species. Above, a waterfall cascades over the tepui summit to a lake pooling hundreds of feet below.

In minutes, the light dims with the sun already low on the horizon. Timenneng points to their bags, and Samuel couldn't be more delighted to sling his hammock on the edge of paradise.

41

EDEN

It's been fourteen days since Samuel left.

Fourteen days of hard work in the fields, and this morning the blisters on my palm have finally popped. Every day I have completed the chores expected of me and follow the lead of the other women, our routine unchanging, until now. Instead of heading to the cooking pot with the other women to prepare lunch, Kaikare waves for me to follow her, leading us to the stream. She removes her skirt and beads before wading waist-deep into the water.

"Tamu'ne Akare." She repeats, laughs, and waves me in.

Throwing my costume aside, I follow her in and submerge myself beneath the cool, clear water only to surface and find her climbing the bank. She gathers leaves from different shrubs before splashing as she lands beside me. She foams a leaf and rubs the soap through her hair, handing the green waxy leaf to me. I use it to wash my hair, forgetting how wonderful the sensation of clean hair is, and the scent is remarkably better than any product I know on the market. She laughs like a child, even though I presume she's thirty-plus years my senior.

The humidity makes it impossible for our skin to completely dry naturally. We replace the black and red beads over our necks and loop the tweed ties of our skirts around our hips. I catch a whiff of my socks and groan before slipping on my sneakers. I still refuse to walk barefoot. If only I could rewind time and contemplate what I could squeeze into my pack, like an extra pair of socks.

Rewind to when I was with my friends.

Following the footprints of Kaikare along the narrow path to the village, I'm surprised when she leads me to another hut. She stands at the door and smiles.

Inside, animal skulls hang on the walls. Trophies of teeth are strung in a necklace with incisors large enough to be of jaguar or caiman. She opens a small woven basket with a lid and pulls out something with a handle. She hands it to me, both hands outstretched like it's precious. Taking the object, I turn it over and catch shards of my reflection in the dirty glass.

"A mirror. It's beautiful." I turn it again, several times, rubbing the glass tainted by time. I scrub the back with my fingers and catch the flower decoupage under glaze that has worn away. I hesitate. It's otherworldly, old, and only an outsider would have gifted it to her. Before I hand it back, I catch the bird-nest hairstyle I'm fashioning. Holding the mirror higher, I check myself in an unstained piece, running my fingers through tangled strands endeavoring to tame my mane.

Kaikare laughs again and takes it from me, copying my action with her hair. Hearing voices outside, she hastily replaces the mirror in the basket, tucks it under a woven mat, and leads me to the village center. Before we reach the fire, the children run up to her shouting and pointing to the river. The children bounce near my face, grab my hand and drag me a few steps until I'm forced to follow. The shaman appears out of nowhere, and there's a discussion between Kaikare and him. I kneel to allow the children to touch my hair yet manage to keep Kaikare and the shaman in my line of sight.

Kaikare shakes her head and comes to stand beside me. Even I can make out the warning in the shaman's voice. She leads me toward the river, and I'm surprised to find Asoo waiting on the sandy bank.

"Asoo." I run up to him and throw my arms around his waist, eager to speak with someone who understands me.

He nods at me, his eyes full of sorrow.

"Is everything okay?"

He hands me my phone. "You have a message. I bring it to you."

My stomach drops before reading the message, then settles when I understand the message from Yasmine is informative, nothing bad.

> We finished the Macchu Piccu trek and are heading north to Iquitos.

> Fantastic! Text me and let me know your plans. Miss you all. Stay safe x

Stay safe. I want to laugh at my advice, thinking touché.

I hand my phone back to Asoo. "Please ensure it sends when you're back in Canaima."

He takes my phone and wraps it in plastic before

slipping it into his bag. "I need to ask a favor of my friend, Samuel. Is he here?"

"No." I hear the disappointment in my voice.

His chin dips to his chest. "It bad. Children dying. Doctor Robert ask for more supplies until his arrive."

"Of course. I'll search Samuel's bag to see if I can find anything of use."

I run into the bushes and almost scream when I bump into Kaikare, forgetting she led me here and clearly couldn't reveal herself. "I need supplies," I say as though I need to announce my good intention despite the language barrier. She remains on my heel the entire way to the hut and watches while I forage through Samuel's case taking needles, alcohol solution, saline, and antibiotics in vials. I find antibiotic tablets and dressing packs. Samuel mentioned more supplies were being sent to him, and I assume his medicine is rarely used. Emptying the contents of my backpack on the table, I shove the medicines into the bag and jog the path to the river.

"Here." I hand my pack to Asoo, puffing like I ran five miles even though it's only one.

"Come. Help the doctor," he pleads. "Help the children. Put wet cloth on face." He acts out the action with a hand to his forehead. "They have fever."

"What?"

I have been vaccinated.

I glance over my shoulder toward the village. "I can't." My thoughts whirl remembering what Samuel said about the Ularan people's vulnerability and how he quarantines himself for days when he leaves.

Asoo places a hand on my shoulder. "Please." The

way his eyes plead, I know he wouldn't ask this of me unless the situation was desperate.

Shit!

"How far is it?"

"Half day."

Listening to my raspy breaths, I focus on doing what's right. "Okay," I say, knowing I might not be allowed to return to Ulara.

Kaikare appears from the bushes. Asoo stumbles back, turning his body toward the canoe. She speaks in a calm tone, her eyes and focus on Asoo. To my surprise, he understands her, and they talk to and fro as though they have met before. Kaikare gives me a long stare, guilt eating at my stomach. She speaks to Asoo in an elevated tone, and I hope she's not demanding I stay.

"She wants to come and help. Her medicine can help."

"What? No, she can't. Kaikare isn't vaccinated." I shake my head, my eyes begging her.

"She says she had needles. A baby. She wants to help."

I'm shaking my head, confused and torn on what to do. "It's her decision, but please ask her more questions as I need her to be safe."

"She's gone for her medicine," he says when Kaikare retreats to the vines and disappears beyond the trees. I anticipate the shaman's reaction knowing I'll probably be blamed.

My thoughts are whirling, second-guessing, and now I'm worried for Kaikare. "The camp, do people wear Western clothes?"

Asoo nods. "They own clothes on their back."

"Give me a minute to grab mine."

When I pass the village center, I notice Kaikare talking with the shaman. Both wave their hands, neither raising their voices. I keep my head down and make my way to Samuel's hut, grabbing a skirt, two tank tops, shorts, my mosquito net, and doxycycline tablets, then I head back to Asoo.

We wait for Kaikare on the sand, my stomach in knots, knowing she has placed herself in bad favor with her leaders. I look over my shoulder every few seconds and almost tell Asoo to go without her because her coming with us isn't the right thing for her safety or the entire community. Only the decision isn't mine, and I've never seen her so determined.

If anything happens to her because of me, then my erratic behavior would be unforgivable.

42

EDEN

The river current assists our journey downstream.

Kaikare sits at the front of the curiara, her back straight, looking out to the water, ready to tackle anything we greet. Asoo and I can't see her expression, yet I wonder if it's her first time sailing down the river away from her home.

What's Kaikare thinking as we sail away from the only place she knows? Her courage amazes me, especially with the shaman forbidding her to leave. In direct light unfiltered by the canopy, her scars in straight lines and Vs shine on her naked back.

What honor do the scars represent?

After retrieving my phone, I check the time. Something I miss even though there isn't any service. If only I remembered to pack a wristwatch and kept it hidden in my hut.

An hour passes, and we have mainly traveled in silence.

"Do you think you could talk to her?" I ask Asoo. "I'm worried."

"I understand some," he tells me. "Her language a combination of all Pemón languages."

"Can you ask her if she feels safe?"

He nods. "I will sit with her and no shout over motor. Come. I show you how to steer."

We swap seats. I take the stick and wrestle to hold it in place for a moment. "Stay here." He points to the left of the river. "Middle, the current stronger. Not close to edge. Away from floating branches and vines."

Asoo settles in the seat behind her, slightly to her right, so he's in her periphery.

I hear nothing of their conversation with the motor in my ear. Occasionally, Asoo bows his head as though words escape him.

We reach a fork in the river, and he points for me to veer to the right, the girth twofold, requiring a firmer grip on the stick to steer us out of the center. There are more sandy beaches and less overhanging jungle, and soon Asoo climbs back and retakes control in time to guide the canoe onto a small beach. He says nothing of Kaikare.

"We walk now. You can dress." Asoo jumps ashore and stands with his back to us. In the canoe, I pull on a tank top, shoving the beads in the front pocket of my pack. I slip into shorts and untie my tweed skirt. Curiously Kaikare watches. I clamber over wooden planks and hand her another tank top. Her chin raises, she shakes her head, refusing my offer. She stands and finds Asoo. Admittedly, her skirt covers most of her bits, and the beads fall over her breasts. She's proud of who she is, and I respect that. Covering her body with Western clothing is more about my insecurities.

We cross a grassland before seeing the brick and clay structures before us. One building is a makeshift church with a cross on the top. It catches Kaikare's eye. She says nothing, yet I can't help wondering what's going through her mind.

Some children approach us in dirt-covered t-shirts and shorts, all barefoot. Three dogs of no particular breed follow the children like friendly mutts.

Kaikare grabs my arm and freezes. "Asoo, the dogs," I call out. "It's okay," I tell her and reach to pat one with my free hand.

Eyes wide, she watches, although she steps away when it bounces toward her.

"Down," I demand.

Asoo chuckles. "The locals speak Pemón or Spanish. Some learn English. Dogs no understand your words."

I take Kaikare's hand and shoo any other dogs in our path until we enter a small brick dwelling.

A thin man sits behind a desk. Asoo speaks in Spanish first, then turns to me. "Eden."

The man nods. "I'm Robert." He runs his fingers along the length of his beard and eyes us through gray bangs.

"Nice to meet you. I've come with supplies." I place my backpack on his desk and empty the medical kits. "I believe you're in need of some help. My sister has a toddler, and I've cared for him when he's been sick. It's not much, but I'm willing to assist where I can."

"Your friend?"

"Her medicine is from the jungle."

Asoo reverts to Spanish so fast, and the only word I catch is *Kaikare*. He turns to her, and his language becomes stilted, speaking in her native tongue.

Kaikare nods slowly, leaning forward in a slight bow.

"I'll show you ladies where you'll sleep, and then I'll

take you to some of the huts where the children are isolated," Dr. Robert says.

Thankfully, our room has a door and hammocks. Kaikare watches as I open and shut the door, the handle fascinating her. I point to us both and the hammocks before placing my hands under my ear and close my eyes. Surely, it's a universal sign. We head out, Kaikare refusing to let go of her basket, and meet Asoo. The dogs are tied with a rope away from us. The children shout and laugh innocently, and the adults shoot wary stares. They seem unsure who they trust least—the native American or the privileged white girl.

The doctor is inside the long hut. From the moment I step inside, I'm greeted with chesty coughs and sniffles. The children's faces and bodies are covered in a red rash.

"Most of the children and adults only have the cold symptoms although many are compromised with poor hand washing and now have pneumonia." The doctor takes the temperature of a girl. "Some of the children have suffered seizures, and the older generation believes it's the work of a bad spirit." He points to a bowl of murky water with cotton cloths cut in strips beside it. "I don't need all my shirts, so I'm using pieces to help cool them."

He pumps a bottle of sanitizer and wipes it over his hands. I look around. There's no running water. "We have one tap that pumps water from beneath the ground. The whole community shares it. We have electricity for three hours a day from a generator. Most of the volunteers come for eight weeks and leave. One brought the measles virus with him. It spreads like wildfire in a community with no vaccination. I treat them for malaria and parasites, diseases known to their community for years. We can't afford communicable diseases from outsiders."

"What do the volunteers do here in only eight weeks?" I ask him.

"They help with the fields, gardens, cooking for so many mouths to feed. The elderly people are tired, some sick themselves."

"I want to help in any way I can." I walk over and examine a rash on a boy no more than three years old. He moans and barks out a cough.

"Thank you for these antibiotics. The packs Samuel sent have helped a few of these kids. We've had nine deaths in two weeks."

I gasp. "Tell me what I can do now."

"Strangely, I need no one to visit for a few days. Their families want to come in and check on their children, only they are taking the virus back out to the community. I can't keep watch here all the time. They can stand in the doorway and no closer. And you can wash down their bodies with wet cloths to help stop the febrile convulsions."

The humidity is still rife and thick in the air. Even I want to wash just to cool off. No wonder the children struggle with high temperatures. I find a bowl and wet some cloths and wipe one small boy's forehead, chest, and shoulders. I glance up to Kaikare watching me.

She speaks to Asoo. The conversation goes back and forth.

"I show Kaikare the women. She needs water and pot for fire."

"Wait. Does she want me to come with her?"

Asoo shakes his head. "I stay and help if she needs anything."

"Okay."

They leave me with the doctor, and I continue

assisting him administering medication. My thoughts wander to Asoo and Kaikare with an inkling they are keeping something from me. Maybe they believe it's something I wouldn't understand.

🌴

By dusk, we sit around a fire in a way no different to Ulara.

Kaikare is on alert, her eyes permanently round like saucers. She holds a dinner plate in her hand and utensils I assume she's never seen before. She eats with her hands from the plate, watching out for the dogs.

There are many similarities to Ulara, and I'm comfortable knowing I'm not out of my element. Tonight, I eat everything on offer—meat, vegetables, and yuca bread. I didn't question the type of meat. Could it be my mindset because I didn't witness what was killed before it was cooked? I'm not sure I'd ever be comfortable consuming monkey, and yet I understand the need for meat when these people have little choice when it's about survival. "Asoo," I whisper. "Is the meat dog or monkey?"

"No," Asoo says sternly. "Fowl. Dogs are treated well. If you harm your dog—"

"Then when your fifth soul goes to the heavens, your dog will be waiting and kill you," Dr. Robert finishes for him. He gives me a knowing smile.

"Good to know," I say with relief.

This piece of knowledge surprises me. The surprises keep coming every day. The little things bringing joy on this holiday have led me on an adventure of wonder.

🌴

The hammock beside me is empty.

I consider Kaikare has gone to pee, then enough time passes for me to comprehend this is not the case.

I check the time on my phone, a luxury for a few more days, and realize it's not quite seven. Throwing off the mosquito net, I head out to find Kaikare.

Eventually, I find her with the doctor, spooning mouthfuls of her tea into gaunt-faced little mouths. Oh, my heart. She's a natural with these children, and I have no words to describe the admiration I hold for her. She is warm and caring, risking her health and respect from the Ularan elders to come and help. Not just to any place, to one outside the safety of her world, where I assume she's out of her comfort zone. Yet here she is, her head high, doing what she can to help these children survive.

"Morning," I say and smile.

"Morning, Eden." Dr. Robert nods toward Kaikare. "Your friend has a great brew. We gave it to one of the children last night, and this morning when I listened to his chest, there was minimal wheezing."

"Already an improvement?"

He raises a brow at me. "We were as surprised as you. Whatever Kaikare has going on here, we'd appreciate more of it. And another child has less mucus secretion than yesterday. Do you know what plant her medicine is derived from?"

"No, but I can find out. When Samuel returns, he'll be able to show you." I watch Kaikare's face light up when each child finishes their cup and babbles away, thankfully. "I think she's happy to help."

"If there's a way of getting that plant to us with instructions on how to boil it, for how long and with what combination of other plants, we'd appreciate it. My appreciation extends to your generosity in providing the supplies Samuel had in stock. You're very kind."

I nod. "It's the least we can do. What can I do to help now?" I ask him.

"Continue spoon-feeding the children the brew." A child coughs repeatedly behind him. It sounds moist and hacking. He turns and assesses the little boy. "You could start with Amos."

"Right." I scoop out a cup of the tea, and with a spoon ready, I kneel beside Amos. "Hey." With a hand behind his head and back, I help him to sit. I keep one hand behind to support him, and with the other, I scoop a teaspoon of the river-colored brew and sit it next to his lips. Dark eyes stare up into mine, almost questioning if he can trust me. I give him a gentle smile and nod. "It will help you feel better." I know he doesn't understand my words. There is one thing I have learned in the weeks of my stay, and that is the tone and body language communicate understanding more than our foreign words.

By late morning, Dr. Robert has arranged for Kaikare to show the women how she prepares and boils the brew. When she has finished preparing the next pot of medicine, it's time for us to leave the camp. At midday, we're on our journey back to Ulara. I know it not from my phone but by the sun directly above us. Kaikare glanced over at me with a smile from ear to ear. Like her, I'm filled with gratification in helping others—the best kind of joy. Only I'm preoccupied with ideas of fundraising when I arrive home in Australia to support communities like this. With Dr. Robert's business card in my backpack, I promise myself I'll research organizations and other indigenous villages in the Gran Sabana.

My fondness for Kaikare and the village has grown, only I can't see myself staying in Ulara forever. Yet, I don't want to just give up on Samuel and me and some kind of future we could have. Maybe we could combine our homes, live a mixed life. At least when I'm home, there are things I can do to help even from the other side of the world. Money might not hold status in Ulara, but for these communities, it can buy pharmaceuticals and medical supplies. Yet, after what I witnessed with Kaikare's brew, no doubt a recipe from the shaman, our worlds need to share all our secrets as there is a place for both to heal the sick and vulnerable.

43

SAMUEL

"Let's do this," Samuel mutters to himself the following morning. The snacks inside his pouch are low, and the water in his bottle is almost gone. They need to find more sources and fast. They make their way up the steep wall to the surface, using branches for support as they clamber over rock and slippery moss. Hours pass, pausing only to sip mouthfuls of water from the drink bottle. Samuel swishes the water around his mouth before swallowing. Everything is now about preserving the energy, so the two barely talk and only focus on getting to the top. They use vines to climb or propel them upward.

The moment Samuel lifts his leg onto the plateau, he lays there a moment in amazement. The tepui surface reminds him of an alien planet. Black rock with a volcanic appearance similar to totem poles or dangerously long, horizontal fractures around a half-mile deep like narrow craters, slice into the plateau. It's like nothing he has ever seen on earth. Walking over the treacherous surface is another challenge but hopefully the last before finding the flower.

In his mind, he visualized the journey, only he underestimated the demand on his body and has to dig deep to pick himself up and keep moving. He finds Timenneng kneeling on one knee assessing a bromeliad, his feet bloody and covered in cuts.

"Pyjai," Samuel tells him. *Medicine.*

He drops his sack beside him and pulls out the leaves that clean and disinfect wounds. Samuel understands if bacteria gets in his wounds, the challenge of combating the infection is tough without giving him antibiotics.

Water sits in the rocky crevices beside them, not a lot but enough for him to dip the leaves and rub over Timenneng's feet. Timenneng winces a little before regaining a stoic expression.

Samuel pulls out the last of the dried berries for them to nibble. They need a moment's rest.

Sitting cross-legged on the jagged rock, Samuel closes his eyes and meditates for a few minutes to gain his energy. At first, his thoughts are blocked, and he sees only darkness. He curses, ignoring the lethargy weighing down his body and his mind. Visualizing the flower and the song of the shaman, his thoughts clear, and Eden's voice finds a way into his head. "I love you," she tells him in his dreams. Finding the flower will complete his purpose to the pharmaceutical company, and more importantly, free him from his demons so he can be with her. He looks to the sky with gratitude. "Thank you," he murmurs.

Timenneng stands beside him and places a hand on his shoulder. He nods, ready to begin the last leg of the journey.

They trek over the rocky landscape, pushing thorny bromeliads and orchids aside to search for the purple flower. The sun moves across the sky above them, and he stands and leans back, his hands on his buttocks to stretch out his lower back. They push on, and he can't help thinking his visions were misleading. Timenneng points to a cluster of flowers, the striking purple color is squished between the pink orchids. He runs to the plant and moves the orchids aside to examine the quality of the plant—the roots of the purple flowers clinging to a rocky crevice.

This. Is. It.

Samuel takes a single breath, and time stills. His past has led him to this moment—his destiny of finding what he has searched for, for many years. With shaky hands, he extracts the flowers with roots intact before sealing it in a weatherproof bag inside his sack. He turns in a full circle, stunned by the bleak, windswept summit where the rare exotic plant survives. There is minimal plant life near the fractures, and he understands water is responsible for the harsh erosion. He follows Timenneng to a rocky meadow abundant with more bromeliads, pitcher plants, and other carnivorous insect-eating plants. The bright red color catches his attention, the same as it would to insects that become prey and respects the plants' diversity to survive. In the distance, green forests line the rocky edge of the mountain, and a river divides the land that feeds Angel Falls. The looming gray clouds tumbling toward tepui is enough for him to cease further admiration.

Time is suddenly of importance being as high as the clouds. They race against Mother Nature to seek protection from lightning and before the temperature drops dangerously low with an upcoming storm. Without clothes or blankets, the men run the risk of hypothermia if they don't make it back to the cave before night falls upon them. Even with the flower in his possession, his duty isn't complete. He made Eden a promise to return to her.

His body aches and his hands shake from exhaustion. The downhill climb is just as dangerous, yet he wants to push harder and lessen the days on his journey home because every minute steals valuable time away from Eden.

His mission, a success.

In his mind, a new goal blooms.

His heart is no longer divided.

All he visualizes is *her*.

44

EDEN

I remember what Samuel had told me about quarantining outside the village and ask Asoo to explain to Kaikare our need to be cautious that we're not carrying any viruses.

She agrees to stay with me in the small campsite Samuel erected, and I can't help thinking like me, she's not ready to face the shaman yet. After watching Asoo sail away with my iPhone, insecurity creeps back in. Stupid, since it could only take photos, provide time, and a light while the battery lasts maybe a few more hours. The photos were memories and a connection to home and my friends. With every passing day, I'm missing them more.

Alongside the river, Kaikare gathers Piri-Piri, a reed-like grass Samuel had explained was used for some basket weaving yet also had medicinal value. She digs up the rhizomes, carries them back to our camp, and grinds them with a rock. In a fast-twirling action of a stick on rock and dead matter, smoke sparks, and her hands cup to protect the small flame. She hands me a dirty clay pot and points to the river. First, I wash it, then return with it filled with brown water, hoping we don't have to drink it. The ground rhizomes are scraped into the pot and placed on the fire. She rubs her stomach, and I nod, understanding her underlying nausea or nerves. While we wait for it to boil, she walks a short distance to bamboo, which appears to have grown overnight. Snapping several pieces, she hands me a piece, a source of clean water. I have no idea how far we are from the stream on the other side of the village. If I venture too far from the camp, I'm afraid I won't find my way back. So, I take it, and she continues to snap more until we have quenched our thirst.

Sitting around the fire, she sings quietly to herself, the sound calming my erratic thoughts. Immediately, I'm thinking about Samuel.

Is he safe? I try to imagine what it's like being out there, climbing a tepui with minimal assistance, catching your food at the same time as being the lower echelon of the food chain. She jabs a cup at me. I sip the earthy-flavored tea and pretend it's coffee, ignoring the gurgling in my gut.

Dusk falls upon the forest, and I remain by her side, only to add fallen branches to the fire, knowing it's the one mechanism of defense I understand.

Our smoke-perfumed hair and skin deter the number of mosquitoes circling our heads. When darkness falls, she stands as though cued and waves for me to follow her into the jungle.

"Really. We wait until it's almost dark to go in there?" I question. I am finding I'm talking to myself more and more because the silence is beginning to frustrate me, and hearing my voice speaking English offers some sanity. "I'm really not a fan because well, you know, there's this thing I'm conscious of... nocturnal predators... spiders and snakes. Oh, and we don't have a flashlight."

Kaikare stops when enough light from the night sky breaks through the canopy and shines on the fruit several steps inside the denser growth. *More passion fruit.* She picks several pieces before being disturbed by a shower of Brazil nuts falling from above, knocked to the ground by monkeys screeching as they swing from branch to branch. She gathers nuts that have landed by our feet, hands them to me, and proceeds to reach up and snap several sprigs of acai berries from a palm. I follow her lead, and we weave through vines to our camp. I'm hungrier than I realized.

No sooner do we finish, she stands again, waves for me to follow her back into the forest away from the safety of our fire. "You know, I'm full and don't need seconds," I tell her, especially since it's somewhat darker. She stares at me, so I push up from my log seat and moan with some reluctance. "I'll come with you because it's the safety in numbers we should be considering."

Even I question my sanity following her deeper into a black jungle, stumbling over swollen roots and slipping on leaf decay even while holding her hand. Arrows of moonlight provide enough light for Kaikare to weave around the giant tree trunks of kapok trees. Monkeys screech louder with our approach. The click and chatter of insects stop and start, depending on our movement. She pulls up, and I stumble with poor coordination, her hand under my chin guiding my focus to the ground.

The leaves glow, their veins lit up like a green x-ray image. Mushrooms dot the floor like a network of Christmas lights. The jungle flaunts bioluminescence across its decayed floor. The forest's night music now has party lights, and even though I'm smiling in awe, I can't help feeling we're uninvited gate crashers.

"It's beautiful," I tell her, hoping she hears the appreciation in my tone.

We return to our site, and my feet welcome the relief of being elevated in the hammock. Side by side, cocooned in a mosquito net, I fall asleep to the Amazonia lullaby.

Last night, I woke several times in a sweat from bizarre dreams. Unexplainable dreams making no sense, only my heart raced so fast it put the fear of death in me, and I re-evaluated everything. How the hell did I end up here in a hammock hugging a woman I barely know and with no medical facilities for days? Where's the responsible Eden? If I died, what would happen? Would they send my body down the river or be cremated?

I take it as a sign the sensible voice of my conscience is warning me the adventure is coming to an end. As much as I've appreciated stepping outside my comfort zone, opening my mind, and living in a world I never believed existed, I have to go home to family and friends.

As we wash our faces and hands in the shallows of the river, Kaikare stares at me with concern. Whether she senses my indifference or it's her own, I'm relieved there's been no sign of the shaman.

Then he appears as if silently summoned.

Jesus, there isn't any rustling of foliage to warn us. He simply steps from the jungle onto the sand. My heart jumps to my throat. He didn't approve of our leave.

Kaikare nods to him, her poker face unreadable. I want to stand behind her, then stop myself. We're in this —trouble—together. He stops a distance away from us, and she plods a few paces closer yet a safe distance as though she learned the distancing rule from Samuel. He speaks to her, and she lowers her head. I follow her lead. Their conversation goes back and forth several rounds, and not once do I detect heat in their words. By the time I glance up, he's disappearing into the jungle once more. I follow her back to the fire, dying to know what was said. She picks up my bag and holds it with an outstretched arm.

I nod and take it. Her expression changes as though she's struggling inside, and I take it as a sign I'm receiving marching orders.

"It. Time," she manages.

My heart leaps hearing her words. I want to hug her until I realize what she's saying, and my excitement falls flat. Leave on foot? The ball of panic—always present— slowly grows. "I should wait here for Asoo."

She frowns at my words. A hand reaches for mine. "Come."

Slinging my backpack over my shoulder, she leads me into the jungle, pushing past vines and weaving around some of the thickest tree trunks I've seen. I stop to rest momentarily, gripping the narrow trunk of one of the more common trees. Kaikare waves her hand, shaking her head. I let go, and on closer inspection, realize the tree is unlike others. Fire ants swarm the branches. "Shit." I brush my hands and shake myself. She gives me a long look before leading me into the sunlight of thinning overgrowth to a garden of sorts with an abundance of orchids, hot-lips flowers, and heliconias.

A distant song halts my step, mixed vowels of no meaning yet harmonic and mesmerizing.

The voice of an angel.

45

EDEN

Whenever my heel hits the ground, I focus on trying to be lighter on my feet, now aware the plants hold value. With every snap of a twig, I wish I had more grace. Maybe if I did ballet lessons as a child, I'd be less of a lead foot.

Standing by a kapok tree, the shaman sings a harmonic tune. His eyes are closed, and both hands are on the tree, fingers splayed over the bark. The size of the tree is so imposing, it consumes most of the sun's rays. I didn't notice Kaikare slip out of my sight until she comes to me holding a prickly heart-shaped pod. This time, I realize she's leading me to the village.

Keep your distance. Samuel's words play over in my mind as I follow her to the cooking fire, where she breaks open the pod to reveal dozens of reddish seeds. After scooping them into a pot of water, she then places it over the heat.

A loud crack has me jumping. The heavens open, and heavy rain drenches me in seconds. With my backpack over my head, I sprint to Samuel's hut.

Everything is like we left it.

I strip out of my wet clothes, not for being cold as the rain is refreshing, more so my clothes need to dry before musk seeps in.

Kicking off my sneakers, I heave at the smell of my socks. I peel them off for the first time in days. Come to think of it, lifting my arm, I get a whiff of me. Ugh. The socks and I both require a good scrub. It's weird I didn't notice until I thought of how society has an expectation of body odor. The subtle musky odor of the Ularans isn't offensive, and I guess it's grown on me. Even still, I'm washing because my feet reek.

Laying my soaked clothes on the wooden table, I tie the skirt around my waist, slipping the beads over my head and shoulders.

My stomach growls, reminding me I've barely eaten. Remembering Samuel left a note to help with some of the foods' nutritional value and what is safe to eat, I scour through his case. "What's this?" It's a handwritten piece of paper. No, a wad of notes on medicinal uses of some of the plants. I flick through the notes reading the descriptions. Many of the plants aid in killing bacteria and parasites, and I understand now how everyone remains relatively well. It's why Samuel reiterated foreign viruses were a threat. Anti-inflammatory, anti-cancer, digestion, blood purifiers, cough relief, bronchitis, diarrhea—there is a plant for almost every known ailment.

Rain continues to pound the palm roof. At times, I worry it's not going to hold. I curl into the hammock with a handful of notes and read more about Samuel's findings, staring at his neat handwriting, imagining the passion driving him to do this.

My gut tightens the more I reflect, missing the man who led me here.

I hold the paper to my chest, close my eyes, and imagine him talking to me. I allow his imaginary voice to envelop me like a warm blanket. Until realization hits— my being here has tortured him. I don't want to be the reason he fails his obligation, knowing the extent of his study and how close he is to finding what he needs for pharmaceutical research. Is love a strong enough reason to be together at this point in time?

Before I come to a conclusion, the rain stops, and Kaikare is at the door waving for me to follow her. I want to hug her when she leads me to the stream.

A pot of red liquid sits on the embankment. She raises a finger, and without hesitation, I wade in, grabbing a handful of scented leaves to wash as I go. Minutes later, she waves me out of the water. "Already? I could lay here all afternoon." She smiles at me, and yet I know it's not a sign she comprehends my words.

Clambering over the edge, she hands me a handful of leaves to dry myself. I'm still not accustomed to being naked in front of people and push down my inhibition and insecurities. She glides the leaves over my back like a squeegee cleaning glass. After drying where I can reach with the leaves, I squeeze the remaining water out of my hair and secure it on my head in a messy bun.

Wrapping the straps of the reed skirt around my waist, I tie a knot while Kaikare bends and scoops red paste from the pot. She adjusts my shoulders, so I'm standing upright and proceeds to paint my back with a sequence of strokes and angles. Freshly washed and painted, I sense it's in preparation for something. I pray it's not an initiation like the one I witnessed with fire ants.

Kaikare continues to paint my front. I close my eyes when she touches my chest, although this time, I don't stop her. I focus on breathing and tell myself it's not weird. At all. The strokes extend to my limbs. I open my eyes and admire the long lines along the length of my legs. Do they stand for more than simple decorative body art? She takes my chin in her palm, angling my face in assessment. My forehead, chin, and temples are dotted. I smile as I look into her eyes, eyes holding understanding, honey-colored eyes different than everyone else's here. She holds my gaze. Seconds pass, and it's like time stands still with no judgment, only understanding of the things we have learned about each other. Her lids close and open in a slow movement, and then she smiles.

🌴

Until today, I was ignorant of how rain and tropical rain differed.

Back home, we would say, *it's bucketing down*. Although the worst of the rainy season has passed, Mother Nature decides otherwise, and the rains have paved a small stream past Samuel's hut to the round house. Kaikare keeps me under the cover of the long house where the fires are protected by high makeshift palm roofs and small moats to lead the water away. And this isn't even the wet season.

A faint sound of cheering comes from the jungle. My eyes are unaccustomed to seeing anything through the blanket of rain falling in sheets rather than drops. Peering into the gray, I make out naked human figures waving spears in the air as they approach.

"Samuel?"

I stand and walk toward the edge, stopping myself from running toward them. Shit, would I have to keep my distance from him? I can't think straight with the sound of my heartbeat in my ears. I'm smiling ear to ear as the warriors emerge from the green carrying animals attached to long sticks of bamboo on their shoulders. Not caring about the deluge of water, the women run to them cheering and jumping about, leading them toward the fire. How long has it been since they left on their hunt with Samuel and Timenneng with them for part of the journey? Sixteen days? It dawns on me the excitement extends from the men returning to their loved ones. The meat is much-needed food, and everyone was waiting for this hunt. Strung up by the feet are a wild pig, two small deer, and the largest snake I've seen.

"Is it a boa?"

No one answers since I'm a good distance from the other women. Even if my words were understood, I doubt I could be heard over the applause. Immediately, the animals are prepared before being secured over the fire pits.

Everyone's bellies will be satisfied tonight.

Twilight is barely noticeable under a canopy of gray.

It reflects my mood, and I'm going stir crazy. We're stuck in the hut, and I am away from the others, not knowing what to do with myself. My stomach rumbles at the aroma of spit-roasted meat. God, I could eat a full animal on my own. Sitting on the ground, I pick up a rock and make squiggly lines in the dirt. Kaikare leans in, and her brows pull tight. "I'm doodling," I tell her.

She gazes up at me. "Doo-lin."

"Yes." I want to hug her. "Yes." I smile at her like an idiot and point to the meat, then rub my stomach. "I'm hungry. Hungry."

Kaikare shakes her head and points to the meat cooking over the fire.

"What? I can't eat anything?" I ask in desperation.

She brings her hand from her shoulder to her hips in a fast ax action.

"I take that as a no." Ugh, what's their word for no? "Awarö?" *Bad?*

She tilts her head at me. The meat isn't bad, I already know that. I wish she could explain why I can't eat it.

She stands and leaves me a moment before returning with yuca bread and potatoes on a palm leaf. She shoves it in front of me, and I take it. Without waiting for permission, I down it quickly and look for more. Kaikare stands and gestures for me to do the same. I guess it looks like seconds are out of the question.

The rain has eased to a drizzle, and we walk through the sludge to the round house. Inside, in the far back corner, the shaman kneels, smoking a pipe. A massive-feathered headdress sits on his head. Small fires dot the dirt, and it's light enough to make out the blue, yellow, and scarlet feathers on his crown. Across his cheeks are strokes of red like mine. He glances up and nods. Is he expecting me?

A woven mat lays on the floor in front of him. It hits me—I'm being prepared for my own ayahuasca ceremony. "God help me," I mutter as I remember Samuel's reaction after ingesting the tea.

A bowl is placed to his left, feathers tied to strings of teeth and bones to his right. He lifts the twine holding feathers, bones, and teeth and shakes it like a musical instrument before breaking into song.

"I'm not sure I'm ready for this," I say to Kaikare as she assists me to kneel before him. "I mean what if I have a reaction? I know I'm going to puke my guts up, and hell, maybe lose control of my bowels, which I prefer not to think about, but it's the racing heart and shit that scares me most. I could have a heart attack because we all react to drugs differently. Your people probably fall in the body of the bell-shaped graph of a desired drug effect. Some fall on the lip of no effect, yet knowing my luck, I'll fall in the minority where it's probably fatal..."

Shit.

I go to stand, only she stops me and wipes the tears I'm oblivious to. She places a hand on my cheek and smiles, a finger circling between us as though she's telling me she'll be here for me. "I hope you know CPR," I murmur. "So, this is it. I die in the rainforest, and my father gets to say, 'I warned you' at my funeral."

I shut up when a cup-sized bowl is handed to me. *I'm already crazy.* I shoot Kaikare a worried look before downing it in one go.

I gag and cough on the vile taste, handing her back the cup. "It's disgusting," I say. It reminds me of a night on tequila. Spluttering, I try to spit the bitterness from my mouth.

She lets go of my hand to refill the bowl by the shaman's side. He blows smoke over the bowl from a pipe and returns to his song. When I down around seven cups, I hold up my hand to refuse anymore. The shaman blows smoke into my face and chest. The ground seems to move beneath me. I fall back onto my rear and close my eyes.

The room spins as if I'm intoxicated, lying in bed and can't sleep—the very worst part of being drunk.

Breathe.

You can do this.

My heart thuds behind my ribs, a quickened beat as though in a race, and I'm sprinting to the finish line. My breaths quicken, and no matter how I try to calm my thoughts, it's helpless to slow my vital organs' reaction to the brew. I'm guessing my heart wants this shit out of me as much as I do.

After a series of flips and turns, my stomach gurgles in warning, and I say, "I'm ready."

Lying on my side seems natural, and I'm not sure how many minutes—or hours—pass before I shoot up on all fours ready to puke.

Beneath me, I sense a clean bowl right before the regurgitated tea finds its way out. I sweat profusely, heave and cough, while my gut continues to twist and contract. Wiping my mouth on several occasions, I sit back on my heels, saying, "Okay. I'm done," until a demon possesses me once more, and I throw myself forward in an exorcism on my soul.

Burning wood overpowers my senses. When smoke hits my face, I'm forced back onto my butt as though a ghost pushed me. The shaman's harmonious tunes fill my head, and I'm swaying back and forth, handing control over to him. A shiver leads to trembles quaking over my body. A warm hand guides me to lie on the mat. Each vowel echoes as though my brain is trying to find meaning in a dark cave. My lips tingle. Spots form before my eyes, a kaleidoscope of brilliant color in the most unusual patterns and brightness I could ever imagine. The brightness is in my head, and before me, as though I could reach out and touch the rainbow on steroids, something alien reaches in for my soul so that it can witness the astral show. Colors twist and turn, slow to almost nothing before returning to their former brilliance. I don't want it to stop for it's not only the color, I'm overwhelmed with emotion and pure joy.

The nausea builds again, only I manage not to puke. The tingling travels up my arms and over my body, and my thought processes unravel as if something is inside of me, coursing through my veins until its fingers probe the lock to my brain. The doors to my world open to allow this alien intelligence to rifle through my thoughts. The spirit is stronger and more powerful than me. I sense its strength without fear, only endless love. Memories flash before me, and along with them, emotions undo my resolve—my time with Ethan and the moment he killed my soul and my life being controlled by my father, never being free to live the way I choose. Tears come with more images morphing to my friends, their faces appearing and disappearing, a movie on fast-forward until I'm visualizing a life-size image of Samuel.

He stares back at me as though searching for my life force, blue eyes holding my focus. My chest rises as though my heart reaches for him. My grandmother's face appears, her beautiful smile telling me I'm doing fine and to reach for the stars. She morphs into a black jaguar, and I sense I'm looking at a mirror image of myself. My soul or whatever part of me is connecting with this higher intelligence glides into dark nothingness in a universe surrounded by stars and other souls. For a moment, I believe I hold knowledge for all there is to know. If anyone were to ask me a question, I'd have an answer. Colored wings coming from the stars soar toward me in the form of beautiful butterflies. They speak to me in the voice of the shaman, and I understand every foreign word. *Evol* is whispered. One word. I don't know what it means, but it shoots emotion into my head. Rain falls in the form of butterflies all whispering to me, nothing comprehensible yet full of meaning.

Life.

I feel life.

The click of insects has its own language as does the chatter of animals. I hear everything differently and feel connected to what lies beyond the border of the jungle. Gone is the fear I held inside. Fear of the unknown. Fear of what could harm me. I understand now we all have a place. A chance to live harmoniously together by respecting each creature and their purpose on earth.

My eyes open to darkness, the shaman's song, and a hand on my shoulder. The trees rustle their leaves, speaking to me. I turn to the jungle, the trees glowing green, their bioluminescence like we saw last night. Each tree is lit up in a network of nerves, and a web penetrates beneath the soil to the roots. It's as if my face is to the ground, and I'm seeing what lies beneath as you would when in the ocean and staring beneath the surface. A central nervous system connects one tree to the next, electric energy firing between each, silently communicating with one another, and tonight, me. I feel every vibration of life. I hear the whisper of the trees, the energy surrounding us, emanating oxygen to the world in clouds of green.

Our lifeforce.

🌴

Everywhere I look is as though we have two suns shining bright light upon us. Before my experience, I perceived the world through a cloudy lens, a heavy fog clouding my thoughts. Today, I woke with more clarity than I've ever experienced in my life. Even now, out in the fields with the other women, the ax is light in my hands, and there's a sense of purpose that I didn't have before.

Looking into the jungle, beyond the trees, I have clarity. A connection. Maybe I'm still high? I don't care because I have found everything I was searching for—my eudaimonia—and I don't want to lose the feeling of infinite happiness.

Kaikare smiles at me, knowing my secret despite no words exchanged between us. By lunchtime, I'm starving, and despite the new sense of energy soaring through my veins, I am shaky after puking equal measures of my body weight last night.

I stop to wipe my brow, the sweat even drips from my chin with my body trying to eliminate the toxins after the ayahuasca cleansing. I have no experience in microbiology, but if I was carrying a disease, I think the tea destroyed it.

Heavy gray clouds loom overhead. Hurrying along, we carry the produce in woven baskets and head back to the village center, dumping our day's work on the ground near the fire to keep the insects at bay.

I'm eager to learn how to prepare the yuca since I'm more in tune with their ways. Before I consider my words, the children come cheering from the direction of the river. Kaikare listens before waving for me to follow.

I want to run to the river. It could be Samuel, and there's a chance he could be sick after being away for so long. We reach the sandy beach, and I stop to catch my breath, the lightness in my chest fades.

"Hey, is everything okay?" I say to Asoo.

Asoo hands me my phone. "Your friend, Amy, say it urgent."

"What?" I take my phone from him and read her messages. Skimming over the words, my thoughts racing to the worst possible scenarios.

> Eden!

> I hope you get this message soon. I'm so scared. I don't know what to do and need you here to help me. I'm in Iquitos alone because Yasmine is with Michael. I don't care that I'm alone, but I'm worried about her, and you're the only one who seems to get through to her when she refuses to listen. She's about to take a tea with a shaman, only this shaman isn't reputable because I have asked around. Some people have died in his ceremonies!

> She won't listen to me, and what's weird is Michael asked for you and Samuel to come. That made me panic because he sounds worried. I don't know what to do, and when I tried to talk her out of it, she got angry with me. She's due to take the ceremony in two days. Please hurry!

I glance up to Kaikare, the well of tears in my eyes blur my vision. "My friends need me. I have to go." I blink the tears away and swipe my eyes. "Asoo, please give me a moment to grab my things, and please explain to Kaikare the need for me to leave. Tell her I'm going to miss her."

I don't think, I just act and leave my friends on the bank to sprint to Samuel's hut. My throat burns as I gasp for air. This is possibly the last time I'll see Kaikare, the shaman, and the smiling faces in this hidden village. After last night, my perspective has switched. Even though I couldn't live here forever, the notion of staying for a few months is appealing. Now, I understand Samuel's desire to live here and be connected to every living thing.

Denied of that choice, my decision is made for me without a chance to say goodbye to Samuel.

I hope the universe knows what it's doing.

46

EDEN

Beneath the scattering of clouds, the broccoli jungle fades, and with it the very place I left my heart. Looking away from the window to my hands, I trace the outline of red Vs no amount of soap could remove in a day.

Yesterday when I entered the resort in Canaima with a painted face and limbs the looks from the staff were priceless. Did they think I was innocent? A grin spreads across my face. The sense of belonging and the memories will stay with me always.

When the plane touches down and I regain Wi-Fi, I'm searching for the next flight to Iquitos.

The airfares are double the usual fare, and thankfully, I have enough savings since I've barely spent a cent these past few weeks.

In the hub of the airport, people bustle around me. I have a few hours between flights, and it gives me a chance to grab some food. I'm craving meat, yet I decide on fruit—a banana and an apple since my stomach has been in knots since I first saw Asoo by the river. Security and the police are everywhere I look. The news flashes on the television, the presenter speaks in Spanish, and I have no idea what's being communicated. Living in a village sheltered from the rest of the world, I'm clueless to world events, although the political world is volatile, and I could be headed straight into a shitstorm. Keeping a low profile, I stick to myself and remain in the terminal for my flight. As much as I want to put it off, I have to call my father. Thankfully, I'm seated away from other travelers as they'll hear him roar. Inhaling a deep breath, I mentally prepare myself for a dressing-down.

"You have reached Winston Monteford, CEO of Monte Hotels. I'm not able to take your call, so please leave a message regarding the nature of your inquiry."

I let all the air go out of my lungs. Shit, it must be around midnight in Adelaide.

"Dad, I didn't want to send a text. Only a quick call to let you know I'm fine. I know you heard I separated from the girls, and you're disappointed with my decision, but I'm safe. I'm meeting up with my friends tonight, and we'll be heading home in a few days. I'll call you from the airport and let you know our arrival time and if there are any delays. Looking forward to seeing Mum and you, and of course, Will, Faith, and little Seb. Love you all."

Pressing my hand to my chest, I feel the measure of my heart being torn between missing my family, leaving Samuel and a jungle village I have grown to love.

People around me have joined a queue to board the plane to Iquitos. Following the line, I walk the aisle, take my seat, and sink into my chair. I relax into the headrest, close my eyes, and refuse to open them as the plane soars along the runway. Finally, I'm a step closer to seeing my friends.

I arrive in Iquitos around nine at night and am

required to pass through customs with my luggage. My suitcase is full of stuff I now consider unnecessary.

Amy is waiting in the airport terminal somewhere. When the crowd disperses, she waves her hands at me, then she sprints and leaps into my arms, almost knocking us both to the floor. I regain my balance, and she lets out a sob, her face nestled into my chest. "I've missed you so much."

"Me, too," I tell her, squeezing my arms around her shoulders.

Arm in arm, we head outside, humidity smacking my face, a reminder I'm back in the jungle.

"We get around on tuk-tuks," she says. "I'll get us one to get to the city. It's like Canaima here, you can't access it by car, only plane or boat."

I nod. "So, you researched Canaima?"

"Yep. I almost came to you." She turns and waves down the three-wheeled motorized vehicle. Amy tells the driver of our destination, and he helps me with my luggage, putting it at our feet in the squishy cabin. He veers into the traffic without looking, and I grab Amy's arm.

She ignores my anxiety and instead nods at my face. "Is this a new form of makeup?"

"I can't concentrate right now, so it's a story for another time." Her brows pull together, and before she says anything else, I ask, "What's important is you tell me everything that's happened with Yasmine."

She shakes her head as though she's exasperated. "She only talks to him, not me, and if I'm around, she bloody whispers. I mean, what the fuck is that about? You'll barely recognize her. Can someone change in a matter of weeks?"

Reflecting on my journey, I nod. "Sometimes, yes."

We stop out front of a colonial-style hotel wall to wall with the other buildings. The hall is beautifully tiled with historical black and white pictures lining the long passageway.

"This is mine," she tells me and opens the door to a quaint room with one queen bed. "It's just you and me, *ba-by*."

I laugh and yet head straight to the bed and flop backward. "I have missed the luxury of a mattress."

Amy screws up her face. "What have you been sleeping on?"

"A hammock." I kick off my sandals—my smelly sneakers dumped in a bin at the airport—and lift my legs onto the bed. "And as much as I want to talk about my adventure first, you need to tell me what the plan is for tomorrow because I'm not going to keep my eyes open much longer."

Amy lands on the bed beside me with more energy than necessary. "Yasmine is in preparation, apparently."

Linking my fingers behind my head, I stretch my elbows wide. "How do you know?"

"Michael calls me. He keeps asking if you and Samuel are coming? He mentions *Paulo* and how Samuel would understand."

Asking for Samuel and me doesn't sit right with me. I'm her friend. I can talk her out of most things if warranted, and besides, Michael is aware of his friend's commitment. "Why is Michael allowing her to go through with it if he's concerned?"

"They both went to some sort of shaman festival. You meet around thirty shamans and choose the one who's right for you. This guy is from New York. We're not sure why she chose him, but he convinced her to go down the river to his little camp. His fee was close to double the others. I mean, I saw some of the shamans. They looked like spiritual, beautiful people, but this guy appeared fake. I don't trust him, and there have been whispers his brew has killed people, although no one has proved it. I hope it's all whispers."

"Wait. You pay?" I'm so naïve.

She nods. "It's a commercial thing here. Part of the reason many come to visit. Camps are set up even for corporate businesses from around the world. And there are women's groups as well as professionally organized ones, yet Yasmine decided to go with this Paulo from New York who could sell ice to an Eskimo."

It doesn't sound like Yasmine. She's smarter than this.

"Do you know where the camp is?"

"Yep. I have a map with directions from Michael."

"You said he calls you. How would he if he's in the jungle?"

"Michael has a satellite phone."

"Oh, right."

Does Samuel have one too?

After texting Asoo that I'm here safe at the hotel and mentioning Paulo's name, I climb under the sheets and curl into a ball. "We'll find her tomorrow," I murmur. My eyelids shutter closed as the energy drains away.

Thick, moist air in the tropics isn't the easiest to breathe at any time, and if you combine it with pollution from the tuk-tuk and motorcycles, it's even more difficult. Amy and

I wait on a landing for a boat to take us along the Amazon River. At least the air is cleaner here.

"I've booked us on a tour boat," Amy informs me. "It's large enough for thirty people interested in visiting a small river village."

I wipe my forehead with the back of my hand. "Oh really. A small village."

"Yeah. I thought it might interest you since the help in these villages comes from missionaries and volunteers."

"Right. It does, but you know my interest before was simply to find Samuel, right?"

She gives me a long look. "I didn't want to mention his name."

Giving her an easy smile, I shrug my shoulders. "I miss him for sure. I also believe when his work is done, he'll come looking for me. For now, we both have to live our lives until that day comes."

"God, you sound mature and so confident."

I laugh once and yet say nothing because we are interrupted by the tour guide, and we're directed onto a boat. It's a civilized means of travel, everyone with their own seat and a canopy to protect us from the sun.

"This is cool, right?" Amy says as the boat picks up speed, and we sail along the water.

I smile at Amy. "Yeah, this is cool." We point out birds as they fly overhead and chat about the rainforest bordering the river, although it's nowhere near as majestic or towering as the jungle where I've lived these past few weeks.

I sit in awe, staring out at the impressive Amazon River. I'm not sure how many miles wide it is. The current and body of water are more powerful than the smaller rivers I voyaged near Angel Falls. A pink dolphin surfaces and swims alongside the boat. We laugh and call out to the dolphin as though it were following us.

After a couple of hours, we arrive at the small village. While everyone disembarks for a village tour, we cross through on tuk-tuk to a tributary river on the other side. Traditional and Western structures line small, sealed pathways along with a church. Children play, dogs wander, and we interrupt a football game with enthusiastic barefoot teenagers yelling as the ball passes sticks for goal markings. The overland segue is waiting for us, and it then takes us fifteen minutes until we board a motorized canoe. I smile at Amy's glee. It's a little more streamlined than my previous canoe experiences, yet it still features a plank of wood as a seat.

My focus is to chat about Yasmine, and yet I'm more relaxed than I should be in the thick, uncomfortable heat. Sailing along the river, the breeze in my freshly shampooed hair, and surrounded by rainforest, it's almost natural for me to seek comfort in this environment. It gives me a sense of awareness to honor myself. Do what's right for me. Enjoy the little things and stop stressing about the future, especially the fear of being loved. It has taken me all these years to realize love is more than something found as part of a couple. It has to start from within. In Ulara, I learned to love myself.

In my heart I know Samuel and I will be together one day. It makes leaving him and his work okay because I'm being true to myself as well. I found how helping others as I did in the Pemón camp is rewarding and important to me. It helped me to understand him better. I'm not sure I understand the level of Samuel's commitment, although over the last couple of weeks, I understand why, as I too have grown to love the Ularan community, the people, and the place.

The jungle has grounded and lifted my spirit. During the tea ceremony, I felt harmonious to the earth, to every living creature, and I developed a tangible unity with the universe. I'll never lose that bond.

"It's not too far ahead," Amy says after speaking with the driver. She carefully steps over the planks to sit beside me. "What are you going to say to her?"

We didn't speak much on the previous boat ride with other people sitting close to us. "Besides what I mentioned at breakfast? I have a few things I've mulled over that might help her rethink her decision. If taking the tea is what she desires, we'll help her find a reputable shaman. There are hundreds of experienced shamans, so I'm curious why she chose a guy from New York. When we find out why, then we can negotiate with her."

The driver pulls into a poorly constructed small pier, and I realize by the buildings high on stilts, this area is susceptible to extreme flooding in the wet season. There are only a couple of structures reminding me of the Ularan village, only sturdier with the assistance of modern tools. I now understand the need for rubber boots that are provided when we booked this trip. The driver waits for us in the boat. We slip on the boots, leaving our flip-flops on the boat, and walk through the muddy water pooling ankle deep.

We only have minutes to convince Yasmine to leave with us.

"Can you imagine wanting to stay here?" Amy whispers while watching me peruse the palm-leaf thatched roof and open walls of the two huts.

I ignore her comment, my senses alerted to a herbal

aroma hanging in the muggy air. I cough at the unpleasantness. A small indigenous woman dressed in a green t-shirt and pants approaches, almost camouflaged by the surroundings. She speaks to us in Spanish.

Amy talks over her. "We're looking for Yasmine and Michael."

Lines deepen on the woman's forehead. The hand behind her back reveals itself as she takes a cigarette to her mouth and sucks while giving us a once-over. She puffs out smoke in my face as though my facial paintwork offends her.

Doing my utmost not to cough, I follow her past similar structures with walls reminding me of log cabins. She points to a treehouse. Amy and I step up the ladder, my feet slipping in the rubber boots, and I grip the side in case I misjudge a step.

On reaching the top, we scramble onto all fours before standing to find Yasmine in a hammock with Michael. My entry isn't delicate, so surprise turns to suspicion when both remain sleeping, especially since the small room reeks of smoke, musk, and sex.

"Did you really come here to sleep?" I snap.

Michael jolts. The hammock sways and both scramble to be upright.

"Eden? I mean, how? Why are you here?" Yasmine croaks. Her hand clasps her throat.

"You sound terrible. Are you sick?" I ask. She shakes her head. "Okay, well, I'm here because our holiday is almost over, and it's time for us to meet up and go home."

She shoots me a warning look with narrowed eyes. Yet I sense she doesn't have the energy to argue. "This is the last thing I wanted to tick off before we leave," she says, with her hand remaining on her throat.

"I know," I say in a calm voice.

"Did Samuel come with you?" Michael probes.

"Why would he?" I snap.

Michael glances at Amy. "Did you give her the message?"

Yasmine scowls at Michael. "What message?"

"I was concerned about you, babe, that's all." His hand slides across her forehead and down her cheek.

Yasmine slaps his hand away. "What message?"

"He told me to tell Eden and Samuel to come as you were putting yourself in danger being here with Paulo," Amy states.

Yasmine glares at Michael. "Danger? You recommended him."

"Babe. You chose him. You were adamant. I know you've been high for days, but this was your decision."

"We're taking you back to Iquitos," I tell her. "I know you want to do this but not here and not today. You're sick, and you need to get well first. You have to cleanse and be healthy. In your condition, it could be dangerous to take the brew."

Her eyes widen.

"Quite knowledgeable, Eden. Just where is Samuel?" Michael asks in a low, deep voice.

"He had an exploration. I know you understand his commitment to his work, and besides, I haven't seen him in almost three weeks."

"Where did you stay while he's away?" He stalks closer to me.

"In Canaima. I told Amy where I was."

"I've been to Canaima. These markings aren't from there," he says, holding my chin and turning my face.

I push his hand off me. "I went to help in a Pemón

village. The doctor needed some extra hands, and most of the volunteers had left."

He raises a single brow. "Right. Nice try."

We both turn when Yasmine groans and Amy wraps a hand around her back.

"I can't believe you kept her here in this condition?" I gasp. Right now, I wish I had some medical knowledge. I wish Samuel were here.

He crosses his arms and juts out his chin. "She refused to leave. It's why I sent for you." I push past him and assist Amy with Yasmine. "She's still high. Give her some time for the drugs to wear off."

"What drugs?" Amy yells at him.

"It doesn't matter. We're leaving now," I tell them both. "There's a driver waiting for us."

"Eden, but I want to—"

"Not here and not today," I repeat. "Michael, you need to help us get Yasmine down the ladder."

I make my way down onto the muddy ground and take Yasmine's arm to balance her landing.

"What's going on here?" I swing around to a man with straggly blond hair falling around his shoulders.

"We're taking our friend," I tell him. "And don't worry, she doesn't want a refund. Keep the money, only there'll be no ceremony."

He looks at Yasmine. "Is this what you want?" he says in an American accent.

"You know what I wanted. Now my friends are here, and I'm not well, so—"

"I have stuff that will help you get better. You have to talk to me, girl. I can't fix what I don't know."

"If..." I say in a stern voice, "... you're the shaman you claim to be, you could heal without instruction. You

316

would simply know as the forest would talk to you." I slip Yasmine's arm over my shoulder and take a step past Paulo, ignoring his glare.

"You and I need to chat," Michael whispers.

"We do," I say but not in the same context.

We arrive at the small village, and a tuk-tuk takes us to the missionary's office as we've missed the boat back to Iquitos. It's a silent ride because I'm too angry at Michael to calmly discuss anything and equally worried about Yasmine.

The door opens, and a middle-aged nun in a traditional long, white dress with a white veil concealing her hair and part of her face steps forward. "You welcome to stay, boat can take you in morning. We have beds for you," she manages in English, her Spanish tongue thick. "Young man can sleep in other room. No see ladies with ring."

"Is there a doctor here?" I ask her when my friends leave to find their room. "My friend has a sore throat, and I'd like him to take a look."

"Yes, child. He go to you after dinner," she says in her broken English.

"Thank you. We appreciate your kind hospitality."

"Would you like some tea?"

Knowing Yasmine is safe with Amy, I take a chair at the table. "Do you mind telling me about your work here, Sister?"

She opens a tin to reveal cookies inside. "You like Alfajore? You call them shortbread."

I smile, my mouth already watering. "I would very

much. Thank you."

It's something to sweeten my thoughts before I question Michael.

The following morning, I tap gently on Yasmine's bedroom door. "Can I come in?"

"Not if you're going to lecture me," she groans.

I open the door and peek in. Yasmine is still in bed. "Hey." I stride to her side and sit on the single wooden bed, lean in, and hug her. "It's not a lecture," I whisper.

"You're lucky I'm too sick to yell at you because I told you my plans in Ilhéus," she starts.

"I know. And I respect that. Only he wasn't the right shaman for you. I know what Michael said…" I add quickly when she opens her mouth to interject, "… because I've also experienced the tea."

"You have?" Her eyes round, and she pushes up onto her elbows. "With Samuel in the jungle?"

I nod slowly and not in an excited way. "It was part of my journey, and the ceremony wasn't with Samuel."

"What did you see and feel?" Her words come out fast.

"All our experiences are different, which is why I want you to benefit from it and not fall sick." I slide tight, dark ringlets away from her face and smile at her. "How is your throat?"

"A little better. The antibiotics are helping some."

"There'll be another time for you, I promise, and it won't be with Paulo. As for Michael, I'll be questioning him because things could've turned out far worse if you went ahead."

"Why did he want Samuel to come?" she asks, her hand resting on the base of her neck.

"I'm not sure. It's another thing I'll be discussing with him. Right now, we need to get you up and showered, so we can catch the next boat back to Iquitos."

47

SAMUEL

The plane descends, and the Amazon River widens far more than the one he calls home. His eyes are fixed on the window, and he looks below as the plane approaches the runway. He should've relaxed more on the flights to regain his energy. The thought of not seeing Eden for many months caused his chest to tighten, and he couldn't breathe. He closes his eyes when the wheels screech, his shoulders less heavy. The voice over the speaker talks in Spanish. He listens to directions and waits for the time to be mentioned—*6:31 p.m.*

He rushes through customs, the first in the line, and takes the first tuk-tuk he sees into the city, praying he has not missed her.

His exploration was a success, despite him not eating anything substantial for days. His critical thinking directed him to what needed to be done. He pushed through hunger, hiked miles with only acai berries to eat, found water amongst the plants with flowering plants in his pack.

The down trip was harder. His thoughts went to her.

She was the best and worst distraction. The image of her ingrained in his brain guided him *home,* knowing she was waiting for him.

He was weak and tired, but it didn't matter, but then he found her backpack missing. Kaikare filled him in. He'd missed her by a day. Asoo came by the next morning, mentioned Paulo, and Samuel has since been on plane after plane.

He hopes she's at the same hotel that she mentioned in a text to Asoo. If not, he doubts he'll find her in a city of half a million people or if she's in one of the water villages dotting the river.

He dreams of holding her, making love to her, yet he can barely remain upright. He pays the driver in American dollars and is grateful the hotel reception is open.

"No reservation? I'm sorry we're fully booked. There's a hotel up the road," the receptionist says in Spanish.

He places one hand on the desk to balance himself. "I'm looking for Eden Monteford," he tells her. "Is she staying here?"

"I'm sorry, sir, we can't give out confidential information."

"Samuel?"

He turns at the sound of her voice.

She runs to him, almost knocking him off balance. Her arms wrap around him. "You're okay."

"Barely, but now I've found you, I'm more than okay." He kisses Eden holding her tightly, wishing he didn't have to let go. He breaks the kiss and leans in so their heads are huddled together.

"You're safe that's all that matters," she rasps.

Safe in each other's arms they allow themselves a

quiet minute to process their emotion. Tears stream down Eden's cheek. His heart is near bursting. His resolve cracks and he cries quietly with Eden in his arms. Gathering some strength, he takes in a deep breath, and inhales her scent.

She's all he needs to survive.

Eden leans back, her eyes flicking over his face. "You're thinner." She runs her fingers over his cheeks. "Come, let's get you up the stairs."

Stairs.

One arm hooked around his waist, she guides him up each step and unlocks the door with one hand. She leads him to her bed and grabs her phone. "I'm sending Amy a text to bring extra food back for you. She's with Yasmine and Michael."

"What was the message about Paulo?" he croaks.

Eden curls up beside him on the bed. "It's a story that can wait." Her hand is under his t-shirt, stroking his ribs. "How much weight have you lost?"

"It happens on these trips, although it's not as concerning as the thought of losing you."

She pushes up so their lips meet. His walls are down. Everything about her arouses him—her scent, her touch. The warmth radiating from her calms him like no other. And the memory of him between her legs. His fingers curl around her hair. She owns his heart and soul. He kisses her with more passion and need than he believed possible. She fuels his energy. In minutes, they are naked, their legs intertwined.

With frantic breaths, he sinks into her, rasping, "I love you," against her mouth. Unlike the last time, he moves slowly, lovingly, inside of her.

Delicate hands hold his face while blue eyes demand

his focus. She waits for his breathing to slow and whispers, "I love you, too."

He collapses onto the sheet beside her. His eyes heavy and overcome with exhaustion. "When do you leave?"

"Tomorrow," she whispers. "I'm sorry."

"Don't be. It was inevitable. It's not goodbye. I'll come and find you. I promise."

Knowing his words to be true, he closes his eyes, his heart finally finding peace.

"Where are they now?" Samuel asks Eden while sitting at the table after eating breakfast.

"In Yasmine's room, I assume. He managed to worm his way out of any blame and said he was doing what Yasmine wanted. Yet he knew you would come. Why is that?"

Samuel crosses his arms and leans back in the chair, his gaze rising to the ceiling while he constructs his explanation. "Michael knows about the shaman in Ulara. Well, bits and not as much as you... only that their ayahuasca recipe is pure and more effective than any other brew. He wants me to divulge what plants are used and the secrets of the village. He's been using subtle blackmail for years. And yes, I stupidly told him some things when I first decided to stay in the village as I needed to report to someone my whereabouts for safety. He has tried different teas with shamans over the years. We met Paul, or Paulo as he's now known, when he first arrived in Peru. He stated he wanted to become a shaman and learn their ways. To be a healer takes many years and a special skill to connect with the forest. It's not a job you apply for and can be trained in a year. Yet Paulo was determined and thought he could make a living if he remained here. He married a local from one of the villages, and it's worked out for him. Only he's not a true shaman. I believe he can be dangerous because he doesn't take anyone's past medical history into account or any underlying symptoms. To him, it's a fix-all brew. He mixes too much caffeine into it, and it not only makes you sick and gives palpitations, but for someone with an underlying heart condition, it can be potentially fatal."

"Amy said people have died in his care."

Leaning forward, he rests his weary arms on the table. "Two deaths. The first happened years ago when someone stood while still high from his concoction and fell and hit their head. He said it was beyond his control and not his fault. The second had a stomach ulcer and died in Lima a few days after leaving his ceremony. He denies both were any fault of his. It's upsetting because the shamans here pride themselves on their work, and sharing it with people who need their help is important. They didn't want bad publicity from a—"

"What? Fraud?"

"That's almost a correct assumption. Although Paulo has studied some, just not enough."

"Can you speak to Yasmine? She wanted to experience a ceremony. I told her I wouldn't stop her, only she couldn't do one with Paulo."

"Understandable, and you did the right thing for your friend. I'll deal with Michael after you leave. You need to care for Yasmine. I'll tell her how to prepare properly and provide a diet to follow if she wants to come back. And strictly, no alcohol. At certain times, Iquitos is busy with tourists searching for the right shaman and willing to pay extraordinary amounts of money to find direction in their life or help them with depression. I know the benefits, and now..." He runs a finger along her cheek. "May I?" He takes out his phone. "Smile." He takes a picture. A memory of her embracing his world so he can look at it any time he wants.

"Your phone?" Her eyes round. "Can I add my details?"

"Of course."

Eden taps in her number and address. Then she calls her phone before handing it back to Samuel.

A grin spreads across his face. "Now, do you want to share what the markings are about? Kaikare mentioned some, but I was in a rush to leave and come find you."

Eden's chest rises and falls as her lips part with a smile. "I understand why people pay if they get to experience what I did."

He links his fingers with hers. "I didn't want you to experience it without me there to help you. Kaikare said you found your spirit."

"Maybe I allowed my walls to come down knowing you weren't there?"

Samuel chuckles. "Ayahuasca is the vine of the souls. She has no barriers. She'll go where she chooses. She reminds me of you," he says, his forehead crinkling.

"Me?"

"It was a long boat ride with Asoo, and so he told me what Kaikare and you did. I'm proud of you, and I'm also upset you left me no supplies."

"Aren't all people your priority? You have your herbs as well. These people needed your medications and Kaikare's help."

He rubs his hand over hers. "I *am* proud of what you

both did. In fact, it shocked me a little. Have you considered studying medicine in some form?"

She squeezes his hand. "I've learned a lot about myself these past weeks. When I found Yasmine with a fever, I had to help her. Maybe I was a nurse in another lifetime." She grins at him.

Without a second to lose, he leans in and kisses her. "You'd make a wonderful nurse."

Sitting beside Eden in the tuk-tuk, he's aware of every minute passing before her flight home. Ulara will not be the same without her, although he'll enjoy hearing the stories of Tamu'ne Akare.

He squeezes her hand tucked securely under his. "Kaikare will miss Tamu'ne Akare."

"And I'll miss her. Wait." Her eyes round. "What did you call me?"

"It's your name." He manages to keep a straight face.

She smiles at him warmly. "I had a name?"

He nods, holding back a smirk. "White tortoise."

Her brow crinkles. "White I understand, but... they thought I was slow?"

"You did take a while to pick up on things." He chuckles at the noise of surprise coming from her throat.

"All right, then what was your name?"

"I have two. Everyone is given a name at birth. One is sacred, private, and not to share. The other is what everyone knows you by. After I was initiated as a warrior, I was given a birth name. My other name is Väi Uarati Kún-imá."

"Oh. It's quite a mouthful."

He chuckles.

"What does it mean?"

"Sun man with a long leg."

She bursts out laughing, and he frowns, not understanding why?

"Because you have a big dick?"

"No." He shakes his head in exasperation. "Because of my fair hair, and I'm tall. You might have noticed the Ularans are smaller in height."

She's still giggling. "Yeah, let's go with that. What about Kaikare?"

"Her name is a combination of tortoise and jaguar. She can be both."

"I'm going to miss her," Eden whispers. "She was like a mother to me."

He holds her gaze, pushes wisps of hair from her eyes. "You're a lot like her in some ways." He wraps his arms around her, smiles leaving both of their faces when the tuk-tuk arrives at the airport.

They stand on the side of the pavement. Her suitcase divides them while she waits for her friends to arrive. Silence shrouds them, afraid of the words to come. He links his fingers with hers, fighting an overwhelming urge to ask her not to leave.

"I forgot to mention something," she whispers. She waits until his gaze meets hers. "When I was under, *dreaming*, I saw butterflies. They spoke to me." She hesitates when his expression changes, a combination of fear and concern. "It was euphoric. And I understood every word even though it sounded Ularan."

"It's not the Ularan language, Eden. It's a universal language of the jungle known by all their ancestors across the Amazon."

"Oh."

"What did you hear?"

"It's hard to explain, although one word was repeated over and over. *Evol.* At first, I thought it was evil until I felt this amazing connection with the jungle. Well, to everything, really."

He takes her in his arms and holds her tight. "I wish you didn't have to go. The jungle has embraced you. The spirit of the jungle has accepted you." He kisses the top of her head before resting his nose in her hair. "*Evol* backward is *love.* You're as one. And now you're leaving..." The words claw his tender heart apart. He wants to tighten his squeeze and never let her go.

"You promised you would come find me," she whispers.

Samuel leans back and meets her gaze. "I did."

"Well, one day I'll come back to Ulara. It's *my* promise to you."

On tippy-toes, Eden kisses his lips, wraps her arms around his neck, and deepens the kiss as though it's their last.

48

EDEN

Adelaide, Australia.

Two weeks later...

"Twenty-five percent of modern pharmaceutical ingredients are derived from sources in the Amazon rainforest today. But only one percent of its medicinal potential has been discovered."

I close the newspaper after reading about illegal forest logging in the Amazon and how it affects the environment. I move the paper to the corner of my father's desk, wipe my eyes to compose myself, and walk out of his office. The past two weeks he's been on a business trip in Sydney, and since my homecoming, we've only spoken on the phone. I've teared up anticipating the questions he'll ask face to face because the only thing he has said on the phone is, *"Are you sure you're okay?"*

I don't want to lie to him, and I don't want to disappoint him either.

Since opening my eyes this morning, I've thought only of Samuel and how much I miss him. Maybe it was my dream about being back in the rainforest. Or that I keep reliving our last night together, the love and the longing for each other, and how we connect on a physical and spiritual level when we're together.

How can the universe be so cruel in letting me find my soulmate and yet keeping us worlds apart?

Still, I'm grateful to have grown and discovered things about myself. Like the strength I knew was inside me and kept hidden in fear of hurting those around me.

"Thank God, it's Friday. That's all I can say." Dana stacks her pens in a container and then closes down her computer.

"Are you doing anything special on the weekend?" The weather forecast predicts the rain will clear by the evening, so it should be fine."

"We're heading to the Barossa for a wine tour. What about you? Or are you still recovering?" Dana stands and wraps a silk scarf around her neck.

I glance out of the window. I don't think I'll ever recover, nor do I want to.

"I'm no clairvoyant, but something tells me it's not jetlag why you're still lethargic. Could it be something or *someone* else?" She gives me one of those looks she must have learned from my grandmother.

"You could say it's both," I say. I haven't shared much about Samuel with my family. I won't until I'm strong enough to talk about him without any tears.

"If you're smart, you'll tell me about *him* on Monday while Ethan is around."

I laugh at her. "You haven't *really* told me what it's been like to work with him."

Dana shrugs. "Can't complain because he does what's asked. He's your father's robot. But if you ask me, he has an ulterior motive for being here. I know a rat when I smell one."

Dana has never forgiven him for breaking my heart. "Maybe I have one as well, so be *nice* to him."

"What are you not telling me?" Her eyes fixate on me while adjusting the collar of her coat.

I smile. "If the pieces line up for me, then you'll be one of the first to know."

"You're going to leave me to deal with him, aren't you?" she asks, pointing the curved handle of her umbrella in my direction.

"I'm not saying anything. Have a good weekend. Enjoy your wine tasting."

"By the sounds of things, I'm going to need it."

Being back at work is harder than I anticipated. I miss you so much. I don't want to be here. I want to be back in the jungle with you—it's something I didn't think I'd say, yet I miss everything about it. Love you with all my heart. E xx

It's the fifth text message I have sent Samuel.

Each message lines up below the other with zero replies in between. I have no idea when he'll respond. Yet, I'm thankful to keep in contact and have a form of communication with him, even though it could be weeks or months before he responds. For now, it's enough.

Grabbing my coat, I head out the door to Faith and Jake's house. She arranged the Friday night family dinner party to hear about my travels since we only caught up briefly last weekend. Mum is picking Dad up from the airport and driving directly to Faith's house. I'm not sure Dad wants to know everything, so I placed *safe* photos in an album to share on my phone.

Faith lives twenty minutes from my parents' beachside residence and only minutes from the city. As much as I admire the Edwardian architecture of her luxurious home, I carry some envy in how everything has come easy for her. It only lasts momentarily because I'm happy for her, and right now, my heart warms knowing I get aunty cuddles with my nephew.

I hesitate before knocking to appreciate the old stained-glass panels surrounding the front door. Beyond the door, there's the patter of tiny feet on the floorboards. My brother, Will, unlocks the door, and before I have a chance to respond to his surprise visit from college, Seb jumps onto my leg.

"Edes," Seb says excitedly and leaps into my arms.

I reach to Will with my free hand to pull him in for a hug. "This is a nice surprise. Are you on a semester break?"

"Good to see you, too, sis. Yeah, a brief break before mid-year exams. Have to say I like hearing stories about your trip. For once, I'm not the one stirring trouble."

I laugh. "It's not intentional. And you've grown again," I say, tilting my head back more so than I remember.

Seb grabs my cheeks with both hands and turns my face, so he has my undivided attention. I kiss his cheek and plant my nose in his hair and inhale his freshly bathed scent. "Aunty Eden's missed you." He raises his head and nods at me. "And you're going to be two soon? You're growing up so fast." Sebastian holds up two fingers. "That's right." I kiss his fingers and carry him into the kitchen, where my sister is placing a lasagna in the oven. The roundness of her stomach is now evident beneath her jersey.

"He's missed his Aunty Eden, too." She smiles at me. "Like your other surprise?"

I smile at Will as he takes a seat at the table and scoops a handful of cashew nuts from a bowl. "She didn't recognize me."

I roll my eyes. "You might be taller than me, but you still have the face of a little-shit brother."

Faith laughs. "Have to ask, though. Are you ready for tonight? You know Dad will fire questions at you—"

"Yeah," Will interrupts. "I want the popcorn ready for that show."

"Shut up, Will," Faith says. "You haven't been here to see how crazy Dad's been acting."

Great. Now I'm more nervous than I was before I arrived.

Will taps away on his phone. "Looks like I'm gonna miss the show," he says and stands. "Brock's out front, and I'm heading to his to watch a footy game."

"You're supposed to be here for the family dinner," Faith rouses. She's already perfected her 'mother' voice.

He pushes up from the table. "It's not going to be a happy one." He glances at me with an apology and sympathy in his expression. "I'll see you both over the next couple of days."

Before Faith has a chance to respond, he's walking the hallway toward the front door. "Good luck, sis." His voice echoes from the hall.

"Thanks," I yell back.

"I don't know why Dad's so worked up about you

when Will is so erratic. He just doesn't give a shit what anyone thinks."

"He's a teenager." I shrug, although I wish I could be more like him. "About tonight. I've placed the photos in an album. I'll show you the other ones I mentioned when I come over tomorrow."

"Yeah, thanks for babysitting on short notice. Jake has another business dinner in the city. In a few more months, I won't feel up to going."

"Honey, I'm home," Jake calls out when he walks through the front door.

Faith rolls her eyes. "He says that every time he arrives home."

Jake strolls into the kitchen and drops his briefcase in the corner. He takes Faith in his arms and kisses her dramatically until she pushes him away. I can't help giggling at his antics. He comes to Seb and gives him a kiss on the top of his head.

"How's my favorite sister-in-law?"

I shake my head at him. "You're such a suck. Yes, I'm good."

He holds out his arms for Seb to go to him and I'm surprised when he curls into my chest.

"We're still catching up on cuddles." I tighten my arms around Seb, and kiss his cheek with a smack of my lips.

"He did ask for you a lot while you were away," Jake says warmly. "And thanks for babysitting for us." He loosens the tie around his neck and unbuttons the top button.

"Not a problem."

He glances at Faith, then at me, and then at Faith again. "Do I have time for a shower before dinner?"

"Make it quick," Faith says. "Mum and Dad will be here soon."

"And I don't want to miss the main act." He winks at me before striding toward the door.

Ugh.

I nuzzle Seb, the perfect distraction, and laugh when he giggles. "That sound..." I tell Faith, "... makes my heart swell. I love it."

She smiles fondly at her son and rubs her stomach. "I hope he's okay when this little one arrives."

"Of course, he'll be fine. He's bound to have some jealousy, though. But I'm sure it's natural. You're a wonderful Mum, and he'll never feel unloved."

"You mean like us?" She raises a brow.

"We were loved. Mum and Dad were busy, but we had Gran. And then Dana helped out when Gran traveled. Then if Gran got sick, we always had someone who was here for us." Seb wiggles, and I lower him to the floor. He runs off to play with his cars scattered across the living room.

"Gran was always *sick*." She makes imaginary inverted commas with her fingers. "You know Dad never fully trusted her to look after us."

I stare at her. "No. How sick?"

"Mum said she had mental health issues. She was never diagnosed, although Mum mentioned postnatal depression to me because she wanted me to know the warning signs, especially since Dad said he was aware she was depressed growing up, although she never took medication for it. He remembers when he was little, she was always crying, and he held some resentment to her in his upbringing. He never knew why, and I think he blamed himself."

I had no idea about any of this.

My memories of her are all happy ones. My gran was one of the kindest and most loving people I knew. "Before I went away, Dad mentioned I was like Gran."

"Yeah, I remember it. Weird. I don't know why he said it."

"He seems to have more power over me than he does Will or you. I've always done what he's asked, and you both do what you please, and he supports you."

Faith wipes her hands on a towel before coming to me and pulling me into a quick hug. "While you were away, I really missed you. It got me thinking how Dad expected too much of you compared to Will and me. I have no idea why." She shakes her head before returning to wash lettuce under the tap. I sit at the table and chop cherry tomatoes and cucumber for a salad. "He'd say stuff about keeping you in check when you returned home because he didn't want you getting this travel bug and becoming 'side-tracked' in life. And how everything will change now Ethan's working for him."

"Ugh." I shake my head. "I thought as much. I'm not going to date Ethan again just because he's working alongside me. If Ethan thinks he can win me over with his sexy, bloody smile when he waltzes through the door on Monday, he can think again."

"Can he? It sounds as though you have given it some thought."

I give her a long look. "Not anymore now that I've met someone."

She gives me a knowing smile.

"I believe he's my soulmate..." I shrug. "It's going to be complicated for a while."

"Bree didn't paint a great picture. I know she gets

concerned easily, but damn, I've been waiting too long to get you alone to talk about him."

"Yeah. He's been working in Venezuela for years, and the fact he's in the jungle didn't sit right with her."

"Don't tell Dad, he'll only stress more."

A knock on the door stops our conversation. "Hello," Mum coos, her voice echoing down the hallway. The heavy door closes with a bang. I stand as though it's a command knowing who has arrived.

I walk to the hallway and stare down the long passage.

"Look who's here," Mum announces.

I rush to Dad like I did to Mum at the airport and wrap my arms around his waist.

He leans down, and his hold is tight like a bear hug. "Edes, my girl. I have missed you." He pats my back like I'm a child in his arms.

"I missed you all," I rasp because my throat burns with new tears forming in my eyes. "Argh, I don't know what's wrong with me?" I swipe the tears because I'm feeling foolish.

"Nothing wrong with missing your father," he says proudly. "I'm just glad to have you home safe."

I smile as though it was never a concern, and yet I know some of my decisions were not thought through.

"I'm happy to be home, too."

Over dinner, we all laugh and chat about old times until it's time for me to show the photos of my trip. My phone is passed between Mum, Faith, and Jake, my father shaking his head.

"I'll look through them when you're all finished," he says.

I know it's his way of saying I need time to assess her trip.

"There are places I never got to visit, so I plan to go back," I say in warning to him.

"Because you thought it smart to leave your friends and travel alone in one of the most dangerous countries in the world?" He raises both brows and gives me one of his looks, which intimidated me as a child.

"I never felt unsafe. In fact, the people were some of the kindest I've ever met. The media make things out to be worse than they are."

"Right." He laughs sarcastically. "Like all the protests and troops in Caracas are a façade, and the warnings not to travel there should be *ignored*."

"No. We avoided Caracas for that reason. I'm saying other parts of the country are suffering when they rely on tourism. It's not unsafe in all areas."

"And where's that, Eden?"

"We saw some beautiful photos in Canaima," Faith interjects.

"Yes," Mum agrees. "Here, I'll show you." She swipes my phone and holds it in front of Dad's face. "Oops, I'm sorry I got out of it." She presses away. "Oh, what are these?"

Faith's eyes round before she looks past Mum's shoulder with an expression indicating I should panic. I reach for my phone, only Dad takes it before I get the chance.

"Dad, I think you should give Eden back her phone," Faith says politely.

Dad swipes a couple of times.

There were several images of Ulara and the people I kept in a separate album. The memories were for me and are not intended to be shared.

Dad's expression falters. Deep lines ingrain his forehead. He slides my phone to me without uttering a single word. He drags his hands over his cheeks to the back of his neck. "I've seen enough."

"Enough of what, Dad? To judge me?" I rasp.

He pushes his half-full red wine glass away. "Grace, I'd like to go."

My mother drinks her sparkling water and stands.

"Please don't," I croak. "I don't want the night to end like this. I'm not a bad person. I'm not sure why you're so upset."

"Let it go, Eden," Mum says gently. She gives me a nod in understanding, and I hope it means she'll explain what just happened when we're alone.

"Eden, I know you're not a bad person. But there is much you don't know about our family, and you went against my wishes when I asked you specifically to stay out of the jungle. Those photos were not taken on a tour." Dad stands without looking at me.

"No, but—"

"I've been up since four this morning, and it's been a long couple of weeks in Sydney. I'll talk to you about this later. Thanks for a lovely meal, Faith. I'll see you all on the weekend."

Faith stands and walks my parents to the door while I lean my face into the palm of my hands. Why is he so hung up on the jungle?

"Are you okay," Jake whispers. "Can I get you a glass of water? A full bottle of shiraz?"

My hands fall from my face, and I chuckle. I forgot

Jake was even sitting at the end of the table. "Sorry you had to witness that."

He looks up as Faith enters the room.

"That was *interesting*." Faith drags a chair and sits beside me. She pats my back in a calming way like she would Seb when putting him to sleep.

"As much as I want to stay and listen because dinner parties with your family are always much more interesting than mine..." Jake says. "I'll leave you two girls to talk alone."

"I know she'll tell you everything, anyway."

"Yeah." He grins at me and walks past patting my head. "Night." He kisses Faith on the top of her head. "I'll check on Seb and then head to bed."

"Night, babe." She turns to me. "You want to explain what those pictures were?"

I sigh. I need to talk to someone without divulging all the secrets of Ulara. "It's where Samuel works as a volunteer... sometimes." I go on to tell her about my experience helping in another community alongside a doctor and see it as a future job for me.

"Actually... there's more to it." I meet her gaze and wait a moment.

"Go on," she says, her eyes rounding.

"I need to know I can trust you because I want you to know the truth about Samuel." I reach for her hand.

Faith squeezes my fingers and gives me a nod. "I'll always have your back."

"Remember when you came home from college and said you can't help who you fall in love with?"

Faith smiles. "And you told me to follow my heart."

I nod because Faith fell in love with Jake when he was dating her best friend. She felt guilty about her feelings, and they never got together until he broke up with her friend. "Well, when my heart decided on Samuel, his circumstances are a little more complicated. It's why I'm going to return to him. Maybe at the end of the year."

"What?"

I blow out the air between my cheeks. "I miss him, and I don't want to feel like this any longer." Her eyes round. "But it will only be a short holiday..."

Sunday night, I meet Amy and Yasmine for a drink at our local hangout at The Bay.

"Have you spoke to Bree since you've been home?" Amy asks.

"No, only by text. She's coming to Adelaide to visit her parents, so I assume we'll all catch up then."

"She'll be asking questions," Yasmine says and places a glass of sauvignon blanc in front of me.

"I wouldn't be telling her what you told us," Amy quips and takes a sip of beer out of a bottle. "Ah, I've missed the taste of Aussie beer."

I chuckle at her content expression. "So, how's the new job?"

Amy shrugs and flicks her ponytail over her shoulder. "I signed another contract leading me up to the Christmas break. I'll be teaching grade four for the rest of the year."

Yasmine grins. "Poor kids."

"Poor me," Amy replies quickly.

"What about your work?" I ask Yasmine. "Did you have great sales while you were away?"

"It appears many of my online customers followed me

on Instagram and were inspired by our holiday. Boho dress sales are through the roof, and I have a huge backorder. I'm thinking of putting someone on to help with marketing."

"I can help you set it up," I say.

"Damn lucky you're moving in with me then." She gives me a wink even though we haven't yet settled on a date. I take another sip of wine and push it away. I'm not in the mood to drink alcohol tonight.

Over the next hour, we reminisce about our holiday. It's the thing about holidays—as soon as you're home, everything goes back to normal, and it barely feels like you were away at all.

Except for my heart. A piece of it is still missing, and I'm not sure the ache will ever go away.

"I better get going. Big day tomorrow," I say and roll my eyes.

"Call me tomorrow night," Amy states and takes another sip of beer.

"Call *me* on your lunch break. I want to know what Mr. Slimeball is up to."

I chuckle at Yasmine's description of Ethan. It's the same description she used for Michael. She has barely spoken to him since arriving home and can now see why we were worried about her.

It's a short walk back to our apartment complex, and I take the esplanade path even though the icy wind is whipping my face. When I open the door, the penthouse is in darkness with Mum and Dad already asleep.

I can't shake the loneliness of missing Samuel even when I'm surrounded by friends. Even worse, tomorrow I have to work alongside the guy who once upon a time I trusted with my heart. After stomping all over it, he thinks he can win me back.

Loving Samuel has helped me to forgive him even though the memory of seeing his naked ass pumping *her* against the wall is still ingrained in my thoughts.

When I'm alone in my room, I close my eyes and replay the memory. I threw his key at them before slamming the door. Seeing his name come up repeatedly on the screen of my phone and rejecting his calls of apology and refusing to discuss it with him even though he told my father he messed up, I can still hear my father saying, "*How bad could it be?*"

Everyone believed he *kissed* someone else. I never ratted on him but simply told my family to let us work it out—meaning for him never to contact me again.

As usual, my father had other plans.

When I stop taking the malaria medication in a few days, hopefully, the vivid dreams will stop because it's a memory I don't want to think about. Or is it the fact I'm worked up about working with him?

A crack of thunder wakes me. I toss for about twenty minutes and can't go back to sleep, so I shower and dress, then I creep down the stairs. When I unlock the office door, it's still dark, and I'm the first to arrive. An hour later, Dana strolls in, mumbling something about Mondays when she walks past my desk.

"You ready for this?" she asks as she slips off her coat and places it over the back of her chair.

"You know how I asked you to be nice? Well, scrap

that," I say and swallow the last of my coffee. My second cup. "At least for today."

"Consider it done," she says, firing up her computer.

By the time Ethan waltzes into the office, both Dana and I are well into the day's work with most emails addressed.

"Eden," he says with the warmth I remember from happy times. "It's good to see you."

He's wearing a lilac shirt and black tie that matches his pants. The way his dark hair is swept away from his tanned face accentuates his beautiful brown eyes even more. Their beauty was the first thing that caught my attention when we met ten years ago.

I stand and hold out my hand. "Thanks for all you did while I was away."

Ethan takes my hand, and he reaches in for a friendly kiss on the cheek. "Glad to have you back."

It grinds on me how he says it as though he's got this covered. I remind myself it's not a bad thing even though this company has been my baby since I left school.

"Do you want coffee while I go over everything I've ticked off your list?"

Raising my mug, I smile. "On my second cup already. Heads up... in my father's eyes you're late even though you technically haven't clocked in. And I worked through your list last week while you were in Sydney. I'm sure Dad will cover everything in his Monday morning meeting." I raise my arm to check my watch even though I'm not wearing one—only to make a point. "Which is in one hour, so best you check your emails now."

The space between his eyebrows creases, only slightly yet enough for me to notice.

"I replied to most of mine yesterday except for a couple that may have come through early this morning."

Working on a Sunday would impress my father.

"He has placed me on the pool and guest house reno."

My gut drops. It was my idea. I even had architects draw up my design.

"With you," he adds.

"Okay..." I'm breathing faster in a combination of relief and pent-up anger. Some projects are my babies. If I'm planning to move on, I need the reassurance everything will be handled in a way that's best for the business.

"Did you peruse my plans?"

"They look great, but I have a couple of ideas to add."

"Yeah," I say, tapping my fingers on the desk. "Same. I've been inspired by the architecture from my holiday. Perhaps we can brainstorm over lunch." I want to kick myself the moment the words fall out.

I give myself a moment and accept I'm capable of working alongside Ethan. Until *that night,* we got on well. We told each other everything. He was my best friend. It would make my father happy if we can work alongside each other.

As an added benefit, it would allow me to get the wheels in motion to gain freedom for myself because that's what I crave—freedom and a certain someone hidden away in the jungle with a tight hold on my heart.

49

EDEN

On Saturday, I hand my mother a cup of coffee and wait for her to take a sip before announcing, "I'm moving into Yasmine's apartment."

She tilts her head, and for a moment, I see a hint of sadness in her expression. "When?"

"In a month or so." I shrug. "After I save a little more to pay my share of the deposit and up-front rent.

"Honey, you don't need to move out if you want to save for something important."

I take a seat beside my mother on the balcony lounge overlooking the ocean. The esplanade is busy with people donning beanies and coats and walking their dogs. I snuggle my chin into the woolen scarf around my neck. "There is something I want to talk to you about. Besides saving to go on another holiday, I'm thinking about studying something different."

"Really, love? What?"

"I always thought it would be architecture, but after my holiday, I'm considering a complete career change. Maybe nursing, although I'm undecided."

Mum peers over the rim of her mug. Her expression is unreadable. "You know your grandmother was a nurse."

I pull a face. "Your mum?" My mother was adopted, and her adoptive parents both died when she was in her early twenties.

"No. Ivy."

"Gran was a nurse?"

"There's a lot you don't know about her, and it's time I filled you in." She stands and indicates for me to follow her inside. She leads me to her bedroom and their expansive walk-in closet, the décor in rose gold. She hands me her mug, then pulls out a small stepladder and reaches for a wooden box on a shelf. It's the size of a shoebox. I place both mugs on the carpet near the wall, so I can take it from her before Mum steps to the floor.

The cedar wood is patchy where the color has faded, and there's some flaking on the side. Still, it's stunning. Four carved timber legs and three letters are embossed on the lid. Fancy swirls are cut into the corners like a frame surrounding the initials.

I.M.M.

Ivy Maisie Monteford.

"Albert had it made for Ivy," Mum says. "It contains memories and some of her belongings. She asked me to give this to you on your twenty-fifth birthday."

"Why then?"

"Most of us have a better understanding of ourselves by our mid-twenties and know what direction we want our lives to take."

I nod. Even though my birthday is only a couple of months away, I'm aspiring toward personal growth. Only,

I'm unsure if I am following the right path. "Am I allowed to see it now?"

"This is why your father has been stressing all year. It's time I explain some things to you. You deserve to know what upset him, and perhaps it will help you to understand him better. I really hate seeing you both like this. You have always gotten on well. The stress isn't good for him."

"It's because I did what he asked and never argued. Only I'm not sure if..." the back of my throat burns before I say it, "... if I want to keep working for the hotel."

Mum places a hand on mine. "You'll work it out. We all need a break from time to time." She finds a key taped to the bottom of the box. "Shall we?" She wiggles the key until the old lock cooperates. Opening the lid slowly, we both peer in as though waiting to be surprised.

The first thing I pull out is a notepad or a diary with a faded tan leather cover and a tiny lock. I press the tarnished brass lock, but nothing happens.

"Your father hasn't unlocked it, and we don't know where the key is. He decided never to unlock it, believing some secrets should stay with his grandmother. I think he was afraid of what he might discover, and back then, he wouldn't have coped if it dragged up sad memories." Her eyes hold empathy and a touch of sadness.

"I understand." I place the diary aside as there is much more to discover.

Underneath the diary is a pile of family photographs. I look closely at each one before passing it to Mum. "We looked so happy. Yet Faith tells me Gran had a history of depression. She never showed it around me."

"Well, you were her favorite," she says with a sigh.

"I never noticed and played on it. I mean, if it's what you're implying by this box being left to me..."

"She saw something in you when you were born that Faith and Will never had. She blessed you when she came to the hospital to visit you as a newborn."

"Blessed me?"

Mum lifts the photos and takes out a photo frame, a lock of blonde hair, and an old brush. "Over time, most of her friends stopped talking to her... said she was a witch."

I laugh because it sounds insane. Mum's gaze lifts, and I realize she's serious. "Oh, how awful for Gran. Was she ostracized? Wait, you believe it, and you think she... what? *Performed magic on me*?"

"It sounded that way as it wasn't a religious prayer she was quietly singing. Ivy told us you were like her, and it has haunted your father ever since."

I shake my head to unravel my confusion. "She loved us and both of you. She helped out when you needed her to take care of us when you worked late hours. I don't understand. She was nothing but kind."

"Ivy was always kind, Eden." She finds a picture of Pop and hands it to me. "I'll tell you what your grandfather told your father and me. He met Ivy when she was seventeen, and they fell in love. He knew the moment they met he'd marry her even though she was different than the other girls her age. Everyone wanted to find a nice boy, get married, and have kids. It's what they did in their era. Only Ivy was always helping someone. She had a kind soul like you said. She was also a little *wild* for those days. She studied nursing, and her shifts during her training meant your grandfather and her were apart for long stints. So, they set up rendezvous weekends. She'd sneak out of the nursing quarters and would visit him. She ended up pregnant with your father, and they had a quick wedding. Only in her heart, she wanted to continue nursing. She had told your grandfather she'd always wanted to travel and volunteer overseas as a nurse."

I run my fingertips over the matte surface of the photograph. Only now, I note the musky scent coming from the box, as though it hasn't been opened in years. The image of my pop holds more than just a snippet in time—it's the beginning of a world of secrets.

"She developed postnatal depression, and so he let her go," Mum continues. "She was gone for almost three years and returned before Winston started prep school. She said her place was with her husband and her son, only she had this sadness about her, and they fought a lot. Eventually, she confessed she'd had an affair during her travels. Had a daughter, Dawn, and lost her at twelve months old. She came home brokenhearted. Although she promised your grandfather she was in love with him, not the other guy."

I gasp and cover my mouth. "Oh, Mum, I had no idea. It's so sad for everyone."

Mum nods. "Your grandfather set some ground rules. She was to give up nursing to be a mum and wife one hundred percent. It turned out she had complications and had a hysterectomy overseas, so they couldn't conceive any other children. She almost died by account. Anyway, she never spoke about her travels. We only know about it from what we found in this box when she passed. The sad thing is your father partly blamed her for your grandfather's death. He became an alcoholic and drank himself to sleep every night. He had a massive heart attack and died at fifty-five. Winston had already thrown himself into our business with a vision of making the building we inherited to be something special. He thought you could also be part of it since you wanted to help out from a young age, even when you were at school. Faith had her heart set on law and had no interest to work in tourism on any level, and besides, he couldn't handle her stubborn nature."

Pride warmed my heart. "Part of why... did it stem from keeping me in close check because Gran thought I was like her?"

"He saw something in you, which also reminded him of your gran, but also reminded him of himself. I don't believe it was so you wouldn't become wild like your Gran."

"*Wild.*" I roll my eyes. "I wanted to travel and see the world. You both have traveled."

"Eden, it's the jungle." She flips through images and scrambles through the box until she finds a picture. "This is Gran. She's in the jungle surrounded by native Americans with spears. None are wearing clothes except for grass skirts, including Gran."

I study the image. Blonde hair falls over her shoulders covering her breasts. Gosh, she looks like me. My heart races. I know where this was taken. Only I don't recognize any faces. One of the ladies holds a white baby.

"Is this...?"

Mum nods. "Apparently, it's Dawn."

My chest tightens. My thoughts race. What would giving birth in a village like Ulara be like? Without the Samuel's of the world, things would've been harder. Then, I remember Kaikare protecting me from that deadly spider. Perhaps they wouldn't have been that much harder after all.

"Now you know why your father gets upset."

"Yeah, I do." I release a breathy sigh.

Our eyes meet, again an understanding passes between us before Mum restacks the photographs. "Apparently, there's a journal about her time in the Amazon, but she gave it to her friend as your pop banned her from talking about it. I think if she hadn't got rid of it, Albert might have burned it." She tilts her head as though recalling a memory. It sounds like an extreme measure, only now I understand why Pop would've been angry. "Brenda and your Gran both nursed together, and the last I heard she was in a retirement village. Your father isn't interested in what happened in the jungle, and we haven't spoken to Brenda since the funeral."

I pick up the diary. It's light, and yet the emotion inside it gives an illusion the pages are lined in mercury. After a quick scrape around the bottom of the wooden box, I'm a little relieved not to find a key. No one has read Gran's diary. The discolored cover arouses curiosity as to when she started writing in it.

I place the diary at the bottom before Mum packs the remainder of the contents into the box. She does it slowly. Is this hard for her? Does she miss Gran too? She pushes the box over the carpet toward me. "It's all yours."

I can't share what Mum has told me to anyone until I process everything. Until then, the box will remain in my closet for when I'm ready to absorb everything. I understand the joy my gran felt while living in the jungle, yet the pain caused to her husband and my father is so messed up that my heart hurts for them all.

The box can stay locked until I'm ready to inspect her memories with an open mind. I make myself a cup of tea in a china cup like the way my gran used to drink it. I fire up my computer to the open documents from yesterday. After speaking with Mum, there's a weight off my shoulders. Hoping the universe is guiding me right, I click and send on my nursing application and quickly close the computer before I second-guess my decision.

50

EDEN

One week later...

I miss you xx

I promised Samuel I'd message him every week, and I'm keeping my promise.

51

EDEN

One week later...

I love you xx

I stare at the screen with a list of messages, all from me. My thoughts snowball to panic. I hope he's safe. Damn, I wish he'd respond. Just once.

52

EDEN

Ten days later...

"These are good," I tell Ethan and trace my finger over the design on the desk in front of him. His ideas for a Bali-inspired resort pool would suit our complex.

"I've always liked the relaxed setting," he says. "The garden is a mix of Mediterranean and Bali if you know what I mean."

"It's unique in a way. Anyway, we can talk on Monday." I stand and head to the bathroom. I've cut back on tea and coffee the last few days because all I seem to do is pee.

When I emerge, Dana is waiting for me. "Everything okay?"

"Yep. Ever since I finished all the meds from traveling, my body is up and down."

She nods slowly. "You have a good weekend," she says as she enters the cubicle.

"You, too." I walk back to the office and finish packing up my desk.

"Any chance for Friday night work drinks?" Ethan winks at me.

"I can't, sorry. I have other plans."

Please don't wink at me.

Shoving everything into my desk drawer, it can wait to be sorted on Monday. I rush toward the door leaving Ethan to lock up.

I don't bother changing out of my office clothes. It's a short drive to Yasmine's apartment. Finding a parking spot on the street, I grab my bag and walk the path to her apartment door and knock twice.

Yasmine answers, and the aroma of herbs and rice wafts into the night air.

"Come in," she says.

"We ordered you a Thai red curry." Amy wipes her hands with a cloth. She points to an Uber Eats bag. "It should still be warm."

"I'm sorry I am late. Ethan and I were going over some drafts."

Amy stands and doesn't respond. She cracks open a bottle of wine. "If you're going to talk about him, I'll need more of this."

"I'm not. When I mention him at work, think of him like you would Dana."

Amy rolls her eyes.

I grab my food and take a seat next to where Amy is sitting. Her phone lights up next to me—she left it open on Tinder.

I check out the guy posing on her screen. "Want me to decide for you?"

Amy snorts. "Our taste differs."

"Oops, I super-liked him."

"You didn't!" She puts down her wine glass and grabs

her phone to check. "Hilarious." She closes the app, and I laugh. "I have a date on Wednesday night, and I want your opinion on what to wear."

Amy disappears out of the room.

Yasmine hands me a wine glass and takes a sip from her half-full crystal glass.

"Have you been chatting about Tinder dates waiting for me to arrive?"

Yasmine rolls her eyes. "Her list is insane. For every minute we waited for you, she cursed Ethan. I don't like the guy, but Amy despises him."

"I'll chat with her. She doesn't need to worry. There's no chance of us getting back together. Besides, if I've moved on, she shouldn't be so worked up about him."

"I need to tell you something," she says. "Michael is messaging me again. He called a few nights ago and apologized over and over. He wants to remain friends and plan a holiday together somewhere else."

"What?"

Amy waltzes into the room holding four tops and a black mini skirt. "What do you think?"

I give Yasmine a look that our conversation will be continued, and then smile at Amy.

"It's a Tinder date, right?" I hold up each top to decide if it's suitable. "I like this one."

"That one's for you. It doesn't suit me." It's a low-cut navy top with frills along the bust line.

"Thanks." I love receiving clothes from Amy. She often buys them, then changes her mind and sends them my way. Amy strips to try on the others, and I do the same to check if the navy top fits.

"Stop buying online and come into my shop,"

Yasmine tells her. "I'll fit you out properly, so there are no rash purchases."

"I know. I love your store, but I do most of my shopping at night when I can't sleep. Damn, girl." Amy stares at me wide-eyed. "Check out your tits."

"What?" I glance down to my ample cleavage and clutch both breasts. "You know, they've been sore the last week. It's like I'm getting my period, except I haven't had one in years because of my implant."

"Does it need changing?" Yasmine asks, holding one of the other tops against her chest.

I stare at Yasmine, my mind ticking over. "Shit." I reach for my phone and scroll through my calendar. "April," I murmur. "I forgot to make an appointment."

Yasmine stares at me. "Sore tits. Anything else?"

"Apart from the crazy dreams from our meds, I want to pee all the time now that the weather has turned cold?"

"I don't want to pee," Amy says.

"Same," Yasmine adds. "You better get a pregnancy test."

"Don't be ridiculous." Only, I have a gut feeling something's not right, so I push the wine away.

Amy grabs her keys. "Right. We're all going for a ride to the pharmacy," she says, leaving her glass of wine untouched.

🌴

On my right, Amy stares at the stick on the table. On my left, Yasmine's gaze is fixed on the same spot. Elbows on the table, we wait the three minutes as directed on the box. I keep looking away as though it's all a joke, and it will read negative.

"I see a second blue line," Amy says, and our heads dip closer.

"I don't see anything."

"I do," Yasmine quips. She grabs the stick and holds it up to her eyes. "There's definitely another line, Edes."

"Show me." I take it from her fingers, and sure enough, it's there. Two blue lines. "Shit." I drop the stick back on the paper. "This isn't good."

"Home tests aren't always accurate. You need a blood test, so make an appointment with your GP," Amy says, trying to calm me.

"I need a check-up as I need to have my rod removed anyway. So, I can mention it then."

Yasmine rubs my back, and my face falls in my hands. "I really can't be pregnant. I'm still living at home, for fuck's sake."

"Not for long," Yasmine says and smiles. "We're going to be one happy family here."

I smile at her kindness. We're jumping to conclusions, yet I panic every way I look at it. How do I tell Samuel? Christ, he doesn't even reply to my texts. It's something I'd have to say and not in a text.

Ugh, how do you tell someone over the phone?

Surely, I can't visit him while pregnant.

"Don't worry unless you have to." Amy removes my glass and pours the wine into her glass. "Go to the doc and take it from there. To be on the safe side..." she raises her glass, "... no more alcohol for you."

I sigh because right now I need a drink.

I set the *National Geographic* magazine on the chair beside me when my phone vibrates. I have every intention of ignoring it until I read Asoo's name on the screen.

Samuel misses you. Good you left Ulara. Samuel followed from his exploration by warrior from Watache tribe. Some cannibals. Shaman's magic scare them away.

He was followed. What does that mean? Is another tribe angry at them? I had read somewhere that cannibalism still existed, only I thought it was deeper in the Amazon. There are tourists and helicopters visiting Angel Falls not far away. Why can't he just leave if his safety is jeopardized? There must be some clause in his contract. Honestly, I think he enjoys the element of danger when he has to ramp up measures for his safety. I shake my head and try to picture him here with me. I want to believe we could live happily together, but I have no idea how long he'd survive in society without it depressing him.

He'd have me.

"Eden Monteford."

I look up to the doctor calling my name and follow her along a hallway.

After another urine test and physical examination, she tells me I'm pregnant and writes a referral to an obstetrician. She removes the rod from my arm and sutures the incision.

"Malaria medication can be detrimental to the fetus. You also ingested ayahuasca, and my knowledge is limited regarding these teas. You can discuss this in more detail with the obstetrician." She peers at me over the rim of her glasses with a tight, serious expression. "My calculation is a January baby, although it's a broad guess considering you haven't menstruated in some time, and the times of sexual intercourse were spread over a couple of months."

I nod. The rough lump in the back of my throat burns, and I'm afraid to speak. The moment I open my mouth, I know the damn tears will come. I've cried more since I returned from South America than I have in a long while. I should've picked up that it was a sign of hormone overload.

"Good luck," she says as though I'll need it.

On the drive home, my thoughts race to Samuel and my father and how to break the news to both. Or do I?

The photo of Gran holding a baby in the jungle is like a snapshot of my future. I can't shake the image out of my head, and I can't help believing it means something more.

Is Dad right... am I like Gran?

I let out a sigh. I don't want to disappoint anyone. If I decide to visit Samuel and tell him about our baby, I have to be aware of the many things that can go wrong. Shit. Is it how Gran lost her daughter? Or was it the malaria prevention medication? Did they even have those meds in the 1960s?

I have to take each day as it comes.

Making my way up the stairs, I head directly to my room to be alone and process everything.

"Eden."

I turn to my father stepping out of his bedroom.

"Do you have a moment?" His brow pulls tight, and his eyes flick over my face. "I don't want us fighting anymore. I haven't properly apologized for my reaction at dinner. Your mother has informed me she has enlightened you on why I felt strongly about you avoiding the jungle."

"Yes, she—"

"It's still no excuse not to trust you. I apologize."

"Dad, I understand."

He runs a hand over his head. "I may have earned myself a few more gray hairs in the meantime." He chuckles low.

I go and hug him. "I'm lucky to have you always looking out for me." I take a step back. Now is a good time than any. I clear my throat. "Though it's time I do what's right for me, and right now, I need a change, and I'm not sure the hotel is my future." I twist my fingers waiting for him to say something.

"My girl, I knew this day would come. I hoped it wouldn't be yet, although your mother did forewarn me. I want you to be happy, so I'll support you on whatever you decide, even if it's nursing. Just promise me if you're unhappy, you'll consider coming back to the hotel."

"Oh, Dad."

"Don't say anything." He pops his arm over my shoulder. "I'm proud of you and know you'll do well wherever life takes you."

"That's because I have your determination," I say and laugh once.

"That you do. That you do."

I give him another hug before heading to my room, my shoulders lighter than a few minutes ago.

Below my bedroom window, the ocean crashes onto the foreshore rocks with a force of energy, creating a boom with each wave. The wind howls against the shutters. I shut my blinds and block out nature's anger.

While wrapping a blanket around my shoulders, I slide onto my knees then pull open the closet door to find the locked wooden box. Something has been playing on my mind. Flipping through Gran's belongings, I locate the brush and turn it to the tarnished decoupage of flowers decorating the back. Even behind the rust color, I recognize enough of the design to know it's similar to the one Kaikare showed me.

Impossible.

Photographs, trinkets, jewelry lay sprawled around me until I find the black and white image my mother pointed out. My grandmother is standing beside a young man wearing a small ring of feathers around his head. The image is old and not taken close enough to identify anyone. Only the blonde hair of my grandmother contrasts with the dark heads surrounding her makes her identifiable.

Nothing is impossible—I learned that in Ulara.

I reach for my computer. I open it to a website on visa applications, knowing what I have to do.

53

EDEN

Canaima, Venezuela

Three months later...

From the small window of the Cessna aircraft, I peer out to the mountains of green vegetation. It's stunning and unchanged. A sea of green seen from the air, the beauty conceals the danger lurking below.

After a few bumps on the landing strip, the pilot pulls up the plane, brakes screeching.

I'm one of two passengers and surprised the flight wasn't canceled, although I assume Canaima tourism will do everything to encourage visitors in light of what's happening in the country.

My interest in obtaining a visa was questioned, especially in light of certain embassies closing. The closest is Colombia, and God forbid, anything goes pear-shaped, and I can't get there. The visa took eight weeks to arrive, allowing me to save more cash in the meantime.

Victor greets me and drives me to the resort lodging.

It appears I'm the only guest arriving today. We chat about Australia and his desire to travel there.

"You tell your friends to come visit Victor's resort," he says enthusiastically while wheeling my small case to reception.

"Of course." I smile at him. "Is Asoo here?"

"He's at a camp. Returning tomorrow."

I wonder if it's the same camp Kaikare and I visited, although there are hundreds dotted along the river and around the Gran Sabana. "Have many of the volunteers and medics returned to help?"

"Yes. Some." He nods, not saying anything else, and I assume some may have re-evaluated their travels with visa problems.

"I'm so happy to be back here." I inhale the clean, fresh air already heavy in my lungs and glance out to the vista before us. I'll never tire of looking at the waterfalls on the other side of the lake. In the distance, three tepuis push toward the clouds.

I swat at the annoying buzz above my head. There's not a guest in sight, and despite wanting to take a stroll since I have the entire resort to myself, I retreat inside to apply more repellent.

Here, mosquitoes are the enemy.

Early the next morning, I make my way across the grass toward the sandy beach of Canaima Lake. Asoo waves out to me, and I smile at his enthusiasm even when it's just after dawn.

"Samuel doesn't know Miss Eden coming."

Not a question. "No, he doesn't. I wanted to surprise him."

"I visit once every two weeks. Now you here, I visit more."

"Thank you. I'd appreciate that."

He takes my hand and assists me to step into the curiara. "You're welcome."

"Your English has improved," I compliment Asoo.

"Yes. When I visit Samuel, we speak in English, not Spanish or Pemón. He teaches me."

"I noticed it's quiet around here. It's good you're using your time to learn."

Asoo shakes his head. "Victor not say much, but everyone sad no tourists come."

I understand their concern when tourism is their livelihood. I settle in the seat in front of him and gaze out to the mountains beyond the lake. It still astounds me when I imagine Samuel climbing the tepui to find a particular flower. The rocky face juts up straight toward the clouds, and to my naked eye, it looks unclimbable. The indigenous believe these mountains house the spirits of the dead. It's why only one Ularan warrior volunteered to go on the journey with Samuel. It's a reminder to me I'm returning to another world where mythology influences their daily life.

We take the Carrao River deeper into the jungle. Beyond the trees, I catch movement. It could be a wild pig, and then the monkeys sound an alert from the trees. Macaws fly overhead from one side of the river to the other. It all feels strangely familiar, like home.

"You know I traveled along the Amazon River in Peru," I tell Asoo. "The width is several miles wide in some parts. The current is substantially stronger."

"She's beautiful wherever she flows."

I smile, loving how he sees joy in everything.

"Have you seen Kaikare again?"

He shakes his head. "Ulara quiet, especially with Watache man spying. It's dangerous now."

"Dangerous how? You have your boat."

"They very good hunters. Every spear strikes pig." He makes a whistling noise, and with his free arm, mimics a spear in the air. "They make bad poison. I could die in minutes."

I stare at him, aware I'm gaping. "And Samuel remained there?"

"They scared of shaman. He has secrets. They scared to die like us. Now they mourn their chief who's same age as the shaman. Watache have shaman's young son, and he still learning. He has gone back to old ways believing if you eat a man, you'll inherit their knowledge and power. They know Samuel a different medicine man, smart with no magic. You tell Samuel to stay with shaman."

I'll be asking why he's still there.

"And bad people cut down the forests for money. Big money," he says. "They forced the Watache from their homes and north toward us. I believe they are passing through toward Colombian jungle where it safe to hide."

"I hope so."

We don't speak much for the remainder of the journey. As the hours pass, I'm finding the seat uncomfortable, having to lean back on my hands clutching the plank of wood. I straighten my spine as much as possible to ease the ache, thankful to finally reach the junction to follow the Churun River.

A helicopter flies high overhead. It's the first one I've seen all morning. "Is that a tourist chopper?" I ask Asoo.

Asoo stares at the base of the helicopter because it has a symbol painted on the bottom that I don't recognize.

"No, it's going to the mines."

His face is solemn. Does this upset him? Before I ask him anything else, he guides us to the entrance of the small tributary river that leads to Ulara. The current isn't as strong as I remember. In fact, the river is low for this time of year. We glide past overhanging branches, thicker than I remember, that protrude like long tentacles into the water.

Asoo kills the motor early and guides the canoe onto the sandy embankment. I take my small pack, the remainder of my luggage is with Victor in Canaima.

"I'll keep my phone on me for now," I tell Asoo. "I'll give it to you to charge when you next visit."

"Do you want me to wait? Samuel not expecting you."

I shake my head. "No need. "I'm sure he'll be alerted soon. I'll stay over here at the small camp for now."

He pushes the boat out into the water. "See you soon, Miss Eden."

I wave goodbye and tread to the camp. Fresh new growth almost conceals it. It seems untouched in months. Pushing vines away, I walk to where I remember the passion fruit grows. Plump fruit covers the vine, and I pick several and tread back to the log seat where Samuel first took me.

I'm unsure of the minutes or hours that pass. I'm not prepared to remain out here alone with no fire or even with fire, now I'm pregnant. Isolation, I understand, only it needs to be in his hut.

Beyond the shades of green and brown, a rustling of leaves alerts me to a visitor. Slowly, I pad back toward the river in case it's not human because I remember Samuel telling me jaguars have been sighted in the past. With my back to the water, I scan the green wall trying to see behind the trees.

Maybe I was imagining a presence. I walk up the small embankment to the camp to retrieve my phone. The sun is low, and I estimate another couple of hours before it's sunset. Looking around, I search for sticks in preparation to make a fire, even though I'm not entirely sure how to create a spark.

"Shit." I throw the sticks to the ground, glance up, and notice him standing by a tree watching me. In warrior stance, legs apart, balance equally distributed, arms by his sides near a spear in his twine band around his waist.

I meet his gaze, hesitant at first. I see it, *feel it,* the emotion where words aren't needed for me to understand what he's feeling because I feel it too.

54

EDEN

Samuel doesn't move as though he's processing. His knees flinch. Those long, tanned, and muddy legs don't hide the faded red artwork that decorates his lean muscles.

When Samuel takes the first step, I forget all the rules and run to him, jumping into his arms kissing him hard.

"I told the kids to stop messing about," he says against my lips. "I thought they were teasing me."

"How are you?" I say in between breaths. My fingers catch in his knotted fair locks. "Asoo told me another tribe was after you."

"I'm fine, even more so now." He breathes heavy sighs into my mouth.

His earthy scent jolts me back in time. I slide down his body until my feet hit the sand. "I know I should be in quarantine, but honestly, I haven't come all this way to remain out here. I'm happy to be isolated in your hut, so please don't make me—"

"Not a chance." His calloused hands frame my face,

and he holds me there for a moment and just takes in every detail.

"I'm sorry. I should've warned you. I thought it would be a nice surprise."

He shakes his head in disbelief. "It's a surprise. I'm just having trouble believing you're here. That you came back to me."

"We promised each other, remember?" I push up on my toes and kiss his lips. "I've had time to think, and I am sorry I'm breaking your quarantine rules. I'll be mindful and keep a distance—"

He silences me with another kiss. "Don't you worry. I can take extra measures." He takes my hand and starts to lead me away.

"Wait." I pull my hand from his to fetch my bag, run back to his side, and match his stride over the mangled roots and decaying leaves. "Will it be a problem with the shaman?" He takes my bag from me and throws it over his shoulder.

With his other hand, he takes my hand and squeezes it. "You're my family."

Family.

"You look well." A little on the thin side, yet he still looks healthy. I smile at Samuel and instantly know I made the right choice in coming here.

"You look radiant as always." He stops walking and pulls me in for a kiss. "I can't believe you're here."

I've waited months for his kiss. I run my hands up his back, his muscles contracting beneath my palms.

"It will be different this time," he tells me and leads me toward the village at a much faster pace.

When we reach the outskirts, the children run to me and bounce up and down. They giggle and shout to me with big smiles across their beautiful faces. I laugh along with them, waving enthusiastically. "Hello, hello," I say to them all.

Samuel is frowning at the kids. He raises a hand in a gesture to stay away. "Senke awarö," he repeats. *Near, bad.* "They have to wait before they can touch you."

Inside the village barrier, there's a change in my sense of gravity. With every step, I'm light on my feet, so light I'm walking on air, and at the same time grounding me to the earth. I match Samuel's stride with the grace of his step. We take a path around the outside of the village, avoiding as many people as possible until we reach his hut. He's still holding my hand as he takes the steps inside. He lets go and places my pack in the corner. It appears the same but different. One striking change is the whiter twine of a second hammock strung next to his. "This is new."

"I began to weave it while you were here. Finished it months ago and hung it in hope... want to give it a try?" He lifts me onto the edge, and it swings with my weight. He holds it steady before he slides on and settles beside me.

"Hoping for a wife?" I rasp, remembering how simple it is to be married here.

"Hoping the person I intend to marry returned."

I stare into his beautiful blue eyes, my heart thumping in my chest. "I promised I would one day, but you also said you'd come find me. I thought I'd see you in Australia before I visited again."

He stares into my eyes, and his eyes flick over my face.

I reach out and touch his cheek. "Luckily, I had a change of heart."

He nods once, kisses my lips, and slides off the

hammock. "Give me time to speak to the shaman and chief."

When Samuel disappears from the doorway, I scramble out of the hammock and walk the length of the hut, noting a new string of red and black beads, animal teeth, and bones hanging on the wall. I question the significance—is this a promotion of sort? My hand lowers and rests on my stomach, a habit that's a reminder to myself and a protective touch to my unborn child. A fluttering makes me smile. Sensing another presence, I turn to the door to a figure watching me. I gasp at *his* presence, and in the few steps it takes for me to reach the doorway, the shaman has disappeared from sight.

Admittedly, he still freaks me out a little. I'm surprised he didn't say anything, or maybe he didn't know I was here. Seeing him unsettles me, and I'm glad Samuel has gone to talk to him. At least he kept his distance, although I don't expect any affection from him like a hug. Come to think of it, I have never seen the shaman embrace anyone, not even Kaikare.

Unsure how long these discussions will take, I climb into his hammock. I inhale so that his scent fills my head, and I'm transported back several months in time. I close my eyes and imagine my time here will be different. I've returned a wiser woman.

Samuel returns and stands in the doorway holding a wooden type cup. God, the sight of him has my ovaries exploding. There is a little dirt around his shins and knees. His hair is a messy bed-sex style. I can see every outline of muscle when he moves. Those blue eyes lock with mine. "The shaman wants you to drink this in case you're carrying any viruses."

Oh right. I scramble up, and my hand goes to my stomach out of habit when I get up.

"Is your hammock comfortable?" He raises one eyebrow and hands me the cup.

"Yes. I just wanted to lay in yours for old time's sake." I smile at him and then take a whiff of the tea.

Ugh. I grab my stomach and heave. It doesn't take much to make me nauseous. I cough to get the vile smell out of my throat. Over the months, I've been careful about what I eat and drink for the baby. Staring into the cup, I ask, "What is it? What if I react?"

"Eden, I don't make the rules, and please be thankful for the leniency they're already showing you."

"I can't." I shove it toward him. "I can't risk it."

For a moment, our eyes lock before his lower to where my hand rests under my naval. His eyes widen, studying me. His mouth gapes, and he stumbles back a step.

"Mine?"

I take a step toward him. "Of course."

Samuel takes the cup from me and places it on the ground, then he wraps his arms around me. His kiss is hot like wildfire. Warm lips dot my cheeks and neck before finding their way back to my mouth.

Samuel pulls away, out of breath. "I'm sorry I wasn't thinking straight. You must be hungry since it's dinner time."

"A little." I shrug. More for him.

"I can't wait for Kaikare to see you." His voice holds the excitement like a boy meeting his idol.

"Shouldn't I remain here?"

"You can keep your distance. "I'll tell her no hugging."

"What about you? You're with me and then—"

"I can keep my distance from the people. I have meds and a bottle of alcohol hand wash. I'm not leaving you alone at night." He walks briskly toward the center of the village.

Twilight never scared me. The dark hours past midnight freaked me out more, and I'm thankful to be in his hut and not alone in the dark at the campsite.

"There's an immune-boosting tea I'll have the ladies make you. It's safe for pregnant mothers. It will also help fight any viruses you may be carrying." He points to a log at the side of the fire, a good distance from the others as they eat dinner.

Heads turn, curious eyes meet mine, and a whisper spreads through the group. A new person visiting can be unnerving to them, and apart from Samuel, no one returns to the village. Yet after seeing Kaikare's trinkets, I know people have visited before Samuel's arrival. My interest is with one particular visitor, and I need to approach the question with sensitivity.

I glance over to Samuel, who is standing away from the ladies cooking over another fire. One hands him a cup, and he drinks it. They give him another, and he holds on to it. Our gaze meets. The fire casts a flickering light, and I catch his expression—a look of relief, joy, and desire. The sight of him takes my breath away. Shadows highlight pectoral and abdominal definition, and I'm already imagining running my fingers along each contour tonight.

Turning away, I'm still smiling when my gaze meets the shaman. His expression is serious and questioning. I nod, lower my gaze, and dip my chin. When our eyes meet again, I sense the probing, like ayahuasca's fingers in my thoughts. Standing before the fire, his headdress is stunning with long feathers and more beads around his neck than I remember the last time.

Samuel appears beside him. They exchange a few words, and he holds up the cup in his hand. The shaman waves his hands over the top while Kaikare appears on his other side. Samuel speaks to her. Our eyes meet, and Kaikare beams a smile at me.

The shaman hands him the cup, and he walks around the outside of the congregation and slides in beside me.

"Everything okay?"

"Yes." He hands me the cup. "Drink this before your dinner."

I take the cup and peer into the dark liquid, hoping it doesn't come straight back up. I knock it back like a shot and cough at the bitter taste lingering on my tongue. "It tastes like poison," I groan. He chuckles and speaks to one of the women who places a huge palm with roasted vegetables on the ground in front of me. She bows her head once before walking away.

"What did the shaman say?"

"He envisaged your return and knows you carry a secret."

I place my hand on his knee and find joy in the way his eyes sparkle. "So, you told him?"

"He already knew, and it's not the secret he was referring to."

The shaman's voice breaks our attention. The shaman raises his arms, holds them wide, encompassing his audience. I never thought of it until now, but he reminds me of the Christ the Redeemer statue in Rio—a bigger-than-life protector overlooking his people, arms open wide, embracing every living soul.

"I have something else to show you," I whisper. "I think you'll be as curious as I am."

"Let it wait for tomorrow. Enough surprises for one day." Samuel's arm snakes around my back, and I snuggle into his shoulder while he translates our bedtime story.

55

EDEN

After bathing in the stream, I change into my newly woven grass skirt and take Samuel's hand to tread through the forest. We stop for him to explain a certain vine or flower or point out the strangest of insects. The passion in his voice is different than my last visit. He's more relaxed, and it's like everything is sugarcoated, and he's not warning me about the dangers.

Smoke from the village fire lingers in the breeze, helping to guide my broken compass. The path to the stream is identified by others where a cut vine or branch guides them. I'm starting to pick up on identifying marks to lead me even though it comes naturally to Samuel and the Ularans. The jungle grows rapidly, even overnight, and I don't trust my instinct to walk alone until I can rely on my sense of direction.

We arrive at his hut, and I flop into the hammock. Nothing is simple. The walk to the stream is an equal distance from the village to the river only in the opposite direction. I stretch out the kinks in my back since last night wasn't about sleep. There were times I doubted the strength of the hammock could support us both with Samuel demonstrating how much he had missed me.

Samuel climbs in to lay alongside me. We both need to catch up on rest. Snuggling into his side, I glance up at him wide-eyed.

"I thought you were tired?" I murmur.

"Lying here beside you is restful," he says, and he takes my hand and squeezes it. "We talked about not keeping secrets. Do you want to tell me what's in your pack?"

Oh, that. "I can't be sure..." I roll off the hammock as ungraceful as I was on my last trip here. I open my bag and pull out the waterproof zip-lock bag containing photos and my grandmother's brush. The diary is packed in a separate compartment and double-wrapped. "I want to explain the story from the beginning." I climb back in to lie beside him.

First, I explain how my sister and brother have lived under different rules than me and how my father asked me to stay out of the jungle. Then I relay the stories my mother told me about my grandmother, her postnatal depression, and her work as a nurse. When I reach the part where she volunteered, met someone, and lost her baby, I show him the photos. We peruse the image for a while before I bring out the brush. "Kaikare has the mirror to match this. It could be coincidental for that period, but..." His face changes when he understands what I'm telling him.

"You believe the photo was taken here?"

"Kaikare told Asoo she's had needles when we went to help with the measles outbreak in the small Pemón community. Do you know how old she is? I mean, measles vaccines released in the mid-sixties, right? My father is fifty-nine. Do you think she's a few years younger than him?"

His eyes widen. "You believe she's your father's sister? Your aunt?" His voice is skeptical.

"Well... my gran's baby died. So, I don't know, but don't you at least think it's strange that Kaikare has the mirror to match? Because I believe the shaman had something to do with Gran."

He holds the black and white photo closer to his eyes. "It's taken too far away to identify anyone. Did your grandmother travel to Papua New Guinea?"

"I don't know the details of her travels. There was another journal, although she apparently gave it to her friend."

"Is her friend alive?"

"My parents haven't spoken to her since Gran's funeral. I understood the hurt it caused my father, so I've worked with what I have. Could you ask the shaman some questions?"

Samuel raises both hands. "It's a delicate matter. Ularan shamans don't marry. They commit their energy to the forest and her medicine. It's why Kaikare never found a partner as she's following in her father's footsteps."

"Like a priest?"

"There have been partners but no marriage. His work comes first."

"Like you when we first met."

He gives me a look. Behind his eyes, I sense the cogs of time turning. "Yes, and yet here we are." He pulls me into his arms. "I'm sorry I haven't messaged. I didn't want

Asoo to visit, and I couldn't risk my phone being lost because we've had torrential rain."

"I heard about the cannibals, which is another thing I want to talk about."

"I didn't want you to worry. I'm fine and know what I'm doing. Your being here changes everything."

56

SAMUEL

"Can we show Kaikare my brush?" Eden hands the brush once owned by her grandmother to Samuel.

Samuel understands Eden's enthusiasm, although he's aware of the fragility of the Ularan people's emotions by searching for answers and being intrusive. Over the months, Eden was gone when the lonely nights merged into one long, dark night until he realized she was living *her life* without him. They loved each other, this he knew and made promises, knowing time holds the power to erode the chains of promise. He'd learned that cruel truth from his parents.

He had tried to go back to how things were before her. Tried to forget how she made him feel by spending countless hours in the garden with the shaman. He ventured out beyond their boundary in search of a miracle despite the danger, to bring testament to why he is there—the reason to his life choice.

The pain he suffered *before* coming to Ulara resurfaced and found cracks in his armor. His strength weathered like a rock battered by the ocean, anxiety seeping into tiny fissures. With his shield weakened, he had to eliminate debilitating thoughts and focus on why he is here, not his own selfish desires.

Each day he woke focused on small wins in progress.

Nothing made sense without her.

Eden had changed him.

"*Yes.*"

The answer he wants to give to every question she asks of him.

But this question is lined with warning.

Lives may change.

Hearts might break.

All for a secret shared by two lovers, forever apart.

He makes a silent promise that the same fate will not be repeated for him and Eden.

Samuel flips the brush in his hands, studying the detail. "Kaikare will be curious. Consider the repercussions. Anger is unacceptable here. Please remember their ways."

Eden wraps her arms around his waist and leans back, so her beautiful eyes capture his. "I know. I've thought it through, and it's not right to put it off because it's like I'm keeping a secret. They deserve to know of the possibility..."

He sighs loudly. "I have no idea how either one of them will react."

He allows her to guide him out the door toward the shaman's hut.

Mid-morning, he expects the shaman to be singing in the garden and is surprised to find him in his hut. The shaman steps through his doorway and greets them with an open hand. No headdress. No beads. Gray hair drooping over his shoulders, bloodshot eyes hinting at wariness.

Eden looks to Samuel before holding out the brush. "It was my grandmother's. Ivy."

Samuel translates her words. The shaman's focus is on the brush, turning it over in his hands. He brings it to his nose, closes his eyes. His serious expression gives nothing away. He points to his hut, and both follow him inside.

Samuel watches Eden's expression as she looks around, taking in the decorative ornaments and trophies lining the walls of the shaman's private space. The shaman crouches and draws a circle in the dirt between them. From a clay bowl, he pinches something in powder form and sprinkles it to form three piles—a triangle over the circle. He bows his head and sings to the jungle, lifts his gaze to Samuel, and nods.

In a brief conversation, Samuel explains how Eden thought it coincidental the brush matched the mirror Kaikare owns even though these brushes were popular in a certain era. He chooses his words carefully so as not to offend him.

The shaman asks about her grandmother. Samuel relays what Eden had told him, although where Ivy volunteered is a mystery. Eden pulls out the photographs from her pack before Samuel can stop her.

The shaman gazes at the black and white image with no alarm in his expression. Samuel asks if he had seen a photograph before, and he nods, explaining many, many moons ago. A few minutes later, he hands the photograph to Eden without another word.

Samuel apologizes. Bowing his head, he excuses himself and asks for forgiveness.

The shaman nods. "I knew be-fore."

Samuel and Eden gape at his broken English. "Ivy come here. I see spirit. You."

Samuel responds in the Ularan language to clarify his words.

Eden gasps. "Is it why you allowed me to stay?"

The shaman nods to Eden.

"Did you have an affair with my grandmother?"

Samuel places a hand on hers, shakes his head in a gesture not to overstep their place. "Perhaps you should head back to the hut. I'll take it from here. You can't interrogate him with questions to satisfy your curiosity."

"We're talking about my grandmother here. I have a right to—"

"And he has a right to keep a secret. Let me speak with him without anguish in my voice."

"There are many things I need to ask."

"I know. We need to tread carefully. Otherwise, you'll learn nothing more. I'll ask him the important questions now."

Eden lowers her gaze and chin before leaving Samuel alone with the shaman.

Free to speak openly, the shaman tells Samuel about the day Ivy landed in his village, and like Samuel, the shaman knew the moment those blue eyes met his, everything in his world would change.

He contemplated giving up his shaman training to be with her without considering her time being numbered in days. He fell in love with the white-haired woman who took away his words of speech. Samuel smiles, understanding infatuation. Their baby became sick, and she left the village to travel elsewhere when she didn't believe their medicine would help. It angered the shaman, yet she had a will as fierce as her jaguar spirit. When she returned, she was different. Something had changed in the many, many moons she was gone. Kaikare had grown. He told her Kaikare belonged with him in the village. Her tears, he remembers. He touches his heart, and there's a heart-wrenching look in his eyes as if he is reliving the memory. He tells Samuel Ivy's spirit remained after she left. Samuel questions him, thinking he means death. The shaman's hand rests on Samuel's shoulder. The spirit of the blue-eyed jaguar that runs with Samuel in his dreams. The other jaguar is Ivy.

The younger jaguar is Eden.

Eden cannot remain here.

Besides the new danger of the Watache tribe, he can't risk a claim made on their baby. Before reaching his hut, he sees her pacing near the doorway.

"So, what happened?" she says, eyes wide.

"You were right about the affair. He loved your grandmother very much and didn't want her to leave. Kaikare is the shaman's and your grandmother's daughter."

"You know I already knew it," Eden says, her hand resting on her chest, the other hand wrapped over her stomach. "Deep down, there was something about Kaikare that drew me to her. I just can't get my head around why Gran didn't bring her home."

"It concerns me as well. The shaman told me Kaikare became sick at some point, and Ivy disappeared for some time with her to get treatment at a hospital. It could be when she received vaccinations."

"Oh my God," she rasps. "It's really sinking in that she's my aunt."

"He knew." Samuel stares at Eden. "When you first arrived, he knew who you were. It's why you could stay."

Eden's eyes round. "And he didn't say anything." He senses anger whirling within her. "I have to go speak with her."

"No." Samuel takes hold of her hand, his eyes pleading for understanding. "Enough for one day. We'll both speak to Kaikare tomorrow."

Again, Eden has managed to shake up his world. Only this time, the secrets have him questioning whether the shaman saw *him* coming long before Eden?

57

EDEN

At sunrise, my energy levels are ridiculously high, so while Samuel sleeps, I roll out of my hammock and pad to my bag. I'm staring at the photo of my grandmother and the shaman and several photographs of my father and grandmother over a twenty-year span. At first, I hesitated in packing Gran's belongings, and now I'm glad I did. Will the shaman want to see the pictures of my grandmother, learn about the life she lived after Ulara? Or will it hurt too much? I glance up to the window and peer out to the rainforest, my view blocked by a silhouette.

Before panic builds, I realize it's Kaikare. She waves for me to come, so I keep hold of the photographs and creep past Samuel toward her. I follow her along the path until thick one-hundred-feet-high kapok trunks obscure us from view.

Kaikare's eyes study mine, questions whirling behind her honey-brown hues.

"Do you know?"

She says nothing. With only her eyes to guide my decision, I hold out the photographs.

I allow her to study each in silence, and like her father, her expression is unreadable. What I'd give to know what she's thinking. I hold out my hand for the pictures. Her fingers wrap around mine, and I'm pulled along the path before asking where we're headed. She leads me to her father's hut, and I know I shouldn't be here, but fate has led me to this moment, and I have to follow my gut instinct in doing what's right for Kaikare. The shaman nods to me and gestures for me to sit.

Cross-legged, the three of us sit facing the other. Kaikare hands him the images, and he speaks to her in a gentle tone, pointing to the man beside my grandmother in the jungle photo. Not once do I detect anger or any emotion. She responds with a nod of the head. How can she be calm? How can he? I want to tell them both how important this discovery is and ask why they aren't upset or excited. I'm about to say something, hoping the shaman will understand part of my words, only I notice Kaikare wipe her eyes.

"Eden, what are you doing?" I spin to Samuel standing outside.

The shaman points to the door, and I take my leave without the photographs.

Samuel isn't as practiced at hiding his concern.

"I asked you not to do this without me," he whispers. He takes my hand and leads me away toward the northern end of the village. "I wanted us to do it together, so I could communicate for you. Causing disruption to peace in the village can mean you being sent away and not allowed to return."

"I only wanted them to learn the truth."

"I know. And I want what is best for you. For us. Please understand our views differ when it comes to harmony and breaking their rules. Kaikare needs to focus on her training. If something happens to the shaman, it's like a library burning down, decades of knowledge gone."

"What do you mean? I'm not hurting him," I rasp.

He leads me to the garden, picks fruit from a vine, and hands it to me. "Please eat. You're my concern like the shaman is Kaikare's. He is old. He could have a heart attack or stroke like any elderly person, and she still has some to learn. They hold emotion inside, and although he is healthy, stress of surprise can lead to a stroke."

My gut tightens, and I want to go back to apologize. In a moment of my thoughts being read, the shaman and Kaikare appear.

"Oh, hi," I say like a dork.

Samuel ignores me and bows his head. He speaks to them in words I don't understand.

"You're now considered family," he says, the dent between his eyebrows deepening. "It seems both are happy about your photographs."

Yet Samuel doesn't seem as happy. In fact, the deep lines on his forehead tell me everything but happy.

※

"It's all I wanted," I say to Samuel when we're alone. "For them to be happy about the truth. For them both to see pictures of my grandmother and know she arrived home safely. And for Kaikare to see her mother and my father, since he's her half-brother."

"Since you arrived I've witnessed a change in the shaman. You have shown them another world. One that's frightening to them, and that has possibly created a problem for us." He swipes the side of his face.

"Us. How?"

"You are family as was your grandmother. I don't want the same fate for our baby, so I'm sending you home. You have to remember, in their eyes, the people of the rest of the world are fueled by greed. Forests are destroyed and burned for land. We bring disease, use guns, and our emotions aren't intact as the Ularans."

"But I have almost three months," I croak out. "I want to be with you."

Samuel takes me in his arms and kisses the top of my head. "I know. And I want to be with you. I also want our baby to be safe."

My hands tighten around his hot skin. "Please don't make me leave. When I'm with you, I'm stronger. I need to stay."

"Eden," he croaks. "I feel the same. More than anything, I want you here by my side." He holds me, so our gaze meets. "Before I met you, I believed I was happy. The day you left, I realized you took a part of my heart and soul with you. I'll never be the same. I've changed for the better."

"Then don't make me leave," I beg.

He runs a finger along the side of my cheek. His kind eyes are filled with love, yet his lips press tight in a straight line.

"Say it. Say I can stay. Please..." I stretch out the last word. "What if something goes wrong with our baby, and I can't reach you. What if—"

"Stop." He exhales slowly, the heat of his breath hitting my face. "If." He leans his forehead against mine. "If you stay, you have to promise me something—"

"Anything," I croak.

"You remain here only if there is no danger to you or our baby. The moment anything escalates, and it includes word from Asoo about border security with rebels outside the village, you are to leave. No questions asked."

"Agreed."

I tilt my head to meet his eyes, watch as his lips meet mine. There's urgency in his kiss like it could be our last. I ignore my gut and allow him to melt away all my thoughts.

"I love you," I say against his lips.

Holding both my cheeks in his large hands, he tilts my head. "And I love you more than anything else I value in this world."

I have eleven more weeks.

It will bring me close to the term of my pregnancy, and I need to consider the risk of flying while in the last trimester of my pregnancy. Do I leave before the airline refuses travel, or stay and *somehow* extend my visa and have my baby here?

Yasmine would understand.

Dad will take more convincing.

Faith has my back, so she'll be able to talk to him.

It's not forever.

I smile, knowing this man who led me on this crazy journey will protect me because I chose to take a risk, take steps outside my comfort zone, and embrace fear— to be here with him.

I only hope the shaman doesn't see me as a threat. My time here is in his hands. Though my gut tells me not to let down my guard because Samuel's love might not be enough to protect me.

Thank you so much for reading Samuel and Eden's story.
Their story continues in Hopelessly Wild.

Next book in the series is ...
Hopelessly Wild (The Wild Series - Book 2)
Perfectly Wild – (The Wild Series Book 3)

ALSO BY LEESA BOW

www.leesabow.com

ACKNOWLEDGMENTS

Eleven years is a long time to write a story, and there are many people to thank during this time.

First and foremost, to my husband, Lynden. Thank you for your encouragement, love, and support of my writing journey.

To my four beautiful daughters, Jamie-Lee, Shauni, Ashleigh, and Demi, for providing constant inspiration. To my wonderful parents, Pam and Vic, and my sister, Vickie, and her family for believing in me and helping in any way possible. Cam, Charlie, and Cruise, I'm grateful that you all are now part of our family and supporting me.

A big shout-out to my friends and biggest fans. Mum, Deanne, and Helen, Dayna, and Alison for believing in me from the day I decided to give authoring a shot. Your love for my story gave me the confidence to take a giant step forward.

To Marilyn, Juls and Tracey, and all my friends, including the basketball and football communities, Sacred Heart community, my nursing friends (the Mudgettes), and my Nestle crew, who have been by our sides from the beginning while I wrote this story from my heart. You have witnessed the story of Ulara evolve from a dream to a reality, and I'm thankful every day for your support and patience. Especially during one of the toughest times of our lives. A shout out to Francina for the cave scene. A similar way to how you met your husband!

To Kim, at Blogging for the Love of Authors, for the feedback while tolerating my insecurities, and to Charli at Beyond the Pages, thank you both for your encouragement, and words of wisdom, and for reading my story in its raw stages.

To Kaylene Osborn at Swish Design and Editing. Thank you for all your expertise, for answering endless questions, and for making my book shine. Most of all, for calming me when I message or call in a state of panic. You are my rock! And a big thank you to Nicki!

To Lauren Clarke at Creating Ink. You moulded my story into a piece of art, and I'm truly thankful.

To Letitia Hasser at RBA Designs, thank you for my beautiful cover. You nailed Samuel!

My appreciation extends to my Facebook reader group, Leesa Bow's Lovelies, and all the blogging community for helping to get my book out to the world. You all make the book world a much better place. A special thank you to Ena at Enticing Journey Book Promotions and all the blogs and bookstagrammers for promoting Beautifully Wild.

To my author friends, who I've chatted with while writing this book. You have been with me from the day I decided I wanted to publish my story. I can't express enough gratitude for all your advice and inspiration. To Nina, Maggie, Jen, Beth, KE, and Jodi you always have my back, and I appreciate you all! To RWA and Yon author group, and all the authors whom I've met at signings, you are my writing family.

To Carol, Kellie, Robyn, Jen, and Megan, thank you for beta reading my story and helping me refine it. You are awesome. And to Adriana for helping me with the Brazilian terms. A special mention to Haley for her insight of an Aussie in Brazil. And to Carla for all the information about Venezuela.

To my readers. Thank you for your endless support, and most of all, for loving my stories. Some of you have been with me from the start of my author journey, and to others, I'm a new author. What I love most is you all embrace my characters and stories and love them as much as I do. Thank you for reading, reviewing, and talking about my books to your families and friends in book clubs and blogs.

I appreciate everything you do for me!

Finally, to my daughter, Shauni, and the special teenagers and parents, we met at the Royal Adelaide Children's Hospital—Gina and Jenna, Michael and Sue, Will and Sherie, and Shauni's oncologist, Dr. Tapp. Thank you for your friendship and for showing me what it is to truly embrace fear. Your strength is admirable, and I'll never forget the bond, the support, and love when faced with the battle of cancer. To all the children in the oncology wards around the world, some of you now live in the stars, but you are never forgotten. You are forever the real heroes of the world.

ABOUT THE AUTHOR

Best selling Australian author, Leesa Bow writes alphas with a fierce determination to win, and the women who will push for them to fight harder. She is known for her steamy sports romance and her latest adventure romance.

Leesa lives in sunny Queensland, Australia. She spends her spare time with her family, and catching up with girlfriends for coffee or a wine.

Leesa loves to keep fit with pilates, and yoga, and keeping the fun with laughter in her life.

She loves nothing more than to curl up with a good book, and a glass of South Australian wine.